If I was an angel sent to protect my people, how could I be mortally injured by so small a thing?

I immediately burst into tears and rushed over to her. I grabbed her shoulders, flipped her over, and crushed her petite, marble body to mine. I ceased my flapping and just rode the wind while I sobbed apologies, which I knew she wouldn't understand, into her satiny raven hair.

"I will always be here for you, as long as you want me," I cried. "I will never leave you again. I will never die on you again."

At that instant, as soon as the words left my mouth, I knew without a doubt that they were true. I saw my distant future and smiled wide through my tears.

I pulled my face from her hair and wiped away her tears before I wiped away my own. "Cry no more, child," I said in Russian before I kissed away a fresh tear. "I stay forever."

"Please don't leave us again. We will follow you anywhere now," her brother said.

"Will you follow me to my tribe and help me protect my people? Will you follow your father's teachings and kill none of my people?" I asked them both.

"Yes, Mama. Anywhere. Anything. We have spent 513 years wanting our mother back, and now we have her. We will never let you go," my daughter said before she squeezed me so hard, my breath rushed from my chest.

I thought I had popped right into two pieces when my wings fell limp.

"Careful, child. She is still very breakable," Deema warned in a sharp tone.

In a reflex reaction to his warning, she quickly released me as she flipped over, and I started to fall. For the first time since I'd started flying, I could not breathe. I also couldn't move my wings.

When Hope grows massive wings and learns to fly, her elders declare her their only hope, the savior of the Hopi people, and make plans to gather everyone in the tribe back to their reservation in southwestern Colorado. After learning of prophecies predicting a war that could end society, Hope is frantic to save her childhood friend, Taniya, who moved away shortly before Hope's wings began to grow. She arrives at Taniya's apartment in New York, only to learn that her roommate, Deema, is a vampire. He quickly falls in love with Hope, professing her to be a reincarnation of his late wife who died over 500 years ago. Hope plans to save her people through her abilities to dream the future and remote view the present, and she doesn't need any distractions. But she feels so drawn to this man. Life becomes further complicated when Hope discovers she's pregnant with the vampire's child. When she realizes that her pregnancy is accelerated and the baby will be born after only two weeks, she fears she will not survive, especially when she hears a prophecy about a blood drinker who will distract her from her mission and turn her into a demon. Could the prophesy be referring to Deema and, if so, does she really have the strength to give him up before the coming war destroys her people…people who are counting on her to save them?

KUDOS for *Our Only Hope*

in *Our Only Hope* by Janelle Samara, Hope is a young Native American woman who has grown a set of wings. The tribal elders tell her she has been prophesied as the only one who can save their tribe in the upcoming catastrophes that are coming to their people. Hope goes to New York to bring back her best friend Tayina and there she meets a vampire who says that she was prophesied to be his mate. Poor Hope. All these prophecies telling her what she has to do and be, and she can't even sit down in a normal chair due to her fifteen-foot wing span. She can't be seen by anyone, even her own people until after they have signed a form promising not to reveal her, so she spends most of her time hiding. I thought the author did an excellent job of describing what it must be like to have wings, both the good and the bad of it. She has also woven a sexy romance with a hunky vampire into the plot to give it extra appeal. ~ *Taylor Jones, Reviewer*

Our Only Hope by Janelle Samara is the story of a young Native American woman who suddenly grows wings. Now, where most people might think this is a good thing, being able to fly and all, our heroine, Hope, deals with the more mundane problems, such as she can't be seen by anyone outside her immediate family, she can't sit in a chair, and can only go outside at night to take care of her chickens and tend her garden. When her wings are finally fully developed, which takes about a year, Hope presents herself to the chief of the tribe and the elders. They tell her that she has been foretold of in prophecies as being the only hope to save her tribe from a coming disaster. Hope is earthy, immature, and resentful of the duty that has suddenly been thrust upon her, aside from the fact that her wings are very inconvenient. She can no longer live a normal life, and she can't help but wonder, why me? Especially since she would much rather get stoned that try to turn herself into a mythical warrior. Her life is further complicated when a vampire named Deema falls in love with her and tells her that not only is she destined to be his mate, but she is also the reincarnation of his long dead wife. Geez, give the poor girl a break. Samara has crafted a complicated story of a young woman destined for things far above her station in life, as well as her own ambitions. The plot is strong, the characters credible and well developed. ~ *Regan Murphy, Reviewer*

ACKNOWLEDGEMENTS

First, I'd like to thank all of the wonderful people at Black Opal Books who have helped me get this book published. They've all been so kind and helpful throughout the whole process.

Second, to my good friend and fellow author, Marissa Bauder. I couldn't have even brought myself to submit anything without your feedback and encouragement. I'm so happy to have you as my friend and sounding board.

I'd also like to thank all of my other friends who have listened to me babble about stories I'm writing, ideas I have for more, etc., for the last several years. Your patience with me has meant a lot.

Finally, I want to thank my husband. Without his love and support, I don't know that I ever would've gotten my edits finished. He's been incredibly patient with me when I'd stare at my computer for hours while I edit. Or when he'd come home to find me furiously typing and I shush him because "I have to get this out before I forget." He has been extremely supportive of my dreams and my work, even though I've never let him read more than the first page.

OUR ONLY HOPE

Janelle Samara

A Black Opal Books Publication

Black Opal Books

BECAUSE SOME STORIES JUST HAVE TO BE TOLD

GENRE: PARANORMAL THRILLER/PARANORMAL ROMANCE

OUR ONLY HOPE
Copyright © 2015 by Janelle Samara
Cover Design by Jackson Cover Designs
All cover art copyright © 2016
All Rights Reserved
Print ISBN: 978-1-626944-03-9

First Publication: JANUARY 2016

Published by Black Opal Books **http://www.blackopalbooks.com**

DEDICATION

For Bennie & Barbara.
I'll always love you.
May you rest in peace.

Author's Note

I debated with myself for a long time over whether or not I should use the name of an existing Native American tribe for this book series. I really like the name of the Hopi tribe because it is so close to Hope, the name of the narrator. But I didn't want to—and couldn't—use existing stories of any one tribe. I needed to have the freedom to create my own mythologies. That being said, nothing that is written about the tribe in this book is factual. I didn't even place their reservation in the correct state. I truly hope that I do not offend anyone. I have an immense amount of respect for Native Americans and their various cultures. That is one of the reasons I needed Hope to be who she is for this novel.

CHAPTER 1

This was so long in coming, so long in the works, I wasn't sure I'd ever understand how it surprised me so much. I'd always known I was different, but I had never allowed myself to fully embrace just how drastically different I was from the rest. Perhaps I had to try so hard to convince myself I was normal so that I could survive my adolescence. But none of that mattered anymore. Being normal would never again be an option, now that I had a fifteen-foot wing span.

As a child, I would have never guessed that I was an angel. I'd always known I was special and different, but I'd had no idea just how different until I neared my thirties. That was when my wings began to grow.

I was quite a sight to see, though. I stood five feet, ten inches tall and I had a healthy build. I was a Hopi woman with long, thick, black hair that I had not cut in fifteen years. It nearly reached my knees. I'd grown up with pale skin compared to the rest of the tribe, but I was always still too dark to pass for white. My eyes were large and dark hazel with long lashes. My bottom lip was large and full, but my top lip was smaller in an almost strange way. My mother had called it a cupid's bow and said other women would always wish they had my lips. I just thought it made me look funny because none of the other women in the tribe had lips like mine. Just like none of the others had eyes like mine.

My wings looked much like one would imagine angel wings. They were covered in feathers like I'd never seen. They were kind of opalescent, and nearly luminescent—an amazing, sparkling white. They were each over seven feet long when fully extended. When I folded them, as I usually did, the tips of my wings were about a foot above the ground and the folded joints were about a foot above my head. They did not emerge directly from my shoulder blades, but rather from the space between my spine and shoulder blades. Moving my shoulders caused great movement in my wings, but that's not how I flew. My wings were full of muscles just like the rest of the human body, so I had to exercise them just like any other muscle group.

I tried to fly a couple of times with no real luck, so I had my younger brother, Will, get me quite a few books about the mechanics of birds and how they fly. After extensive research and a lot more exercise, I gave flying one more attempt. Well, as the saying goes, the third time was the charm. I took off from my roof, glided down a bit over my garden, and then soared off into the night sky.

I flapped my massive wings to gain altitude and I was taken aback with the beauty of my surroundings. The mountains that ran to the north and the west took on a whole new appearance from this angle and the sight of it nearly brought me to tears.

I flew around for about ten minutes before I decided to pay my big brother, Brian, a visit. Since it was Thursday night, I knew he would be out back barbequing. I circled around the neighborhood a few times to make sure no one else was outside to witness my landing.

As I tilted my wings to lower my altitude, I saw my brother walk out of his back door with an empty plate and head for the smoking grill.

My landing was, without a doubt, highly ungraceful and the shock of my unexpected arrival caused him to drop the plate he was carrying.

"Damn it, Hope!" he grumbled as he picked up his plate.

He was a bit unnerved and kind of angry that I'd flown to his house. His furrowed brow, pulsing temples, and flexed jaw would've been enough to terrify anyone who didn't know him as well as I did. It took me a minute to calm him, but he composed himself once I assured him that no one else was outside to see.

We went into the house, once he removed his food from the grill and then sat down for dinner. Well, he sat down. I stood since there were no chairs or stools on which I could sit. He had brought the only stools he had over to my trailer so I could sit down at home. We hadn't intended on me leaving my place and visiting others.

I told him all that had happened since he'd last visited me. I explained about my flying attempts and Will bringing me all of the books from the library. I babbled on for a while about how my wings worked and how I was able to fly. While I rambled on incessantly, jumping from subject to subject as was my style, Brian appeared to only half listen, as was his style. But I knew my brother well and I understood, as many did not, that he rarely appeared to pay attention even though he absorbed everything that was ever said to him. One of the only times he even looked at me was when I told him about my second flying attempt.

"Man, I thought I was screwed. I couldn't stand up on my own and I couldn't drag myself into the house, either. Will just happened to show up and he helped me inside," I told Brian while he paused and stared at me with a blank expression.

He turned his attention back to his food with a shrug. I understood what he was thinking, though. Yes, what I did was stupid, but everything happened for a reason. So it wound up being okay.

By the time we were done eating, I felt I had filled him in on recent events as much as I could. He sighed as he stood up and turned toward his bedroom.

When he emerged, he held the pipe that our grandfather helped him make as a child, as well as the cigar box where I knew he kept his supply of herbs. It was a peace pipe, like our ancestors had used to smoke their sacred herbs. It was ornately decorated and made from a very long antler that came from far away. Only once was tobacco ever smoked out of this sacred pipe. When Grandfather tied the last knot on the pipe's decoration, he filled the bowl of the pipe with wild tobacco and the whole family smoked it to let our ancestors know that this pipe belonged to this family.

Ever since our teens, we had exclusively used the peace pipe for smoking cannabis when we needed to meditate on a problem as a family. No one smoked from our pipe unless they shared our blood.

Without saying a word, Brian opened the back door and stepped outside. I followed him since I was well used to our tradition, even though it had been almost two years since I'd visited him. We sat down on the four-foot tall stone wall that marked the edge of the patio and watched the night sky.

After he passed me the pipe and exhaled his first puff, he broke his silence of the past hour. "We cannot continue hiding you. I think it'd be best if you presented yourself to the tribal elders. Immediately."

I choked on the smoke I was inhaling, due to my shock at his words. I started to protest, but he held up his hand and shot me a glare to silence me as he continued to speak. At six feet, five inches tall, he was thickly muscled and had a bevy of expressions that could freeze almost anyone. He'd certainly always managed to get me to stop short.

"When our grandfather helped me make the pipe when I was a child, he told me many stories of our people. Each knot, each feather, each bead, each thread, every little thing about this pipe is a story or prophesy. This right here?" he said as he pointed to the long white feather that hung from the pipe right next to a black one of the same length. "This tells the prophesy of the winged flying woman who will unite and save our people as our calendar nears an end."

I was about to ask him about the black one when he turned toward me and regarded me with a contemplative gaze. "We cannot put this off any longer. Now that you can fly, you must present yourself to them. The calendar ends in a little over two years. They've been expecting you for well over twenty years now. It's up to you now to save us all from destruction, little sister."

I was stunned. I couldn't believe that he'd known all this time that this was predicted to be and he hadn't told me. I was on the verge of being angry, but I was so filled with such fear that I wasn't sure the anger had any room to grow.

"What do you mean, I am to save everyone?" I gasped as my grip on the wall beneath me tightened.

He shrugged. "They'll be able to explain it further. You know I'm still just an elder-in-training. But, yeah. It's up to you now to prevent the destruction of our entire tribe."

"You seem just a little too calm about that," I said slowly as I tried to decipher his composed, blank expression.

He shrugged again before he took another puff from the pipe. "Either you will win, or we all will die. Why should I stress? I cannot stop it either way. Only you can. Only you can save us all or allow us all to perish."

"What about Taniya?" I whispered in my fear.

I couldn't help it that she was among my first thoughts. She'd been my best friend since we were toddlers. I also hadn't seen her since right before my wings had sprouted. That was when she'd moved clear across the country to New York.

"You're going to have to let her die," he said in a soft, sad tone as he looked up at the stars.

CHAPTER 2

When I awoke Friday morning, I only had thirty minutes to eat breakfast and get ready before my big brother arrived. I frantically ran out to the henhouse to gather some eggs. I was in such a hurry that I forgot to cover my wings. It'd been over a year and a half since I'd stepped into the sunlight outdoors. I realized my mistake once I was nearly done searching for eggs. I quickly glanced around and breathed a sigh of relief when I saw that no one else was within sight. I ran back inside and threw a handful of bacon into the pan.

Just as my breakfast finished cooking, my brother arrived. He waited patiently as I ate my food and got dressed. I was so nervous that I almost forgot to conceal my wings again before I stepped outside. Brian laughed as he caught me by my shoulder and suggested I cover myself. When I put on the cheap cape I usually wore, he noticed that it left the bottom few inches of my wings exposed. It took us a few minutes to find something that would cover my wings entirely so as to not alarm other tribe members who would no doubt see us as we walked to the Hall of the Elders.

After we'd tried to hide my wings with everything else in the house, we concluded that the only thing that would cover them was the blanket our great-grandmother had woven by hand with wool she had sheered, dyed, and spun. He carefully took it down from the wall, and I felt like a little kid again as I remembered the first time I'd wrapped that blanket around myself. It not only covered my wings entirely, but it looked and felt very appropriate, considering the circumstances.

When we stepped out my front door, I could feel several pairs of eyes on me and I could hear them wondering what was happening. I thought about their murmurs as we walked, and it occurred to me that they really had no idea what to think.

I'd been in this house ever since I turned twenty-one and started receiving a share of the casino profits. I'd always had lots of people over on the weekends and been very generous with my garden vegetables at harvest time. Now, for nearly two years, I'd been completely unseen, yet obviously still lived there since I grew a full-yard garden and I'd taken to keeping chickens. My car hadn't moved since I quit my job, and I never had a group of people over anymore. My garden was tended every day, but no one ever saw or heard me do it. Part of me thought it was funny, while the rest of me felt guilty for staying in hiding for so long.

It was a five-mile walk to the Hall of the Elders and, about a mile down the road, I wished I'd remembered to bring some water. As I turned to ask Brian if he had anything to drink, he handed me a skin of water before I could speak. I smiled to myself as I drank the cool water under the increasingly hot desert sun. It was past ten in the morning in the middle of June in southwestern Colorado.

I wished I didn't have to wear that heavy wool blanket over my huge, feathery wings and I relished the thought that maybe after today, I wouldn't have to wear it anymore. As soon as I'd completed the thought, my brother stopped in his tracks and turned to face me. "You must continue to keep them covered because non-natives still live scattered throughout the reservation on land they've rented from tribe members who have moved away."

"How'd you get so much better at reading my mind?" We'd always had a connection, but nothing like this.

He turned and started walking again. "As your wings have grown, so has my telepathy. I've been exercising my mind as you've been exercising your wings. I've learned how to pick out thoughts from different people, even from great distances."

I considered for a moment how that could be useful.

"You have no idea the terrors the government's plotting," he whispered to me as we walked past more gawking people.

I asked him to tell me what they thought as we walked past and he laughed loudly. He said that they thought I had a tumor or elephantitis or something horrible growing out of my back. "And that limp from your bad landings isn't helping," he said with a chuckle.

None of them ever considered for a second that I was hiding wings, and I breathed a sigh of relief. I knew in my heart that it was wrong for others to discover my secret before I could reveal myself to, and seek counsel from, the elders.

After walking for almost two hours, we arrived at the Hall of the Elders. Brian never lost a beat or slowed his pace once the Hall was in sight. He didn't realize I'd stopped in my tracks until he opened the door. I looked at him in despair. I was afraid of not knowing what to say and what to do. The butterflies in my stomach started to make me feel queasy.

"You don't have to speak if you don't want to. I called ahead this morning and requested a private audience with the elders."

Knowing that they were expecting us, and we would have privacy, gave me enough courage to walk through the doors.

As we walked into the conference room, I beheld the twenty-five old men seated at a long, thin, triangular table. It sat up on a dais so that even though they were seated, we were all still at eye-level. When I locked eyes with my grandfather, I burst into tears.

"Why are you crying, child? And why has it been so long since you came to visit me?" he asked quietly.

"I'm crying *because* I haven't come to see you for so long," I replied.

"And why is that?" he asked me again.

I took a couple of heaving, broken breaths before I lowered my head and untucked the blanket from between my back and my wings. As the blanket started to fall off, Brian caught it. I spread my wings, and they touched both of the sun-faded tan walls.

CHAPTER 3

When I blinked the tears from my eyes, I saw that no one had seemed very affected by my revelation.

"Why has it taken so long for you to reveal yourself?" my grandfather asked. "You're twenty-eight, Hope. How and why have you kept this hidden for so long?"

"My wings have only been fully developed for six months, and they took just over a year to grow," I told him.

A murmur of disapproval swept through the room. A man who appeared to be in his fifties stood up. "This has to be some kind of trick," he declared. "Our protector was to be *born* with wings."

Then our chief stood up from his seat at the blunted spearhead of the odd triangular table to silence the room. "It matters not whether she was born with wings or grew them," he announced in a stern voice. "The important thing is that she stands before us now. Our time grows short and the calendar is nearing an end. If there is any hope for the survival of our tribe, it is up to you to protect them."

At this, he turned to face me and bowed his head in acknowledgment.

I dropped my wings when he motioned toward me. How could I possibly save my people?

An elder next to my grandfather stood. "You have the holy light of our creator buried deep within you. If you can learn how to accept this and forsake all of your ego that remains, you alone will be able to save the lives of many," he said in answer to my silent question. "Many may die that you cannot save, but all will die if you do not accept your destiny."

I wanted to sit down, or fall to the ground, but the gray Berber carpet didn't exactly appear welcoming. My knees felt weak and my head started to spin.

My brother heard my silent plea not to let me fall and placed his hands on my shoulders to steady me as I started to tilt forward.

I didn't understand how to do what I needed to, or why it was *my* responsibility, *my* burden, to save my tribe.

"Long before you were born, you made a choice to come back to this tribe and live the life you lead," the man next to my grandfather continued. "Thousands of years ago when our calendar was written, the founders of our tribe vowed to return toward the end of the longest calendar to guide our people back to the ways of the planet."

His words echoed in my head and I feared I would lose consciousness, so he paused for a few moments while I composed myself.

"Look around this land we were confined to by the Whiteman. See the consumption and greed that our tribe has succumbed to. Observe the greed the casino has caused in the many tribe members who don't even work because of their share of the profits. Watch the women who sit around our section of Four Corners and sell trinkets to tourists, telling them the tribe made the jewelry when it's all really been imported from a factory in Mexico, just so they can make more money.

"Only a handful of our tribe still grows a garden or hunts. Our traditions have been almost completely lost, and most of our people have become just as evil to our planet as our oppressors. We are nearly out of hope. But you, Hope, you *will* save us. Please don't doubt yourself. You truly are our only hope."

He gave me a small nod with an expression on his face I had trouble placing. It couldn't be respect, I thought. I'd done nothing to earn respect from this gathering of wise old men.

"What about the other founders? If they all vowed to return, how is it that I'm the only hope? Where are the rest to help me save everyone?" I blurted out after a few moments of deafening silence.

"We are already here," my grandfather said quietly. "You are the last to reveal yourself." Everyone stood up. "All of us in this room have fulfilled our promises to return and help our protector. We are all here for you, to help you, to guide you, to give you support when you have doubt. We will all be here for you until the day we die." His voice broke a bit at the end.

I knew in my heart that if times were going to get tough, as they all kept alluding to, they wouldn't last long with as old as they were. The average age of a council elder was seventy.

I reflected on this for a moment before I continued my inquiries. "Will I be revealed to the tribe? Will I be able to leave my house during the day? Is there any way we can ban others from our rez so they won't discover me and try to do tests on me or something?"

"Yes, maybe, and absolutely not," the chief said. "We will call a tribal meeting for Monday night. We will shut down the casino and have the meeting there in the theater. Everyone will be required to attend. We will announce to the tribe what is coming and how we are to survive it. We will reveal you, under the condition that if anyone tells someone outside the tribe, they will be punished by death under tribal law."

I gasped and stumbled backward at his bold statement and the nonchalant way he said it. "How can we *kill* our tribe members?" I mumbled.

"Because it is our law and our way. As a native tribe living on a reservation, we are not subject to the laws of America. We live by our own laws, our own ways, and we have a law that states if you betray your tribe, you can be killed by the tribe under the order of the Council of Elders. If anyone were to betray us by revealing the prophesies we will discuss, or by telling an outsider of our resident winged woman, then they will die. Of course, we will inform everyone of this before we tell them the secrets.

"It's okay, Hope. We have it all planned out. As you must realize, we've been waiting for you for quite some time now. We were starting to wonder if the winged woman had moved away or been aborted or if something else horrible had happened, like a frightened mother cutting off a child's wings."

The chief had a wondrous way of speaking. He was so gentle and soothing in one sentence, then so curt in the next. But he never really seemed rude. He was just an intense, wise man who seemed to always know what to say.

I had no doubt in my mind that this would go fairly well. I could start to see it in my head and the weight in my soul started to lift just a bit. I knew that the tribe would accept me after the council told them what was to come.

As soon as I started thinking about my dreams, another question spilled out of my mouth. "Am I a prophet? I see many things in my dreams that come true. I also see many that do not, but then I can also see in my waking mind, later, how I deviated from that path and why it did not come true. I've also seen things that have happened to people that I don't know and I've never met."

I shifted my wings uncomfortably and silently asked my brother for some more water. "The deluge in India—the tsunami that killed so many people the day after New Year's—I saw it. I saw it a couple of weeks before Thanksgiving. I didn't know what I was seeing. I mean, I didn't know when or where it was. I assumed it was just one of many disaster dreams I've had off and on for so long now. But when it happened, I knew. I saw a photo on the Internet that was an exact snapshot of my dream. I've seen many more floods, and I've seen fires. I've seen great earthquakes, and I've seen starvation. I've seen tornadoes and hurricanes like modern man has never had before. I've seen horrible things inflicted on the American populous by its own government," I babbled.

"As have I," Brian said as he handed me a glass of water.

"As have we all." The chief sighed sadly. "Yes, you are a prophet. We have much to discuss, but first, I think we need to have lunch. How does chicken sound?"

CHAPTER 4

After a wonderful lunch of rotisserie chicken and roasted potatoes, we resettled in the conference room. I was very thankful that they'd found me a stool so I could sit down.

The chief handed me a file labeled *2072* as he passed me on his way to his chair on the other side of the room. "The contents of that file are what we have done to prepare. In the back of the file is a flash drive that contains everything that's there in print. That drive has never been, and can never be, put into a computer with an internet connection. It's merely a precaution, but one that we do not take lightly."

He gave me a stern look and I nodded in understanding.

"There is a form in there which we will copy and distribute to all tribal members before the secrets are revealed. It states a warning that if they expose our secrets to anyone who is not a tribal member living on our tribal lands, they will be killed. It must be signed, and anyone who refuses will be expelled from the tribe and banned from tribal lands."

I'd found the document he was talking about and I glanced it over as he spoke. I knew in my heart it was fair. If someone willingly endangered the lives of the entire tribe, then they should be punished.

"So what do we do until then? How do we tell everyone they have to be there?" I asked.

As the youngest elder started to answer me, I found my answer in the file.

"There is a list that has the address and number of and ages of the occupants of every property on tribal lands, as well as some other information such as phone numbers, places of employment, everything," he said. "We will start by making phone calls. Those that cannot be contacted by phone will be contacted in person.

"Every business on the reservation will be shut down, if necessary, so that everyone may attend. We will have a meeting with the tribal police force. They will secure the casino entrances, as well as the other closed businesses. Any police left will take home those who refuse to sign so they may gather their things and leave the reservation."

The chief then took a turn to speak. "We will probably pass out the forms to everyone as they walk into the theater. After everyone has arrived, we will explain why they have been given these forms and, that in order to attend the remainder of the meeting, this form must be signed and returned. Anyone who does not want to sign it will be expelled from the tribe. They will be allowed the rest of the night to pack their things, and they will then be escorted off the reservation. They will be banned from ever returning.

"It will be explained to them that the reason for all of this is because we are about to reveal to the tribe all of the prophesies that have been guarded by the tribal elders for hundreds of generations. If any of these secrets were revealed to someone outside the tribe, it could mean the destruction of us all. Once everyone signs them, the forms will be collected, and we will begin telling them our stories.

"When the time is right, we will bring you out. To prove that you are real and you are not a magic trick of some kind, we may ask you to walk through the crowd so that some of them may touch your wings. We will also ask you to fly for them."

"I don't know if I can take off from the ground," I interrupted. "I've never tried. I've flown twice now, once to my brother's house last night and then the flight home. Both times, I climbed a ladder and glided down from the roof like a hawk from a treetop."

"Then you can fly as your intro, down from the catwalk or you can climb some stairs on stage," Brian suggested.

"But you've seen my landings. I'm in serious need of more practice," I argued.

"Then you've got three nights to practice your ass off." My brother snorted a quick laugh when he saw my appalled expression.

"We will take some supplies tonight to the other side of the western mountains and we will light a fire for you so you can find it from the sky," my grandfather suggested. "The land is ours as a tribe but, as you know, no one lives in that narrow valley. You will have three nights on your own to practice taking off from the ground as well as landing safely. We will leave you with plenty of coffee and a seven-day supply of food, as we anticipate you will need lots of extra energy for all of your exercise. If you are unable to take off from the ground, then at least focus on your landing. We cannot have you getting hurt every time you land."

"What about the three nights and days I'm out there alone? What if I get hurt then?" I asked.

"Will and I can take turns coming out to stay with you to make sure you're okay, and we'll bring our own food and water," Brian offered.

I sat quietly for a few minutes, trying to absorb all that I had been told before I spoke. "So, when the sun is set tonight, I need to fly west over the ridge and just look for the fire?"

"Yes," the chief replied. "One of your brothers will be waiting. You will spend three days and nights flying. As long as you are careful and listen to your instincts, you will be fine. You may even be surprised at how fast you improve." At this, he gave me a wink.

I sighed wearily. "Is there anything else you need from me today, or can I go back home to get some sleep before the sun goes down?" I grimaced when I remembered that I still had to walk another five miles in the heat.

Brian caught me by surprise again when he said that it was all taken care of. "I called Will during lunch. He'll be here in ten minutes with a mattress in the back of my truck. You can lie down in the back and we'll have you home in a matter of minutes."

"Sounds good to me."

CHAPTER 5

When I awoke that night, the colors in the sky were still fading so I decided to heat up some leftover roast before I climbed up to my roof. I filled two skins with water and then I smoked a joint while I watched the blackness spread in the sky. The chief had told me to trust my instincts when it came to flying. I deeply hoped that, being in that kind of meditative state, I'd be able to go with my instincts more easily.

When I felt that it wasn't going to get any darker, I climbed the ladder that was still up from the night before, spread my wings, and flung myself off the roof. As I soared higher and higher, I could feel the moistness on my face and shoulders from the low, wispy clouds in the sky. It took me just a few minutes to reach the mountain ridge and, when I crossed, I saw the fire instantly.

As I slowed for my landing, I thought again about what the chief had said, and I just let my instincts take over. While I flew, I was parallel with the ground. But to land that time, I stood straight up and tilted my wings at an angle I never had while I was in flight. It felt so right, and I instinctually flapped my wings just how I needed to in order to make a perfect and graceful landing.

Will had been watching the sky, waiting for me to arrive, and he applauded my landing. "How can you say you have a terrible landing? That was amazing!" he exclaimed without slowing his clapping.

"I actually can't believe I did that." I laughed as I held up my hands for him to stop clapping. "But the chief told me to follow my instincts, so I did. Instead of trying to figure out how to land, I didn't think at all. I just...I don't know...I just did it." I felt a wide smile break across my face as I spoke, thrilled with what I had accomplished.

"Well, that's still pretty cool. I still can't really get over this all. I can't believe this happened to my own sister. What the hell is going to happen to us now?" he wondered.

"Far too much to explain to you now. I've got a purpose here and I'm not worn out or hungry yet. We can talk then, okay?" I smiled at him, knowing he'd understand.

He smiled back and gave me a nod as he turned his back to go and sit by the fire again.

I figured if my wings could let me land gently, then I should be able to take off gently as well. I turned, so the wind of my wings wouldn't blow down the tent Will had set up, and started to flap with all my might. It wasn't working, so I observed the angle of my wings, and tried to adjust them so that it would work. Only with this attempt, my wings ran into my shoulders, so I lost my full range of motion. I decided to go back to the first flapping angle, but I tilted my torso forward slightly, bent my knees, and pushed off from the ground.

It worked! Before I knew it, I was soaring through the sky again. It was definitely a more difficult take off than gliding, but at least I was airborne. I'd never felt freer than I did when I was flying. This was something I could definitely get used to, I thought with a giggle.

I flew in a few circles before I went in for another landing. It was just as flawless as my first arrival that night. "Can you lay down a marker for me?" I asked Will. "So I can see how accurate my landings can be."

He laid down a gold dollar that sparkled in the firelight. I was able to land on it time and time again.

The hours passed quickly. After countless take-off and landing successes with no failures, I told Will that he could go to sleep if he wanted. I was going to fly until mid-morning so I could enjoy the sun, and then I would get some rest.

I was afraid to leave the valley in the dark. I might get lost. So I passed the hours that first lonely night of flight, soaring lazily from one end of the valley to the other. I practiced my turns, and mostly watched the sky for some hint of light. I was all too anxious to fly under the blue sky for the first time and feel truly free.

Once the sky finally started to lighten, I decided I wanted to actually watch the sunrise. I flew up to the highest peak of the mountains on the western edge of our little town. When I landed, I decided to crouch so as to not be so obvious. I felt like a gargoyle perched on a rooftop, but soon forgot all about that because it was such an amazing sight to behold.

As the sky turned shades of red, orange, pink, and eventually blue, I watched the light spread over the land of my people. It was the most beautiful thing I'd ever witnessed.

When I started noticing movement in the town spread out below, I turned and leapt from the cliff behind me. Since I felt I had done fairly well with all of my take-offs and landings, I decided to see how long I could fly before I felt tired. In an effort to run from the sun and waking people, I found a river and followed it west.

Before I knew it, I'd reached Bluff, Utah, and had to turn back. I was shocked at how fast I'd gotten there, so I decided to test my speed in the valley where I was supposed to be staying. I seemed to be getting everywhere so quickly, but I just couldn't tell what my speed was while I was so high up in the sky.

After the quick flight back to my valley, I noticed that the sun had yet to peek over the mountains to wake my brother and a mischievous thought came to mind. I eyed my path from the sky and traced it several times at lower and lower altitudes. I determined that I would have room to do what I wanted, so I went for it.

I flew as fast as I could, flapping my wings with all my might and producing as much wind as I could. I grazed his tent, which made a loud popping sound from the force of the wind my wings created.

As soon as I was past the tent, I quickly spun around and

stood upright to land. Will jumped straight up, causing the tent stakes to rip out of the ground. I almost fell over laughing as he stumbled out of the tent and shot me a death glare.

"S—sorry to w—wake you," I sputtered through my laughter.

He glanced at his watch as he pushed his long, black, tangled mass of hair out of his eyes. "I've only slept for 4 hours," he grumbled before he added more wood to the fire and put the coffee on.

"Sorry, man. I forgot. I just had a good idea and I wanted to see if it'd work," I said as I tried to stifle a giggle and keep a straight face.

"And did it? Or was waking me a mistake?" He leaned over and dug through the coolers for breakfast.

I couldn't control my expression, so I hid my face by digging out the cast iron skillets. "Well, it kind of worked. I wanted to make a lot of wind with my wings close to the ground. I never thought it'd make that noise with your tent. I thought you'd wake up 'cause it was windy outside, not be scared awake and fuck up your tent. Really, man, sorry." I put the skillets on the fire.

Will gave me a sideways glance when he threw some bacon into one pan and some butter in the other. "It's okay, I guess. I've still got to get home and grab my uniform so I can make it to work by eight."

"Cool. Well, I'm going to fly around some more before you take off." I laughed to myself as I—literally—took off.

Flying in circles and figure eights was starting to bore me, so I decided to try some tactical flying. I flew to the far end of the valley and gained as much altitude as I thought was safe without being seen. When I reached what I felt was my maximum speed, I quickly laid my wings against my body to cover my arms and streamline my rapid decent. Before I was in any risk of hitting anything, I re-opened my wings to glide out of my decent and speed back up to the altitude where I'd begun.

The adrenaline rush was amazing. As I reduced my flapping and glided back to the end of the valley, I could feel my heart pounding in my chest.

I wondered what kind of damage I could do to people trying to do harm on the ground.

I had a sudden vision of a long, slightly curved blade in my hands. I flew over a field of men, slicing many of them open. I was instantly reminded of the fabled flaming sword in the bible—though mine was just steel—and decided I should acquire a quality Japanese sword.

As I gained some more altitude and made a wide turn, I imagined my next practice run. When I wrapped my wings around myself for my second decent, I kept my hands at my waist. When I opened my wings, I went through the motions of drawing a sword and slicing at the air with it as I flew over the ground. I had another idea and I quickly landed. I surveyed the valley in which I stood for a moment before I pushed off into the sky again.

When I landed in our little camp, I could see that breakfast was ready. I poured myself some juice while I considered my words to my little brother.

"I need to find a sword, but until then I need to just practice with a branch or something so I can make sure I'm not going to slice open my wings."

He gawked at me like I'd grown green skin and four more eyes. "Why do you need a sword? Wouldn't you rather get a gun?" he asked incredulously.

"No," I said sternly. "I sort of—had a vision. I need a *sword*. A sword never runs out of ammo. Call the elders today from work, if you can, and tell them your sister has asked for a Japanese sword—a katana. Tell them I've mastered what they told me and I'm working on defense now. But do *not* say the word flight, okay? Be very careful to never mention flight or technology. Do you understand?" I dished out my share of food and perched on a nearby rock.

"Oh yeah, I get it," he said very seriously. "Well, I'm already done eating. I'm gonna head home and I'll call Grandfather before I go in to work. Brian should be here around noon," he said as he put on his shoes. I ate my food in record time while he finished gathering his things.

"Okay, well, tell him that if I'm asleep when he gets here,

to wake me up for lunch. I think I'm going to get some rest." I stood up and dumped my plate in the wash bin.

"Sure thing, Sis. I'll see you later." Will climbed into his Jeep, then bumped and rumbled his way out of the valley.

CHAPTER 6

"Rise and shine, White Eagle."

I opened my eyes to find Brian standing over me. "What?"

"The elders finally gave you your tribal name. You are White Eagle," he said as he turned to pour more beer over the chicken roasting on the fire.

"Well, that's cool. So how long have you been here? What time is it?" I asked, still rubbing the sleep from my eyes.

"I've been here for an hour. It's almost one in the afternoon on Saturday," he replied. "Are you hungry?"

"I'm starving. I flew all night until I felt like my wings were going to fall off," I said as I climbed to my feet.

"Do they hurt now? Are you still sore?" He sounded very concerned.

"Surprisingly, no." I flexed my wings, stretching and slowly flapping them to make sure my muscles were functional. "But the void in my belly is about to drive me crazy. Is there anything ready to eat now?" I inquired as I grabbed my stomach.

"There's some flatbread in the foil over there and there's some fruit in the orange cooler." He pointed to the ice chests on the other side of the tent.

I ran over to the coolers and threw open the lid to the one containing the fruit. I dug out an apple and a container of strawberries and plopped myself down on the stool my brother had brought for me.

While he continued to tend to the chicken and poke at the potatoes buried in the embers, I started to ramble on about the previous night. Between mouthfuls of fruit, I recounted my take-off and landing successes, as well as my rapid dives and my decision that I needed a sword. He told me I'd have one by the end of the year, and I might need it shortly after it arrived.

"The decision has not been made yet, but it has been discussed that you may need to stay in the valley to practice, as long as weather permits. We will continue to care for your garden and chickens. We will even bring you your harvests. But you have to be ready. We have to make sure you're ready by doing everything we can to help you prepare." His words were matter-of-fact.

"So are you part of the council now or something? You don't even have a tribal name yet," I blurted out.

"I do, actually. It's Silent Wolf. And you always knew I would be someday, but they figured that in these times, when the council may empty of old elders in a year or less, it would be prudent to allow their successors to start attending meetings so they are fully aware of the state of affairs. After you are revealed to the tribe day after tomorrow, the other men my age will join the council as well." He removed the chicken from the fire as he spoke and slid it onto a metal plate. He poked the potatoes and said they'd be about ten more minutes.

I tore into my half of the chicken like I hadn't eaten in a week. The fruit had barely taken the edge off of my hunger and I had no doubt that I'd need more food after I devoured the chicken my brother had cooked. The beer-soaked skin was crispy and delicious. I normally didn't like the skin, but I decided my body must really need the calories as I sucked it down. Before Brian had finished half of his share, I'd devoured every bit of meat and fat. Nothing was left on my plate but bones and cartilage.

Without even thinking, I picked up a chicken bone and started smashing it onto a rock that jutted from the ground next to me. When it broke open, I started scraping the insides out with my teeth before I realized what I was doing. I glanced up and saw my brother staring at me in complete disbelief.

"What the fuck are you doing?" he asked when our eyes met.

"I have no idea. I wasn't even thinking. I just did it." I was just as shocked as he was that I was sucking down a chicken's bone marrow.

"It's okay. I'm sure you just need the nutrients or something." He shrugged as he went back to eating.

"It's high in glucosamine and condroytin. I'm sure I need lots of that with these relatively new bones and all this joint movement," I said as I smashed open some more chicken bones.

After I cleaned out all my chicken bones, I ate two large baked potatoes and a whole flatbread. I finished scraping the potato skins with my teeth and noticed my brother was done eating as well.

"Would you like to go for a walk while we digest, Silent Wolf?" I asked as I dropped my plate in the wash bin.

"Yes, I believe I would, White Eagle." He smiled as he followed suit.

While we walked toward the far, northern end of the valley, we both kept an eye out for a branch suitable for me to use to practice with until a proper bokken arrived. "I feel very strongly that I need to inspire faith in the tribe that I can protect them, so I need to get good fast," I told him while we searched.

After about 500 yards of walking, we saw a branch that was perfect just a few yards up the western hill. I took out my knife, flew up a few more feet to the branch, and grabbed it. When I landed, it broke partway at the joint where I wanted to cut it, so I gave it a few more tugs until it was free of the tree. I gave it about a dozen whacks with my Bowie knife to make it the length I wanted before I proceeded with stripping its bark. I left only the bark that my hand covered so I'd still have a good grip.

As we turned to walk back down to the base of the valley, I glimpsed two people standing on top of the far ridge. I looked closer and realized they were standing perfectly still, and they were staring right at us! Before Brian realized what was happening, I was in the air and going straight for them. '*No one can see me. No one can discover me before I am revealed,'* I reminded him as I sped toward them.

I could hear my brother's reply in my head as I landed in front of the shocked couple with a picnic basket. *'Bring them back and don't allow others to see you.'*

CHAPTER 1

Y ou *must* come with me," I urged, inches from their terrified, blood-drained faces.

They didn't budge. They were hardly even breathing.

"Now!" I grabbed their arms and started dragging them down the side of the mountain. I peered over my shoulder to make sure it was only them. "Go to him. You were not meant to see this. You may have to stay here now until the tribal meeting. Here, take this," I said as I shoved the picnic basket toward the man I vaguely recognized.

"The o—one on M—Monday? Is t—this what that's all a— about?" he stammered while he stumbled down the hill.

"Yes, that's part of it. I mean, I'm only part of it." I stopped and turned to face the stunned couple. "If you promise not to run away, I can fly you down one at a time. This is a treacherous slope, and flying is much faster."

They both turned and looked at each other apprehensively. "Are you sure it's safe?" the small-framed woman asked me.

I smiled warmly. "I have been sent here to protect you. Of course, it is safe."

She gave me a timid nod and I wrapped my arms around her waist. "Put your arms around my neck and don't let go. Relax your legs to ease my take-off and landing."

She did as I told her and, in a matter of seconds, we were at the base of the valley where my brother was waiting. I flew back to retrieve her male companion and then, once again, for their picnic and my makeshift bokken sword.

While we guided them south toward camp, I apologized for the unintended discovery in their day. "I'm sorry your picnic has been disrupted. I'm pretty sure I know what's going on here and what you two had planned for the day. I regret than I cannot allow you to have this day. Until the elders have been consulted about this unexpected discovery of yours, you will have to stay with us. We cannot allow you even the slightest opportunity to have doubt in my holiness and run away. You see, if the Whites and the fat-cats in charge of this country found out about me, the entire tribe could die."

At this, my new companions stopped in their tracks and I watched the blood drain from their faces again.

"Don't worry. We have many precautions in place so this will not happen. As I said, I'm here to protect you." I smiled again in an effort to ease their minds, but I was sure they could see the doubt and panic in my eyes. After all, this was completely new to me, too.

I didn't really know that I was holy, even though I was claiming to be. I certainly didn't feel like it. I still felt like my same old self. Growing wings hadn't made me any wiser or changed who I was at all. No new and divine wisdom had been bestowed upon me, just a few occasional whispers in a language that I didn't understand. It actually scared the hell out of me. I was terrified that if I repudiated what everyone thought I was—if I denied being an angel—then the tribe would doubt my abilities to save them. I didn't want them to doubt me because I didn't want to doubt myself. If the elders believed that I could save them, then I had to do everything that I could to do so. I hoped I would get new powers as I gained confidence and knowledge. So until I could figure it out for myself, I'd just have to fake it until I made it. After all, the only precaution that the elders had in place seemed to be me.

We walked back to our small camp in silence while I mulled over my doubts. The three of them sat down around the dying fire. I, of course, could not sit down.

"What are your names? Where do you work?" Brian asked as they got settled.

I continued to pace back and forth on the other side of the fire.

"I am Bob and this is my girlfriend, Nallia. I work as a dealer at the casino, and she works at the smoke shop on the southern end of the rez." He continued to seem apprehensive while he spoke.

Nallia looked like she was going to go into shock. She just stared at the ground, lightly rocking forward and back as Bob kept her pulled close to him and absentmindedly rubbed her arm to comfort her.

"Make sure she doesn't fall asleep. Shock can be fatal even if there's no injury." I stared into his eyes as I spoke and saw the terror burning inside them. "She will be fine," I assured them. "I can't stress enough that I'm here to protect you, to save you. I am going to do everything in my power to ensure these end-times are as painless as possible. Bob, can you come with me for a moment? I'd like to speak to you."

Bob squinted up at me and gave a quick nod before he stood.

"Brian, keep Nallia talking," I instructed. "Ask her about her life, or their relationship. Try to bring her back to this moment so she can relax."

I heard him start by asking if she was hungry or thirsty as I rounded a corner in the rock wall with Bob. When I thought they couldn't hear us, I began my line of inquiries. "You came out here today for a day of exploring, picnicking, and proposal, didn't you?"

He looked utterly shocked.

"You were going to hand her a rose during the sunset with a ring tied to it, weren't you?"

At this, he plopped down on the ground and stared down at his legs as if he didn't understand what was happening. He gazed up at me with pleading in his eyes. I reached out, grabbed his forearm, and helped him up. He continued to stare at me in disbelief.

"How do you know all these things? I didn't tell anyone about my proposal idea. Aren't you a bar waitress at the casino?"

"I am kind of an angel incarnate, but real angels aren't like what Christian mythology says they are. The elders told me that my holiness slept inside this mortal body until I was able to stay hidden and self-sufficient in order to grow my wings undiscovered. I quit my job almost two years ago when they started to grow too large to hide. I know these things about you and many others because I am also a prophet, as well as a powerful psychic. I can read people's minds. This is how I will save you. This is how I will save the tribe along with those who seek our help with pure hearts. Many will come here, and many more will die trying to come here. Many that come will be turned away because of the evil in their hearts. You see, evil is infectious.

"But that's not what we should be discussing over here. I just wanted to tell you that if you'd like for me to find a nice peak to sit on, I can fly you up there for the sunset, and you can still propose as you intended while we keep an eye on you from afar. I truly am sorry we've put a damper on your plans. This was supposed to be a wonderful day for the two of you. Plus, I'm losing valuable practice time." I rustled my wings uncomfortably as I thought about how badly I wanted to separate myself from the ground.

"Yes, that sounds fine. I just hope she's still up to it," he said before we turned back to camp.

I heard laughter ring out as we were about to round the corner, and I knew Nallia would be fine.

"...and then h—he walks into the kitchen w—with *shit* all over t—the front of him a—and dripping from his hair!" Nallia sputtered between giggles and then burst into laughter again at this mental image of him.

"Damn it, Nallia! Why do you have to tell that story to everyone we've ever met?" Bob's face flushed, but I could tell it was embarrassment and not anger at his lover.

Nallia continued to giggle as she explained that Brian asked her what was the funniest thing that had ever happened to her.

My brother smirked. "I didn't know how else to lift her spirits."

I laughed at the whole ordeal. "I'd like to hear the full story someday, too. But first, there are other matters at hand. What time is it, Silent Wolf?" I inquired.

He looked at his watch. "It's almost 2:30. Why? Are you still hungry?"

"Not just yet, but I'm sure I will be soon. Right now, what I really want is to fly." I turned to our new guests. "Would you like to join us for a late lunch and then when the sun starts to set, I'll take you to your picnic?"

"Sure, that sounds good," Nallia piped up. "I'm starting to get hungry."

"Okay. Brian, would you mind roasting a few more chickens? I'll eat at least one, maybe one and a half, so maybe you should make three this time. Is that cool? Are there enough?"

"Yes, there's five more chickens in the cooler. Do you want potatoes, too?" he asked no one in particular.

We all said yes, we'd like baked potatoes.

While my brother shoved the spit into the chickens, I pushed off and went soaring into the sky. I glanced back down and saw Bob and Nallia staring at me as I flew. I soon realized that I'd left my bokken behind. As I glided back over the camp, I spotted it leaning up against the rock where I'd smashed my chicken bones.

I flew around in a wide circle and checked to make sure I could descend the pitch of the slope. After I determined I could, I landed near the top of the ridge. I sucked in a few breaths and took off down the side of the mountain. I flapped with all my might and gained rapid speed as I soared down the steep hill, never more than eight feet off the ground.

As I neared the bottom, I could see our guests' eyes getting wider as they realized how fast I was traveling. I swooped down and grabbed my bokken in a relatively smooth motion, but the force of the wind I left in my wake ripped the tent stakes out. I angled my wings to slow myself and quickly swung around to land facing them. "Sorry." I smiled. "I'm still learning my speed. I've been flying for less than a week."

They continued to stare at me in shock and I laughed nervously while I wondered what they'd say if I told them it was actually closer to a day than a week.

"Well, as you can see, I'm gaining proficiency very quickly."

I walked over to the tent and re-staked the side I'd torn up. I found some excess rope and cut it off with my knife. I crouched next to the fire and burned the cut end of the polyester rope so it wouldn't fray before I tied it around my waist to hold my bokken.

"So what's with the stick?" Bob asked quietly.

"It's my temporary bokken sword until a real bokken gets here, and then a real katana will arrive," I said while I got my rope tied.

"What is a bokken sword?" Nallia asked.

"It's a Japanese wooden practice sword shaped like a samurai sword," my brother answered.

"Watch this," I said with a wink.

I pushed off into the sky and flew north up the valley. I gained altitude before I circled back around and went into a dive. Since I planned on going lower to the ground than I had before, I didn't want to gain too much speed and crash. When my rapid dive was complete, I spread my wings to glide over the ground. I drew my bokken from the rope tied to my waist and sliced furiously at head and stomach level—if someone had really been standing there, that is. I continued to glide about six feet above the ground for nearly one hundred yards before I stood up and landed a few feet from the camp.

I could feel the smile on my face, stretching from ear to ear, as I walked over to the fire.

"That was impressive," Brian said.

"Yeah, that was amazing! You could've killed dozens of people if that was a battlefield you had flown over!"

I was a bit shocked to hear those words come out of Nallia's mouth, but the enthusiasm she said it with really floored me.

"You seem just a touch too excited about that," I mused.

"Well, if you're meant to protect us, then shouldn't you be a great warrior?" she asked very seriously.

"Yes." I smiled widely. "I will be a great warrior. That's very insightful of you to notice." I put my bokken back in the rope loop I'd made for it. I turned to my older brother. "How long on that chicken?"

"Well, I just put them on, so at least another hour and a half," he said as he opened a beer to pour over the chicken.

"Cool. Well I'm going to go wear myself out." I laughed and turned to take off into the sky.

CHAPTER 8

As I soared over the valley, I decided I wanted to know how fast I could fly and if I could keep my top speed for long distances, or just short ones. When I reached the southern end of the valley, I asked my brother mentally to time me from when I thought *start* to when I thought *stop*. He pushed the thought that he was ready, and I dove off the mountainside as I thought, 'Start now.' I flapped with all my might and tore through the stillness of the cloudy afternoon. When I zipped over the camp, it was a blur. I kept flapping my massive wings for a few moments, and, before I knew it, the northern end of the valley was right in front of me.

I yelled out, "Stop!" as I quickly angled my wings so that my momentum would take me *up* the side of the mountain rather than slamming *into* the side of the mountain. But I held the angle for too long since I wasn't used to maneuvering at such high speeds. I wound up flying upside down and away from the mountain. I pressed my wings against myself and spun so I was right side up again before I sped back to the camp.

As I closed in on the camp, I decided to try a new landing. When I stood upright and angled my wings to slow myself, I dragged my heels in the dirt so that when I kind of came to a stop, I just kept the momentum to walk a few more steps over to the camp. "How long did it take me?" I asked, only slightly out of breath.

"There's no possible way you flew from one end of the valley to the other. It is impossible for you to fly that fast." He appeared fairly irritated with his arms crossed over his chest.

"How long did it take?" I insisted.

"It took one minute and twenty-nine seconds. This valley is five miles long. And if a car travels a mile a minute at sixty miles an hour, then…" He stared off into space as he thought before he announced, "You were flying about 200 miles an hour!"

His jaw fell open at this realization. I heard Bob and Nallia both gasp. I was also shocked and wondered how I could even breathe at those speeds.

"I have no idea," Brian replied aloud.

"How fast does a plane fly?" Nallia squeaked.

"Commercial planes fly at over 500 miles an hour, while smaller planes with fewer engines fly slower," Bob said. We all looked at him. "My dad used to be a pilot. He wanted me to follow in his steps, so I learned a lot of shit like that when I was a kid."

He stared at the ground and lightly kicked a small rock with his foot while he spoke of his father and I wondered absent-mindedly what had happened between them.

"Brother, I want you to time me from when I take off to when I land. I will fly to the south end, then to the north end, and then I will land in camp. That should be about ten miles and we'll see how long that takes me, okay?"

"Okay. I'll see you in a few minutes then." When he nodded that he was ready, I pushed off and flapped with all my might.

I soared down to the south and tried the same move I'd done on accident at the other end. It worked wonderfully and I decided it was a much quicker way to turn. I'd have to try that move at a slower speed later to see if it still worked, I thought as I passed over the camp. After I made my second turn, I realized I'd forgotten to keep my speed up. As I flapped my wings furiously and flew back over the camp, I could feel the knots in the rope at my waist starting to loosen, so I held tightly to my bokken as I made my descent.

When I landed in the camp, my brother said that it had taken me three minutes and nineteen seconds to make the ten-mile trip. "I bet if you were flying in a straight line, it would shave some time off of that," he pondered.

"I bet you're right. Perhaps we can test that one day, as well," I said as I retrieved some apple juice from a cooler. I gulped down over a pint of juice before I removed the bottle from my lips. "I haven't told anyone this yet, but as odd as it is, my body has stopped producing waste. I mean, like, I don't have to use the bathroom anymore." I laughed nervously. "You know, ever since I started flying," I added.

"I bet it's because of all the energy you need now. Your body must be using everything instead of turning so much of it into waste. That's actually pretty interesting, like Alexandria's Genesis or something," Brian mused.

"You know, that's kind of what I was thinking. Except my eyes aren't violet and those stories are fake," I replied as I put the juice to my lips again.

"Then what do you call the color they are if you don't call it violet?" Nallia asked.

"Well, my eyes are hazel. They're brown at the edges, green in the middle rings, and the smallest rings around my pupils are golden. That's generally referred to as hazel," I said in a somewhat smart-assed tone. "It's weird enough that they're not brown, but I think someone would notice if my eyes were purple."

"No, they're not hazel, Hope," Bob said as he stood. "They *are* a pale shade of purple, almost lavender. How could you not know that your eyes changed color?" he asked incredulously.

"Well, I haven't been able to fit into my bathroom in almost a year and that's where my only mirror is. Also, it's not like I've worn makeup since I quit my job, so I've had no real reason to inspect my face recently. I can't believe no one else noticed and told me," I said as I pulled my large Bowie knife from its sheath that hung in the small of my back.

When I inspected my reflection in its shiny steel surface, I saw for myself that my eyes had turned a wonderful, lovely shade of light purple. I turned the knife to see my whole face. How beautiful I was! My acne had completely cleared up since

I'd stopped wearing makeup, and the lavender of my eyes complemented my skin tone perfectly.

I re-sheathed my knife and asked my brother if he'd noticed the color change.

He denied seeing it.

"I suppose I'll have to ask Will when he gets here. When is that, by the way?" I asked before chugging more apple juice.

"He should be here around sunset," Brian answered as he turned the chickens.

"Okay I'll be back in a while. I'm gonna work some more." I put the remaining apple juice back in the cooler before I smiled at our guests and pushed off into the cloudy sky.

I decided I wanted to see how high I could fly, and since these weren't thunderclouds, I had no fear of flying into them. I made a wide spiral up into the sky until I disappeared into the mists high above the valley. Once I realized I could no longer see the ground below me, I wondered if I could go through the top of clouds and still be able to breathe. I continued to spiral up, and within seconds, I broke through to the blue sky above. The wetness clung to my skin and my feathers as I soared above the fluffy billows and into the warm summer sun.

As I coasted through the sky, doing dips and turns and just having a good time feeling free, I noticed a commercial jet flying toward me. I was instantly filled with conflict. I wanted to dive back down into the clouds and go hide in the valley so I was not discovered by the others. I knew that's what the elders would want me to do. But another part of me wanted to be seen by some of the plane's occupants for a myriad of reasons.

For one, it would be funny because that was a total movie scenario—people on a plane seeing something or someone outside and they go crazy. For two, they wouldn't really know exactly where they were, so even if anyone believed them, they wouldn't know where to search for me. Also, who was to say it wouldn't inspire faith in some people? I wondered. Maybe seeing a smiling angel outside an airplane window could save someone's life.

With that thought, I decided to do it. I determined the path the plane was on, and quickly flew toward it. I was thrilled to realize as I flew that the altitude wasn't affecting my breathing. I pumped my wings as fast as I could to gain speed. If Bob was right about how fast those planes fly, it was going more than twice as fast as I was, so I would only be seen for a blink of an eye. Too bad I couldn't sit on a wing or something, I thought.

While I tilted my wings to turn, I saw that the plane was still a few miles behind me. I continued flapping with all my might. The whole time, I kept my head down to watch out so that I wouldn't get sucked into the plane's massive jet engines. But it did not appear to be getting any closer. I did a quick loop-de-loop and saw that the plane was still flying right for me. I did a few circles in the path of the plane before I started beating my wings again so fast that the tips were a blur. The plane roared behind me as it closed the gap between us.

I stopped flapping for a second so I could peek over my shoulder. I saw the pilots through the front window with gaping mouths and wide eyes. As the plane screamed past me, I made eye contact with at least six passengers through the tiny, oval windows. When the plane was ahead of me, I dove a bit lower and flapped with all my strength in an effort to catch up with it.

Well, it must have been my lucky day, because the plane appeared to slow and lower its altitude. I decided it must be starting the descent for the landing. I swooped up next to the other side of the plane and tried my best to match its speed. As I caught up with the front of the plane, I once again stopped my flapping so I could glimpse the occupants. This time, when the pilots saw me, I smiled and waved before I slowed and fell back along the rest of the plane. This time, when I drifted past the windows, nearly every person was staring outside. I figured someone must have freaked out about seeing me, and now everyone was searching for a little hope.

As the plane continued to descend, I realized I needed to disappear before I wound up leaving the bottom of the clouds. I broke through the top of the clouds, saw the trail of pollution the jet had left, and traced it back while I counted to 100. I had no idea, really, how far I'd flown and I had no doubt I was hundreds of miles from home. After I reached a spot I felt was possibly close to where I'd ascended, I started a slow decline. I was very fearful of bursting through the bottom of the clouds and finding myself in the middle of a big city where people might see me.

When I saw the clouds thinning, I realized that my fears had come true. I was flying over a cluster of skyscrapers in a city I didn't recognize. I tilted back up into the clouds so no one could see me while I tried to decide what to do.

Before I knew it, I'd come to a mountain pass with a road running along it. I didn't see any cars, so I went in for a closer inspection and hoped I could find a road sign that told me where I was. I couldn't read the large, green sign from the sky, so I swooped in for a quick landing. The sign stated that Denver was one mile ahead, and I figured that was the city I'd flown over.

Just as I started to freak out over how far I'd come, I heard a car coming. I knew I couldn't make it to the clouds before they saw me, so I quickly crouched down next to a large bush and wrapped my wings around myself to cover my human body.

The car chugged and sputtered around the corner before it died right next to the sign I'd been studying.

I heard the driver exit the vehicle and start to slowly walk toward me. I was panicked and my heart pounded in my chest as he cautiously approached me. I knew I must face him, but not allow him to know I was a Native American. I silently thanked God for my purple eyes that would help to confuse my race.

I sprang up from my crouch and spread my wings wide. The lone man yelled in surprise and stumbled a few steps backward. I spoke to him in Russian, knowing he wouldn't understand me, and said that I was sorry, but I didn't speak English. Again, I silently thanked God for an old co-worker who had taught me a few phrases in her native tongue.

I pointed at his car before I walked over to it. I laid my hands on the hood, prayed that this would somehow work, and I willed the car to start and make it to his destination. The engine roared to life. I turned to the stunned man and slowly said

"Ow-tow mek-en-ik" in a thick Russian accent. "Go. Ow-tow mek-en-ik," I repeated.

He nodded that he understood as he climbed into his car and watched me soar off into the sky. I flew north in an effort to further confuse him.

When I was far enough away that no one could see me, I turned back south and flew toward Four Corners. I had no idea how long I'd been gone and I had no idea how long it would take me to find my empty valley again. I figured fastest was best, so I started flapping with all my might. In a matter of minutes, I found myself rushing over the tourist spot at Four Corners, and I knew I'd be home soon. I ceased my flapping as I turned back to the northeast and just allowed myself to ride the wind as I coasted through the clouds toward my people's valley, and then on to my own.

CHAPTER 9

I landed in my camp and proceeded directly to the cooler for some more apple juice. "How long have I been gone?" I asked between swigs of juice.

My brother chortled. "Over an hour. You got lost, didn't you?"

"So what if I did?" I snapped back.

"It's nothing. It's just that, well, I heard you. I heard you wondering if there was any way I could send some kind of mental homing beacon to you so you could find your way home without being seen. But that didn't happen, did it? You were seen again, weren't you?"

I was surprised at how calm he was about me being seen.

"Yes. I was seen. I was seen by people in an airplane for a few seconds while I was above the clouds and I was seen by a man on a mountain road outside of Denver. His car broke down right in front of me and I helped him. I laid my hands on his car. I willed it to work, and I only talked to him in Russian so he'd think I was of a native tribe in Alaska or Siberia. It's fine. No one has any idea that this is where I'm from. No bad will come of this, I assure you." I looked my brother right in the eye the whole time I talked and I saw that he believed me. I was amazed that he hadn't yelled at me for being such an idiot.

"You're right. You are an idiot. I should be yelling at you. Only, I have enough faith in our prophesies to believe that everything will be fine." Brian walked over to the cooler and popped open another bottle of beer for the chickens roasting over the fire. As he dribbled the beer over the birds and turned the spit, he glanced at me over his shoulder. "Lunch should be ready in about fifteen minutes."

I decided I'd rest for the remainder of the day since I'd just flown a couple hundred miles. "After lunch, I think I'll go to sleep so I can fly all night." I situated myself in my tall chair. "What is Will going to bring us tonight when he arrives?" I asked as tilted my head back to rest it on my wings.

Brian walked over to a rock and took a seat. "He's bringing more dry ice and regular ice for the coolers, as well as another cooler full of meat. I figured you'd get sick of eating chicken all weekend, so I asked him to bring some red meat, too."

"Good. So, I think after I've slept for about four hours, you'll have to wake me so I can eat again. After I've eaten, I'll fly Bob and Nallia up to that peak there so they can have their picnic." I pointed to a ridge that was tall and did not appear to be accessible by foot. "That way, they can still have their night and they won't be here to surprise Will when he arrives." I then silently told my brother what Bob had planned and he smiled at me.

"That sounds fine," he said after a minute.

We ate lunch mostly in silence until I started smashing my chicken bones. My brother and I laughed as we explained what I was doing to our once-again surprised guests. They peered at each other like they were wondering what other weirdness I would surprise them with next. I chuckled as I went back to smashing my chicken bones.

After I ate two whole chickens, a baked potato, and two apples, I bid my new friends good night. I turned and asked my brother, "Will you please have a half pound of bacon and a dozen eggs ready for me when you woke me up an hour before sunset?"

He smiled, nodded, and wished me pleasant dreams.

While I got settled in the tent, I heard the three of them head north up the valley to go for a walk. I was grateful that they left me to fall asleep in silence.

CHAPTER 10

I awoke several hours later to the smell of coffee, bacon, and eggs. I crawled out of the tent and glanced up to see my brother smiling at me.

"I was just about to wake you," he said as he handed me a tin cup of coffee.

"No need," I mumbled. I stood up and took the cup from him. "The coffee was calling my name."

I quickly drained the cup, ignoring the heat of it as it seared my mouth and throat. I dished out as much food as my plate would hold and went over to crouch on a perch rather than sit in my chair. I greedily scooped the scrambled eggs into my mouth, pausing my hand only to chew the bacon. My brother walked over and handed me a skin of water which I immediately drained before handing it back to him.

"Why don't you use a fork?" Nallia asked shyly as I continued to scoop food into my mouth with my bare hand.

I almost choked on my eggs as I stifled a laugh. I swallowed my mouthful and quickly replied, "Sharp metal doesn't belong in your mouth."

I finished my breakfast in record time and went back to clear the pans. The rest of the bacon and eggs didn't even fill half of my plate, so I ventured over to the orange cooler for some fruit. I grabbed an orange, an apple, and filled the rest of my plate with grapes.

I found the apple juice I'd been drinking earlier and finished draining it before I returned to my perch. I gobbled down the rest of my food and checked the sky. It was nearly time to take our guests to their picnic.

I dropped my plate in the wash bin and quickly scrubbed my hands clean. "Are you two ready?" I asked.

"I think so," Bob said with a clear nervousness in his voice.

"It's okay, man. You'll be fine. It's going to be great," I told him gently with a pat on the shoulder. I turned to Nallia. "I'll fly up there first to make sure it's solid and safe and that the mesa is plenty large enough for you two to be comfortable without fearing that you'll fall off the edge. But in order to give you two some privacy, I have to leave you somewhere that you cannot get down without me. Do you understand?"

Nallia nodded firmly. I could tell she was not upset that I couldn't trust them completely. I got the feeling that Brian had explained a lot to them while I'd been flying and sleeping.

We walked for about ten minutes until we came to the base of where I thought I should take them. "Wait here for a minute," I said before I flew up to the small mesa. I stomped around on it and I jumped up and down all around the edge of it. It seemed very sturdy. It was a good size at about fifteen-by-twenty feet and there was indeed no way down but flight. I dove off the side and glided down to where the soon-to-be-engaged couple stood.

I asked Nallia if she was ready and she grinned widely. I flew her up first and then flew Bob up before we realized they'd left the picnic basket back at camp. "Back in a flash," I said before diving off the side of the mountain again. I returned a minute later and handed them the basket.

"When you want to come down, face the camp, and picture me in your mind. Imagine that you are pushing your thoughts to me and Brian and ask that I come for you. I should be here shortly after you call for me in your mind."

I smiled warmly and they gave me a nod of understanding. I winked at Nallia before I dove off the side of the cliff and sailed toward the setting sun.

I flew around for a few large, lazy circles until I saw my little brother's Jeep bumping along into the valley. I flew around behind him and called out to him not to slow down. He glanced over his shoulder and then understood that I was try-ing to land in the back. My landing wasn't as graceful as I'd intended, but that was just one more thing I'd have to work on.

When we pulled into camp, Brian was surprised to see me standing in the back of Will's Jeep.

"Look what I found, Brian! Can I keep it?" Will called out as he came to a stop.

We all had a good laugh and then proceeded to empty the vehicle of the coolers full of stuff our brother had brought.

As we sorted everything out and resituated all of the cool-ers, Brian and I explained to Will what all had happened that day. He didn't seem pleased about these intruders, but I told him we didn't have a choice. "If they had returned to the rez and spread the news before agreements were signed, it could've been disastrous," I explained.

"So when are they coming back?" Will asked.

I laughed. "Whenever they call for me. I'm guessing that'll be around the time the darkness has mostly spread through the sky. Maybe a little sooner, depending on how excited he is that she accepted his proposal."

After all the food was put away, Brian told us goodnight and drove his truck out of the valley with the empty coolers in the back. We started to set up our next meal since Will had not eaten dinner yet, and I knew I'd need plenty of fuel for my night ahead.

Will had a road atlas and a compass in his glove box, so I determined my flight path for the evening while dinner cooked. I told my younger brother that I wanted to see if I could fly to Las Vegas and back without being worn out. He was pretty apprehensive about it since I was not supposed to be leaving the reservation. But when I told him about my unin-tended trip to Denver, he agreed that using a map and a com-pass would be a better idea than just blindly flying into the night and getting lost.

Just as I was figuring out exactly which direction I needed to fly, I heard the call from both Bob and Nallia at the same time.

"I'll be right back, Will. I'm going to go retrieve our

guests," I said before pushing off into the darkening night sky.

I landed on the small mesa a few moments later and I was greeted by Nallia's beaming face.

"You heard us!" she exclaimed. I smiled at her enthusiasm as she continued to speak in the same breath. "See what my Bobby gave me?" She thrust her hand inches from my face. I took a step back as I reached out to hold her shaking hand and inspect the ring.

"It lovely," I mused. "The light from the moon gives it a wonderful sparkle."

"It's three diamonds for the three years we've been dating," she gushed.

"Really, I'm very happy for both of you. I'm glad you could still have your special night, even if you might now have to stay here with us for two more nights. But for now, we should be heading back to camp before it's pitch black out here. Who's first?" I asked with a warm smile.

"I'll go!" Nallia squealed. "I love flying with you. Can we fly all the way back to camp?"

"Sure. Would you mind putting your arm through the basket so it hangs from your elbow? It'll save me a third trip back here," I said as I placed the basket on her arm how I thought it would work best. She did as I asked and, in a matter of seconds, we were landing in the camp. "Back in a flash," I said to my brother as I pushed off to retrieve Bob.

When I landed with him half a minute later, I introduced our new friends to my little brother. We sat down around the campfire and discussed the plan for the evening. I told them that the tent was plenty large enough for the two of them and Will could wait to sleep until Brian returned in the morning.

"At first light Sunday morning, Silent Wolf will attend the Council and let them know what's going on out here, as well as find out how the meeting with the police force went tonight. He will tell them how cooperative you two have been and that we feel it should be fine for you to return home once you sign the forms you'd be signing Monday night anyway. Or, even if you do sign your forms, you may still have to stay here until the meeting. I really don't know. That's up to the elders. When he is done at the Hall, he will return here to let us know what's going on. Then, we'll figure out what to do next.

"So whenever you two are ready to get some sleep, the tent is all yours. There's a pile of sleeping bags and pillows I use to make my pallet. Feel free to use and rearrange whatever. I only ask that you don't have sex in there. That's really not something I want to be sleeping on later." I winked.

They both blushed and nodded in understanding.

I went back over to the rock the map was laid out on and continued to figure out my route. Once I worked out the directions to go toward and return to, I quickly memorized some town names on either side of and beyond Vegas in case the wind blew me off my bearings. I tied Will's brand new stopwatch to my belt loop and made sure I could hold it in front of me, as well as tuck it in my back pocket without pushing buttons. I was very happy to see he'd picked one that was perfect for me to fly with. "Wish me luck, Brother," I said with a touch of nervousness.

"You don't have to do this, you know. You could just fly around the valley." His face was filled with concern. "What if you get tired? What if you get hungry? We haven't had dinner yet," he argued.

"Asking me to stay in this valley and get good is like putting a speed boat in a pond forty feet across, five feet deep, and telling me to practice maneuvering it. It can't be done. The top speed I can reach in this valley is 200 miles an hour. When I was flying above the clouds, I kept pace with a commercial jet going at least 500 miles an hour. I need to stretch my wings, William. I need to test my limits in speed and distance.

"I will fly as fast as I can there and I will time it. Then I will fly lazily home and time that as well. I will see how I feel, and I will see how long it takes me. Flapping lazily for me is still probably a mile a minute, maybe a bit less. Actually, if I were to fly fast both ways, then I bet I'd be back just in time for dinner. Trust me, I'll be fine. I'll see you in a couple hours," I said as I turned to go.

"Fly safe," I heard him whisper as I started flapping for my exit.

CHAPTER 11

I cruised lazily around the valley for a minute before I pulled out the stopwatch and hit "Start." I shoved it back into my rear pocket before I streamlined my arms and legs and flapped with all my might.

I could definitely feel a difference in my wings every time I flew. As I shot through the night sky, I wished I had some way to weigh only my wings to see how much muscle I was gaining.

I zipped over the land below me and realized that I couldn't make out anything clearly. I knew I would have to identify Las Vegas by its bright lights. But if I didn't keep a watchful eye out for the shining jewel in the desert, I might go too far and get too worn out. I checked my compass to make sure I was still headed due west and then I checked the stopwatch to see how long I'd been out. It'd been over twenty minutes. I climbed higher into the sky so I could see Las Vegas if it wound up being on either side instead of right in front of me.

After another five minutes of flying, I could see a beam of light shooting up into the sky from beyond the horizon. As I continued on, I realized that it was the light from the hotel shaped like a pyramid. I tore through the clear night sky and very soon found myself soaring over the blurred lights of Sin City. I ceased my flapping so that I could pull out my stopwatch and check my time—thirty-eight minutes and fourteen seconds. I was thrilled.

As I made a lazy and wide turn, I fumbled with the stopwatch as I tried to save the time, but restart it as well. Once I got it figured out I hit start, glanced at my compass to make sure I was headed east, and I took off through the sky. I put my head down and tried to ignore the gnawing hunger inside my stomach as I pushed my wings to their limits.

After twenty minutes of flying, I decided to slow down so I could survey the land stretched out below me. Finding my valley would not be as easy since there was no beacon to guide me. Another twenty minutes passed before I saw the village at the northern end of our reservation stretched out below me, so I turned south until I came across my valley. As I made some additional large, lazy circles high over our camp, I remembered that I needed to stop the stopwatch. This time it read forty-six minutes and two seconds.

I landed in the valley and strolled into the camp to find my brother removing a roast from the open fire.

"You got here just in time," he smiled.

"Psshh! You're tellin' me. I'm half-starved over here, Brother. I just flew about 900 miles in less than an hour and a half," I exclaimed. I filled my plate with food and grabbed a gallon of water out of a cooler. I sat down on the stool Brian had brought me, set my water on the rock next to me, and tore into my food like I hadn't eaten in weeks.

Will stared at me in complete disbelief as I ripped through my food like a savage animal.

"You might want to slow down so you don't choke."

I glanced at him and saw his face was filled with genuine concern.

"It's okay," I said and paused to chug some water. "Fine. I'll slow down if it'll make you feel better. But I really am incredibly hungry here," I added when he raised his eyebrows.

"You look…gaunt. Like, I don't remember being able to see your ribs before. And your cheekbones are more prominent."

"No doubt my body uses my other tissues to fuel me when I run out of ready calories," I said around some half-chewed food.

"Like when someone is starving to death?" he gasped.

I simply grunted in agreement.

I finished what was on my plate and then went back for another helping. I asked Will if he wanted any more meat and, after he carved off a few slices, I plopped the remaining four pounds of the roast on my plate along with the rest of the vegetables he'd roasted.

When I settled back into my chair, I began to speak as I pulled apart my meat into a pile of shreds.

"You know, I don't even shit anymore," I blurted out.

My little brother studied me like he didn't know if he should laugh or apologize.

"Everything that I eat I process as fuel, and now that I fly so much, I eat more than you and Brian combined. I could end up being an incredible burden on the tribe if times get tough. But, then again, I guess if I'm protecting them, it's worth it, huh?" I mused.

Will nodded faintly at my question that even I wasn't sure if it was rhetorical or not.

When we had both finished eating, we went for a walk to digest and not be in the camp being loud and disturbing Bob and Nallia while they slept. We discussed my trip to Vegas as well as my return. We also talked about my worries of the meeting in less than forty-eight hours.

"I'm afraid that many in the tribe will refuse to sign the forms. I'm also afraid about…well, what about tribe members who moved away? Will we call them back to protect them?"

"So you're worried about Little Sparrow?" Will scoffed.

"She's practically my sister!"

"She's *not* our sister." His tone was slathered with irritation and bitterness. We both knew that he was the only reason she had left the reservation a month before my wings had started to grow. He also knew that I blamed him for driving her away. She was the one person who did not share my blood that I would have been able to trust with my secret.

"I don't give a fuck how bad your break up was. Taniya's been my best friend since we were three years old. I can't just let her die out there," I yelled at him. I took a deep breath so I could continue with more composure. "I'll fly her back here myself if I have to. I won't let her just fade away. She's a part of this somehow," I nearly whispered.

As I spoke quietly, I drifted farther away in my mind. I could see her sitting in a crappy apartment in my mind's eye. I knew she didn't have loads of money to live in a nice place, so her New York apartment was surely a dump. While I thought hard about her, I saw her pick up her phone and dial it. She appeared worried and impatient. Then I heard her mumbling, "Come on, Hope. Pick up, pick up, pick up. Damn it! Voicemail."

This stunned me like a body slam and I snapped my eyes open. I realized that I'd stopped walking. I was just standing in the middle of the valley with my brother staring at me, confused.

CHAPTER 12

U m, are you okay? What just happened here? You've been, uh, gone, I guess, for a couple minutes. Where did you go just now?" His face had changed drastically from the last time I'd seen him and it was once again filled with concern.

I gawked at my brother, no doubt matching his confusion in my own expression, and he continued to speak.

"I said your name a few times after you trailed off, but you didn't respond until I shook you."

"I went—I went to New York." I blinked a couple times in disbelief as I heard the words leave my own mouth. "I saw Taniya sitting on a daybed in a shitty apartment. She picked up her phone and tried to call me. I think I really saw her. I think she felt me thinking about her and wanted to talk to me." I stared at the ground for a moment before I could meet Will's gaze. "I think I really saw her."

"How long has it been since you've spoken?" The irritation was starting to creep back into his voice again.

"We talked twice after she left. The last time we spoke was right after my wings started to bud, but they hadn't broken through my skin yet. Then her phone was disconnected." A thought suddenly came to me and I turned away from Will as I spoke again. "I'll be back in a minute. I've got to see if I can reach Brian." I drifted off in my mind and set my focus to my older brother. He quickly appeared to me. I saw him sitting on his back porch, smoking the peace pipe.

He looked up once he realized he was being watched and stared directly at my spectral self who was peering at him. "I see you figured out how to remote view. So what do you want?" he mumbled.

'*I need to use your phone and maybe your computer. Can I come over? Are you alone?*' I replied with my mind.

"You'd better make it fast. I'm tired," he whispered.

I snapped out of my trance and turned to Will. "I'll be back in a little bit. I have to go see Brian. Would you mind walking back to camp by yourself?"

He shook his head no and shrugged his shoulders, as if to say "Why would I care?"

"Okay. Also, would you mind cooking up some bacon and a dozen eggs for me?"

Will agreed and I took off into the night.

Within a few minutes, I landed in my back yard and ran into my house to grab my beat up, prepaid cell phone. I had a missed call from a number I'd never seen before. I was out of minutes, so I wrote it down, grabbed all of my cash, and shoved everything into my pockets. I ran out to my yard and took off again. I landed at Brian's a few moments later and found him sitting exactly how I'd last seen him in my mind.

"So what the hell is going on?" he asked with a touch of annoyance.

"I need to call Taniya."

He stared up at me in surprise. "I thought we decided to leave her out of this?"

"No, *you* decided to leave her out of this. Besides, I started thinking about her and suddenly she was there, in front of me. I think she must have felt me thinking about her, because I watched her pick up her phone and try to call me," I babbled.

"But you two haven't spoken in almost two years," he interjected.

"I know. So I have to call her. I may have to fly out there tomorrow night to bring her back. Her house is empty since her mom died last winter, and I can't just let her die out there," I continued.

Brian chuckled softly as he glanced down and shook his

head for a few seconds. He focused on me again and raised his eyebrows. "What about Will?"

"He's not at all happy with my idea, to say the least," I replied. "But I don't really give a shit. I told him not to fuck my friend, and he did. Then he broke her heart and she set his car on fire the night she moved away. I know, I know, I know. But this is beyond petty bullshit like this," I said all in one breath. "So do you have your phone out here?"

He handed it to me.

I turned around as I pulled the number out of my pocket and dialed it. My hands were shaking when it started to ring on the other end. After two rings, Taniya picked up the phone.

"Hello?"

I hadn't realized how much I missed talking to her until I heard her thin metallic-sounding, far away voice.

"Taniya?" I squeaked.

"Hope? Is that you? I just tried to call you, like, ten minutes ago! I wasn't sure if it was still your number 'cause it was an automated message so I didn't leave a voicemail," she gushed.

"Yeah, it's me. I've missed you so much! But hey, the reason I called is because I'm going to be in New York tomorrow night and I really want to see you." My voice continued to break as I spoke.

"Um, yeah. Sure! Definitely!" she squealed. "How come you didn't call me sooner? Do you need a place to stay?" She sounded extremely excited that we'd get to hang out. I was so relieved that she didn't consider the massive coincidence of her calling me first when I'd wanted to call her.

"I'm afraid I can't stay and I'll only be in town for a few hours. Can I just get your address so I can Google it and I'll give you a call when I get close? Oh, and do you have roof access?" This time when I spoke, I was much more stable and my voice only broke twice.

"What's going on? Why do you need roof access? Why will you be here so briefly?" The excitement in her voice was finally replaced with suspicion.

I was glad I was such a fast thinker when the words just spilled out of my mouth. "I've got an eight-hour layover at the airport. You're the only person I know in the city, and I miss you like crazy, so I figured there would be nothing better than kickin' back with my sister and burning one under the stars." I attempted to laugh lightheartedly, but I was sure it sounded forced when it escaped my lips.

She laughed. "Oh. Well, that's cool. Man, you wouldn't believe the bomb-ass weed they've got in the stores out here. Way better than anything we grew on the rez or got in the stores in the cities around there."

We chattered on for a few more minutes before she gave me her address and I bid her goodnight. As I handed the phone back to my brother, I asked for one more favor. "Can I look this up and print it out before I take off?"

He sighed and waved me inside as he stood to retire to his room. I knew he had a big day tomorrow, so I did my best to be quiet as I printed out a satellite image of the top of her building and some maps of the surrounding area.

When I landed back at the camp with a fistful of computer maps, Will knew what was going on. "You really are going to fly out there and bring her back, aren't you?" he asked incredulously.

"Yes, William. I am. And I don't give a fuck what you say," I spat. "This is stupid crap! Are you really willing to let my best friend die just because she burned your car?"

"It was fucking irreplaceable. That car was a mint classic with all original parts. That bitch broke out the window, dumped a gas can in it, and lit my shit on fire!" He got louder and louder as he spoke. I tried to quiet him so he wouldn't wake our guests and that just angered him further. "Don't you fucking shush me. How could you think that I'd ever want to see her again?" His fists were clenched at his sides and his whole body was rigid with anger. I could even see his nostrils flaring as he fumed.

"It's not like you were Mr. Perfect! You promised her all sorts of shit you weren't willing to follow up on just to get in her pants. I warned you not to fuck my friends, and you still did. This is going to fucking happen and you *will* be civil to her, Will," I said in a low tone. I stared him down as I spoke and I watched the hostility decrease in his face. "She has been my friend almost as long as you have been my brother. We share a connection that cannot be explained. I will not allow her to fall like the rest when she may be capable of remote viewing like me and Brian. That is an essential tool in the protection of our tribe. Would you like to be the one to explain to the elders that we have to be without someone who could help save the tribe because you're angry at her?"

He sank into his seat and huffed out a sigh. I knew he would do as I wished and not be rude to her when we landed Monday morning.

I sat down and quietly ate the food he had prepared for me. Once I had polished off the bacon and eggs, I added more wood to the fire and washed the dishes that were starting to pile up in the wash bin.

When everything was clean, I dug through the coolers to see what food was left. There were two chickens, a cooler full of fruit, one half full of potatoes with a few handfuls of carrots, and a cooler full of pork and beef. There was also a cooler full of gallons of water, one jug of apple cider, a bottle of V8 juice, and three more bottles of beer. I pulled out the last of the chickens and shoved the spit through them. When I put them on the fire, I noticed that Will was leaning up against a rock with his hat over his face. *I guess he's going to sleep*, I thought. I poured some beer over the chicken and buried three potatoes in the embers of the fire before I took off to fly some more.

As I soared through the cool air of the early summer night, I thought about the coming tasks of the next few days. I knew that if a flight to Las Vegas and back used so much energy, for the flight to New York and back I would need even more fuel to sustain me.

I decided I would spend the rest of that night and all of the next day eating as much as I could and only fly while my food was cooking. I made large lazy circles as I climbed higher into the night sky. I found a good current and just rode it for a few minutes without flapping my wings.

After several minutes of deep thought, I landed to tend to

my food. While I sat next to the fire and turned my chickens from time to time, I noticed that my little brother was lightly snoring as he slept in that awkward position.

I figured that if this trip was going to happen in eighteen hours, I would also need a lot of food waiting for me when I landed. If Taniya felt me when I saw her before, could I make her hear me, too? I wondered.

I gave my chickens one more turn and poured some more beer over them before I sat down and got as comfortable as I could.

CHAPTER 13

I focused on Taniya and, in a matter of seconds, I saw her sitting on her daybed, watching late night reruns of old sitcoms on a crappy TV across the room. I drifted my view to between her and the TV and she sat straight up.

"Hope," she said flatly.

She didn't seem to see me, but she definitely was thinking about me again.

I forced my thoughts into her mind and said, *'Taniya, I am here in front of you. I can remote view now, so I can see you and your apartment. If you can hear me, nod your head.'*

She bobbed her head up and down slowly to indicate that she could hear me.

'I do not have a layover at the airport tomorrow. A month after you left, I started to grow wings and now I can fly. I want you to close your eyes and focus on me. I believe you are able to remote view as well and I want you to see me as I am.'

'Okay.'

At first I thought I had imagined it, but as she continued to speak, I realized that I faintly heard her speaking inside my head. *'Are you sitting on a rock in a valley with huge wings folded in an X behind you?'* Even the voice of her mind was shaking in shock.

'Yes, I am.' I spread my wings and stretched them out above me as I continued to push my thoughts to her. *'I am a prophesy fulfilled. I am the savior of our people. I am to be revealed to the tribe Monday night, and I want you here. No, I need you*

here. I'm coming to get you tomorrow night. Anything you want to take with you to the reservation, you need to ship to your mother's house in the morning. I will take off from here at sunset, or if it's cloudy, I'll take off earlier. But it is over 2,000 miles from here to there. The farthest I've flown so far is 900 miles to Vegas and back. The fastest I've flown that I know of is 550 miles per hour, so it could take me between three and four hours to get there, then another three or four to fly back. Plus, I'll need to eat massive amounts of food when I land. That's why I contacted you now. I was hoping you could have some good Chinese delivery food waiting when I get there.' I laughed after I finished my thought and I saw her chuckle a little bit, too.

'*Well, there's not enough darkness to fly here and back in one night. Can you fly here tonight? There's almost five hours until sunrise.'*

Her voice sounded stronger in my head and I decided she was getting the hang of this cross-country communication.

'*That's a good point. I will also, no doubt, be exhausted after such a trip. I'll tell you what. I've got some food cooking right now. I should be done with that in an hour or so, and then I'll head that way. When the sun starts to lighten the sky, go to your roof and wait for me. Turn to the west and send out your thoughts to guide me to you. We'll chow down on some food and then we'll get some sleep. When the sun sets again, we can leave for the reservation and we'll land here in my practice valley.'*

I saw a smile spread across her face while she listened to the thoughts I pushed.

'*That sounds great! I'll make some coffee and stay up to wait for you. Good thing I'm off work for the next two days,'* she thought.

'*I'll see you soon, Taniya.'* I smiled, broke the connection, and stood from my rock to tend the chickens again. They were coming along nicely, as were the potatoes.

CHAPTER 14

I walked over to where my brother was sleeping and stood silently over him while I contemplated whether I should wake him or not. I knew I couldn't wake Brian, and Will was my only other option. Then I realized that if I woke Bob and Nallia, I could circumvent the anger and argument with my little brother. I walked to the tent, unzipped the door, and saw the couple sleeping sweetly in each other's arms.

"Bob, Nallia, wake up. I need to talk to you," I whispered as I shook their feet.

They slowly moved and unwound themselves from each other before sitting up.

"What's going on?" Bob asked as he rubbed his eyes. "It's not morning already, is it?"

"No, but something has come up and I needed to tell someone. I'm going to be leaving in a little bit, and I won't be back until this time Monday morning. I have to fly farther than I ever have before, but I must only fly long distances at night so that I can't be seen. I will sleep and eat in a safe place with a tribe member who remote views. She will likely return with me. But I will be safe. Tell my older brother when he returns in the morning that I will be waiting for him to contact me at eight p.m. eastern standard time. He can inform me then of what the elders said about the meeting Saturday night and how attendance is looking for Monday night. I will see you soon, okay?"

They both stared at me blankly.

"Do you understand? Will you remember all of that to tell Brian?"

They bobbed their heads up and down in perfect unison. It was almost enough to make me laugh at them.

"I'll be leaving in a while after my food is done, so I'll do my best to remain quiet until you have fallen back asleep."

They thanked me. I zipped the tent closed as I backed out of it.

I returned to my chickens and turned them a few times while I emptied the beer on them. I sat down on my stool and munched on about a dozen apples while I waited for the chickens to finish cooking. After I had polished off all of the apples in the camp, I pulled the smallest potato out of the embers with a stick. I sat it on a rock to cool and tore the wings and legs from the two chickens still roasting on the fire. By the time I had finished all of that, the rest of my food was ready and I ate it as fast as I could. I managed to drink almost a gallon of water with my dinner and felt incredibly bloated by the time I had finished.

I placed the string of the compass over my head and let it hang from my neck. I studied the maps one last time before I took off into the sky. I turned east and flapped with all my strength. As I climbed higher into the sky, I found some thin, wispy clouds that felt wonderful on my face and shoulders.

Many different worries regarding my future ran through my mind. So, okay. I'd figured out how to remote view, read minds, make others hear my thoughts, and fly really fast. I still wasn't feeling any kind of greater knowledge. When I swung my fake sword, I felt like a little kid playing ninja after watching a movie. I knew I wasn't moving how I should. But who was there to teach me? If I'd had a vision of needing a sword, shouldn't I be gifted with the know-how to use it? I felt more and more frustrated every day that I woke up without having had some kind of great revelation on how to actually save my people.

The time seemed to pass quickly considering the strenuous activity I was performing. After what seemed like thirty minutes, I checked the stopwatch and it had been three hours. I was shocked. Before I knew it, I was flying over water that never seemed to end. I checked my compass and quickly turned north as I sent out a thought to Taniya. '*Where are you?*' I pleaded in my mind.

'*I'm here,*' I heard her think as I felt her presence to the north and slightly east. I continued flapping my wings with all my might while I tried to ignore the gnawing hunger in my stomach. I urged her to continue sending me a signal since I had no idea where I was. After a few minutes, I felt her beacon grow in strength and I knew I was drawing close to her. The sky was beginning to lighten to my right and I was certain the sun would soon blow my cover if I didn't find her in time. Just as I thought this, I passed over her and stopped flapping my wings as I turned to go back to her.

I landed on the roof behind her and she jumped in surprise as she turned to face me. "Sorry I scared you," I said sheepishly and folded my wings behind me.

She approached me hesitantly. "Oh my God! Your wings are amazing! Though, you look scrawny as hell. How long did it take you to get here?"

I pulled the stopwatch out of my pocket and wrapped my arms around her in one smooth motion. "I've missed you so much, Taniya! You look good, too. It took me almost four hours to get here. I guess my top speed must be closer to 600," I mused and broke the hug.

She reached up to the top of my left wing and ran her shaking hand down the length of it, lightly smoothing my feathers with her delicate fingers.

"I am so happy to see you," I said. "I really hope you'll come back with me. I'm also starving. Do you have any grub?"

She laughed a little bit, nodded, and waved for me to follow her. "Don't worry about people seeing you. No one lives on the top three floors and none of my neighbors are awake this time of morning," she said as we walked down a decaying staircase. "Sorry it's a dump, but this city is expensive as hell. My shitty little apartment here is over $1600 a month for rent." She laughed when she turned to see my jaw drop in disbelief.

"I know. It's ridiculous, right? Do you still like cashew chicken?"

We stopped in front of her door and she fidgeted with the locks to grant us access.

"Hell yeah, I do!" I exclaimed as we entered the dingy little shit-hole where my best friend lived. "I don't smell any, though. Is it on the way?"

"No, it's leftovers. But I figured you could eat on that while we waited for more to arrive if you needed it." She walked over to the fridge and pulled out a bag of take-out with dragons printed on the side.

I laughed. "Well, I'm glad I brought a fist full of cash, 'cause I'd likely eat you out of house and home otherwise," I sputtered through my laughter. "You'll understand better when you see me eat, but I require exorbitant amounts of fuel to fly at the speeds that I do. In the last twelve hours, I have flown over 3000 miles. I've also eaten over four pounds of beef roast, six pounds of potatoes, eight pounds of apples, two whole chickens, several gallons of water, a pound of bacon, and two dozen eggs. And I don't have to use the bathroom anymore because everything I eat and drink is processed for fuel. I sweat a lot, though.

"Also, you saw me with your mind's eye earlier and I wasn't gaunt, was I? I fill back out quickly when I eat." When I finished speaking, I looked up to see her face frozen in shock.

"How is that possible?" she mumbled.

"Well, I don't really know. But how is it possible that I grew wings at my age? Or at all?" I asked. "How is it possible that I can fly and see the future and remote view and all sorts of other shit? How is it possible that my eyes have changed color? None of this is logically possible, but it's happening so I've just learned to accept it. I guess nothing should really surprise me anymore when it comes to unexplainable creatures or acts. I wouldn't be surprised if I came to discover that vampires and werewolves were real," I joked.

Taniya appeared to stiffen at my mention of these fictional creatures, but she quickly composed herself before she suggested that we get some food ordered.

We dug through her drawer of take-out menus and found a stack of Asian cuisine restaurants. She pointed out to me which ones were the best, which ones were close and fast, which one was cheapest, and a whole slew of them that were mediocre in all of the above. I picked the one with the best quality food and perused the menu for a few moments before deciding on my order.

"You might want to write this down. It's long and complicated."

She dug through the drawer until she found a pen and a Post-it note pad.

"Two orders of cashew chicken without onions or mushrooms and with extra cashews. I don't care if they charge extra. Three orders of beef and broccoli with sides of extra teriyaki sauce. Um…three quarts of beef lo mien, four orders of crab rangoon, a dozen egg rolls, and four orders of sweet and sour shrimp with extra shrimp, water chestnuts, and bamboo shoots."

She nodded that she'd gotten it all written down as she set down the note pad and picked up the phone. When she was done placing the order, she hung up the phone and told me that it would be forty-five to sixty minutes before the food arrived. I groaned at the length of the wait and she laughed.

"What did you expect with an order that size? That's enough to feed a dozen people! You heard me on the phone arguing with them that this wasn't a prank. Lucky for you, I order from them at least once a week, so most of them know me. She said they'd have to send at least three people to bring us all the food. They deliver it on bikes, you know."

I was silent for a moment while I processed what she'd just told me. "Well, would it be cool it you called them back and said they can bring it to us as it gets ready? I mean, like, stage it, you know? One guy could bring a load and we'll pay for it and tip him, then another guy could come with some more, and we'll pay him and tip him for what he has brought. That way, the fried stuff isn't getting cold while it's waiting for all the dinners to be ready. You know?" I suggested.

"Actually, I think that would be a great idea," she said as

she started to pace tightly in front of the sink. "I think they'd like that better, too, since they'd be getting paid several times and know that if we jack them the first time, they won't lose more food and money from having multiple driver's robbed." She gazed at me then and the smile spread wide on her face. "Yes! I'm calling them back," she cheered as she picked up the phone and hit redial.

While she explained to the woman on the other end of the phone what we now wanted them to do, I dug through her refrigerator and freezer in search of something else to eat until the food started to arrive. I found what I guessed was some kind of meat or maybe tomato sauce that was vacuum sealed and wrapped in layers of crumpled plastic wrap. As I dug through the freezer some more, I found a few more of them, but decided that whatever they were, they'd take longer to thaw and cook than it would take for my food to arrive. I found a frozen dinner stuffed in the back and I quickly popped it in the microwave.

Taniya hung up the phone and I turned to face her. She was beaming. "They'll be here in twenty minutes with the lo mien, rangoon, and egg rolls," she squealed.

"Awesome! I hope you don't mind that I'm eating your last frozen dinner, but I didn't think you would."

She shook her head and chuckled as she clapped me on the arm.

"Also, whatever those frozen packets are in there, you might want to get those packed in dry ice and shipped off or just throw them away."

Taniya stiffened again at the mention of these frozen packages. "Um, those aren't mine. He'll be back for those tomorrow or maybe later today. I forgot when he said he'll return. He can also ship me anything I need from here," she replied sheepishly.

I squealed in excitement. "You have a boyfriend?" I asked. I couldn't believe she hadn't mentioned him sooner.

"Well, not really. He's more like a roommate." She blushed. "Well, he *is* a roommate," she corrected. "But he's in Russia right now getting some things settled to take care of his old house there." She mumbled her reply and stared at the ground. "He's a really weird guy and I'm actually glad he's not here to disturb us. Deema tends to become the center of attention whenever he's around."

"Oh. How did you two meet?" I tried to ignore her suspicious behavior since I figured I would be filled in eventually as to what exactly was going on here.

"We used to work together at this diner. It was my first job when I got here. He started there a couple weeks after I did and I found his accent hypnotic. I had a huge crush on him for a while, but then he seemed to be such a player that I refused to let myself get attached to him. As we grew closer and hung out more, I realized that I wasn't so much attracted to him as I was the idea of him. I mean, I still really like him, but only as a friend. We've been living together for eighteen—no, twenty months and nothing has happened in the two years we've known each other."

"Oh. Well, he sounds nice, I guess," I quietly replied.

The microwave beeped to indicate that my food was ready. I devoured it in about a minute and placed my spoon in the sink.

We chattered on like we were in high school again and I caught her up on what had happened with the development of my wings.

CHAPTER 15

S o, tell me how it started," she insisted with an exuberance that I'd missed so much in her absence.

"Well, it began in the form of dreams in the same manner and style of so many prophetic dreams that often infiltrated my sleep."

Taniya nodded quickly. She knew all about the dreams I'd always had.

"I saw myself with massive, almost luminescent, opalescent white wings extended from my back." I spread my wings as I continued to illustrate my vision. "I was standing on a fence-post in front of a group of soldiers that were trying to attack our people on the reservation. They could feel—and see—my obvious difference from them and believed that the words I spoke were true. They decided to not only join us, but to also help protect us from other attackers." I lowered my wings and met her eyes again.

"When I awoke from this dream I felt different, and when I beheld my reflection in the mirror I almost fell over in surprise. My spirit body, or soul, or whatever you want to call it, had sprouted massive wings. I could feel the weight of them in my spirit and I quickly discovered that I could move them. I flapped my spectral wings and I could feel the connections to my back as well as my other torso and shoulder muscles."

"Holy shit," she muttered. "Even in spirit form? You could really feel it?"

"Yeah, I know, right? Fucking crazy. So over the next few

weeks, I started feeling an actual physical difference in my back. There was often a tingling sensation where my wings would soon emerge."

"I remember that!" she squealed. "The last time we talked, you said your back felt weird."

"Yep. And once they did start to break through my flesh, I was only able to hide them under my shirt for about a month. But after that, all bets were off and I couldn't wear any shirts that covered my back at all, no matter how loose fitting they were." I turned to the side while I tugged at the halter top I was wearing to show her how it cut around my wings in the back.

"I had to quit my job as a cocktail waitress at the casino and revert to the ways of our ancestors since I could never leave the house during the day or go into town. I hunted and tended my garden at night while the rest of the reservation slept. Luckily, I was never at risk of losing my house because my share of the tribal casino profits had always paid all of my bills. My job had just been so I could have luxuries like Internet and cable as well as save money to someday move off the reservation to go to college.

"It turned out to be a very satisfying life, with the exception that I had virtually no human contact for nearly two years. My brothers would come to visit me sometimes, but I missed my friends from work. I've missed *you*. I missed the nightlife of going to the casino with my girlfriends and having a blast, bar jumping and gambling. I miss going to the grocery store and getting to buy stuff like Dagoba chocolate, Smart Balance peanut butter, and strawberry Jell-O. I miss Kashi frozen waffles with real Vermont maple syrup. I miss not having to kill, butcher, and grind all of my own meat.

"But I think most of all I've missed being outside in the daylight. I even had to be careful on nights with a bright moon by covering my shockingly white wings with a black Halloween cape. I could sit inside all day long on my stool and stare outside, but that was never good enough. I've often wished that I could still go have a picnic in the desert, or even just sit on the ground at all without having to hold my massive wings in the air.

"In fact, I can't sit in most chairs with a back—and certainly not any with armrests—without having to hold my wings out to the side. Imagine that, every time you sat in a chair, you had to hold your arms parallel to the ground the whole time. You can raise them up higher, but you can never put them down for as long as you're sitting in the chair. That is how awkward it is for me to sit in a chair with my wings. I also can't sit on the ground for the same reason. There's nowhere comfortable for the bottom half of my wings to go when I sit down. So, I can only sit on tall barstools that give ample room for my wings to hang behind me. Brian brought me one that has a half back so I can actually lean back in it without bothering my wings.

"Sleeping has also become its own issue."

Taniya laughed. "I was just going to ask about that."

I grinned at her. "Well, I could no longer sleep on my back, because it made my wings hurt like hell when I woke up. As my wings grew larger, I also couldn't sleep flat on my stomach either because I felt like they were crushing me.

"I eventually worked out a method of piling pillows on the floor so that I could lean on them while I slept. I pile up several body pillows as well as several regular pillows and sleep facing the ground at about a sixty-degree angle. I'll rest the wing closest to the ground on the floor with my other wing either on top of me or flopped back on top of my other wing, depending on how cold or hot I am.

"Blankets became tricky and semi-uncomfortable since the cloth would catch on my feathers and pull on them. I finally figured out how to lay the blanket around my waist and only pull it up in front of me to cover my torso."

"How long did it take you to fly?"

"I just started flying successfully within the last week."

"Successfully?" she asked and arched an eyebrow.

I laughed. "Yeah, well, I had a few failures first."

She giggled, but motioned for me to continue.

I sighed before I spilled the details. "The first time I tried to fly, I climbed up a ladder to the roof of my trailer, steadied myself, spread my wings, and jumped off. I wasn't able to fly, but I was able to slow myself enough by flapping my wings that I didn't get seriously hurt. I took it as a learning experience and spent the next few months flapping my wings as much as I could tolerate all day long while I waited for darkness to come. I had to remove anything that could be blown around in my living room and I even had to tape my curtains to the wall so they wouldn't blow around and reveal me."

Taniya snickered again. "I can just picture you duct taping your faded-ass blue curtains to that ugly green wallpaper."

I couldn't help but laugh, too, before I continued. "The second time I tried to fly, I made it about 100 yards to the edge of my property before I tumbled to the ground. This time, I did actually hurt myself. I sprained my right ankle and knee as well as my left wrist. Since I had gained speed traveling over the ground, I'd kept the momentum as I crashed into the ground. I decided that my problem was that I needed to learn how to properly catch the wind with my wings.

"Within an hour of my second attempt at flying, Will just happened to stop by. He helped me bandage myself and hobble inside. I asked him to find me as many videos and books as he could about the mechanics of bird flight. The next night he brought me two bags full of information for me to study that he'd borrowed from the library and I spent the next month pouring over it all."

There was a knock at the door and we both sprang to our feet. I shoved a handful of bills into Taniya's hand before I ran to hide in the bathroom.

CHAPTER 16

W hen I heard the door close, I exited the bathroom in eager anticipation of the food I smelled. "I hope they brought lots of soy sauce," I said as I ripped into the bags of food. I frowned at her and shook my head. "Not one single packet."

She flashed me a smile before she calmly walked over to the window and flung it open. She crawled out onto the fire escape, waited a moment, and called out something in Mandarin. I then heard her holler down to the guy who delivered our food that we'd double his tip if he brought us a few handfuls of Kimlan Soy Sauce packets on the next trip. I heard a faint reply echo up from the street before she re-entered the apartment.

She smiled as she walked back into the kitchenette. "Not a biggie. He'll be back in fifteen minutes with more food and a bunch of the good soy sauce."

My mouth was still hanging open disbelief. "How the hell do you speak Mandarin?"

She laughed loudly and dipped an egg roll in some sweet and sour sauce. "I took some classes to learn basic Mandarin, Cantonese, Arabic, Hebrew, Spanish, French, and Italian. Plus, Deema has been teaching me Russian. In all eight languages, I can say that I only speak a little, ask directions, count to 100, and a few other simple things for basic conversation. Mostly, I know how to order food." She giggled. "Oh! And I can tell people to go fuck a goat. I thought it would be an easily translated insult that people anywhere would understand." She gave me a wink and finished eating her egg roll.

"That's amazing!" I said after I finished drinking the broth from my first container of soup. "I take it that it comes in handy?" I asked before I started to slurp my noodles.

"In this city? It most certainly does! But if I move away from New York, I doubt it will do me any good at all," she replied.

I choked a little bit on my mouthful of noodles before I managed to swallow it all. "*If* you move back?" I asked in surprise.

"Well, I'm coming back with you tonight for sure. But, I don't know if I'll stay or not. I mean, I love it here! I can get any kind of food I want any hour of the day in this city. I can walk three blocks in any direction and find a different language being spoken in the streets. I don't know if I really want to give this up." She spoke firmly, and with conviction. She really was in love with this city and the life she had built here.

"I'm sorry, Taniya, but if you come back to the rez, there is no coming back here. Times are changing and the final war is coming. If you are four hours of flight away, I cannot save you or protect you. But you are my soul-sister, and I cannot leave you here to die! By the order of the elders, I am to stay in that five-mile long valley to the west of our town. They do not know I am here because I could not wait for their permission. I saw you try to call me the first time. You tried to call me because you could feel my presence. I knew you could do things—I know you can do things that we've yet to discover. You are important not only to me, but to the entire tribe. They just don't know it yet. *You* just don't know it yet."

The whole time I spoke, she sat there with her hand frozen halfway to her mouth. "But what about Will? I never went to court over his car. What is he going to do to me if I have to spend the rest of my life in the confines of the tribe?" Her voice was quiet and shook as she spoke.

"You need to apologize to him and he will treat you with civility. Don't make snide remarks and ignore any you hear him say. I don't know if he will apologize for what he did to you or not, but you definitely need to be the bigger person here and let him know how sorry you are for destroying his one of a kind car," I calmly replied.

"It wasn't one of a kind," she mumbled.

"Actually, it turns out that it was. All the rest of the cars in the country that were that same year and model had been damaged or pimped out or altered to be legal. His was the only one that was mint—the only one that was still perfect and 100% factory original. He got the insurance from it, but he never found another classic car he liked that the owner would sell."

I could see the regret in her face as she stared at the floor. It told me that she was genuinely sorry for what she'd done.

"But," I added, "I never really did understand what the big deal was with that car. Those old things from the 1970s haven't been legal to drive with original engines in over fifty years. And he refused to ever modify it. All he ever did was drool over the damned thing and tow it to a car show once or twice a year."

She opened her mouth to speak, but before she could, a knock came at the door along with a man shouting something in Mandarin.

I turned to hide in the bathroom and she opened the door to pay for our second load of food from Xiang House. She tipped him $20 this time and said what I could only assume was thanks or goodbye as she closed the door.

She laughed. "This time it looks like we got the cashew chicken and a whole bag full of soy sauce." Then she sighed as she set the food on the counter. "I will apologize to him. I hope he not only accepts it, but I hope he apologizes to me, too," she said more seriously.

I grabbed a small bowl out of her cabinet and started filling it with soy sauce. After I'd filled the bowl about halfway, I grabbed a large mixing bowl off a different shelf and turned back to the food. I opened up the cashew chicken and saw that they made it exactly how I'd asked. I poured it all into the giant bowl and let the steam envelope my face.

"This smells awesome! I can really tell that they use quality stuff. Mmm. I can't wait," I exclaimed.

I poured in a few packets of soy sauce and stirred it with my hand.

Taniya snickered at me as she asked me if I wanted some chopsticks or a fork. I laughed right back at her and told her I avoided forks and other metal utensils in my mouth whenever possible and chopsticks would just slow me down. I started to scoop food into my mouth as she giggled at the ridiculousness of my actions.

After I swallowed my first few handfuls, I paused to defend my actions. "I'm starving, girl. You've got no idea how hungry I am and how much food I'll need to eat to gain the energy to make it back home tomorrow at twice the weight."

As soon as the last word left my mouth, I was stuffing it full of rice, chicken, and vegetables again.

We ate in silence for the next five minutes until another knock came at the door, accompanied with the heavily ac-cented shout of "Xiang House delivery." I walked into the bathroom with my bowl of food and waited for the front door to close.

"It smells like we got the beef this time," Taniya said as she turned back toward the tiny kitchenette. She set the bag on the counter, but we left it untouched since we still hadn't finished what we'd already started.

I gulped down the rest of my soup before I went back to finish my rangoon and cashew chicken. As I threw my soup containers into the sink, I noticed that Taniya had stopped eat-ing. "Are you okay? Or are you just full?" I asked, picking up my mixing bowl of food.

"I'm fine, I'm just full. And thinking a lot, I guess. I'm scared of what's going to happen when I go back to the reser-vation. What if you get in trouble for coming out here to get me? Maybe I shouldn't go with you." She sounded really sad about what she'd said, so I'd felt confident in opposing her.

"You are coming with me, Little Sparrow, and I refuse to take no for an answer," I insisted. She blinked up at me, dumb-founded. "I can't do this without you. I won't do this without you, Taniya." The expression on her face said that she felt like a little kid again as I scolded her. I put my hands on my hips and ruffled my wings a little bit. "Will you come with me to-night?"

"Well, there's something else you need to know first." Her eyes darted over to look behind me.

CHAPTER 17

"Mommy, why does that lady have wings?"

The voice of a small child came from behind me. I turned sharply to see a little boy clutching a teddy bear and rubbing his eyes. He was the spitting image of Will when he was a toddler. I turned back to Taniya. It was my turn to gawk at her, dumbfounded.

"She's an angel, baby. She's here to save us from our lives in this rat hole," she said to the little boy. Then she turned to face me as she spoke again. "This is my son, Dancing Bronco. I figured since I'd never return to the rez, I'd give him a tribal name myself. He's your nephew. He's Will's son." She choked back tears. "I left because he wanted me to get an abortion."

"He told us you did. I thought you left because he still broke up with you," I blurted out.

My wings touched the wall behind me. I realized I'd been backing up. My left hand shot out and I gripped the frame of the front door to help me stay on my feet. My mind was spinning with all of the complications this was sure to bring.

Her son shuffled across the room and crawled into her lap on the daybed.

She cuddled him. "I couldn't go through with it, but I told him I did. Leaving was my only option. I considered adoption, but once I felt him moving in there I knew I could never give him up. How can I face Will now? And how can we bring Dancing Bronco with us?" She started to stroke his hair and I watched him fall back to sleep in her lap.

I was trying to figure out what to do next, when a knock at the door made me jump. "Xiang House delivery."

As she tried to stand without disrupting her son, I heard another voice talking in the hall. "I'll get that. Hang on just a second." The slightly accented voice was that of a man and it drifted into my ears like giant silver bells—deep, but beautiful and intoxicating. A few seconds later, keys started jingling in the locks. When the last one was undone, the door opened a few inches. It stopped, just as Taniya reached it.

"Hang on, Deema. I've got to undo a couple more locks."

She closed the door and undid the last two locks before she swung it open. I could see through the space between the hinges that a gorgeous man was paying for our last delivery of food for the morning. He was just over six feet tall and he had pale skin that almost seemed to shimmer in the flickering fluorescent lights of the hallway. His eyes were dazzling. His irises looked like polished black stones that were embedded with teeny tiny diamonds. His hair was blacker than mine, stick-straight, and waist length. His smile was intoxicating and his movement had the fluidity of a classically trained ballet dancer.

I stood there like a statue as I peeked out from behind my wing at him. I wasn't facing him when he entered, but I was still afraid to move lest the delivery guy glance behind the door and see me.

When the door closed behind them, Deema saw me for the first time and froze in his tracks. "What the fuck is an angel doing here?" he demanded in a low growl without taking his eyes off of my wings.

"Language!" Taniya yelped at him.

"How do you know that these wings are real?" I asked without averting my gaze from his glittering eyes.

He seemed as if he was about to spit at my feet. "Because there's only one strap on your shoulder and it's obviously attached to something on your lower back. You're also not wearing a bra and you have a halter top on. Those are obviously real, flesh and blood wings."

I spread my wings wide, touched them to the ceiling, and

sucked in air for a reply. "I am here to save my family from certain death, asshole."

"Language!" Taniya said again as she put her hands over her still-sleeping child's ears.

"I am Hope, Only Daughter of Dancing Bear," I continued in the same breath.

His face relaxed when I said my name and I knew she had spoken of me to him before. He also finally met my eyes for the first time and he appeared shocked for just a split second before he regained his composure. Though, a tenderness seemed to grow in his eyes for the rest of our conversation.

"I have to bring her back to the reservation later tonight so she may attend the tribal meeting on Monday night. We were just trying to figure out what to do about the growing complications of this when you walked in."

He strolled over to the counter and smoothly shoved a few things aside to set down the bags of food for which he had paid over eighty dollars.

"So now that you're here…um…would you mind watching my nephew until we can book you two a flight out there?"

He gently laughed at my idea.

"Well, you don't have to be a dick about it!" I huffed.

"I'm not being a dick," he said and continued to chuckle. "I don't have to book a flight there. I can fly over 200 miles an hour. I bet I could beat you there."

CHAPTER 18

"Whatever. I can fly over 600 miles per hour," I scoffed before I entirely realized what he had just said to me. "Wait a second. What do you mean you can fly?"

He continued to laugh for just a second before he stopped and peered at me strangely. "I—take it—that you—that Taniya didn't tell you that I am a vampire, did she?"

He was so hesitant, so unsure, that I felt like he'd wanted to ask me something else instead. He gazed into my eyes in such a tender and familiar way, but I knew I'd never met him before.

I shook my head. It felt like trying to move through gelatin.

"Well, I am over 500 years old. Thirteen years ago, after I reached my last milestone, I learned that I could fly when I tripped and just floated above the ground. I drink blood, but I only kill people who are bad and kill or steal from other people. I can also read the minds of the weak so I know who is evil, but those who are stronger with the mental arts seem to have a natural block around their minds. Like you, for example. You must be very strong with your mind because I can't even get a glimpse inside, no matter how hard I try. Taniya's difficult, but you're imposs—"

"I am a remote viewer, as is Taniya, and my big brother, Brian," I interrupted.

"That's great," he said absently and settled down in the only armchair in the room. "So, I help support Taniya and her son with money I take from the corpses of my victims. I also rob blood banks when really bad criminals start getting low and, if I have to, I can survive on the blood of animals."

I glanced back and forth a few times between Taniya and this self-proclaimed immortal who sat across the room before I decided he was done filling me in on their arrangement.

"Okay, so you can fly. That's great. Do you have super strength and super speed on land as well?"

He nodded in a slow, lazy manner as he held my gaze.

"Fantastic. You could be of much use to us. Will you stay with us? Or will you return here to live in the city filled with evil men?"

He shrugged one shoulder. "I don't know. I suppose I'll do what I always do." A haughty smirk crossed his face and quickly disappeared. "Whatever I want."

I filled my huge bowl with the beef dinners and dumped some sauce on it before I walked over to the middle of the room and sat down on the nasty, stained carpet. I held my wings high over my head so they wouldn't touch the floor. I was glad that I had chosen to wear long pants.

"It should take you about twelve hours to fly out there at 200 miles per hour," I said between mouthfuls of food. I caught Taniya's eyes to address her directly. "I don't think your son can go that long without food, water, potty breaks, or sleep. Perhaps I should fly him out there since I'm faster and he's lighter, thus less likely to slow me down. I'll leave him with the elders and I will not speak of him to Will."

I turned back to Deema. "And you—does sunlight really harm you?"

He shook his head.

"I wouldn't think so since the sun has been up for nearly an hour, and you just got home," I mused.

"The sun causes my skin to appear translucent, almost clear like glass when it's really sunny outside. I can get by if I hide in the shadows of buildings, and in this city, it's not that hard. It causes me no discomfort or pain whatsoever. But, I must admit, I miss its warmth against my skin on summer days like today." He stood up and walked over to the window. When he pulled up the blinds, I saw what he meant as his skin faded from white to a milky translucence.

I continued to shovel food into my mouth as I listened and pondered some more about our newly developing plans. "I'd like to have a snuggly to carry him in. I'm pretty sure we could fit him in a large one. And a windbreaker or some parachute cloth to keep his face from getting windburn," I said when I was nearly finished with my giant bowl of food.

"You were right, Hope. I really can't believe how much food you have consumed," Taniya said as I stood to pour more food into my bowl. "But your cheeks aren't so hollow looking."

I laughed, emptied two containers of sweet and sour shrimp into my bowl, and splashed it with more sauce. I put the last two containers of food in the refrigerator before I went over to the bed and sat down next to her. "I'll need to sleep after this, and I should be starving again by the time I wake. By the way, did I tell you I got a tribal name finally? I am White Eagle," I beamed before shoveling more food into my mouth.

At the mention of my name, Deema sprang from his chair and stumbled backward into the wall. "What did you just say?" His musical voice was shaky and it caught me off guard.

"My name is White Eagle," I said after I swallowed my mouthful of food.

"That can't be. You can't be! I thought I was supposed to be White Eagle!" He stared at Taniya with wild eyes. She gaped at him in confusion. "Or that you were to be White Eagle, at least!" he shouted as he continued to study her.

"What are you talking about? Settle down, man. I've never seen you act like this."

"You don't understand. When I was a boy, my grandmother told me many stories of my future." He started to pace quickly in the tiny apartment. "I'd always thought she just made them up, but so many have come true throughout my immortal life, I've started to wonder how many more of them would reveal themselves to be true. Lately, I've wondered if all of them wouldn't eventually come true. She told me of a woman with skin like the river clay, with hair as dark as the night, and as straight at the arrow flies. She told me this woman would bear me a child to care for. Grandmother said she would fly beside me through the night skies. I returned here tonight to turn Taniya into a vampire because I remembered some more of the story when I was in Russia visiting her grave behind my castle."

"You have a castle?" I interjected.

"Yes, one of the oldest stone castles in Russia. I thought that I was supposed to do this, but now I am having doubts. How is she to fly with me if it took me 500 years to fly myself? And here you are with wings. You *are* Hope—the only Hope. I just don't know what to think about this." He stared at the floor while he continued to pace.

His creased brow disturbed me more than I felt it should. I finished my food while the three of us were silent and the child continued to sleep. Once I was done, I walked over to the kitchen sink and cleaned up the remaining trash on the counter before I rinsed my bowl and washed my hands.

I went back into the living room. "Where should I sleep?"

She stood up and gestured to the daybed. "Right here is fine." She woke her son. "Are you hungry?"

He wearily nodded his head. The boy shuffled after her to the kitchen. She helped him up onto the stool at the bar I had just cleared off and poured him a sippy cup of milk.

I lay down on the bed after I arranged some of the pillows to lean on as I slept. When my head hit the pillow, I suddenly realized just how exhausted I really was. I was out within a matter of seconds.

My dreams were filled with flashes of disturbing imagery. I saw Deema with his face, hands, and chest covered in blood. He was vicious and terrifying as he snarled and bared his perfectly straight, ruby red teeth.

The next thing I remembered seeing was the same scene that had started the growth of my wings, only this time, I appeared to be pregnant.

The next flash was of Taniya sitting on a shower floor. She was naked, crying, and hugged her knees to her chest as she sobbed. Blood swirled with the water as it went down the drain. The blood was coming from a human-looking bite wound on her collar bone, as well as two spots on her back.

I quickly realized that the source of the blood on her back was tiny wings that had broken through the surface.

CHAPTER 19

I awoke in a panic and jumped up to find Deema still sitting in the same chair.

"How long have I slept?" My voice didn't sound at all groggy like it usually did when I woke up.

"You slept for almost exactly eight hours," he said after he glanced at the clock on the wall.

I looked for myself and saw that it was four in the afternoon. I made a bee line for the kitchen and grabbed my leftovers before I dug through the drawer for menus of Italian food. I sat down at the counter and proceeded to stuff my face with one hand while I flipped through the menus with my other hand. When I had eaten the last bits of rice from the boxes, I dropped them in the trash and turned to Deema.

"Where's my family?" I asked nonchalantly.

In the blink of an eye, he was on his feet and inches from my face. "They're gone. She went out to find a snuggly he'd fit in, as well as some belts to make some kind of contraption for your wings."

His icy fingers softly traced up my arms and then back down.

"What kind of contraption?" I asked with a small voice.

He chuckled lightly as he leaned in to whisper in my ear, "She wants to make straps for your wings so you can walk in the streets. She said that if people think they are part of some costume, they won't think anything of it. Of course, you can't move them at all, or you'll blow your cover. She wanted to surprise you, so act surprised, okay?" His voice was soft and the tickles from his cool breath sent little chills down my spine. He felt me quiver and wrapped his icy fingers around my shoulders as he pulled back to stare into my eyes. "They are climbing the stairs. This never happened, okay?"

I nodded my head dumbly and he grabbed my face. What followed was the most passionate kiss I'd ever received without opening my mouth. It ended far too soon and when I opened my eyes, he was back in the chair across the room.

I heard keys jingle in the door and struggled for a second to regain my composure. I turned back to the menus and scooped them off the counter. When Taniya came in, she was carrying her son in a snuggly and had a huge grin spread on her face. She turned around to show me it wouldn't interfere with my wings.

I beamed at her. "Awesome! So, what's your favorite Italian place around here?" I asked and held up the menus.

"Ooh," she enthused, her eyes lighting up. "Definitely Luigi's two blocks over and three blocks up. Too bad they don't deliver," she said with a slight wink at Deema.

"Damn. Would you mind going to get me some carryout from there?" I tried to sound disappointed as I shuffled through the menus. There were at least four places called Luigi's.

"I don't think that will be necessary," she said as she plopped a bag down on the counter in front of me.

I opened it and saw what appeared to be some shiny leather straps that were all connected and covered in silver studs. I pulled it out of the bag. "What the hell is this?" I asked

"It's from the shop on the corner called Master/Slave. I figured we could make a couple of adjustments to make it look like your wings are attached to that instead of you. As long as you don't move your wings, no one will think anything of it if they can see these obvious straps. What do you think?" Her excitement was barely containable. She even started bouncing up and down on the balls of her feet while she waited for me to reply.

I beamed back at her. "I think it's awesome! Help me get this thing on."

It took the three of us several minutes to figure out how to put it on and where it needed to be cut. But, by 4:30, we had gotten everything situated just right and had my long, thick hair draped over my back to cover where my wings really attached. We walked down the stairs and got nothing more than a few brief, curious glances when we emerged into the light breeze of the afternoon.

We walked the five blocks to Luigi's without anyone staring at us for more than a few seconds. With my faded and ripped, skin tight jeans, my bra-less halter top, and my super long hair, they all just assumed I was a stripper or something, Deema explained after a few blocks. I laughed it off and tried to ignore the void in my belly.

As we entered the last block, I told them that I would try to eat slowly and I would use utensils, but toward the end of the meal, I would order enough food for several imaginary people we left at home.

"Is that cool?" I asked as we turned to enter.

Deema winked and held the door open for us. "That's fine. Do whatever you like. I've got plenty of money," he whispered in my ear as I passed him.

I laughed. "So do I."

He followed me closely and fixed my hair over my wings.

CHAPTER 20

We were greeted by a slightly short, mostly round man in his sixties with thick, salt-and-pepper hair. He smiled warmly at Taniya and said something in Italian before he noticed me standing behind her. His face started to drain of color but his smile returned a bit weaker when I stepped out from behind her and "adjusted" my straps as if they were uncomfortable so he could see my wings were "fake."

He seated us at a pair of tall bar tables he pushed together so I could sit without messing up my "costume" and we started off with an appetizer assortment. I ordered the biggest plate of spaghetti and meatballs they had, and Deema ordered the same. Taniya ordered the chicken primavera and we ate our appetizers that had arrived so quickly.

Once the waiter left again, I asked Deema why he had ordered food and he laughed loudly at me. A few of the other patrons scattered throughout the restaurant stared for a moment, but soon returned to their own food and conversations. He whispered in my ear that we could keep switching plates when no one was watching and he would always keep a fork full of food in his hand.

"That way, you can eat two full plates and no one will be wise to the fact that you are a bottomless pit and I am incapable of eating," he whispered as he lightly traced the back of his icy fingers down the opposite side of my cheek. He pulled me by my chin to face him and rested his freezing forehead on mine. I feared, for a moment, that he would kiss me again, only this time, Taniya was sitting right next to me.

He saw my eyes widen and he released my face from his delicate grip. Deema turned to the food and grabbed a piece of fried provolone. I peeked at him sideways as I smeared some roasted garlic on a triangle of pita bread and he dipped the cheese in some marinara. He laid his hand on my thigh as he turned to feed me this little piece of cheese. I could feel the icy cold of his hand through the denim as he lightly rubbed up and down my leg.

I turned to Taniya with pleading in my eyes. '*What do I do?*' I thought to her.

She gave me a small nod as she thought, '*It's okay. Go for it.*'

'*You said he's a player, though,*' I thought as my eyes narrowed.

She shook her head and lowered her eyes while the corners of her lips turned up slightly. '*No, not with you. Look, just trust me on this one. He and I had a long talk while you were asleep. Seriously, Hope. Go for it. You'll understand soon enough.*'

I turned back to Deema and saw a smirk on his face as he waited for me to accept his offer of cheese and marinara. I smiled at him timidly as he started to guide it toward my eager mouth and starving stomach. Just as he was about to feed it to me, he pulled it back and placed the undipped end between his lips. He leaned toward me. I met him halfway and bit off the end of the cheese without touching him. I started to sit back to chew, but he grabbed my chin a little too roughly and pressed his lips to mine. As he gave my chin another tug to open my mouth, he pushed the rest of the cheese inside with his lips before he sat back and dabbed at the grease on his mouth with a napkin. I swallowed the food he had just force-fed me and gaped at him in astonishment.

"What is your deal?" I asked in a hushed but exasperated tone.

"What's wrong with me wanting to feed my lover?" he asked sweetly.

"I'm not your lover, for one thing," I replied quietly and with a touch of acid in my voice.

"I also found a way into your head," he continued as if I hadn't spoken. "I watched all of your visions of the future you had today while you slept. I know what becomes of us," he said as he leaned in for another kiss.

I put my hand to his chest and whispered to him, "I only remember three snippets of my dreams and none of them involved us being lovers."

I marveled at how solid his chest felt. It was like a marble statue draped in cloth. I could feel the ice-cold of his skin through his polo shirt.

He leaned in for another kiss. "Then you weren't meant to know it, only to live it."

After he broke away a few seconds later, I blushed. "I'm sorry, but I'm starving. I've got to eat."

He smiled at me, gave me a mock bow, sat back in his seat, and moved to stir his water lightly with his finger. I drained my glass of water before I grabbed the garlic I had prepared for myself. Deema glanced around the restaurant then he switched our glasses and signaled to the waiter that he was out of water.

Our food arrived about fifteen minutes later as Taniya, Dancing Bronco, and I were finishing off the appetizers. She asked for an extra plate for her son and proceeded to cut up small bites of chicken and pasta for her little boy. The waiter returned a few seconds later with a bread plate and she scooped his food onto it. The child placed his own napkin in his lap before he proceeded to carefully eat his food. I was surprised at how mature he seemed for his age and I asked her when he was born.

"He'll turn two in the fall. Even though he was born almost two months early, he has continued to surprise all of the doctors with his maturity. They told me he has the motor skills of a three year old the last time I took him in. And when he was one, they told me he had the speech abilities and walking stability of a two year old. He said his first word when he wasn't quite four months old and by ten months, we could hold lengthy conversations. He is truly an amazing child," she said, smiling down at him and watching him eat his food carefully with his hands.

"Indeed! I've never seen a child his age be concerned with eating carefully so as to not make a mess," I mused as I observed him.

The boy glanced up after he finished chewing and stared right in my eyes. "I've always been a careful eater ever since your aunt choked to death on her dinner. You know that, Hopal," he said solemnly.

"What did you just say?" I asked, stunned. Only my father had ever called me Hopal.

"You heard me, baby girl. Does it really surprise you that I'd reincarnate as a member of the family?"

He addressed me as any adult would. I couldn't believe that this was my father's soul inside this tiny little boy. I continued to stare at him in shock.

"We can discuss this later. Right now, you need to eat," he said after I'd stared at him in silence for a few moments.

I turned back to my food and tried my best to eat like a normal person instead of a savage beast. After I'd eaten about a third of the food on my plate and drained both of our water glasses, Deema quickly switched out plates before motioning the waiter over for some more water. I pushed the food around a bit more to look like it had been eaten from before I returned to stuffing my face.

By the end of the meal, Deema had switched our plates at least six times and no one was suspicious of the fact that he was neither eating nor drinking. When Taniya ordered an entire cheesecake to-go for dessert, I remembered that I needed to order more food to take with us as well. I got four orders of lasagna, two orders of meat ravioli, and one order of cheese ravioli. We waited for about twenty minutes before they emerged with our to-go order, then we paid our bill and left.

CHAPTER 21

The walk back to the apartment was more difficult that the walk to the restaurant. My wings were starting to grow more and more uncomfortable as the leather straps dug into my skin. They were starting to rub me raw in a couple of places. When we finally reached the front door of her building, I started unbuckling the straps the moment we walked inside.

I glanced up and saw a man watching me curiously. "Deema, can you hold these things up for me so they don't drag? These damn straps are killing me," I said to cover my actions.

He laughed and grabbed my wings while we climbed the stairs.

Once we were safely inside the apartment, I finished shedding my straps and flipped my head over to put my hair up in a ponytail. When I stood back up straight, Deema slid in front of me and leaned down to hold his nose barely an inch from mine.

"Are you still hungry? Or are you hungry for something else?" he asked sheepishly, lightly brushing his cold, pale lips against mine.

I sighed low and long before I pushed him away from me. I had never been so attracted to a man, but this man could easily kill me so I decided I should keep my distance.

"I need to eat all this food in preparation for my trip. My brother will be contacting me at eight p.m. and I need to be ready. I haven't bathed in almost a week and I was really hoping to fit in a shower before my brother remote views me. Actually, I'm going to take a shower now. I'll eat when I'm done, and I'll talk to you when I'm done with my brother." I spoke fast as I rushed around the apartment and tried to keep space between us.

"That's fine." He wore a smirk when he appeared in front of me again. "My house is your house. There are fresh towels in the cabinet in the bathroom. I'm sure your friend has some clothes you can borrow."

He brushed his lips against mine again and I longed to press into him.

I fought my desires and turned to the bathroom. I quickly disrobed once the door was shut. Turning on the water for it to heat up, I called out to Taniya and asked her to leave me some clothes outside the door. I heard her say '*Okay*,' in my head, so I sent her a thought back that she was getting much better at this.

I climbed into the over-sized tub and relished the hot water running over me. I hadn't been able to take a shower in about a year since I couldn't fit into my tiny shower stall anymore and I had been sponge-bathing myself out of the kitchen sink.

I let the water soak my hair before I scrubbed the roots with shampoo. Oh, how wonderful it felt to not have to wash my hair with a colander in the sink. I rinsed my incredibly long hair, found a fruity conditioner, and slathered it throughout my hair. I scrubbed my body twice with an exfoliating gel to make sure and rid myself of dirt and sweat.

I heard the door open as I started to scrub my face.

"It's just me," Taniya said. "I didn't want to put your clothes on the carpet, so I'm leaving them here on the counter."

"Okay, thanks," I said through the water running over my face. "What time is it?" I turned off the water and heard the door close.

"It's almost seven," I heard her call back.

I stepped out of the shower, pulled a few towels out of the cabinet, and twisted my hair up. I squeezed out as much water as I could into the tub, piled my hair on top of my head, and wrapped it in a towel. I took the second towel and quickly ran it over my body before I wrapped it around myself. The third towel I used in a mostly failed attempt at drying my wings. I couldn't spread even one wing in the compact bathroom, so I decided to just get dressed and try to shake the water out of my wings on the roof.

I exited the bathroom to find Deema leaning against the doorway.

"Are you hungry for me yet?" he asked with a cocky grin.

I pushed him aside and kept walking toward the kitchenette with my dripping wet wings. He ran his hand down my spine from my neck to the bottom of my wings, so I spread my wings and just shook the water off on him.

"I'll talk to you later, Deema," I called over my shoulder.

He laughed and bowed deeply to me as he backed toward the living room and his empty chair.

I opened my lasagna and decided it was still warm enough to be delicious. I devoured all four orders in about ten minutes, and it took me another twenty minutes to polish off all of the meat ravioli and half the cheesecake.

When I cleaned up my empty containers and washed my sauce-covered hand, I turned around to find Deema in my personal space yet again. "Dude, seriously," I said, exasperated.

"Dude, seriously," he mocked and leaned in to kiss me.

I tried to dodge him, but he still managed to catch my lips with his. He pressed against me for what seemed like minutes, but must have only been seconds because when he broke away, I realized I had stopped breathing. I inhaled sharply before I recomposed myself enough to grab a gallon of water out of the refrigerator. I drank the whole thing.

After I finished the water and dropped the jug into the recycle bin, I went to the living room to check the time. It was a quarter 'til eight, so I sat down on the bed and started to prepare myself for my talk with my brother. I turned to Deema, who sat down in the chair, and I explained what I was doing.

"I've got to talk to my brother on the reservation. He's supposed to remote view me in fifteen minutes and I need near silence to concentrate. I've never done this longer than a few minutes, so I'm not sure what to expect. If I collapse, if this drains me, can I count on you to catch me so I don't get injured?"

In a fraction of a second, he was next to me on the bed with his arm around my waist. "I would never let you fall." The expression in his eyes was what I could only describe as love.

"Don't look at me like that." I blushed and averted my gaze. "And you can sit in your chair. I know you can move quick enough to help me should I fall."

He smiled and gave me a nod before he rose to his feet and walked back to his chair.

CHAPTER 22

*W*hite Eagle.' The stern voice was Brian's, so I held my hand up to Deema before I closed my eyes and focused on connecting with my brother.

'*I'm here,*' I sent to him.

'*Yes, I can see you. I've been here for a few minutes. Who the fuck is that guy? This is not the time for distractions,*' Brian snapped. The anger in his voice boomed and echoed in my head.

'*This is Deema. He's a vampire who kills evil doers and animals. I believe he can be of much help to us and, apparently, he thinks we're destined to be together or something. He's been living with Taniya ever since our nephew—who is also our father's reincarnation—was born twenty months ago,*' I informed him.

'*Okay, well, that's a whole bunch of insanity. I guess we'll have a lot to discuss when you all return. When is that, by the way? The tribal meeting is in twenty-six hours and you need to be well rested. You look like hell! What's wrong with your wings?*'

'*They're wet. I took a shower.*' I made a face and pointed to the towel on my head. '*I'm leaving here with Taniya's son when the sky darkens. We will arrive by the time the sun starts to rise. I'm going to try to take the trip a little slower so I don't get worn out so fast and so I can leave Dancing Bronco with Grandfather before the sun rises,*' I replied.

'*I will be in the valley when you return. I am to be there with you all day since Will didn't want to be around Taniya. There was no mention to the elders of you leaving the valley because I didn't want to upset them. You can bring him with you to the valley, so fly as fast or as slow as you want. Just give me a heads up, and I'll have food waiting for you.'*

'That's fine. I'll need you to send me a signal so I can find you anyway. I was flying out over the Atlantic for a while before I picked up Taniya's guiding beacon. How is attendance looking for the meeting? How did the meeting go with the police force?' I inquired.

'Everyone here has been contacted and they are now trying to contact tribal members who moved away from the reservation to ask them to come back. So far, everyone who has been contacted has agreed to come to the meeting or return to the rez as soon as they can. The meeting with the police went well and no one has any doubts in the elders. That has been a blessing. I guess our tribe isn't as lost as we thought they were. Eat up, get some rest, and don't get eaten, you hear? I'll see you in a while, little sister.'

I laughed. *'Okay, Silent Wolf. I'll do that. I'll see you in a while.'*

Once I felt like he was gone, I stood up onto my tiptoes and stretched my arms and wings. When I lowered my arms, I found them resting on Deema's shoulders. I sighed. "You again?"

He wrapped his arms around my waist and picked me up so fast that I instinctually wrapped my legs around his waist so I wouldn't fall. The towel on my head fell off with the fast movement and my wet hair tumbled down behind me.

He smiled at me and held his face a few inches from mine. "Well, if you don't want to be close to me, how come you're trying to ride me?" he asked me quietly.

"I just don't think I can deal with this right now. I have an entire tribe to save along with a million other things on my mind at the moment. I can't have you clogging up my brain. I've known you for twelve hours and I should not be feeling this for you. How am I supposed to focus on my tasks at hand with a distraction like you floating through my brain?"

I leaned in closer to him as I spoke without realizing it. By the time I was finished, my lips were resting millimeters away from his and I could feel the coldness emanating from his skin.

Despite my words and the conviction I felt behind them, I gave in to my carnal desires and crushed my lips against his. Fireworks exploded behind my eyes as I pressed my hot face against his icy skin. I heard him let out a quiet moan.

He walked over to the bed and gingerly set me on it before he broke away. Then he knelt on the floor in front of me and gazed into my eyes. "I think you should rest up before your big flight home. We've got about an hour and a half before you'll have the darkness you want. I'm going to go pick up some Mexican food for Taniya before they close. Do you want some?"

"Yes. Get me a couple dozen soft tacos with sour cream and no beans," I replied, almost automatically, as I stared at him dumbfounded.

He left the apartment and I flopped back on the bed. It was uncomfortable for me to lie on top of my wings like that, but I didn't really care at the moment.

As I stared at the ceiling, I heard my brother's voice in my head once again. *'What the hell was that? Are you really going to get involved with that bloodsucker? The elders will never allow this. I'm sure of it. So just what the fuck do you think you're doing? What are your plans here?'* he demanded.

'Honestly, Brian, I don't know. I've never felt like this and it's totally illogical and irrational, but he has a kind of gravitational pull on me. I have to consciously hold myself back from him at all times so I don't just melt into him. I don't know what the fuck I'm going to do. But perhaps they will let him stay when they see how useful he is for our protection. He can even hunt for us and help us slaughter livestock for food by draining them of blood. He's not just a monster. He's still very much human. Even if he is over 500 years old,' I replied.

'Okay. Do what you're going to do, then. But know that I don't approve and I will not defend your actions. You're on your own for that.'

'That's fine. I understand.'

CHAPTER 23

The slam of the front door jarred me from my slumber and I bolted off of the daybed. I hadn't even realized I'd fallen asleep. I sat back down on the bed once I realized it was just Deema with an armful of food.

"Two tacos for Taniya, and two dozen tacos for Hope," he said, smiling as he set the bags on the counter.

At the mention of her name, Taniya emerged from her son's room and went toward the kitchen. We sat down at the bar and devoured our food while Deema watched us.

"So I guess you'll be leaving now that you're done eating and it's dark out?" he asked with a touch of sadness to his voice.

"Like you won't be right behind me?" I said playfully as I approached him. "I'll see you in about twelve hours, right?"

I pressed against him and waited for him to nod before I kissed him goodbye. I put on the snuggly and got it comfortably adjusted. Taniya placed her sleeping son in it and strapped him in tight. She handed me a windbreaker. "Are you ready?"

I sighed. I put the jacket on backward and secured it to keep his head covered. "I think so."

They walked with me up to the roof to see me off. When I gave Taniya a hug goodbye, her son woke up. He rubbed his eyes and peered at each of us. "What's going on?"

"Hope is taking you back to the reservation," Taniya explained. "Deema and I will follow, but we'll be several hours behind you because she's faster."

He nodded wearily and quickly fell asleep again. Deema gave me one last frigid kiss on the cheek before I dove off the roof.

As I soared west, I felt like I wasn't alone. I searched the sky over my right shoulder and saw nothing but the city fading away behind me. I looked over my left shoulder and still didn't see anything. I tried to shake the feeling as I pushed on through the chill of the night. The farther I got from the city, the more the feeling of being followed faded.

After over three hours of pushing my wings to their limits, I noticed the end of the plains and the rise of the mountains. I decided I must be over either northern New Mexico or southern Colorado, so I sent out my call to my brother, *'I'm getting close. Please start me some food and send me a beacon.'*

I immediately felt him pulling me toward him and turned slightly south to follow his call. Another forty-five minutes passed before I saw my reservation stretched out below me. I quickly slowed—before I overshot my target—made some wide turns, and spiraled down to the valley floor.

When I strolled into camp, I saw my brother sitting at the fire, poking at the embers. He turned to greet me.

I took off the jacket and started to loosen the straps on the snuggly. "Can you give me a hand with him?"

As I started to pull Dancing Bronco from his confinement, Brian hoisted the sleeping child out of the snuggly and held him to his chest while I finished undoing the straps. Once I released myself of its confines, I walked over to the coolers and drank almost a gallon of water.

"What time is it?" I asked between gulps.

"It's just past eleven," he replied without looking up from the sleeping child who shared our blood.

"Are Bob and Nallia still here?"

He walked over to me so he wouldn't wake anyone by talking too loud. "Yes. They are sleeping. They signed their forms, but they chose to stay. The elders said they could return home, but they said they wanted to stay here with you."

Dancing Bronco awoke from his slumber as Brian walked toward me. He squinted up at my brother with sleepy eyes that quickly widened when he saw his face. "My boy!" he cried as he leapt up to wrap his arms around Brian's neck.

Brian kissed him on his forehead and returned the hug. "I've missed you, too, Daddy," he said with tears in his eyes.

It was certainly an awkward exchange. As I dug through the coolers for something ready to eat, I wondered how we would ever get used to these oddities that had become our lives. Our father's soul was in the body of our twenty-month-old nephew, and he remembered everything about his previous life. I had wings and I could fly over 600 miles an hour. I was now apparently dating a 500-year-old, bloodsucking immortal. I could have entire conversations with someone clear across the country using only my mind. I could remote view people, and I was getting better at reading minds with every day that passed. What an odd life we're in for, I thought as I sat down in my chair.

Brian removed the food from the fire while Dancing Bronco watched him and I watched them. While I ate my pork chops and potatoes, I noticed that our nephew had fallen asleep curled up next to the fire. My thoughts drifted to Deema and I wondered when he would arrive. I decided that he would probably get here a couple hours after the sun had risen.

When I finished my food and dropped my plate in the wash bin, I turned to face my brother. "I'm really exhausted. Would you happen to still have that mattress in the back of your truck?" I asked him.

"Actually, yes, I do."

"Awesome." I walked over to his truck, climbed into the back, and flopped down on my stomach. I spread my wings as much as I could so that their weight didn't suppress my breathing.

I eventually fell asleep with Deema on my mind. I knew that it was wrong of me to bring him here. I also knew that something deep in my soul yearned for him to be by my side. Only, I couldn't pinpoint why. Maybe it was the fact that he could help me to save my tribe. I was so terrified that I'd fail them. I knew I would have to defy them if I had any chance of keeping them all alive.

CHAPTER 24

I slept a dreamless sleep that night and, when I woke in the morning, the sky had already faded its last pinks from the sunrise. I crawled out of the back of the truck and stretched my wings in the warm sunbeams that were starting to peek over the eastern ridge.

I scanned the camp and saw my brother sitting around the fire with Dancing Bronco, Bob, and Nallia. I walked over to them and said good morning before I grabbed the V8 juice out of the cooler. I sat in my chair and drank it all. "What's for breakfast?"

Bob grinned. "We were just talking about that. We're considering going home to grab stuff for French toast."

"Oh, man! Nothing has ever sounded so good as that does right now," I exclaimed.

"Well, I guess it's settled, then." Brian stood up. "I'll give you a ride back to town so we can get to cooking quicker."

He and Bob climbed into the truck and bumped out of the valley.

Nallia turned to me. "Brian mentioned that someone else would arrive soon with the child's mother. So who is this guy?" she asked coyly.

"They kissed," Dancing Bronco said quietly.

It took me about half a second to realize that his tone was the chagrin of a parent and not the shyness of a child.

"Oh my god!" Nallia squealed. *She must not have noticed his tone*, I thought, as she continued in the same breath, "So you've got to tell me all about him! What's he like? What's his name? How does he fly? Is he another angel like you? Brian wouldn't tell us anything. He seemed rather irritated that this guy was coming."

"Well, Brian is mad because this guy is an immortal."

She gawked at me and her mouth fell open in surprise.

"He is a vampire, actually," I continued. "He says that he is a Russian who is over 500 years old and, that when he was a little boy, his grandmother told him stories of me, so he's convinced we're destined to be together or something. I feel inexplicably drawn to him, as well. But I honestly don't really know what to do about all of this. He's so charming and nice, but he's a killer. I mean, he's killed countless people in the last 500 years." I let out an exasperated sigh. "So what's to stop him from killing me? You know?"

She continued to stare at me in shock for several long, silent moments before the child sitting between us broke the quiet of the still morning air. "He only kills bad people." He gazed up to meet my eyes. "He could never harm you because he loves you and he wants you to love him. He will never allow anyone else to hurt you either."

I was shocked to hear these wise words come from his tiny mouth. Not five seconds after he finished speaking, a cloud of dust erupted in the valley about ten yards to the north of where we sat. Before the dust cleared, a blur of movement brought Deema and Taniya to my side. Taniya scooped up her son and covered him in kisses as I stood to greet Deema.

He picked me up, put me on a rock, and held me by the waist. We stood nose to nose.

"I missed you," he whispered before crushing his frigid lips into the warmth of mine.

I melted into him as he slid his arms between my wings and my back. When he pulled back from the kiss, he stared into my eyes.

"You're crazy," I told him.

"Crazy like a fox," he smirked while he stroked the small of my back.

"Well, where are my manners?" I pulled myself away from

him. "Nallia, this is Deema, and this is Taniya. She is also called Little Sparrow and she's been my best friend since we were two or three. Guys, this is Nallia. She and Bob accidentally found us the other day and they have elected to stay here with us until the meeting tonight when I'm revealed to the tribe. Bob is off with Brian getting stuff to make French toast and they should be back in a little bit."

"Oh man! Nothing has ever sounded so good!" Taniya gushed.

I let out a loud peel of laughter. "I said almost exactly the same thing earlier."

She joined me in my fit of giggles. We chattered for a few minutes about what to expect at the meeting that night and, before we knew it, they had returned with our ingredients for breakfast. We quickly whipped up a large batch of batter while I finished the introductions. Brian greeted Deema with a grunt and a handshake.

My always-protective big brother squeezed the vampire's hand with all his might and Deema just laughed. "I'm sorry, but you really don't want me to squeeze back. I could shatter every bone in your hand without showing any strain, which your face is full of right now."

My brother broke the handshake and glared at him as Deema walked over to the large rock next to my chair.

"Not that one," I cried out. I was pretty sure I knew what he was planning to do. Seconds later, he proved my assumption right when he zipped across the valley, pulled a rock as tall as he was out of the ground, and threw it up into the air. It made a huge arc before it smashed to thousands of pieces 100 yards away.

"Are you satisfied that I can protect your sister now? Do you believe I am what I say I am?" Deema asked as he slowly lifted into the air and floated back to my side.

"I have no doubt you are what you say you are. I just don't like what you are. My people will not accept you. First of all, you're white. And a pale, bizarre white, at that. And what the hell is going on with your skin now? It's like I can see through it. Second, you are a killer. We must keep you hidden from all and this valley will be your home if you choose to stay here with my sister. The elders will ban you from the land if they find out what you are and that you are here," Brian demanded, his voice angry and firm.

"Why? Are there stories of him that you won't tell me? Like the stories of *me* you didn't tell me?" I interjected.

Brian's eyes narrowed a little bit and I saw his jaw flex. "You'll find out in about seven hours when all the stories are revealed to the tribe. The meeting starts at four and is expected to last until ten. We need to get there at noon to have our own meeting with the elders and fill them in on your absence, as well as your return with Taniya and Dancing Bronco. They will come with us, as will Bob and Nallia. Deema will stay here, out of sight." When he spoke the vampire's name, he practically snarled it.

"I will go where I wish," Deema growled back.

Brian glared at him. They appeared to be arguing silently, so I stepped between them.

"I will not have this between you two! I don't care what the stories say, he's staying. And if he wants to come, he can come, goddammit!" I pushed my energy toward my brother to let him know how serious I was and, much to my surprise, he backed down.

"I don't approve, and neither will they, just to let you know. I was—I was just trying to save you some pain, but I guess there's really nothing I can do now, is there? You're going to be stubborn and do stupid things." His lip curled and his nose crinkled. "Here comes Hope, making bad choices like she always has. I can't believe they think you can save us."

"No, Brian, there's nothing you can do to stop me. I'm not even sorry. This is just how it's going to be," I answered flatly. What I really wanted was to scream at him, but I couldn't say what I wanted to with everyone else around. How could I tell my brother that I also thought I had no chance of saving our people? At least, I knew I couldn't do it alone, regardless of how much I tried to prepare myself for this mysterious war.

He snorted in disgust as he heard my thoughts. "That's a shame," he muttered. He pulled the first batch of French toast out of the pan. "Eat up," he said and shoved the plate at me. "We've got to be at the casino in less than three hours."

I sat in my chair and ate in silence while they cooked the rest of the two loaves of bread they had brought. Once everyone else had their fill, I finished off what was left.

Deema remained at my side the whole time and occasionally shot a few glares toward my brother. When I had finished eating, I dropped my plate into the wash bin.

Without a word to anyone, I took off into the sky toward the northern end of the valley.

CHAPTER 25

I landed on a ledge a third of the way up the mountain and crouched there like a gargoyle. A few seconds later, Deema landed next to me and sat on the edge of the outcrop, letting his legs dangle.

"I'm glad you followed me," I said as he laid his head on my wing. "I was hoping you could tell me why Brian hates you."

"Other than the fact that he's just trying to protect his little sister from a man capable of hurting her?" He laughed. I shot him a glare and he stopped laughing. "There is a story in your tribe that the protector will fall under the spell of a demon who hunts in the night. The demon will swallow all of her blood and turn her wings black like the night. After this, the protector herself will become a demon that drinks blood in the night."

I gawked at him in shock. "The black feather," I murmured.

"What?"

"Nothing. Never mind. So according to my people's legends, you're going to turn me into a vampire someday?" I squeaked.

"No, I won't." His voice was filled with conviction. He dropped off the cliff and floated up in front of me. As he stood me up straight, he gazed into my eyes. "I know I've only known you for a day, but I will never hurt you, Hope. I will protect you to my last breath," he promised.

"But you will outlive me," I interjected. "I am not immortal in this body."

"I refuse to believe that," he replied.

I searched his eyes for a moment before I decided he wasn't lying to me. He really thought I couldn't die.

I turned to jump off the ledge. "We should get back."

He held tight to my hips and pulled me back to him. "Must we?" he asked sheepishly.

I blushed. "I think it might be best."

"Well, I think that we can stay out for a while longer and avoid your brother if we want to," he said.

He pushed me back against the rock wall of the mountain behind me. When he crushed his lips to mine, I couldn't resist wrapping my arms and wings around him as we embraced.

I felt the wind swirling around me. I opened my eyes to see that we were no longer on the mountainside. I gasped in astonishment as I glanced around. We were about twenty feet out from where we'd been standing, just hovering there and slowly spinning around.

"Would you like to go for a spin with me? See what it's like to fly without using your wings?" He smiled. "It's like…dancing on the moon."

I nodded dumbly as I tightened my grip around his ribcage.

We slowly drifted through the valley for a while before he landed on another outcropping on the western ridge. "Do you trust me?" he asked as he stared into my eyes.

"Not really," I confessed.

He chuckled at my honesty. "Then I guess you'll just have to," he said with a wink.

He continued to hold me around the waist as he leaned backward and pulled me down on top of him until we were parallel to the ground. We soon drifted a few feet higher and I realized we were flying. He hovered us above the ledge, held me close to him, and gave me frozen kisses all over my face.

"I don't think we should do this," I blurted.

Deema laughed. "Like I'll ever let you go!"

"Please, put me down," I said quietly.

He stared at me for a long moment and tried to see what I was thinking. When he decided he couldn't penetrate my mind, he shrugged and gently set me on the ledge.

Without even looking at him, I dove off and flew as fast as I could away from him. I could feel him following me as I went south and zipped over the camp. As I landed at the southern end of the valley, I heard my brother push me a thought. *'We need to leave soon and you shouldn't be wearing yourself out. Get back here.'* I could even hear the anger in his voice in my mind.

'Yeah, yeah, yeah. Get the fuck out of my head and give me some damn privacy,' I retorted.

Deema landed in front of me as soon as my thought was done. "What the hell is going on? What's with all the mood swings here? I know you're not on your cycle because I could smell it if you were," he said as he approached me.

"What if you are a demon? What if you do bite me in a fit of passion or something? What if you do wind up turning me, and my people die because I allowed you to stay here with me? I can't allow that to happen. My priority must be my people, my tribe, not some monster who lives by stealing the lives of others. How many lives have you taken, huh? How many people have died to keep you alive?"

He appeared thoughtful for a few seconds before he replied and I wondered if he was trying to actually count them up. He let out a long sigh before he answered my string of questions. "I am not a demon or a monster. I am but a man—a man who cannot die because of some kind of unexplainable virus. I would only turn you if you were injured so badly that you would die prematurely and you asked me to. I will never distract you when it's time for battle or negotiations. And I will fight for your people, too. I will protect your people as if they were my own. And lives?" He chuckled. "How many lives have *you* taken to sustain your own? How many chickens have died to ease your hunger? How many cows? Hogs? Lambs? How many eggs have you eaten in your life? How many have *you* denied a natural life and death just so you can survive?"

I blinked at him in disbelief. He had an amazingly good point. Yes, he took lives, but so did I. That was just life. Animals killed other animals to survive.

"Fine. You can stay," I conceded. "But try not to be a distraction. And we need to be getting back. Brian is pissed that I'm gone."

Deema swept me up in his arms and sped me back to camp. Before he set me down, he kissed my neck in front of everyone to prove he was strong enough to resist biting me. Everyone gasped at his move except for Taniya and her son.

"You know, you guys, I did live with Deema for almost two years," Taniya said in his defense. "He's not a bad guy. He just enjoys the taste of a bad guy's blood. I've seen him with lots of women and none of them ever left our apartment with a bite mark or even a tiny thought that he might be a vampire. Despite his cold skin, none of them ever even considered he wasn't human."

"She's right you know," Deema said as he approached my brother. "A good person like your sister, or like you, does not appeal to me. I prefer the blood of the evil doers. They taste and feel sweeter to kill. I would die before I ever harmed her or allowed harm to come to her. Please, Brian, I beg you to not make this any more difficult than it already is. We have many terrible things ahead, and we cannot afford to be fighting amongst ourselves. Peace?" Deema held out his hand. He'd sounded very sincere.

Brian eyeballed the hand thrust before him then stared at Deema. He studied his face for a moment before he extended his hand and accepted Deema's proposal. "Yeah, man. Peace," he said apprehensively. "But I'll be watching you," he added with narrowed eyes. Brian turned to me. "It's time to go. We don't want to be late."

I threw a bucket of sand on the fire and then we all walked toward the truck. I climbed into the bed of the truck and lay down on the mattress while Bob, Nallia, and Brian climbed into the cab. Taniya sat next to me with her son in her lap and Deema lay down on the other side of me.

"You could just fly or run there if you want, you know?" I whispered to him when he rested his head next to mine.

"I know, but why would I want to leave you?" he said sweetly.

CHAPTER 26

We bumped and rumbled out of the valley and on to the casino while my heart pounded in my chest. Just like the first time I'd gone to meet with the elders, I had no idea what I should say or do to explain myself. As we made the last turn into the parking lot, I felt as if I would vomit because I was so nervous. I swallowed hard and tried desperately to compose myself as I slid out of the truck bed and was rushed inside the back door.

As soon as I entered, I was greeted by the council and ushered to a windowless room fifteen yards down the hall. There was nowhere for me to sit in the nearly empty room, so I crouched down in my fear of passing out or vomiting. It took me a moment to realize that no one else who rode there with me had been allowed into the room. Only a few of the elders stood around me. I peered up at my grandfather. "Where are my friends?"

"They will join us shortly. But first, I think you and I need some family time," he said as the other old men filed out of the room. "We need to catch up on some things. Red Elk, would you mind finding her that tall stool with a half-back?" he asked of the last man to leave.

"I'm sorry!" I blurted out once the door was closed. "But how am I supposed to not accept his help if he's willing to fight for your lives, too? Also, how could I just leave her out there to die?" I cried.

"I am not angry with you," he replied with kind eyes. "I am

disappointed that you disobeyed me by leaving the valley, but I am not angry that you returned with Little Sparrow and her son. You will always be my granddaughter, and I will always love you. Even if you allow this demon to make you like him, I will never turn my back on you," he explained.

I stared at him in shock for a moment before we were interrupted by Red Elk bringing me a chair so I could sit down. When he opened the door and carried in the stool, Deema took the opportunity to zip into the room. He stood next to the door for a second while the old man set down the chair. As I stood up to walk toward the chair, Deema made another move too quick for human eyes to see. Before I knew what had happened, he had scooped me up into the seat of the chair and set it back on the floor. My grandfather gawked at him in surprise as Deema linked his arm with mine and stood by my side.

"What's the meaning of this?" Grandfather demanded. "This is a private meeting. You will be permitted into the Council meeting in a little while, albeit grudgingly." His voice was quiet, but stern as he stared down the immortal.

"I'm sorry, sir," Deema said with a waist-deep bow. "But I felt I needed to explain myself to you so that you can understand that I am not a threat to your family or your tribe. I am here to help you and I would die before anyone takes my love from me. I only drink the blood of animals and evil doers. I do not have even the tiniest desire to turn her into the monster that I am to you. And I have promised her that the only way I ever would turn her is if she is dying from a battle injury and she asks me to—"

"Then that is what is to happen," my grandfather interrupted. "Our prophesies say that if you show up here, it is only a matter of time before our protector becomes a bloodsucking demon of the night herself."

"Yes, and my people's stories tell that she will fly with me for the rest of my days, so now I have little doubt now that it will someday happen. But it will not be today or anytime soon. You know she is a prophet and that she dreams the future. Well, when she was asleep in my apartment yesterday, I watched some of her dreams of the future. I know that she has at least a year or two left before she will die and I will have no choice but to turn her." He sounded truly sad and I could tell that he really did not want to turn me into a vampire. He turned to face me. "You know I would never hurt you, right? You know I love you, right?" he asked with pleading eyes.

I gazed at him long and hard before I found the breath to reply, and my voice shook with my lack of conviction. "You have been nothing but nice to me, Deema. You are incredibly sweet and attentive. But despite how much I feel like I've known you forever, I just can't let go of the fact that we've known each other for less than two days. You cannot learn to love someone in two days. This is irrational and illogical. And I—"

"And growing wings, flying 600 miles per hour, remote viewing, et cetera? This is all normal? This is all rational and logical?" Deema interrupted.

"Well, no. But—but I—" I sputtered. "This just isn't normal!"

"Normal simply doesn't exist here anymore," my grandfather offered.

I looked at them in despair and let out a long sigh. "So is this over? Is he accepted? I'm very tired and I'd like to get some rest before tonight," I said wearily.

"Yes, we are done here for now. He is allowed to stay, but you will find no warm welcomes here, Vampire," Grandfather replied with a hard glare at Deema.

We left the tiny room and walked down a narrow, backstage hallway until we reached a larger room at the other end of the hall. We walked through the door to find everyone sitting around a large, round table. Nallia was sitting in Bob's lap, Brian stood in the far corner, and Taniya pulled her son into her lap so that Deema could have somewhere to sit.

The chief apologized to me as Deema squeezed my stool into a gap in the chairs around the table. "It's quite crowded, as you can see, but we were not expecting you to bring so many guests with you today." When I did not reply, he continued. "We have already introduced ourselves here. Perhaps you would care to introduce your pale-faced friend?"

I glanced down at the handsome, shockingly white face of the immortal to my right before I scanned the circle of my native kin. "Everyone, this is Deema. He's over 500 years old, and he has vowed to protect our tribe as if it were his own," I said slowly. They all stared at me blankly. "I understand why you are all apprehensive that he is here, and I am sorry for that." I paused while a few of the old men grunted and grumbled in disapproval. "But he will not harm anyone that I am here to protect, and he will only kill those who have come to harm us."

"And until then?" Red Elk asked calmly. "Surely he will have to feed before we are attacked or invaded by greedy white men trying to save themselves. How can we be sure he will not kill you or someone else before he has evil men to feed on?"

"The blood of good people tastes bitter to me," Deema answered carefully. "I have only killed an innocent person once, and I have regretted it for over 500 years now. I beg you to trust me." He slowly stood and made a deep bow. When he stood up straight, he leaned over and kissed the top of my head. He glanced around the room before he slowly leaned in toward my neck. Amidst shocked gasps and a few verbal protests, I held up my hand to silence them and he tenderly kissed my neck.

When he stood back up and all were satisfied that he had not bitten me, he spoke again. "I will feed on animals until the evil ones arrive and try to destroy us. Any animal in the tribe that needs to be slaughtered for food, I can drain of blood for you. I can hunt like no man you've ever seen and I can bring you a dozen deer ready to butcher in less than an hour. Please do not hate me for the monster I appear to be. I beg you to accept me as the man who is in love with your resident angel. All I want is to be the protector of your protector."

Looking at him, I could feel the sincerity emanating from him like warmth from a roaring fire.

After a minute or so of quiet grunts of disapproval and a few murmurs of "I don't know" scattered throughout the room, the chief stood again. "We will permit you to stay. But, if we decide you must leave, or if you kill any of our people, then you must go without argument. Can we agree to that, Vampire?"

"Yes, Chief. I will gladly agree to that because I know that I could never kill an innocent again. I believe I have been sent here to protect you, as has Hope," he replied with another bow. "Would you care to shake on it?"

"No, Vampire, I would not," the chief grumbled as he settled back into his seat.

CHAPTER 27

Now, on to the business at hand." The chief looked around the table. "Tonight, the entire tribe will gather here in the theater to be told the stories and prophesies of our tribe. This is a long process, as there are many to tell. We will implement a monthly meeting for the tribe to tell more stories and inform them of new developments. We have decided that before entering the theater, the forms must be signed and returned so there is no confusion once everyone is inside. After the whole tribe has arrived, and those who refused to sign have been formally announced, banned, and removed from the casino, we will tell the legend that has become your life, Hope."

When he turned to acknowledge me, I opened my mouth to speak and he closed his.

"May I request that the tribe not be told the story of the demon that kills me? Can we please not scare them with this misunderstood prophesy?" I begged.

"We will not tell them tonight, but we may tell them someday. We will not introduce Deema tonight, either," my grandfather replied. "But we will tell them what you are someday," he said sternly as he scowled at Deema.

I sank a bit in my seat before the chief continued. "Tonight we will tell them only of you and of those who will come to try and destroy us. When we call for you, I want you to walk out on stage and spread your wings for the tribe. You will then take off from the stage and fly over the seats. Make a few circles and let them feel the wind you make with your wings. Actually, can you create wind without flying?"

I gave him a brief nod, stood up, and turned to stand behind the stool. I wrapped my arms around the back of it to steady myself and started to flap my massive wings. The wind that I created quickly swept all the papers off the table and sent them flying toward the opposite wall. I peered up and saw that they were all more than satisfied with the results.

"That is very impressive, White Eagle," my grandfather said as Brian gathered the papers from the floor. "I have no doubt that you will inspire faith in the tribe of your abilities to protect them." He smiled at first, but his grin shrank when he saw the loving expression Deema wore as he gazed at me. "How fast can you fly?" Grandfather inquired.

"In the valley, my top speed is about 200 miles an hour, but going cross country, I think it's about 600 miles per hour. I made the 2,000 mile trip to New York in just under four hours."

A gasp spread through the room.

"How can you breathe at such speeds? How is your hair not ripped out and your skin not shredded?" Red Elk asked with wide eyes.

"Honestly, I have no idea." I felt my cheeks grow warmer and I gave him a shy smile. "But I have no trouble breathing at high speeds or at high altitudes and the pressure doesn't seem to affect me either. But when I'm on the ground, I can still injure myself, so I'm not invincible. It's something I may never understand, but I am learning quickly to no longer question the unexplainable things I can do."

Brian stepped up to the table. "We may never understand many things that will happen from here on out. Just as we can never understand how our ancestors knew thousands of years ago what would happen to us in the present. But what we must do is to accept the gifts we have been given. We need to be thankful for and utilize our gifts of remote viewing, mind reading, prophesy, and flight," he said while he gestured around the room to indicate those of us with abilities.

Everyone quietly chattered about his wise words. I watched

silently as Dancing Bronco climbed out of his mother's lap and stood on the table. He walked to the center and the room fell silent.

"I have a number of things I'd like to say. First of all, I'd like to formally introduce myself. In this life, I am called Dancing Bronco and I am the child of Little Sparrow and William, your grandson," he said with a nod to my grandfather. "My father does not know of my birth, but I'm certain he will accept it when he learns who I am." The toddler walked over to Grandfather and stopped a foot in front of him. "I may be your great-grandson, but I am also the reincarnation of your late son. I remember everything about my previous life. I also remember every day of my short life thus far. It's good to see you again, Dad." He paused just long enough to hug his neck. "That being said, I wish to say my piece about Dmitri." He turned around and walked over to Deema. "Sorry, I know you prefer Deema since it is more easily pronounced by those around you." He gave a slight nod to the vampire then turned back to the elders. "Deema has cared for my mother since the day he met her. By the time I emerged from the womb, I already felt as if I knew him. He has been there for us every day of my life. He has helped her pay the rent and keep me in clothes that fit. He buys her food and makes sure bills get paid on time. He has truly been a blessing to us and, without him, we might have ended up on the streets. If he had not paid for her hospital bills, she might have tried to give birth to me at home."

He glanced over at Taniya and she gave a shameful nod to indicate that it was true. "People have given birth for thousands of years without hospitals," she offered as her defense.

"I trust him to protect our tribe as he has protected us," the child continued. "When I was two months old, someone tried to knock my mother over in the street and steal her purse while she was holding me. Deema saved us from crashing to the pavement, which would have crushed my fragile, preemie body, and then he caught the thief all in the blink of an eye. He snapped his neck, drained his blood, and then threw him into a dumpster with a flick of the wrist. My mother was so stunned by his actions that she'd just stood there frozen and did not cover my eyes, so I saw the whole thing. That was the night she discovered that he was a vampire, and we never feared the city streets again."

Everyone sat and stared at him in complete shock. I guessed no one told them about his soul during introductions.

After about thirty seconds of silence, my nephew started to speak again. "I know all of this is a bit of a shock to you, but so was my death three years ago. I know that you all expected I would be here for the calendar's end. Well, this was my only option. I would also like to ask you all to trust Deema as I trust him. He has been like a father to me. Please, Dad, Chief, everyone, accept him for the *man* that he is. Please don't reject him for the virus that he contains. He is not a monster any more than Hope is a monster." When he finished speaking, he walked back over to his mother, climbed down from the table, and sat in her lap again.

"We will take your kind words on his behalf into consideration, Dancing Bear," the chief said after a moment.

"Um, it's Dancing Bronco, actually," Taniya said weakly. "I combined the names of his grandfathers to name him— Dancing Bear and Silent Bronco."

"My apologies, my dear," the chief smiled. "If there is nothing else anyone has to say, I believe we can adjourn this meeting. There are some buffets in the main restaurant still filled with food. We sent the entire staff home an hour ago to get ready for the meeting at four. You have free run of the restaurant, the theater, and this room for the next two hours until people start arriving to check in.

"Hope, if you need to sleep, there is a very large, plush couch just outside the theater doors. We'll make sure you are awake before people start to enter the casino." He waited to see if anyone else desired a turn to speak and, when he was satisfied that no one did, he stood up and left.

One by one, the rest of the elders stood and exited as well. After I glanced around one last time, I followed the old men out and found my way to the buffet. I scanned it for a moment before I decided that I wasn't as hungry as I was thirsty. I drank a few glasses of water and then wandered over to the couch where they'd told me I could sleep.

"I figured you'd come here," Deema smirked.

I sighed as I flopped down on my stomach. "I've got two hours to sleep, so I'd like to get to it."

"Okay, my dear. I'll be here when you wake up," he replied.

I wanted to tell him to stay out of my head while I slept, but I fell fast asleep before I could bring myself to speak.

CHAPTER 28

ope, there are people coming. You've got to get up."
I felt a hand on my wings and I groggily rolled off the
couch. Deema caught me and flashed me a smile as he
ran through the theater, up the stairs, and off to the right wing
of the stage. As everything blurred past us, his kind, pale face
was all that stayed in focus. When he gently set me down, I
took the opportunity to stretch and flex my wings after my nap.

I closed my eyes and searched for my brother. He sat at the
front door of the casino, helping the elders who had just started
to get everyone signed in.

'*Brian*,' I thought, '*I need a few minutes to practice. Can
you keep everyone out of the theater until I say I'm ready?*'

I saw him stand from the folding table and excuse himself.
He ran through the casino and caught up with the few who had
already been admitted. "Excuse me, guys?" he called out after
them. "I'm sorry," he said when he stopped them. "They're not
quite ready in the theater yet, and we'd like to ask you to wait
out here in the halls until they are. Cool?"

"Yeah, bro. That's cool," replied a man I'd never seen before.

"Mind if we hit up the cold buffet?" the woman with him
asked. "That salad bar looks good."

"Not at all, have at it. This is *our* casino, right?" Brian replied with a wink.

I broke my connection and turned to Deema. I opened my
mouth to speak, but he spoke instead.

"I know. I heard him talking. Have at it," he said with a wink.

I assumed he was mocking my brother so I shot him a playful glare before I pushed off into the air.

I only flew around for a couple of minutes in the relatively small area of the 10,000 seat theater. It was the largest indoor theater in the southwest—outside of Vegas—but it felt tiny to me when I was airborne. I made a few circles, a couple figure eights and several low passes over the seats. I landed on the stage again and surveyed the empty theater that would soon be filled with my tribe members. I let out a sigh as I sent the thought to my brother that I was ready, and then I walked off stage right to where Deema was waiting for me.

"Are you ready for this?" he asked as he put his arms around my waist. I shook my head no, and he continued. "Checking in to a Vegas hotel under a false identity with intent to commit capital fraud on a head full of acid? I sure hope so," he said in his best Dr. Gonzo voice.

I laughed hysterically as he kept me from falling over. When I could finally speak again, I sputtered, "I—I love Hunter S. Thompson! He was so funny and such an amazing writer." I paused and gazed up into Deema's sparkling black eyes. "So, will you always be able to lift my spirits like that?"

He stroked my hair with his hand, gave me a nod, and said, "I hope so." Then he laid his freezing lips on my neck just below my ear.

I heard the door to the theater open and voices echoed in the vast emptiness of the giant room. I snapped back to reality and stood upright. I cast a quick grin at Deema, then I ran off behind the curtain to peek through at them. When I found the seam, I carefully held both sides so as to not expose my wings when I poked my head through. I was pleasantly surprised to see my friends walking down the long, center aisle to get front row seats. When Taniya and Nallia saw me, they ran up the stairs, across the stage, and slipped through the curtain.

They squealed and jumped up and down like high school girls who'd just gotten asked to prom by the star quarterback.

Nallia beamed. "So are you excited? You get to fly in front

of everyone tonight! And now you won't have to hide inside your house all the time."

I let out a sigh and felt my lips twist into a frown. "Excited?" I murmured. I felt like a pit was opening up beneath me and I began to feel a little nauseous. Deema had been doing a good job of keeping my mind elsewhere. But once I needed to say it out loud, it hit me like a ton of bricks how impossible it all seemed. "No, honey, I'm not excited. Tonight, our people will learn that many of them will die very soon. They are going to be told that there is but one woman who can save them, and she cannot save all of them. Our people will be scared out of their wits tonight. And soon? Soon our people will starve when enough food cannot be grown. I'm sorry, but I can't find excitement in anything that is in my future right now," I said bitterly. Of course, I couldn't even vocalize my most nagging doubts—those about myself. I still had no idea how I was going to save them. Dreaming the future was no real help when I couldn't even control what I saw.

"What about me?" Deema asked as he appeared at my side.

"Well, even you have your drawbacks," I said in complete seriousness. "According to the stories—"

He cut me off by placing his icy finger against my lips. "Find happiness where you can," he whispered as he leaned in for a kiss.

"Well, I guess I should get back to Bob, then," Nallia said quietly.

"Yeah, and I should get back to my son," Taniya said. "I should be with him in case his father arrives and one tries to approach the other."

"I'm sorry. I don't mean to be a Negative Nancy, I just…" I trailed off.

Taniya gave me a reassuring smile. "It's okay, sweetie. We understand."

CHAPTER 29

Once we were alone again, I told Deema that I'd like to sit down. A couple of seconds later, he had my stool from the conference room sitting next to me and he made a deep, bowing gesture toward the chair. I thanked him, turned to sit in the chair, and waited for the night to begin.

"You act so regal. Were you royalty?" I asked as he positioned himself between my knees.

He smiled at me then gave me a small nod and a shrug to confirm my suspicion. "Sort of," he mumbled as I put my hands on his hips. "Things were different. More like a lord of the land, I suppose."

"And that's why you have a castle in Russia?"

"*Da*," he replied in Russian.

I felt the corner of my lip raise a tiny bit. "*Ti zni, ya gavayu nyemnoga pau Russki.*"

"*What?*" he echoed throughout the theater. "You speak Russian? How come you hadn't told me yet?" he asked more quietly.

I gave him a half-hearted shrug. "*Nye zniyu.* I guess I just didn't think to. I really don't know much more than Taniya does. Oh, but I can count to 199, though."

He chuckled. "Oh yeah? She can only count to 100."

I pulled him closer to me and laid my head on his shoulder. "Well, speaking of counting, how many people do you think have arrived so far?" I knew he'd been trying to distract me in order to raise my spirits. I just couldn't stop thinking about what was coming. I knew so little of what to expect or how to behave.

"There's about 200 people that have signed in now and there are at least 1000 outside in line to sign their forms. There is a line of packed-full cars over a mile long to get into the parking lot. Your brother is searching for a megaphone so they can read the paper to everyone and just have them sign as they file inside. This will take much longer than an hour to get everyone inside," he informed me.

I sighed as the doubt and dread inside of me swelled. "I wish I could have slept longer."

"It'll be over soon, and then you can go home and sleep in your bed."

"I don't have a bed," I told him. I glanced over at the curtain that separated us from the gathering tribe. "But a flat floor is better than rocks, I guess."

"There you go! Find happiness where you can," he whispered as he leaned down for a kiss.

Since there was finally no one to interrupt us, and I had given up on refusing my feelings for him, I gave in fully as I held him tighter and crushed my lips to his. Fireworks exploded behind my eyes as his icy face and frigid hands pressed into my feverish face, but that soon faded as his lips left mine and left a trail of tingles in their wake. It felt like ice cubes that couldn't melt were being traced from my lips, to my chin, up my jawbone, and down my neck.

I let out a small moan and he brought his face back up to mine.

"How are you doing, baby?" he asked and gazed at me with his sparkling, black eyes.

"I'm doing okay," I slurred. "You make me feel like I'm drunk," I managed to say a little more clearly.

He let out another echoing laugh before he kissed me on the forehead. I marveled at how his skin affected mine. It always left me with an odd tingling sensation that lingered for a few seconds. It was unlike anything I'd ever felt before.

"You're a distraction," I observed.

His eyebrow lifted. "Is that a good thing or a bad thing?"

I tilted my head back and regarded him for a moment. "I'm still not sure yet. Maybe some of both."

When I moved in to kiss him again, my younger brother bolted through curtain and skidded to a stop.

CHAPTER 30

"Did you know about this?" Will asked me with wild eyes. He turned slightly to scrutinize Deema. "Who the fuck are you?"

The vampire took a step back and turned to face my brother. "My name is Deema. I am the man who has been raising your son."

"So what? Now you're fucking my sister, too?" Will demanded.

Deema huffed a single laugh through his nose, shook his head, and smiled at him kindly. "No. No, Will, I have never been intimate with either one of them. Taniya and I are only friends, and I have merely kissed your sister. I am here to protect your tribe, just like Hope. But I will not be revealed to the tribe tonight, so I would like to invite you over after the meeting tonight. Then we can explain to you everything that's happened the last couple of days."

Will eyeballed him for a moment and gave him a short nod. "That's fine. I'll see you later." He turned to walk back into the theater but he abruptly stopped after a few steps. My brother quickly spun to face me. "Did you know about him? My—my son?"

"No, Brother, I swear I did not. She didn't even tell me when I arrived. I only found out about him when he walked out of his room and startled me." I could feel my sympathy shaping my expression while I held his gaze. "I'm sorry she ran and hid. I'm sorry she lied to all of us. And I know she's sorry, too. Have you spoken to her yet? Or did you just see them?"

"I asked Brian where you were and he told me backstage somewhere. So I was on my way back here when I saw Bob waving at me from the front row. I went over to say hi, and I saw Taniya sitting there with a toddler in her lap that looks just like me. I knew immediately he was mine, and then…well, then I ran back here."

"This needs to be talked about. Like seriously talked about," I said. "That's not just your son. He is the reincarnation of our father and he remembers every moment of his life so far, as well as his entire life as Dancing Bear."

Will's head went back, as if he'd been smacked on the forehead. He blinked a few times and scratched his chin. "Um," he mumbled.

"I'm going to get them back here. Then we're going back to the conference room to talk while people finish signing in. Okay?" I walked back over to the first break in the curtains and poked my head through. "Taniya," I called.

She didn't notice me.

"Taniya!" I said a bit louder.

She looked up and gave me a small wave. I motioned for her to come backstage and sent her a thought to bring her son. She did as I asked and climbed the stairs with her boy on her hip. I asked them all to follow me back to the room before we started this discussion, as we did not need it echoing throughout the theater.

They followed me down the hall in silence and, as soon as I closed the door behind Will, Taniya burst into tears. "I'm sorry. I'm sorry. I was hormonal and angry at you, and I was scared. You made me suffer like no one else ever has by telling me to kill my baby, and I didn't know of any way to make you suffer other than killing your car. Please don't hate me anymore! I don't want to be with you, but we have to be civil now. He's yours, Will. This is your son," she cried.

"I know. Hope just told me after I saw him," Will replied quietly.

"Mommy, let me down," the child whispered. She obliged

and he walked over to his father. Will knelt down as the child approached and greeted him with a hug.

"Do you know who I am?" Dancing Bronco whispered to him.

My brother gave him a few jerky nods as tears welled up in his eyes.

The boy smiled. "I am not only your son, but in my last life, I was your father and I remember my whole life. As well as your whole life. I still remember your first steps, your first words, your first haircut, your first everything."

"And I missed all of yours," Will replied shamefully.

"That's okay, Daddy. You're here for me now, aren't you?" the child asked.

"Yes," my brother choked out and hugged his child again.

"Well, that went much better than I expected," I said as I turned and walked out of the room.

CHAPTER 31

I wandered around backstage for a while before I found a spiral staircase that led up to a series of catwalks. I folded my wings back and climbed the narrow stairs that twisted tightly toward the ceiling. When I reached the top and turned to walk across the metal walkway over the stage, I found Deema standing in front of me. I gave him a small frown, squeezed past him, and peeked over the curtain at the growing crowd scattered below.

"How many now?" I asked quietly.

"Um, there's about 2,000 people signed in now, but it's creeping up on four o'clock and thousands more are waiting for entry. It should speed up, now, though. Sounds like they've got a good process going outside and no one has refused to sign. I don't think anyone outside right now has any intention of refusing to sign, either."

"Awesome." I felt only a small amount of relief from his reassurance.

We stood in silence for almost an hour while people continued to enter the theater and find seats. After a while, all of the seats on the floor were taken and people started wandering up to the many balconies and private boxes. I scanned the room and saw that people were seating themselves directly in front of me on the far, opposite side of the theater.

"We need to remain still or disappear quickly before they see us," I whispered.

"Which do you want?" he asked without moving.

"I don't know," I replied after a few seconds.

"Well, does it really matter now if a few people catch a glimpse of you?" he asked incredulously. "I mean, everyone here signed their paper, and you're about to fly for them anyway, right?"

"Yeah, you're right." I turned to him. "Are there stairs on the other side?"

He kissed my forehead. "Yes."

We walked across the catwalk and started to go down the stairs. He stopped on the second step and turned around as I bumped into him. "They've seen you."

"Oh, well."

Once we reached the bottom, I turned back toward the conference room to see if my brother was still in there. I knocked, cracked the door, and stuck my head in.

"The meeting should be starting soon. You all might want to get out there before you miss anything," I said with an apologetic nod.

As if I had cued him, I heard Brian begin to talk over the speakers in the theater. "Attention, everyone. Could I have your attention, please? We will be starting the meeting in about twenty minutes. If you haven't found a seat yet, there are still some open boxes on both sides, as well as a number of empty seats in both center balconies. Also, sorry it took so long to get everyone signed in, but the sooner we can all get settled, the sooner we can get started. We expect the meeting to last about three or four hours, but we will try to get through this as fast as possible. We'd like to ask that no one leave the theater unless we announce there is a break or an emergency. Everything we have to say here tonight needs to be heard by each and every one of you. So, if you think you are likely to need the restroom in the next two hours before we call a break, then I suggest you go now."

I heard the microphone click off as the five of us walked down the hallway to wait in the wings of the stage for the meeting to start. We ran into Brian as we rounded the corner, and he led Taniya, Will, and Dancing Bronco back to their seats.

I sat on my stool and continued to wait nervously. I had always had such terrible stage fright, but that night it had nothing to do with me doubting my flying skills. My fear stemmed from the fact that my entire tribe was about to be told that many of them may die soon. I wanted to burst into tears.

"Hope, settle down." Deema pulled my hand from my wing. I stared at him, confused, and he pointed to where I'd been plucking my feathers out. "You're like a nervous parrot."

"Sorry," I mumbled, fidgeting my hands in my lap.

"Are you going to be okay to fly?" He sounded very concerned.

"I'll be fine." I tried to smile up at him.

His eyebrows pulled together. I decided that my smile must have failed. "Would you like me to distract you?" he asked. He leaned in for a kiss.

I accepted his distraction. A few seconds into our kiss, I heard the microphone switch on. I peered up to see my brother standing center stage once more.

"Five minutes, everyone. We've got five minutes until the elders will take the stage and start the meeting. Please find your seats. We've got five minutes. There are no more seats left on the main floor, but there are still a few available on both upper balconies."

He switched the microphone off before exiting stage left. He stomped right over to Deema, grabbed him by the shoulder of his shirt, and tried to drag him away from me.

Deema stood his ground. "Would you mind waiting until later to yell at me? Look, I'm sorry, man, but she needs me right now. I'm not going anywhere." As always, Deema spoke to my big brother with respect, despite his refusal to comply with him.

Brian grumbled so low and deep in his throat, it sounded like an animal's growl. Deema shook his head in dissatisfaction and turned back to me.

"Brian, will you go sit down, please?" I asked with my face buried in Deema's marble chest. When I felt like my brother was gone, I peeked up at the vampire who was holding me. "Is everyone seated and ready?" I asked.

He put a comforting arm around my shoulders. "Almost. There are three people still headed for their seats and the elders are walking down the aisle toward the stage. It will start very shortly."

I sighed. "Good. The sooner it starts, the sooner it will be over."

CHAPTER 32

When the elders had climbed the stairs, my grandfather turned and asked if I was ready. I gave him a nod so the chief picked up the microphone and turned it on.

"Is this thing on? Good, good. Thank you, everyone, for gathering here tonight. I am extremely pleased to report that not one single person refused to sign the confidentiality/non-disclosure form for the meeting tonight. From here on out, we will need to start having regular meetings every month to keep the tribe informed of what is happening. But no more forms need ever be signed. I do not wish to cause anyone concern or worry here tonight, but the tribe must be informed of what is to come.

"As all of you know, many of our stories, legends, and prophesies have been guarded by the elders for hundreds of generations. For thousands of years, we have kept many stories to ourselves so as to not cause alarm and so that others outside the tribe would never discover our prophesies. Over the last 100 years or so, some of our guarded prophesies have been leaked and the pale ones are well aware that we are prophesized to survive and they are meant to die because of their evil and destructive ways.

"When their government deceives them and kills massive amounts of the American population, many will come here. Some will come to join us, and some will come to destroy us and steal our lands and crops. Many of you here tonight may die before this is all over, but we have protection to keep us all from dying. We have a defender who is here to help us. She can fly over 600 miles an hour and she can carve down dozens of men on a battlefield in a matter of seconds with a sword. She can see the evil and lies in the hearts of men and she can help us keep out those who mean to harm us. She will save countless lives when the battles arise. She is here tonight, and I would like to introduce her to you now. Some of you know her as Hope, Only Daughter of Dancing Bear, but she is now White Eagle." He turned to me and waited for my entrance.

I walked out onto the stage and kept my eyes averted from the crowd. When I reached the center of the stage, I spread my wings as I continued to stare at the ground. Gasps and murmurs spread through the crowd. I started flapping my wings at a leisurely pace until the chief asked me to show them my wind. I pumped my wings faster and faster while I slowly lifted my head. I could see my wind moving the hair of people at least a dozen rows back.

Then I heard Taniya's voice rise above the murmurs of the crowd. "Fly, girl! Fly like an eagle!"

I flashed her a quick grin before I crouched down and pushed off. I circled over the crowd, flying high, then low, and then sweeping a wide circle as close to the balconies as I could. Every person in the massive theater was watching me in complete shock as I soared back and forth over their heads. I flew around for about five minutes before I landed back on the stage.

I stared out over at the crowd. My friends in the front row started cheering and stood to applaud me. Much to my surprise, the rest of the 9,000-plus people there followed suit. I stood on the stage in shock for a moment as the entire reservation rose to their feet and celebrated my presence and my skills. I blushed and bowed before I asked the chief if I could go to sleep yet. He smiled warmly and gave me a nod that, yes, I could go. I turned back to the crowd, spread my wings to help keep my balance, and bowed deeply to their continuing applause before I left the stage.

I walked out the back door with Deema. We flew to the val-

ley to grab my bokken before we went to my house. I anxiously ran inside and pulled my hollow book down from the bookshelf. I turned around and saw Deema watching me with a curious expression.

"Dying to read?" he asked suspiciously.

"No, I need to slow down my brain. I need to smoke so I
can meditate."

I opened the book to reveal a quarter ounce of cannabis, a
pack of rolling papers, and a finely crafted glass pipe. I rolled a
joint, walked outside, and lay face down in the hammock. I
hung my arms over the edge and placed the joint in my mouth
through the mesh. My first attempt to light it burned my face
and Deema quickly snatched it away from me. He lit it and
placed it back in my mouth before I could even protest.

"Hmm, I think I love you," I said as I exhaled my first hit.

He laughed. "You'd better!"

"Ha! Who says I was talking to you?" I teased.

"Who else would you be talking to?" he asked incredulously.

"Ah! Why, my sweet, tasty Mary Jane here," I said as I
rolled sideways and held up the joint. "It tastes like chocolate
cake. Haven't you ever had a piece of cake so good that you
just love it?" I licked my lips. "Gotta love genetic engineering,
man. They can make anything taste like anything. Grandma
told me once that it used to taste terrible—like grass clipping
and pine trees."

He let out an exasperated sigh before he lunged toward me,
flipped me out of the hammock, and swept me off my feet.
When he stopped moving, he was holding me by my waist so
that my feet were off the ground and we were nose to nose. His
long hair swirled around us for a second before it settled and
rested down his back. "First of all, when do you think I would
have ever had a fine chocolate cake? I'd never even heard of
chocolate when I was still a man. Secondly, does a little pot
really mean more to you than all of me?" he asked with pleading eyes.

"Oh, Deema, of course not!" I said as I tossed the joint onto
my patio. I wrapped my legs around his waist, my arms around

his neck, and my wings around both of us. He slowly danced me around my back yard in the light of the falling sun as he kissed me with passion and longing. When my lips could no longer take the iciness of his, I forced myself to pull away from him.

"You look and feel as if you're carved from marble," I mused while I stroked his face. "You have the face of an angel, you know?"

He laughed. "Said the woman with the huge, white, feathered wings."

"Um, we're not interrupting, are we?" I heard Taniya squeak as the four of them rounded the corner of my house.

"Oh! Hey, lady. Brian, Will," I nodded to them. "No, um, we were just waiting for you." I started to untangle myself from Deema. "How'd you get here so quick?"

"I parked as close to the exit as I could so we could be among the first hundred or so out of there," my younger brother replied.

"Well, no, I meant—the meeting is over already?" I chuckled. "I thought they had four hours of stories to tell and it got started well over an hour late."

"And I thought you were going to sleep," Brian sneered. "But since you couldn't stay and most of us were restless, once you left, they just told your story, discussed when the next meeting would be, how people would sign in, how people should arrive next time, and stuff like that," Brian informed me with a little less attitude.

"Oh," I replied. "So, who wants to go blaze on the roof? There aren't any non-tribal people on this side of town so I don't have to hide here."

I beamed at them. I was nearly giddy at the idea of getting to walk outside every day to enjoy fresh air and sunlight after being cooped up inside all day for almost two years. I almost wanted to weep with joy at the thought of how much this would change my daily life. No longer would I have to check for eggs with a flashlight. Never again would I be forced to sleep all day so that I could practice at night. I could finally fly around during daylight without sleeping in a tent.

"That sounds cool. But do you think you're able to carry me up there?" Will asked.

I just raised an eyebrow at him. "I don't think that will be necessary."

Will gave me a confused look and Deema leaned over to whisper in my ear, "He doesn't know what I am."

I just shook my head in exasperation, turned around, and pointed at the ladder that was leaning against the back of my doublewide trailer. Will laughed at his selective blindness and started climbing the rungs.

"You're not being realistic enough," Brian whispered to me before he followed Will up to the roof.

CHAPTER 33

I walked back over to the patio and grabbed the joint off the stones before I flew up to the roof to join them. We watched the fading sun and smoked in silence until the joint was too small to hold. I turned to my new lover and asked him if he could grab the hollow book I'd left inside. He disappeared and reappeared in about a second then handed me the book.

Will gawked at him in shock while Brian scowled at him in disgust. "What—how—how did you? How did you just do that?" Will stuttered.

"Because he's a demon," Brian spat.

"He's not a demon," Dancing Bronco and I said simultaneously. The child spoke calmly, but my tone was very defensive.

Deema just laughed at our responses before he gave his own explanation. "I am a vampire. Contrary to popular belief, vampires are not demons. I am immortal and I have impenetrable skin because of some kind of virus.

"The disease known as AUTO Virus is a man-made and corrupted variation of the vampire virus. They were trying to duplicate the actions of the virus that rules our bodies and devours and controls every cell in them. Only their mistakes created an incurable and incredibly deadly disease that is inadvertently doing another one of their desires—killing millions of people to decrease global population.

"I am but a man. A man who cannot die, but a man nonetheless. One side effect of the virus is that the only food I can consume is raw blood. Another is that my skin takes on various levels of translucence in varying levels of direct sunlight.

"I also have several other unusual effects from this virus. At 200 years of immortality, I discovered I could read minds. The older I get, the farther away I can hear people's thoughts. Thirteen years ago, when I hit 500 years of immortality, I discovered that I could fly. I have had super speed and super strength since the night I was turned," Deema said matter-of-factly, never taking his eyes off the colors of the sunset.

Brian continued to seethe at him while Will stared at him in shock.

Deema turned to Brian. "Do it, then." His voice was calm. His body language was open and nonthreatening as he leaned back on his hands.

"Fuck you, man." Brian growled and spat on Deema.

The vampire stood, charged at my brother, and swooped him off the roof. In the blink of an eye, they were standing in the backyard. Brian stumbled backward in confusion.

"If you want to hit me, then hit me. You can't hurt me, so you might as well get it out of your system. Go on. Use me as a punching bag. You'll hurt your hands far worse than you could ever hurt me," Deema said calmly with his hands clasped behind his back.

Brian glared at him for a second before he attacked him and tried unsuccessfully to knock him to the ground. He pounded on his chest, kicked him repeatedly, and did his best to beat on the immortal who stood in front of him. But Deema was unmovable. He stood perfectly still and took all the abuse my brother could dish out while the rest of us watched in astonishment.

When my brother had exhausted himself, Deema spread his arms and opened his hands in an apologetic manner. "I'm sorry you couldn't make yourself feel better by hurting me, but I promise you I will never hurt her."

He tried to help Brian up from the grass where he had fallen. Brian smacked his hand away, stood up, and spat on the vampire again.

Deema sighed as he wiped the saliva from his face. "Why

don't you just read my mind to see my intentions are true?"

"I can't read your mind. I can only hear your thoughts when you push them to me, and you can push anything you want," Brian grumbled.

I flew down from the roof and landed between them, facing my brother. "Please, Brian. You can read my mind. Look into my head and see how much I trust him," I said as calmly as I could.

"I know you don't fully trust him and I don't have to see into your head right now to know that," he replied bitterly.

'Have you ever considered that someday I may want to become like him? Maybe our love will continue to grow until I decide that I can't die and leave him behind. Have you ever considered that?'

"Yes, I have. And I can't let you do that," he replied aloud. He seemed as if he was about to spit on me, as well.

"Well, there's nothing you can do to stop me, so you might as well get over it," I said before turning my back on him and flying back up to the roof.

'Always so damned stubborn. Stupid. Evil bastard. Ruining my sister. Destroying our hope.'

Will watched me with wide eyes. "How could you be with him?" he asked me incredulously.

"I feel drawn to him. I can't really explain it. I mean, I don't know him all that well, but maybe it's love. We could also totally use his help," I replied.

Deema landed at my side. "Help that I am more than willing to give," he whispered, kissing the top of my head. He turned to my younger brother. "You're not going to hate me like he does, are you?"

Brian was still loudly thinking cantankerous things about us as he stomped through my yard.

Will peered down at his son. "You've known him since you were born. Should I trust him?"

Dancing Bronco held his father's gaze. "As I told your older brother, yes, you should trust him. He has a good heart from what I've seen. He only kills animals or evil men. He will be of much use to us for as long as he is with us."

"Okay, then. That's all I need. Welcome to the family, Vampire." Will thrust out his hand.

They shook hands and we sat back down on the roof to smoke. Brian stalked down the street to walk back to the casino for his truck.

CHAPTER 34

A few minutes later, my neighbors started arriving home from the meeting and they noticed us sitting on my roof. After they got out of their car, my next door neighbors came over to my front yard instead of going into their own house.

"Hey, do you have a minute?" one of them called out.

"Sure." I stood, spread my wings, and glided down from the roof to greet them. I smiled in what I hoped was a comforting way as they continued to stare at me in thinly veiled shock.

"How did you hide your wings for so long?" Daniel, the forty-eight-year-old father of four asked.

"Well, they started growing a couple of years ago. I quit my job when I couldn't hide them anymore, and I've hid in my house ever since. I finally figured out how to fly on Thursday night, revealed myself to the elders Friday morning, and spent the whole weekend practicing in the western valley," I explained.

"How will you protect us?" Susan, his wife, asked.

"I can fly at great speeds and with extreme accuracy. Would you like to see my attack move?" I asked with a touch of excitement.

"Sure," they both answered. He sounded excited. She sounded a bit more apprehensive.

I ran into the house to grab my bokken and then I pushed off into the sky. I flew up to about a mile above the ground before I flipped over and started my dive toward the pavement of our street. At the far end of the block, I reached my desired seven feet from the ground and spread my wings as I slashed at the air with my wooden sword. Buzzing over them, I ceased my slashing before I resumed it on the other side of the growing group in my yard. I made one last turn at the end of the block and showed off with my heel-dragging landing. They all watched me with wide eyes as I approached them with a huge grin.

"Again, again! Do it again!" my nephew cried out.

I smiled at him and obliged his request. When I landed the second time, I asked my neighbors if they'd like to join us in the backyard.

They all declined my request, giving various excuses as to why they needed to return home.

"Sure, well, feel free to stop by anytime." I smiled. "Oh, and if anyone on the block has something delivered to their home, if you know an outsider will be coming to the rez, I would appreciate a heads-up so I can avoid being outside when strangers are near."

They all agreed that would be wise, as they all knew what the repercussions were for being the cause of my exposure to the outside world.

Taniya and Will said they were going to leave as well, so we bid them goodbye before we went back into my house. I flipped on the TV and searched for a news broadcast so I could see the weather.

While I waited to see how much I could fly the upcoming week, a news report flashed onto my screen. The reporter sat there behind her big anchor desk and told all the viewers at home that three separate angel sightings were reported across the country over the weekend.

"While no one was able to take a picture of the alleged angel, one of the reports came from an airplane out of Phoenix that was headed for Fort Collins, Colorado. The pilots claim to have seen the angel twice as they started the descent for landing, and for just a few seconds each time. Over forty passengers on the 757 American Airlines flight also claimed to have seen the alleged angel," the reporter said.

The screen flashed to a woman standing in an airport, and she told the world what happened. "I was just staring out the window, looking at the low clouds beneath the plane, when all of a sudden this woman with super long, black hair and a twenty-foot wing span drifted past the window toward the back of the plane, smiling. I heard a few other people yelling out that they just saw an angel, so I yelled out, too. Then less than a minute later, as everyone was staring out the windows, the other side yelled out that they saw her, too. We all saw exactly the same thing. I know it's real and God has sent us an angel to protect us in this century full of terror and war," the giddy woman babbled.

The reporter said that they also got a report from a man in Denver, Colorado who claimed that an angel fixed his car long enough to make it to a mechanic. The screen flashed again and the nervous man I had spoken to in Russian appeared on my TV.

"My car broke down while I was drivin' through the mountains. I stopped right in front of the sign sayin' I was a mile outside Denver. I got out of my car and I noticed what seemed to be a giant white bird curled up under the sign. I was surprised and thought maybe I'd found some injured, massive bird, but when I walked up to it, an angel jumped up and spread her wings. She had purple eyes and long, black hair down to her knees and she spoke to me in what sounded like some commie language. She touched my car and it started running again. She said 'auto mechanic' in a really thick accent and flew off. I drove into town, and as soon as I pulled into an auto shop, my car died and rolled into a parking space."

"What language did you say she spoke?" asked the interviewer off camera.

"It was some commie language like Russian or something," he said.

"How big would you say her wings were? Was the angel larger than life?" the reporter asked.

"She was almost six feet tall and I'd say each wing was also about six feet or so," he answered.

"Thank you, Mr. Delgado. Back to you, Sara," the field reporter said as the camera turned to her, and then the screen cut back to the woman behind the news desk.

"Thanks, Sharon. We also had a report out of New York from a man who declined an on-camera interview. But he did visit our sister station in Manhattan to tell them his story earlier today. He claimed that he saw an angel land on a building rooftop across the street from his apartment just before sunrise yesterday morning. The angel allegedly hugged a woman who had been standing on the roof for over thirty minutes, and then they entered the building. He claimed that later that day, about an hour after sunset, he saw the angel walk back out of the building, and fly off the roof clutching a child, before he witnessed an un-winged man take off into the sky with a woman in his arms. He asked that his name not be revealed so that no one he knows thinks he's crazy." She stifled a laugh before making her segue to the next story.

"Do angels really exist? One orphanage says yes," she said as she turned to a different camera. Another field reporter appeared on the screen and started her story of an orphanage that almost closed but stayed open due to donations.

I stared at Deema with wide eyes. "What am I supposed to do?"

"Stay out of sight from now on," he said with a smile. "And I think I've got a great way to keep you inside." He pulled me up from my seat, wrapped his frigid bare arms around my waist, and pressed his lips to mine.

After a few moments, I broke away and shyly asked him if he was capable of sex. He broke out in an elated grin and released me before he ripped off his shirt.

CHAPTER 35

I blushed. "No, I mean—I'm not asking to right now," I stammered. "Is it—well, your skin is ice cold, so, I mean, is it…" I trailed off.

He laughed at my question, bobbed his head up and down, and pressed his hips to mine. "Yes, it is just as cold as the rest of me. It is also just as solid as the rest of me."

"How did no one ever notice?" I wondered, trying to ignore the longing for him in my loins.

"You know those little hand warmers?" he asked, his shimmering black eyes gazing down at me.

I nodded dumbly while I tried to keep my focus on his words.

"I would hold one of those down there for a little bit, or if I found women who liked ice-play, I'd keep a bowl of ice next to my bed and melt several pieces on them. They always thought I melted one on me, too," he said before pressing into me a bit harder. "Eventually, I'll warm up once I've been inside you long enough, and I can last all night long." His lustful gaze twisted into a bit more of a cunning leer.

"Really? So, you don't, um, ejaculate?" I whispered shyly.

"No, I don't. I haven't ever since I was turned," he said before he kissed me again.

I gave in to his advances, and he slowly floated us parallel to the ground like he had on the side of the cliff. He slid down the spaghetti straps of the shirt I'd borrowed from Taniya before he rolled the shirt down to my waist.

My skin erupted in goose bumps as my hot flesh touched his freezing chest.

"Are you sure you're not asking to?" he mumbled between kisses while I pressed my hips into his. I unbuttoned my pants as I bit his solid neck in reply. He chuckled at me again, gently rolled over in the air, and laid me down on my pallet.

What followed that night was by far more pleasurable than anything I could have ever imagined. It had been almost three years since I'd broken up with my last boyfriend and been touched by a man, so I relished every kiss and touch of my immortal mate. He left tingling trails of kisses and caresses all over my body while he gave me repeated climaxes like I'd never experienced.

After over an hour of mind-blowing intercourse, Deema stopped and shuddered as if he, too, had just climaxed. He gawked at me in shock as he climbed off of me.

"What the hell was that?" I asked as I grabbed a blanket to cover my freezing skin.

"I don't know. It felt like an orgasm. But it's been a long time. Such a long time."

"Do you think that you just…you know…inside of me?" I asked cautiously.

He stared at me for a long minute before he slowly nodded his head. "Yes, I think I did," he mumbled.

"But I thought you said that wasn't possible," I said with a touch of concern. The image of my pregnant self, standing on a fence post flashed through my brain. "Do you think it's possible that you could impregnate me?" I asked incredulously.

"I don't know," he whispered. "I saw your visions that day, you know? And I saw you pregnant, as well as us kissing and making love many times. But since I have never ejaculated as a vampire, I figured maybe you would cheat on me, or immaculate conception or something. I don't know. I just thought that it wouldn't be possible. But I saw the child in your visions, and I saw myself raising her. I didn't think she could be mine. I didn't think this could happen," he babbled.

"I saw myself pregnant, as well. I also saw you covered in blood and snarling, and I saw Taniya with a bite from you, crying in the shower as wings started to grow from her back," I admitted.

"That's a future that won't happen now," he said flatly. "I saw that vision of Taniya, as well, but it will not come to be. When I made a conscious decision to never turn her, the vision faded from your mind."

"But that vision woke me up," I objected.

"No, the vision of giving birth woke you up. You just don't remember that one. I guess you weren't meant to," he mused.

"So I'm gonna get knocked up by a vampire? What does that mean for the child?" I wondered out loud.

"I have no idea," he said as we lay down and got comfortable.

I yawned and settled onto his chest and arms. "You'll be my pillows tonight, huh?"

"I'll be your pillows for the rest of time," he said before he kissed my forehead and I drifted off to sleep.

CHAPTER 36

I awoke the next morning to find Deema in the same position as when I had fallen asleep. *He must have watched me the whole time I slept*, I mused when I opened my eyes to his handsome face.

He beamed at me. "Good morning, Hope."

"Good morning, Dmitri," I mumbled and unwound myself from him.

"Did you sleep well?" he inquired as he helped me to my feet.

I stretched to wake my muscles and groaned. "Yeah, I did."

He walked to the kitchen. "Coffee?"

"Absolutely," I said as I shuffled after him.

After I drank a little coffee, the hunger in my stomach made itself quite known. I threw some bacon into the cast iron skillet on my stove before I wrapped myself in a sheet and walked out back to my henhouse. I found eight eggs from my twelve hens and went back inside to fry them up. I was thrilled when I found a bag of bagels in my freezer, so I thawed and toasted them in the toaster while my bacon and eggs cooked.

I gobbled down my breakfast and asked him what we should do that day.

"Monsoon season is coming, and it's supposed to rain today, so I don't think I should go out flying." I walked over to the back door as I spoke and peeked out at the growing clouds.

He flashed to my side and slid his arm around my waist, turning me toward him while he closed the blinds with his other hand. "How about we turn off the phone and hole up here by ourselves for the day?" he asked sheepishly.

I smiled at his suggestion and welcomed it with a kiss. He unwrapped the bed sheet I wore like a toga, floated himself up between my legs, and lifted me off the ground while I straddled him. We drifted over to my pallet and he pushed his icy phallus into me.

The sex continued for hours and we both climaxed several times. When I could no longer ignore the void in my belly, I reluctantly asked him to stop. I collapsed onto my pallet and asked him if he could cook me some food.

"I'm starving and I can't move my legs," I moaned, barely managing to lift my head.

"Sure." He flashed to the kitchen and started rummaging through the cabinets. "There are some jars in here that look like soup. Do you want one of those?" he asked, holding one up.

"Could you make two?" I mumbled as I felt myself falling asleep.

He awoke me twenty minutes later with a big bowl of steaming, home-canned soup and a chunk of bread. I thanked him, took it from him, and devoured it.

"There's at least another two bowls worth on the stove," he said, sitting down next to me. When I finished my first bowl, he stood and poured me another serving.

By the time I finished that, I felt I was able to move again and I fetched my cannabis. I smoked a joint in silence while I digested my food. When I was relaxed, I rolled over and started to fall asleep again.

"Hey, what are you doing?" he asked as he shook me lightly.

"I'm tired," I mumbled as I settled onto his chest. "You should let me dream."

"Well, I'm not," he joked. He pulled my face to his and grazed my lips with a frozen kiss.

"Just give me a couple hours, okay? You're more exhausting than flying," I teased.

He laughed at my comment. "So, I'm good exercise, am I?"

"Well," I said with a yawn, "you did make every muscle in my body convulse for minutes at a time. Now, come on, Deema, we've got centuries to have sex for days on end if we want. But right now, I still have to sleep six to ten hours a day. I also need to sleep so I can have my visions."

"Okay. Sweet dreams, lover," he said. He lightly stroked my hair and I fell fast asleep.

CHAPTER 37

What felt like seconds later, I was startled by a pounding at my front door. I looked at the clock and saw that I had been asleep for almost seven hours. Another dreamless sleep. How strange, I thought. I wrapped the sheet, which was still laying by the back door, around myself and shuffled to the front door.

"Hang on! Damn!" I yelled out, irritated, as they continued to steadily bang on my door. "Who is it?" I asked without opening it.

"Open the door," was the reply from a deep, unfamiliar voice.

I scanned the room. Deema was nowhere to be found.

"Identify yourself," I called back. "You woke me up from a sound sleep. I'm not answering the door for a stranger. How dumb do you think I am?"

"We're with the US Marshalls. We have a warrant to search the premises. We have reason to believe you are harboring a terrorist," the man said through the door.

"Well, I'm the only one here, and you can shove your warrant up your fucking ass! This is tribal land and you have no jurisdiction here!" I yelled at him.

"Actually, yes we do. Under the New Patriot Act, we can search any dwelling in the world if we suspect terrorists inside." He sounded almost smug.

"Fine, but at least give me a couple minutes to get dressed," I said as I backed away from the door.

Where the hell is Deema?

"Not a chance! Bust it down, boys!" he roared as I grabbed my shirt and my pants.

I bolted out the back door at the same moment that they burst through the front. It forced me into my first running start for a take-off. I pumped my wings as fast as I could and flew almost straight up into the sky to try to get out of sight and the range of bullets. I flew up so high that I started to feel ice crystals on my face and arms, so I turned to fly more horizontally.

I was thoroughly freaking out. I had no idea what was happening, or what I should do. Was this the beginning of the second invasion by White men? It was so soon—too soon.

Where the hell was Deema? I'd woken up sleeping on pillows that propped me up just how he had been holding me. What if he'd gone out to hunt and left me defenseless? How could he find me if he couldn't read my mind?

How had the government found me? Were they really spying on everyone with satellites? The never ending questions raced through my mind and each new question never brought any answers, only more questions.

After I'd been airborne for about a minute, I heard Brian's voice in my head. *'Come back home. It was just a test.'*

I was infuriated beyond belief as I turned around and flew back to my house. I slowed my flight and managed to put my clothes on while I flew.

I landed in my back yard, and instead of dragging my heels, I ran straight to my older brother. I beat on his chest as I screamed at him, "What the fuck is your problem? What the hell do you think you're doing? I don't have a front door now, you son of a bitch!"

He laughed at me as he permitted me to release my anger on him. "We have to make sure you can be ready at any time, day or night, sleeping or awake. And you didn't do very well," he explained.

I ceased my pounding and looked at him curiously as I thought about what he had said.

"But I got away," I said after a moment.

"But you left your bokken. From now on your bokken is

your sword. It must always be with you so that when your sword gets here, you will be in the habit of always carrying it with you. And, you didn't call out to anyone who can hear your mind to let us know you were in trouble. We also have a new door in the back of my truck in case you screwed up and we actually broke down your door," he replied.

"Okay," I said slowly. "So is this going to be a regular occurrence? I mean, I don't want to get desensitized and then when something really happens, I think it's a drill, ya know?"

He smiled. "I don't know. We'll see, I guess."

"And where is Deema?" I asked suspiciously.

Brian's eyebrows pulled together and he seemed genuinely confused. "How should I know?"

CHAPTER 38

I'm right here," came Deema's voice from my roof.
I stepped back to glare up at him and planted my hands on my hips.

"Where were you when they were pounding on my door?" I demanded.

He jumped down from the roof and peered into my eyes as he tried to wrap his arms around me. I pushed him away and asked him again.

"I went hunting," he replied. "There are two deer I left in the woods, but I heard you calling out for me, so I came back without them," he replied before he tried to hold me again.

"Just give me a minute! Damn! You don't always have to be on me, you know," I chided, pushing him away again.

He sighed and backed away. "Fine. I'm sorry, but you know I've got to eat, too. I'm sorry I left you alone," he whispered with gentle eyes.

"You left me defenseless while I slept! Don't ever do that again! Protector of the protector, my ass," I screamed as I smashed my fists against his marble chest.

"I'm sorry, Hope. I won't. I promise," he said gently and I collapsed into his arms. His skin was still cold, but not nearly as frigid as it usually was. I'd have to ask him about that later.

Once I was able to compose myself, I scanned the other men my brother had brought with him. I recognized most of them as First Grandsons of Council Elders and I figured the rest were the three I'd never met. They all gawked at me in open-mouthed astonishment as I stood there in the arms of the pale, White man who had appeared out of nowhere.

'Brian, do they know what he is?'

He shook his head once.

'Can we keep it that way?'

He rolled his eyes at me. *'We can try. For now.'*

I turned to the group of men who appeared to range from sixteen to forty-five. "I'm sorry, where are my manners? This is Deema, and he's here to protect us just like I am."

"How is he to protect us? Is he Pahana?" the oldest of the new elders asked cautiously.

"Um, I don't know the story of Pahana, though I've heard the name before. But have you ever seen that old TV show, *Heroes*?" I asked them. A few of them nodded while the rest of them watched me with blank expressions. "Well, Deema has many abilities that are completely unexplainable and it's kinda like that," I said, thinking quickly.

"Like what? What can he do?" the teenager asked excitedly.

"He can fly without wings. He never needs sleep. He has tremendous strength and speed. He can read minds and…" I trailed off while I tried to think of other advantages he had that could help us.

"Super hearing and sight," Deema whispered in my ear.

"Oh, yeah. Super hearing and super sight, too," I added.

"That's really cool," the young man replied with an even more obvious excitement.

"Well, I'm very hungry. Could you go grab those deer?" I asked as I turned to Deema. "I can mix up a quick glaze or something while you tear out the backstraps and then I can grill them up while they fix my door." I gestured to the group of men who formed a rough semi-circle around us. "Would you all care to stay for dinner?" I asked them.

They accepted my offer and we each went about our business.

The sun had completely set by then. I turned on the flood light out back so I could gather some food from the garden. I cut up some carrots, zucchini, baby red potatoes, and okra, wrapped them in foil, and threw them next to the grill while the charcoal flame calmed down. I made a glaze with molasses, whiskey, brown sugar, and some spices.

When I walked back out to the grill, Deema was standing there with two gutted deer in one hand, and four backstraps in the other. I thanked him with a kiss before I took the meat inside, rinsed it, rubbed it in spices, and rolled it in the glaze before I placed the meat and vegetables on the grill.

After about thirty minutes, the young elders came around back and waited with us while the food finished cooking.

"Smells good," my brother said as he sat down on the hammock and all the rest agreed with him. When all the food was ready, we sat around the patio to eat. One of the men asked Deema why he wasn't eating. Brian looked at him with a cocky grin and waited for his reply.

"I can wait to eat until later when we make burgers," he replied smoothly.

"Ooh! Burgers!" I exclaimed.

He laughed boisterously at my reaction. "Anything that you all don't eat, I know Hope will need for energy to fly and practice. Actually, even after all of this, I have no doubt she'll need more food in a few hours if she plans on flying tonight."

Everyone seemed content with his answer. We finished our meal over a discussion of how my wings grew and how I learned to fly. We all said our goodbyes around ten o'clock.

I was once again alone with my lover.

"So, do you want to go flying for a while?" he asked coyly.

I could tell what he really wanted was to stay home and make love some more.

"Will you come with me?" I asked as I wrapped my arms around his neck.

"Of course."

CHAPTER 39

W e walked out my backdoor and took off into the sky. It was an entirely different experience flying with someone else. I kept hitting him with my wings, no matter where he flew around me. I laughed as I dipped and turned from side to side, trying to avoid hitting him. He finally slipped up underneath me and found a perfect spot to fly so I didn't run into him.

We flew like that for a few minutes while he covered my face in delicate, icy kisses. I slowly increased our speed as we circled over the reservation.

Soon he started having trouble keeping up. I made a sharp, vertical, 180-degree turn like I'd figured out in the valley. As I flipped over to face the ground again, I went straight into a diving descent toward my house. I landed in my backyard and ran inside to grab my bokken. After I tied it to my waist, I ran across my yard as I pumped my wings and lifted into the air.

I found Deema circling my neighborhood, and I asked him if he would help me practice.

"You don't even have to ask," he said before he followed me back to my valley.

I found some dirt that broke apart into little chunks and I asked him to throw them at me while I flew.

"Are you serious?" he asked incredulously.

"Absolutely. I need to be able to dodge attacks. People could be shooting at me, or throwing rocks, or whatever. I need to be able to dodge shit, ya know?" I said as I walked toward him with a handful of dirt clumps. "We can start with dirt so I don't get hurt, then we can move on to rocks and stuff."

"But I can't throw things at you! I might hurt you even with dirt," he said as his eyes filled with concern.

I sighed. "You have to," I insisted. "I must practice and I need your help."

He considered my words for a long moment before he sighed. "Fine," he conceded.

I beamed at him and then ran away as I pumped my wings. As I lifted into the sky, I felt the first of many dirt clumps hit my leg. I threw all my weight to the left and made an incredibly sharp turn as a ball of dirt flew past my face. I looked down and saw him running after me as he continued to throw dirt clods. I dipped and dodged as best I could, but about two out of every three still hit me. After several seconds passed without any dirt flying at me, I went in for a landing.

"I'm out," he said as I strolled over to him. We searched the valley floor, found another pile of dirt that crumbled the same way, and filled his shirt with them so he'd have more ammo.

"Every time you throw a piece of dirt, will you yell out 'boom' or something?" I asked.

He eyed me inquisitively.

"So I know when something's coming at me. If someone is shooting at me, I'm going to hear a gun going off repeatedly and have an idea of where it's coming from. If you're behind me, just throwing dirt or rocks, I'm not going to know when or where it's coming from," I explained.

He agreed that it made sense, so I took off running again. I was rather starting to like this take-off method.

When I reached about six feet above the ground I heard a "Boom!" at about seven o'clock behind me. I tucked my left wing and it caused me to make a very sharp turn to the left. The dirt clump flew over the back of my head and I drew my bokken as I completed the turn.

Before I could gain any more distance between myself and the ground, he threw three more dirt clumps at me. I quickly turned my wings, threw my body weight, and headed straight up into the sky as I missed all three shots. Once I gained my bearings, I dove back down to the valley and skimmed along the bottom, dodging dirt balls. I even broke a few with my bokken when I couldn't dodge them. After less than five minutes, he ran out of dirt and we had to gather some more. We practiced like this for an hour until I decided I needed food and drink.

We flew back to my house and ground up some of the deer for burgers. I ate five burgers while he watched me in mild amusement.

"You're so beautiful when you eat," he mused.

I snorted a laugh. "I stuff my face like a slob!"

"Yes. You give in to your animal instincts for sustenance."

"Speaking of which, I'd really like some fruit. Oranges, bananas, and ooh! Pineapple. I *really* want some pineapple and strawberries!" I exclaimed.

"Sure," he said with a chuckle. "I'll go get some later."

"How?" I asked after I swallowed my last bite.

"I've still got almost $100 left."

"What will we do for money after that? I mean, I spent almost all of my money in New York buying takeout. I left the rest with Taniya because I knew she'd need to get utilities turned on at her mom's house."

"How would you feel about a trip to Las Vegas?" he asked coyly. "I can surely find sinners with pockets full of money there."

"I don't know how comfortable I am with watching you kill," I said weakly.

"Well, as we both know now, you will be killing like I do someday, so you may as well get used to it. But if it's too soon, then you can just circle the city. I'll find you when I'm done."

I watched his eyes as he spoke and I got the feeling he was sad he couldn't share this part of his life with me.

"It's too bad we didn't bring the straps from Taniya's so I could walk around Vegas like I did New York," I said.

"I don't think that's wise," he said quickly. "We need to keep you out of sight, remember?" he whispered before he kissed my forehead.

"Right," I said quietly. "So, how does your feeding work?

Do you have to feed every day? Or if you feed twice one day, then every other day? Can you drink a whole bunch of blood and then not feed for a week?" Once the questions started, I couldn't seem to close my mouth and I blushed at how silly I sounded when I heard my own words.

He laughed at my queries. "Well, if I only feed on one deer a day, or one man a day, then I do just fine. I've never gone more than a week without blood, and I nearly went mad. And I can only drink as much as my system will hold," he replied once he contained his amusement. "So, do you want to go to Vegas with me?" he asked as he leaned in and brushed his lips against mine.

"Oh, I'll fly with you anywhere." I sighed before I pressed my lips against his.

We stood to leave, but I stopped and looked at him like I'd forgotten something.

"What is it?" he asked.

"How do you turn someone? And have you ever turned anyone before?" I asked with a touch of desperation.

CHAPTER 40

He let out a small, forlorn sigh and shook his head lightly in despair. "My blood must enter your bloodstream. You must be bitten so that my blood will start to turn you before you bleed to death. I bite my tongue and run it over the wound before you are at risk of death." He seemed despondent as he spoke. I wondered if he was watching himself change me in his head.

"And have you ever made a vampire before?" I pressed.

"Yes, twice. I've failed twice, as well," he said with a slight tremor to his voice. "My—my family. I tried to change my wife right after I was, but I did it wrong and she bled to death. I did not know that she—I didn't know that I had to give her my blood, too." He appeared as if he would cry, were he capable. "I waited a few years, and after I'd asked my maker how I was turned, I tried again on my brother. I ripped open my wrist and poured it on the wound I'd made on his throat. I—I watched it start to heal. The virus started to take control, but he died of blood loss before the wound could heal closed.

"I then waited for ten more years until my son and daughter were sixteen. They were adults in our day. They were twins and my wife's sister had taken them in after the death of Ana and my disappearance. I approached them in the woods one day and asked if they remembered me. They said no, and I told them I was sorry I'd been gone since they were three. Before I could explain to them why, the sun came out and they saw my skin change. They called me a monster and threw things at me.

I was emotionally crushed. But nothing could deter me from being with my children. I had missed most of their lives and I was not about to give up my chance and end up losing them again. I snuck into their room that night and successfully turned them both into vampires.

"They both hated me even more for what I'd done to them than they did for my leaving them. So they left me. It's been 500 years now, and I've never seen them since that night. From time to time, I'll find things moved around at the castle, or I'll find freshly drained animals in my woods that I didn't kill—Stuff like that. I'm fairly certain my children are still out there, but I don't know if they've forgiven me yet or not." He sighed. "Perhaps they never will."

"Have you ever left a note for them at the castle? Have you ever asked their forgiveness?" I pressed. "And didn't you say you'd only killed one innocent?"

"My brother was not an innocent. He was a dishonest man, but I loved him nonetheless. And no, I doubt that they can read. Also, why *would* they ever forgive me? I left them in a helpless, unwanted state—twice. I *am* a monster, even if only for what I did to my children." He looked like he was about to explode with anger at himself.

"I'm sorry, lover," I whispered and leaned in to kiss his cheek. "I didn't mean to bring up such pain. I'm sorry," I choked.

He nearly had me crying with his sad story.

"It's all right. You needed to know." He stared off into the sky for a few moments. "Well, shall we go, milady?"

A couple of hours later, when we reached Sin City, the mood had lightened considerably. We landed on the roof of Circus, Circus, and I waited patiently for nearly an hour while he went down to hunt. When he returned, I welcomed him with a long hug.

"Your skin—" I started.

"I know. It takes a few minutes for the blood to cool to my body temperature, so it warms my skin briefly," he explained.

"Well, I don't know if warm is the word for it."

I laughed as he lifted me into the sky. He joined me in my

amusement and kissed me gently as we soared away from the city lights and back toward the reservation.

We landed in my yard shortly before five in the morning. We walked inside and he threw several wads of money on the table while I rolled up my last joint.

"So, how much did you make?" I asked casually.

He chortled. "You act like I won it gambling or something."

I threw him a dispassionate scowl.

He ceased his chuckling and shrugged one shoulder. "I'm not really sure. I guess I should count it," he said and snatched it up again. He thumbed through the money and nonchalantly announced that we had $28,000.

I didn't notice that I had dropped the joint I was smoking until I felt it burning a hole in my jeans. I frantically snatched it up and almost fell off my chair before I turned my shock back to Deema.

"H—how?" I sputtered.

"I picked bad men," he said casually.

"But that's so much money!"

"Not to millionaires."

"You killed millionaires?" I gasped.

"No, I killed a couple of guys who work as a team robbing millionaires," he explained. "You know? I think Vegas might be an even better place to hunt than New York was."

The shock was still setting in for me—$28,000! This would change our world.

"We need to start buying massive amounts of food," I said after a moment. "We need to fill every empty building on this rez with stockpiles of food."

"Why?" he asked, a bit surprised.

"So my people don't starve. So I don't starve," I said very matter-of-factly.

"But I can hunt for you," he said with a confused expression on his face.

"Yes, but you cannot hunt grain for bread. Just like you cannot hunt fruits and vegetables for thousands of people. My concern must be for my people, not just for myself," I explained.

"Good point. Should we start ordering stuff in the morning?" he asked.

"I think maybe the best way to cover the massive amount of food we'll be ordering and stocking would be to open a fake restaurant. We'll report the money you steal as profits and use it to buy more and more food," I suggested.

"That's a good idea. It would look odd, otherwise," he mused. "Or we could just use the casino restaurants to order canned fruit and large amounts of grain. That way, we could start ordering stuff right away. And to get rid of any way to trace the money, you could just gamble away every cent of what I bring back," he suggested. "If you pump the money into the casino, then it's an easy way to give it to the tribe without a real paper trail."

"How would I get away with that? Lots of tourists go to the casino," I objected.

"Good point. Well, Taniya could gamble it away. Or, on the days of the tribal meetings, the casino could be closed down for twelve or twenty-four hours to the public, and you could dump money into the slots then. The whole family could run around the floor, pumping money into slot machines to get rid of it," he suggested as he moved to sit on the floor.

"Cool. Well, I think we've got a plan. We can call someone in the morning to get it all set up. But what do you think my people will have to say about using money that has been acquired in such a way? I mean, is vigilante justice still justice?"

"It is justice," he asserted. "If the only way to know the evils in a man's heart is to read his mind, then only those who can see into his head are capable of passing judgment and bringing him to justice."

He spoke firmly and I knew he truly believed he did his part to bring justice to those who avoided getting caught by mortal authorities.

"I understand. I just hope they do, too," I replied.

"I think they will. Some of the elders can read minds, too, you know." He stood and walked over to the kitchen before he returned with a glass of water for me.

"Thank you," I said as I took it from him.

"Sure. Well, I know you need lots of fluids and most people don't drink enough."

I stared at him, apparently with an ambiguous expression on my face, for several minutes before he started to laugh uncomfortably. "Um, penny for your thoughts? You're looking at me strangely and I'm not sure what to make of it."

"I, uh, I was just thinking…" I trailed off as my gaze shifted to the floor.

"Yes?" he prodded after a moment.

"I was thinking about your children," I said quietly. I glanced up at him and he didn't appear to sadden at their mention, so I continued. "If it was 500 years ago this year, that means they can fly now, or they will soon. If they have developed similar killing values as your own, perhaps they *are* ready to forgive you. It has been several mortal lifetimes. Surely they can forgive you by now," I offered.

"I see," he said pensively.

"Can I go to Russia with you? Can we wait at the castle and search for your twins?"

"It is a day for me to fly there, and a day to fly back. You cannot carry me to make it faster, but I can carry you to save you from needing massive amounts of food to refuel. Also, will they even allow you to leave for that long? We could be out there for a week or more, and if there's an emergency here, it will take a whole day to get back," he argued.

"I think the sooner we go, the better," I replied. "That way, we can make it back before the next meeting. Also, the sooner we go, the less likely it is that they'll need me immediately. I mean, I don't even have a real sword yet."

"Okay, Hope," he said after a moment. "We'll ask for permission for you to leave so you can practice flying in the Russian wilderness. Since they are already uncomfortable with my presence here, I don't think it would be wise to tell them we are trying to bring back my vampire children. Besides, the world already thinks the angel is from Russia, so if you're going to be seen flying, it might as well be there. And for a nice bonus, the area is very isolated and sparsely populated, so any locals who see you who might know of the undocumented castle would not spread the news until long after we're gone." His smile grew very wide after he finished speaking.

I thought for a few moments about his idea. It was pretty solid, so I agreed to his proposal.

I fried up some ham and eggs, ate my dinner, and then fell asleep on his chest.

CHAPTER 41

That night, I finally dreamt for the first time in days. I felt like I'd slept for a very long time with all the visions I had. When I woke, I asked Deema how long I had slept.

"Almost five hours," he said quietly as he gently brushed my hair from my face. "You had many dreams."

"I know. I can remember all of them, I think. I feel like I've been gone for days, watching nonstop movies of the future. I'm actually still pretty exhausted. It feels as if I haven't slept at all," I mumbled groggily. I pulled myself up from the floor, shuffled into the kitchen, and put on a pot of coffee before I turned back to my lover. "Did you watch everything in my dreams?"

"Yes." He smiled sheepishly. "I can't help myself. I can see into almost anyone's head at any time—except yours. For some weird reason, I can only glimpse your thoughts while you're asleep."

"I know. It's okay. I'm not mad or anything. I just want you to tell me what you saw," I said before I settled into my chair.

"Well, when you fell asleep, I saw you standing next to my castle in the warm summer sun. The light glistened on your wings like millions of tiny diamonds—" he started.

"I know what my wings look like," I teased. "Can you just stick to the point?"

"Sorry. Well, I saw my daughter walk out of the woods. She demanded to know who you were. I don't think she could read your mind, either. You told her that I had brought you there so that we could find her and her brother, and she ran off into the woods. Then I saw myself hunting and I brought you back a deer. We cooked it outside because all the chimneys were clogged with debris from a 500-year absence of use and—"

"Can you survive in any temperature? Like, does the hot or the cold ever bother you?" I interrupted.

"No, it doesn't bother me," he said. "I've never tested it, though."

"Okay," I mumbled and shuffled back into the kitchen to pour some coffee.

"I saw my children walk out of the woods as I sat back down from throwing wood on the fire. I could tell they were trying to read my mind, and I was trying to read theirs, but it didn't work. They stared at me in confusion for a moment, and then they disappeared into the woods. The next night, they appeared again, only to run away again before we spoke."

"What are their names?" I interrupted again.

"Sasha." He sighed. "They are my Sashas."

"They're both named Sasha?" I asked incredulously.

He laughed. "Yes. Ana was very insistent that we name them Aleksander and Aleksandra and Sasha is the nickname for both names. So they were both Sasha." He smiled at the memory of his wife and I felt a little twinge of pain. He turned to study me at that moment, almost as if he could feel my emotional change. He smiled at me warmly as he stood and walked over to me. "You know, you look so much like her," he said, caressing my face with his icy hand.

I instinctually pulled away from his hand and he seemed surprised.

"I'm sorry," I mumbled.

It bothered me that he would compare me to her, but I knew it shouldn't. I didn't really want him to know that, though.

"W—why?" he stammered.

"Why what?" I whispered as I stood and turned to walk into the kitchen. I was rummaging aimlessly through the cabinets when he came in behind me.

"Why did you pull away from me? And why are you sorry

that you did?" I tried to avoid answering him by remaining silent, but he quickly appeared at my side. "Are you jealous of my wife who has been dead for 500 years?" he whispered in my ear.

I turned and tried to stare at him blankly.

"You shouldn't be, you know? I'm quite sure that you are her reincarnation," he said. He slid his arms around my waist and pulled me close.

"Why?" I asked, on the verge of tears. I wanted to push him away again, but I couldn't bear to.

He stared into my eyes and caressed the small of my back. "Because the last few times you slept, you awoke saying you hadn't dreamt. But you did. You dream all night long once you reach a deep sleep. You just don't always remember them."

I could feel the tears welling up more as he continued to speak.

"I saw us together when we were both alive. I saw our wedding day, and the births of our children. I—I saw you when I k—killed you, too," he choked out.

"How can you be sure it was me?" I said quietly.

"Quick, what was my wife's name?" he asked.

"Anastasia Marie," I blurted out.

"How could you know that? I have only called her 'Ana' to you."

I blinked at him, dumbfounded. How *did* I know that? What if I really was his wife 500 years ago? What if those really were my children?

"So, what do I do now?" I asked after a few moments of thought.

"I think now you should turn off the coffee pot and cook up some breakfast," he said. "Then, I think we should visit the elders to give them some money and ask if we can go to Russia for a couple weeks."

"What if they say no?" I asked cautiously.

He laughed, released me, and reached over to turn off the coffee. "They won't say no."

"I hope you're right," I said in a daze as he leaned in for a kiss.

CHAPTER 42

I went out to the hen house and gathered some eggs while the last of my bacon fried on the stove. He allowed me to cook my breakfast in silence. I thought deeply the whole time.

Would my children recognize me as well? Would they forgive their father for turning them into vampires? Would they agree to return to my reservation with us? The questions swam through my thoughts while I absentmindedly finished cooking my breakfast. When I sat down to eat, Deema ran his hand down my right wing and asked me if he should call my older brother.

"No need," I said before I crammed my mouth full. Instead of explaining myself, I cocked my head toward the front door while I chewed. The unmistakable sound of my brother's truck was pulling up to my house. "I already did."

"Okay," he whispered. "Come on in," he called out once we heard Brian walk up to the door.

My brother came in with our grandfather and they greeted us warmly.

"To what do we owe this visit?" Deema asked politely.

"Hope's bokken has arrived," my brother said as he handed Deema a long, thin bundle wrapped in cloth. Deema took it from him while I continued to shovel food into my mouth, and he thanked my brother graciously.

"Why are you two getting along so well all of a sudden?" I asked between mouthfuls. "Not that I'm complaining," I added. Though, there was so much food in my mouth I'm sure they didn't understand me.

"Taniya and her son have been staying with me while she waits for her house to be ready. It needs massive cleaning and there won't be any utilities until next Monday. Dancing Bronco told me many things about Deema and he has convinced me to trust him. I will not object to this, uh, relationship, any longer." He sounded sincere when he spoke, and I trusted that he was.

"Thank you, Brother," I said after I swallowed the last of my food. I walked over to the kitchen and cleaned off my plate before I walked back into the living room. "Grandfather," I said as I hugged the old man. "I need to ask a favor."

"What is that, my child?" he replied as he kissed my forehead and released me.

"I need to travel to Russia to practice flying. I need a more expansive wilderness to practice in so I can avoid being seen again," I requested.

"Did you pick Russia because that man in Denver said you spoke to him in Russian?" he asked cautiously.

"So you saw the news, too?"

"Yes, Hope. We all saw the news." His voice had taken on a more stern tone.

"Yes, that is why I picked Russia. Also, it is very isolated where we will be and if anyone does see me, word will not travel until we are long gone," I explained.

"Will the immortal accompany you?" my grandfather asked.

"I will never leave her side." Deema put his arm around my waist and gazed down at me. "No one will harm her as long as I'm around."

"Okay," my grandfather quickly replied. "How long will you be gone and when will you return? How long will it take you to return if there is an emergency here?"

"It will take us a day to fly there and a day to fly back since I cannot fly near as fast as she can. We will be gone for a few weeks, but we will be sure and return before the next meeting," Deema answered him.

"When will you leave?" my brother pressed.

"We'll leave as soon as I stuff my face some more. I won't have to fly myself there, but I'll still have to go a whole day without food, so I'm going to eat another meal or two before we take off. Brian, will you take care of my chickens while I'm gone? I don't want the eggs rotting and their automatic feeder may run out of grain."

"Sure, Sis. Anytime."

"Awesome. Well, if there's nothing else, I'm going to cook some more. Would you two like to stay for lunch? We could eat on the patio," I suggested.

They both accepted my invitation, so I popped my last loaf of bread into the oven to thaw and poured my last three jars of soup into a big pot to heat up.

I asked my brother if he had any cannabis and, much to my surprise, my grandfather pulled out a silver cigarette case filled with joints. "I don't know why you're so surprised. It's been as legal as alcohol since I was too young to even buy it. And besides, it helps with my arthritis." He lit one and handed me another.

We all got high while the food finished cooking and then we sat around the patio to eat our early lunch.

"So, Grandfather," Deema started cautiously. "We need to start building a very large and well-stocked food supply for when the White men shut down all trade. Many will starve if we don't." Deema paused.

"I'm listening," my grandfather replied in a calm, receptive tone.

"Well, you know I only hunt men who are evil. I am their judge, jury, and executioner. Last night we went to Vegas so I could hunt and I took $28,000 from them."

My brother choked on his food when Deema said the amount, but my grandfather was undisturbed.

"They worked as a team drugging and then robbing people. Sometimes they killed them in terrible ways. I had to stop them," Deema explained as he turned to Brian. "But now, we have all this money and the only thing Hope wants to buy with it is food storage for the tribe. So, can we hand over money from my prey to the tribe by pumping it into the slot machines to cover where it came from, and use the casino to order tons and tons of grain and dried fruits?"

"I think that is a very wise thing to do," my grandfather said. "Everything that goes into the machines is tracked electronically and the readouts are part of how we tabulate the income. We can't just slip in the money you..." He cleared his throat. "Well, yes. The money will have to be laundered through the casino so that it seems like it was legally acquired for the tribe. We will have some warehouses built next to the casino and we will fill them with food as fast as we can."

I beamed between bites. "Awesome."

We finished our food and I bid them goodbye. After they left, I remembered my bokken. I went over to where Deema had laid it down, gingerly unwrapped the cloth bundle, and found inside the most beautiful hardwood bokken I'd ever seen. I replaced my makeshift bokken with my proper one and secured it to my waist.

"Looks nice," Deema said with a wink. "Are you still hungry? There are a couple more bowls of soup in here."

"Baby, I'm always hungry." I laughed, walked toward the kitchen, and quickly ate what was left of the soup before I opened all my cabinets to survey what I had left. I was down to bare basics—rice and pasta was almost all I had. I didn't even have any more pasta sauce left. I put on some rice to cook, and then I finished off the last of my bread. When the rice was done cooking, I ate it as fast as I could.

"I'm ready," I said after I cleaned my dishes.

"Are you sure?" he asked, glancing around my trailer.

"I think so. Why? Am I forgetting something?" I asked pensively.

"Only this," he said as he leaned in for a kiss. I welcomed his affection and returned it as I wrapped my arms around his neck. "Okay," he said after he broke away. "Now we're ready to go."

CHAPTER 43

We took off straight up into the sky around noon on Wednesday. When we reached a high enough altitude that no one could see us from the ground, he turned east. It was a gorgeous and cloudless summer day.

We soared through the sky for many hours in near silence. By the time we reached the Atlantic coast, it had been dark for over four hours. Much to my surprise, Deema landed on the rooftop of his and Taniya's apartment building.

"What are we doing here?" I asked cautiously. "What if that guy sees us again? Or if somebody else does?" My voice was filled with concern.

"I'm sorry, but I need to hunt. Can you wait here for a few minutes?" he asked me gently.

"Okay," I said slowly.

He kissed my forehead, thanked me, and quickly jumped off the side of the building. Less than ten minutes later, he reappeared with warmed skin, and we took off into the sky once more. After another twelve hours, we flew over Europe and I asked him how much longer. I was exhausted, but I could not sleep while he carried me through the sky.

"Just a few more hours, my love," he said into my ear over the howling of the wind.

"But the sun is setting for the second time since we left," I protested. "I thought you said it would only take one day to fly there."

"Yes, when we travel with the sun. But we are going

against the sun, so we see it sooner than every twenty-four hours. Twenty-four hours ago, we left your house, but we have traveled many miles and through many time zones. I'm sorry, Hope, but we'll be there soon," he promised.

"Okay," I said as I nestled into his chest.

After five long hours, we reached his castle in the Russian wilderness. The sun had been up there for over an hour when we landed. I flopped to the ground as soon as he released me and immediately fell into a dreamless sleep.

Ten hours later when I awoke, Deema had a fire going about twenty feet away from me. I examined it more closely and realized he was roasting several large chunks of deer meat. I pulled myself up from the cool grass and walked over to him.

"Any sign of them?" I asked as I rubbed the sleep from my eyes.

"No, not yet," he said with a touch of sadness.

"Don't worry, Deema. They're close. I can feel it. They'll be here soon." I hugged him. "Is there a spring or a clean creek around here somewhere? I'm dying of thirst."

"Sure. It's just through those trees there." He pointed to the west. "It's about fifty yards into the woods."

"Sweet," I mumbled and walked off into the woods. I found the creek with ease and drank from my hands for several minutes. I was startled by some movement in the trees to my left, and I peered up to see Aleksandra standing about thirty feet upstream from me.

"Who are you and what are you doing here?" she asked in Russian as I stood to face her.

"My baby girl!" I cried out in Russian as I ran toward her with tears welling up in my eyes.

"Stop! Answer me!" she demanded.

"I your mother, Sasha. I reborn and I here for finding you. Your father tell me what he did to my Sashas many years ago and we here to make us family again," I gently replied in broken Russian. "You speak English? My Russian very bad," I said as I slowly started to walk toward her again.

"*Nyet*," she replied cautiously. I could see in her face that she was trying to read my mind, but she could not.

"Please, Sasha. Please forgive your father. It not his fault that he a vampire. And it not his fault I die. He tried change fate, and fate not allow. I not become immortal 500 years ago because I reincarnate as angel to save my tribe when calendar end." I spoke to her as gently as I could in my broken Russian, and I tried very hard not to spook her or scare her away. I had already managed to change my vision, and I hoped that I could also convince her to come back to the camp with me. It wasn't until much later that I had time to pause and think about our exchange. I realized then that I'd said many things to her I had never learned how to say in Russian.

"What are your people?" she asked slowly.

"I'm Hopi, but different. I save my people, but I need help from my vampire family. I still mortal body and your father not change me until I very hurt by someone else," I answered as I stopped about ten feet from her.

"Why?" she asked as she started to back away.

"He fear my wings turn black and I angel no more," I answered. "Come with me, please. Come to castle and speak to your father," I asked hopefully.

"*Nyet*," she said angrily before she turned away from me and walked off through the woods.

When I tried to follow her, and I begged her again to stay, she disappeared in a blur of movement. I went back to the creek and drank some more water before I returned to the castle to tell Deema what happened.

CHAPTER 44

I saw your daughter," I said as I walked out of the woods.
"*Our* daughter," he corrected, a crooked smile spreading over his face. "I know. I heard your whole conversation. Super hearing, remember?" He winked. "I see you were successful in changing the future."

"Yes, I was. I hope she comes back. I missed her entire life." I sighed and perched on one of the smaller fallen stones from the castle next to the fire. "I just—I just want everything to be okay, you know?"

"They'll be back, my love. Don't worry," he said as he stood to kiss me. He threw some wood on the fire before he turned back to the rock and sat next to me.

I turned to him to tell him that I felt like they were coming back right now, but I saw him freeze and stare toward the woods before I could speak.

I followed his gaze and, sure enough, they were standing at the edge of the tree line.

I quickly pumped my wings and pushed off into the sky. I landed a few feet in front of them and asked them, "Will you please join us while I eat my dinner?"

They stared at me in confusion, so I repeated myself in Russian. They looked at each other for a few moments then they turned back to me and nodded. We walked quietly back to the fire and they sat down across from their father.

"I'm sorry," Deema said in Russian. "I did what I thought I had to before I lost either of you forever. I love you both more than you could ever understand. I hope with my whole heart that you will forgive me and come back to me."

"Why did you leave us in the first place? Why did you not stay to raise us here in this castle instead of sending us to live with our poor aunt in a shack?" Aleksander asked. His voice was so similar to his father's that it was almost creepy.

"I could not stay with you because I was afraid to be around humans at all. I had not learned yet that I could live from the blood of animals and, even if my love for you could have controlled my thirst for blood, I knew I could never go into town to market or they would see how my skin had lightened so much and how it would become clear in the sun. I am very sorry for what I did and I was sure you'd never speak to me again. I hope this will not be the only time we speak so that you can see that I am a good man," Deema quickly rambled in Russian.

He also translated it for me in his mind as he spoke. I was very grateful, as I could only pick out a few words here and there.

"We will consider it," his daughter quietly replied. She looked very much like me, as did her brother, only their skin was unnaturally pale just like Deema's.

"How long has the meat been on the fire?" I asked Deema in English.

"It's been a while. It's probably ready by now," he replied.

I slowly stood from my perch and walked over to the fire. I pulled the sticks he had the meat propped on away from the fire and set the tied Xs so that I wouldn't get burned as I pulled meat from the bone. The twins watched me with ambiguous expressions while I stuffed my face with meat in the shrinking light of the evening.

"Why are you here, angel?" Aleksander asked quietly after a few moments.

"I don't understand. Here, Earth? Or here, castle?" I replied after I swallowed my mouthful of food.

"Both," his sister answered.

"I not sure I explain in Russian. I not fluent and it very long story. Your father answer you best. He knows what happen to bring me here to Earth and castle," I said slowly and carefully.

They both shifted their gaze to Deema as he began to speak. He explained to them the prophesies of my people and of their own great grandmother. He told them of how my wings grew and how we met. He told them about my dreams and how fast I could fly. He explained my determination to find them once I had learned of them.

He rambled on for at least twenty or thirty minutes while the sun set and I finished eating the meat I had pulled off the fire. When he finally stopped speaking, I stood and walked to the creek for a drink of water.

As I walked back, I could hear them speaking in quick, hushed voices, but they stopped when I got about twenty feet away.

"Where is more food?" I asked Deema in Russian. I didn't want the twins to feel excluded by my speaking in English. He laughed and asked if I was still hungry. I blushed and nodded my head. "*Kak ehto skaziet 'fly' pau Russki?*" I asked him quickly.

He answered me just as quickly.

"I hungry, for I fly later. You know I here fly for open space," I replied in my terrible Russian.

"I buried the meat under the fire," he answered me in English. He looked as if he was trying not to grin and his expression was priceless. It also kind of made me want to smack him, and that idea made me find it even funnier.

I grabbed a long stick, approached the dying embers, dug through them, and found a layer of boned meat slowly cooking under a pile of hickory bark and grass. It was wonderfully tender, but not all of it was cooked yet.

I spread my feet a bit wider to get better balance as I perched over the fire pit. I peeled some bits of cooked meat off the top and rearranged the uncooked meat closer to the surface. It was delicious!

I quickly covered the meat in embers again before I went back to the creek. I found an inch thick slab of slate a little bit downstream that was about fifteen inches across. I rinsed it in the creek and strolled back to camp.

The twins watched me in confusion once again when I threw the large piece of slate on top of the pile of embers and pressed on it lightly.

"Why do you do that?" Aleksander asked me slowly.

"I don't know how to say—" is what I thought I said, but they all burst out in a fit of laughter.

It was a wonderful sound to hear, until Deema sputtered through his vocalized amusement, "You just said you don't know how to speak!"

I laughed a little bit as well and I felt my cheeks color. "Perhaps you should translate for me?" I asked my immortal lover.

He smiled. "Anytime, my wife."

I rolled my eyes a bit at his response, but I knew what he meant. "I am pressing the meat to make it cook faster and I am sterilizing the stone so there is nothing to make me sick when I put my food on it," I said, facing the twins.

Deema repeated my explanation in Russian and they bobbed their heads in understanding.

"I also want to tell you that I am sorry I missed your life. I'm sorry I was not here to raise you and teach you how to be good people. I know you never liked my sister very much." When I realized what I said, I gasped as Deema translated.

He turned to me, slightly confused. "How did you know that?"

"I don't know. It just came out. Perhaps being around them is bringing back memories that are buried not in my brain, but my soul," I hypothesized.

He translated again what I had said and then he suggested that they stay a while longer so that I might remember more of my former life in Russia. They agreed to stay the night and I beamed at them as I removed the slate from the dying fire.

"You fly?" I asked the twins as I dug through the embers in search of meat.

"*Nyet*," they replied in unison.

"What month were they turned?" I asked Deema.

"This month, I think," he replied with a pensive tone.

"We will test your flight later," I said in English. Deema

quickly translated for me before he explained to them how he learned he could fly.

I pulled all of the cooked meat out of the embers before I re-covered the rest and added some more logs to the fire. I handed my slab of meat to Deema before I flew up to the tallest fallen stone. I perched next to him, then he placed my large plate of meat in front of me. I thanked him with a smile and started eating like a savage.

"Why do you eat so much so fast?" Aleksandra asked me.

"I fly very fast and my wings use a lot of energy. I must eat huge amounts of food or I cannot fly for very long. I eat with no manners because I have lived alone and eaten alone for so long," I explained and Deema translated.

She regarded me with a curious tilt to her eyebrows. I couldn't help but wonder what she was thinking.

I continued eating my food while I pondered. When I was nearly done, Deema jumped down and snatched the remaining meat out of the embers with his bare hands. Each piece he grabbed, he threw over his head and they all landed on my slate. Every time he thrust his hands into the glowing embers, it sent up showers of sparks due to the force and the speed he used.

We all gasped in shock and amazement at his unexpected show of power.

"Why does the fire not burn you?" I whispered.

"It does," he said as he turned around and held up his hands. They were blackened with ash and I thought I could see a few bones at the tips of his fingers. They almost instantly healed and reformed. He wiped the ash on his jeans and held them up again. "They heal quickly, though."

"You feel pain?" Aleksander asked.

"No, I do not," Deema replied. "Why? You?"

"Yes, but I only feel her pain, and she feels mine," Aleksander said as he pointed to his sister. "It has been that way since we were five years old."

"That is interesting," I said in English. "That usually only happens to identical twins. And identical twins have to be the same gender."

Deema translated for me and they thought about what I said for a few moments.

After I had eaten a few more handfuls of meat, the girl spoke. "Why do you look so much like me? Your skin is even the same color mine was when I was mortal," she asked as she continued to stare at me.

"Deema says that I seem to be very much like I was when I lived 500 years ago. I am actually quite pale compared to the rest of my tribe and I do not tan or burn. My family always thought it odd that my skin tone never changed as I aged," I replied. As Deema translated, her eyes got wide. "Why? What's wrong?" I sputtered in Russian.

"I also never tanned or burned from the sun, and neither did my brother," she whispered, so low I could not make out a word she said, but Deema told me.

"That is, indeed, very strange, then," I said after a few seconds.

How could it be that genetic traits like that could be carried by the soul? I wondered. After several moments more of deep thought, I chalked it up to just another mystery we'd probably never understand.

"There are many things that have happened, are happening, and will happen to us in the future, which we will never understand. We must just accept what was, enjoy and use what is, and be prepared for what will become," I said in a spurt of inspiration.

Deema translated to them and they nodded their heads along with some murmured approvals.

"That's very wise," Deema said to me as he leaned in to kiss my cheek.

I paused in my mastication and smiled as I welcomed his affection. I swallowed quickly and told him I was just trying to paraphrase what the elders kept telling me. He gave me a nod of understanding and I finished my food in silence.

After I was done eating, I strolled back to the creek one last time for some water before I went flying for the night. Before I took off, I asked Deema if there were any fruits or berries that might be ready to eat around there.

He shrugged and asked his children if they knew.

"Not for two more months," she replied.

I frowned in disappointment then bid them goodbye. "I'll be back in a few hours. I need to go fly." I took off with a running start.

CHAPTER 45

As I soared off into the gentle coolness of the evening, I drew my bokken slowly. I made a sharp left turn and slashed at the tiny new branches and leaves of the treetops below me.

I made another sharp turn straight up into the sky and attempted to do a barrel roll. A gust of wind caught me just right and blew me over onto my back so that I was falling in mid-air. I quickly tucked my wings, flipped over before I opened them, and glided just inches over the top of the tree in which I had almost landed.

I breathed a quick sigh of relief then turned toward the stars again and flew high into the sky. When I felt the chill of the high atmosphere, I turned back to the ground and made a tight spiral down.

When I reached about 5000 feet above the ground, I spotted the campfire at the castle and made a bee line for it while I tried to maintain my altitude. Once I was above the camp, I started to spiral down again. I landed next to the twins and put my bokken back in my belt.

"You fly with me," I said in Russian as I smiled at the girl.

"I not fly," she replied simply.

"Yes, I know you fly," I assured her. "Please, try?"

She glanced uneasily at her brother and he motioned for her to go with me. I took her icy hand and led her to the giant stone where her father was still sitting.

I slowly grabbed her by the waist while Deema told her

what to do so I could lift her. Much to her surprise, I only flew us the ten feet up to my perch. I released her and turned her toward the edge. I took her by the hand, gave her a knowing smile, and jumped off of the rock. She tried to stand on the rock and only release my hand, but I held tight until I'd pulled her off behind me.

I glided gracefully to the other side of the little camp and she quickly fell below me.

When she was face down and inches from the grass, she stopped moving right before she would have hit the ground. She moved to push herself up from the ground, but her hands never made contact. She just floated upright and kept floating up.

Her brother yelled out in shock—and possibly in pain—as she floated up higher and over the fire toward him. She grabbed him by the shoulders and laughed as she threw him up in the air. He "landed" nearly the same way that she had and he, too, floated up into the sky.

I was beyond thrilled. I pushed off into the sky and joined my immortal children as they learned to fly in the clear, cool, starry evening. I motioned for Deema to join us and he waved his hand at me in a dismissive manner. I begged him with my mind as I chased after them in the light chill of the evening.

After we got a couple miles away, Deema finally joined us. We dipped and dove around each other over the seemingly endless forest.

We flew around for about two hours. Sometimes, we were playing an odd game of tag, and sometimes we just enjoyed the sights from the sky.

Around midnight, the twins started to head for a clearing full of deer below us. I decided to remain aloft while they hunted and I tried not to watch them while they fed. I looked over at Deema and he watched them with longing.

"If you thirst, nothing is stopping you from joining them."

He turned and flew over to me. "Thank you, my love," he said before he kissed my forehead. He dropped from the sky so fast that a thought flashed through my mind that he may crash into the ground. But he quickly landed on the back of a deer, wrapped his arms around its neck, and proceeded to drink from it.

He pushed his thoughts toward me. '*You should watch. You will have to do this someday, you know.*'

I searched for the twins in the clearing and quickly spotted them taking down deer together. It was spooky how they attacked different deer at the same time, then drained and dropped them in unison. I watched in shock and awe as they each took down three deer in this fashion.

After all of the immortals had their fill, Deema disappeared in a flash with two deer in tow. He reappeared a few minutes later, snatched up two more deer, and disappeared again. Once all the dead deer had been cleared from the field, my vampire family joined me again in the sky.

Deema flew underneath me and stared up into my eyes. "I will set up a smoker and we can preserve all of that meat for you."

"I think I love you," I said dreamily as I stared down at his sparkling eyes.

He grabbed my waist and pressed his lips to mine. "You'd better," he chided.

"They'll stay with us forever," I whispered after I slowed down and let the twins get far ahead of us.

"How do you know?" he asked, perplexed. "I thought you only saw the future in your dreams."

"I can see changes in the future when they alter from my dreams. When someone makes a decision that takes them down a different path than they were on before, I can see the change. I am sure they will stay with us now." I smiled. "They have decided to."

He grinned back at me and wrapped his arms around my waist. I wrapped my wings around him and let him carry me as I covered his marble face in warm, soft kisses. As we flew blindly through the night, our passion increased and I found myself grinding my hips into his. He laughed, loosened his grip on me, and pulled back from my kisses.

"Would you like to calm yourself? Or would you like to go to the ground?" he asked.

I pressed into him again and lunged for his lips. "I think you know what I want."

"Have you forgotten that we're flying with our children?" he reminded me.

"Oh come on! They are over ten times my age! How could they possibly be offended by my displays of affection?" I argued.

"They are from a much different time, and they have not been interacting with society as I have for the last several hundred years. They live in the woods like animals and take clothes from vagrants they kill when theirs are nearing rags. They—they aren't very much like me." Deema sighed heavily.

He gave me a peck on the lips before he released me and pulled my wings from his shoulders. We raced to catch up with our immortal children. They appeared to be having the time of their lives as they soared through the clear night sky.

"Sasha!" I called out as we neared them. They both turned to me and we all four burst into a fit of laughter. "Very fun, yes?" I asked them in Russian.

"Yes, yes, yes!" they cried out together into the night.

"Are you happy I came back? That we came back together?"

"Yes," they replied again in unison.

"I want you to stay with me. Will you?"

"For all of time, Mama."

I peered into Aleksandra's eyes as she spoke alone this time.

They were covered with a dark red film. She blinked and one bloody tear rolled down each cheek.

I immediately burst into tears and rushed over to her. I grabbed her shoulders, flipped her over, and crushed her petite, marble body to mine. I ceased my flapping and just rode the wind while I sobbed apologies, which I knew she wouldn't understand, into her satiny raven hair.

"I will always be here for you, as long as you want me," I cried. "I will never leave you again. I will never die on you again."

At that instant, as soon as the words left my mouth, I knew

without a doubt that they were true. I saw my distant future and smiled wide through my tears.

I pulled my face from her hair and wiped away her tears before I wiped away my own. "Cry no more, child," I said in Russian before I kissed away a fresh tear. "I stay forever."

"Please don't leave us again. We will follow you anywhere now," her brother said.

"Will you follow me to my tribe and help me protect my people? Will you follow your father's teachings and kill none of my people?" I asked them both.

"Yes, Mama. Anywhere. Anything. We have spent 513 years wanting our mother back, and now we have her. We will never let you go," my daughter said before she squeezed me so hard, my breath rushed from my chest.

I thought I had popped right into two pieces when my wings fell limp.

"Careful, child. She is still very breakable," Deema warned in a sharp tone.

In a reflex reaction to his warning, she quickly released me as she flipped over, and I started to fall. For the first time since I'd started flying, I could not breathe. I also couldn't move my wings.

CHAPTER 46

Deema sped toward me. He had me flipped over and cradled in his arms before I could fall even twenty feet.

Aleksander flew over to where Deema had stopped to hover with me. "What's happening? Is she hurt?"

"I don't know, but she's not breathing," he quickly replied. "Breathe, baby, breathe!" Deema screamed loudly as he continued to stare at me with panic carved into his marble face.

His powerful voice boomed in my ears and I needed to scream from the pain it caused. My lungs somehow managed to draw in some air, but that very act brought my attention to a much more demanding agony. After less than half a breath, the horrible torment hit me full force and the remainder of my inhale was a choked scream. Once my lungs were filled with oxygen, I let out a deafening scream of my own. Only mine was wordless. I didn't need words. The trauma was all too evident by the tormented sounds that escaped my lips.

I could suddenly feel every break in every rib in my chest. I could feel my crushed spine rubbing together like gravel. Then I remember feeling like I was falling faster than should be possible for several seconds before I felt a sharp jolt. Deema laid me softly on the hard earth and asked me where I was hurt. But I couldn't answer because I was trying not to breath. I knew that if I did, I would only scream and cause myself more pain again.

"Open your mouth," he said so fast I could not comply before he grabbed my jaw and wrenched it open. I heard a terrible and unfamiliar ripping sound before I felt a cold, thick liquid being poured onto my face. Some of it trickled into my mouth. It was lightly salty, but the main thing I noticed was that it almost felt like it was alive. It tingled on my tongue like microscopic carbonation. Then it seemed to get even colder as it slid down my throat. By the time it reached my stomach, I felt like my insides were being coated in a layer of ice. As I swallowed my second mouthful, my mouth clamped around the source of this icy liquid—Deema's wrist.

I ignored the pain that had seemed un-ignorable only seconds before and sucked at his wrist with all my might. I felt like my teeth would join his blood on the journey down my throat due to the ferocity with which I drank. It took only seconds before I felt my ribs knitting back together. The gravel up and down my back rearranged and reformed itself into vertebrae around my spinal cord by my fifth gulp of vampire blood. My wings perked back up and I regained my feeling in them once my spine was almost done healing.

Then Deema suddenly tore his wrist from my mouth and I let out another blood curdling scream. "*No!*"

My scream echoed off the trees. I lunged at my immortal lover in search of more of his icy blood and roared again. As soon as I'd completed my charge and scream, I realized what I was doing and regained control of myself. I planted my feet firmly on the ground and closed my eyes while I took a few deep breaths.

"I'm sorry," I finally said without opening my eyes. "I don't know what came over me. I'm okay now."

"What came over you is bloodlust," Deema said cautiously as he slowly and loudly walked toward me. It struck me as odd because I'd never been able to hear his footsteps before.

"Am I changing?" I turned to him and finally opened my eyes. "Everything is different. You sound different. The trees look different. I can see everything."

"I don't know. I've never fed anyone my blood before and I've never seen anyone else do it either. But I've seen it in movies and books where drinking won't change you. So, I guess we'll have to see. Perhaps your senses will be increased for a while. Or maybe, if there was a cut in your mouth or digestive track, you will change slowly." He appeared concerned yet confused. The details of his face mesmerized me like never before.

"So we just wait? What if I have to go back to my people as a fucking vampire now?" I demanded once I was able to break his gaze and focus enough to actually process what he'd told me.

"I'm very sorry," Aleksandra whispered in Russian from several yards away. "I forgot my strength," she said with a broken voice.

I turned to look at her. Her shoulders shook with sobs, but no more tears ran down her face.

"How did she cry before? Why can't she cry now? Why can't you cry?" I demanded as I turned back to Deema.

"As vampires, we cannot cry. We are able to cry once in our entire existence. I cried the night I killed you. I suppose it is only appropriate that our daughter cried on the night she killed you, too," he answered as he took the last few steps to me and reached out to embrace me.

"I need some time. Please don't follow me."

I slunk away from his touch. They all respected my request and let me walk off into the woods by myself. I wandered aimlessly for hours until I found a small clearing by a creek. It smelled rotten and was certainly different than the sweet water I'd drunk near the castle. I realized then that I was likely hundreds of miles from there. I lay down in the cool grass and cried softly in despair until I fell asleep, alone and unprotected in an unfamiliar land.

CHAPTER 47

I awoke the next day and found that I was not only still alone, but I was also hungry. *That must mean I haven't changed*, I thought with a sigh of relief. I scanned the small clearing in which I stood and observed that my senses were indeed still affected by the vampire blood I'd ingested. I could see every detail in every leaf. I could almost feel the texture of the bark with my eyes. I could hear a squirrel chattering as it cleaned its face in a tree behind me. It baffled, pleased, and scared me that I could hear its movements so clearly. There was no doubt in my mind as to what that little squirrel was doing.

I glanced up to make sure I could make it through the trees before I pushed off into the sky. When I entered the sunlight, my first thought was another rush of relief that my skin still looked the same. Then I noticed that it was either almost one p.m. or just after 11 a.m. But I had no bearings or landmarks to go by, so I decided to fly perpendicular to the sun and wait for it to move. I was fairly sure that we had flown east the night before, so I decided that once I figured out where the sun was going I would follow it.

I had no desire to be found. I did not want to call for Deema's help. I wanted to find my own way back, even if it took hours, because I knew that I would welcome those hours alone. I needed time to ponder my dreams, my future, and the unusual feeling in my belly. It was well beyond the simple gnawing hunger to which I had been growing accustomed.

Even lower than the hunger pains, I felt bizarre and wrong.

As I slowly flew high over the endless forest, I absentmind-edly ran my hands over my slightly swollen and unusually rock-hard lower torso. It was then that I suddenly realized what had happened. One of my dreams from my latest sleep flashed back into my memory and I saw the events of the next few days unfolding. I watched in my mind as I told Deema that I was pregnant and explained to him that I would give birth in a couple of weeks. I'd watched myself give birth to a child still encased in a placenta. I saw Deema rip the sack off with his teeth and I recognized the sound as the same as when he tore open his wrist to heal me.

I snapped out of my daze when my face got whipped by several tree branches in quick succession. While I had slipped away in my mind, I'd also slipped lower in the sky and started grazing the tree tops. I quickly adjusted myself and flew higher while I searched for the path of the sun. I sighed deeply and made a ninety-degree turn to the left as I found west. I flapped a little harder to fight the wind I was in and I pulled myself higher to find a current that suited me.

I was afraid to think of my dreams again, lest I get side-tracked and lose track of time. But I did ponder my desire to be alone. Why should I have wanted to be alone? Didn't I love him? Didn't I want to share this news with him? I wasn't an immortal. His blood had only healed me. And I was carrying his child. I should have been thrilled. But, instead, I was terri-fied.

Perhaps after my being alone for so long, so rarely having any company but my own, I had grown to like it. That thought of never being alone again once I went back to him that day terrified me. But why should it? I'd wondered. A few days ago, I had cherished the thought of never being alone again and al-ways having him by my side.

I flapped lazily on my journey west while I kept my eye on the horizon for smoke. Deema had promised to make a smoker to preserve all that meat, and my hopes of finding them had been pinned on finding that smoke. After I flew for a few more minutes and there was still no sign of smoke, I saw another figure in flight on the horizon. As I could not see into the minds of my vampire family, I could not be sure who it was. I turned slightly to fly toward the vampire as he sped toward me. A few seconds later, I saw that it was my son. We'd had very little interaction since our reunion, so it puzzled me slightly that he would be sent to find me.

"You are still mortal?" he asked incredulously.

"You speak English?" I asked in shock.

"Yes, but not all English. Father has been teaching us while you have slept. We learn very fast with minds that never forget," he said as he flew ten feet to my left.

"Yes, I am still mortal. But I have increased senses, and I do feel a change happening in my body," I confessed.

"So you will change slowly," he said thoughtfully.

"I don't know if that is the change I feel. But I must return to the castle quickly. There is much to discuss and I need food very badly. Is this as fast as you can fly?"

"No," he said as he sped up to lead the way to the ruined castle.

After about thirty minutes of wordless flight, I saw the smoke drifting away on the horizon and Aleksander dropped from the sky to run the remaining distance. A few seconds later, I landed at the far edge of the field and walked into the woods for some water without looking at anyone.

Once I'd had my fill of sweet spring water, I took a deep breath and turned back to the castle. When I emerged from the tree line, I saw the three of them standing like statues.

CHAPTER 48

They all just stared at me without speaking or even blinking. I walked slowly back to them and wondered how I would say this. When I reached my vampire family, I stared at each of them for a few seconds before I started to speak.

"I have many questions before I will give you any answers," I said as I rested my eyes on Deema.

"Very well," he said cautiously when I didn't continue.

"Did you watch me sleep last night? Did you listen to my dreams?" I asked quietly. I tried to keep the tremors of fear out of my voice, but as I listened to myself, I realized that I sounded slightly angry.

"No," he whispered with a touch of shock.

"Then you have not seen how the future has changed," I said flatly with my eyes on the ground.

"No," he said in a shaking voice. The tone of this two letter word was filled with layers of emotion—shock, terror, loss, and fear of the unknown riddled the sound of this tiny word.

"How long until something is ready for me to eat? I'm starving." I continued to stare at the ground since I could not bear to look into his onyx eyes.

"It is ready now," he said in the same trembling voice. He stood aside and gestured to a pile of meat that sat on my thick slab of slate. "The rest is being smoked over there and should be ready around sunset." He pointed to a large pile of green branches with smoke coming out of the top.

"Good. We shall leave then." Deema let out a small sigh of relief when I said we. "But right now, we need to eat," I said as I pushed past him and toward my waiting protein.

"We?" Deema asked apprehensively after a few moments.

I peered up at him without answering and took another bite of venison. When I took yet another bite without a reply, he spoke again. "What do you mean by that? We," he gestured to himself and the other immortals, "won't need to feed again today after all we drank last night," he said in an increasingly confounded tone.

"What day is this?" I asked, ignoring his question again.

"It is Friday," Aleksandra answered when her father seemed unwilling to.

I thought about this for a few moments while I devoured a few more handfuls of meat. A week and a half, I thought to myself with a sigh as I glanced at my belly.

"What is a week and a half?" Aleksander asked me suddenly.

My mouth dropped open and I stared at him in shock. "I thought you couldn't read my mind," I finally blurted out.

"No, we could not *understand* your mind," his sister corrected. "And now we understand many of the words you think. Except, how can you mean 'until I give birth'? You are not very pregnant yet."

Deema was instantly by my side with his arm gently draped over my shoulder. His other hand flew to my chin and gently turned my face to his. "Are you pregnant?" he asked with longing in his sparkling eyes.

I took a deep breath and got briefly distracted by the powerful, delicious smell emanating from his skin. *How have I never noticed that before?* I wondered for a split second before I remembered the vampire blood I had consumed. "I have known you for barely a week," I started with a shaking voice. "In these last days, you have changed my life like I'd never thought was possible before. You have shown me things I never would have believed existed before and you were able to succeed in doing something no one else ever could. You were able to make me happy, even if only for a brief time and—"

"Are you leaving me? Us?" he interrupted.

"*Nyet!*" the twins cried out together. They were both instantly there, surrounding me. "We will not let you leave us again," my son whispered with tremors in his voice.

"I am not leaving you," I reassured them. "But we cannot stay here. We must leave. I must consult with the elders in regard to this new set of circumstances," I said as I placed my hands on my hardened belly. "My gestation will be two weeks instead of the normal forty weeks. I have ten days until I look nine months pregnant and give birth to a suffocating child still encased in the placenta."

They all stared at me in complete shock. While the twins might not have understood all of my words, they no doubt saw the images of my dreams in my head as I remembered them.

"But that isn't possible!" Deema finally said after a few silent moments of shock.

"Possible or not, you would know that it is true if you could read my mind. And we have to remember that there is no such thing as impossible anymore. There are only things that we will never understand. The important thing right now is that I consult with my living family and my tribal elders. Also, I need to eat, so…"

They glanced around at each other for a moment before they backed away and let me get back to stuffing my face.

While I polished off the meat on my plate, the three vampires turned to statues in various locations around the field. They all appeared to be in deep thought, but I was as well. I was terrified of how my body would react to this far too rapid expansion. I was worried about how I would care for this half-angel/half-vampire child.

Would it eat human food? Would it drink blood? Would it be immortal? Or would it continue to age rapidly and have a short life? Would my body have time to start producing milk? Or would this rapid growth inside of me kill me? Would I no longer be a mortal after ten days? The questions circled in my mind while I kept reaching for more food until I realized that my slate was empty.

I walked the 150 yards to the creek and quenched my thirst

again. I knew they would continue to give me the respect of being alone, so I decided to take the opportunity to contact my mortal family.

CHAPTER 49

I didn't even consider the time difference until I realized it was pitch black when I focused on my big brother. I quickly let go of my hold on him out of fear of waking him. I turned my attention on Taniya then, and hoped that she would still be up.

'*Hope,*' she said as soon as I caught her location.

'*Taniya, I have some big news. Huge news. Holy shit, have I got a ton of news,*' I said gloomily.

'*What's going on? You look different. Your spirit feels different,*' she said as the concern spread across her face.

'*I guess the most imminent worry is my change. I am pregnant. But as a half breed child, the gestation is twenty times faster, so I will give birth in ten days. Well, two weeks total instead of forty, but I've got ten days left,*" I babbled nervously. I ran my hands over my bump to show her how not-flat my abdomen was now. I could feel her shock reverberate through our connection as my words and images sank in.

'*But that isn't possible. He told me before that he couldn't even—*' she murmured after a few moments.

'*I know. He told me that too. But I also saw the shock on his face when it actually happened. We don't really know what's going to happen. The one thing we do know is that I'll live. Whether it is as a mortal or not, I don't know. But I will not die and I will give birth on the reservation.*'

'*Well, at least we know that,*' she said with a sigh of relief.

'*Yeah. Another pretty big deal is that we're not coming*

back alone and we are leaving in about ten hours or so. We should be back in a day and a half. The two we are bringing back with us are also our children. When Deema was mortal, the soul that inhabits my body now inhabited his wife's back then. We had a set of twins, Aleksander and Aleksandra. When they were sixteen years old, he turned them both into vampires out of fear of losing them forever,' I explained.

'Why did he never tell me any of this?' she wondered.

'I'm not sure. I guess you'll have to ask him that. But they haven't spoken to him in all this time, and now they've sworn to never leave me again. We had a good cry and it all got a little emotional, and my daughter accidentally crushed my spine and ribcage when she hugged me too tightly. Deema fed me his blood and it healed me, but I still feel different. All of my senses are extremely enhanced, but I'm also still eating, sleeping, and drinking water. So, we don't really know what to think. Only time will tell what's happening. If these enhancements fade, then I'll know I'm not changing. But if they continue steady or increase, I'll know I am changing slowly.'

'Wow,' she gasped. *'That's a lot to take in.'*

'Ha! You're tellin' me!' I chortled.

'So you'll get here Saturday afternoon sometime?' she said after she thought for a few moments.

'Yes. All four of us will. We will return to the valley so my neighbors do not see my vampire children. If the coast is clear, they will join me in my home until dark when their father will take them to Las Vegas to hunt. Will you inform Silent Wolf so he may pass the info of my return on to the Counsel? I will try to make it to the Hall when I return Saturday, but I may be too exhausted. I'll get ahold of you Saturday morning while we're flying and let you know how I feel. I may have to meet with them on Saturday night or Sunday morning, instead,' I informed her. *'I should appear about three or four months by then,'* I said more to myself.

'How is your body going to react to this rapid expansion?' Her voice in my head was filled with concern again.

'I'm not sure. But if you wouldn't mind—the back door is open at my place. My car keys are on the dresser in my bed-

room. *I'm going to need lots and lots of pure cocoa butter and vitamin E oil. I'm hoping that if I can keep my stomach saturated in shit like that, maybe it will stay elastic enough for my skin to not split wide open."*

'*Sure. I'll go pick some up when I get up later today. But, I am getting pretty tired. And it looks like I'm going to have one hell of a weekend, so...*' She trailed off.

'*Yeah, I understand. I'll see you tomorrow.*' I broke the connection and recomposed myself before I went back to my immortal family. As I walked up the subtle incline from the tree line to the castle, I noticed that they were all still unmoving.

CHAPTER 50

I walked straight over to my daughter and took her face in my hands. "I have no anger toward you. You understand that, don't you? I could *never* have anger toward you. I love you just as much now as I did 500 years ago. Do you understand me?"

She continued to gaze at me with unchanging eyes—the most sorrowful eyes I'd ever seen.

"Sandra!" I said in a sudden decision to give her a new nickname. After all, I couldn't very well call them both Sasha anymore. "*Ti podamaiu*? Do you understand?" I asked again.

She gave her head a slight nod. "Yes. And I am sorry. I never meant to hurt you. I never meant to change your future." She seemed like she would start crying again, but I knew she wouldn't be able to.

"Everything happens how it needs to happen for shit to end up how it needs to be. So, no worries, okay? I am not upset with you at all," I assured her.

She nodded. "Okay."

I released her face. When I turned away from my daughter, I focused my attention on my son. "Aleks," I said as I stroked his marble cheek. "Thank you for finding me when I started searching for home. Thank you for being here. Thank you for forgiving your father and making us a family again."

He gave me a brief, timid smile and dipped his head, but made no move to return my affection when I kissed him on the forehead.

I turned my attention on my lover, my Deema. "And you," I said, exasperated. "You've got a lot of explaining to do to my mortal family when we get back to Colorado. This is so totally beyond fucked up. And we really need to get this show on the road. Right now, I don't really give a shit about preserving all of this meat. Anything that's already cooked, I think I should eat now. The rest can be left. We need to get home before my stomach expands any more," I said in a rush.

"I don't think that is wise. If you are still hungry, then by all means, eat some more. But you cannot go a whole day without food or sleep while you are pregnant like this with a rapidly growing baby. It's like every hour is a whole day's worth of baby development. You wouldn't go two weeks without food in a normal pregnancy," he pointed out.

"Okay," I conceded. "We'll wait until the meat is done smoking. Do you have something to carry it all in while we fly?"

"Yes," came the voice of my son behind me. "We have cloth to wrap it in and we will carry food and water for you while he carries you."

I turned around and noticed that both of the twins had lost their stationary poses. They seemed much more at ease now that they knew I would not be running away from them all.

'Thank you. And yes, I will stay. I will never run from you. I do love you both. I am very sorry that I am so delicate, so fragile, and so breakable, that I cannot get a hug from my children. I am sorry that you are afraid you will hurt me. Part of me can't wait for the day that I can hug you both and never be broken again,' I thought to them. I did not want to alarm Deema any more than I already had.

'Why only part?' Aleks thought back.

'Well, another part of me knows that my tribe will be frightened by my change. I am their protector, their angel. The elders are very unhappy with the idea of me becoming a vampire.'

'But you would be immortal like us! The humans coming to attack you cannot hurt you if you cannot die,' his sister chimed in.

"I'm glad I have *three* vampires on my side now," I suddenly said aloud. Deema eyeballed me inquisitively and I just shrugged it off. "I was just thinkin' is all," I offered.

I walked over to the smoker and took a closer look at the setup. There was a three layer structure of woven branches covered in still-dying leaves. Every single one was in its first year of growth and thus less likely to burn.

Inside the unusual dome were sticks stripped of their bark and pierced through hanging pieces of venison. Layer upon layer, row after row, the sticks of hanging meat filled the large cavity of the smoker. The bottom few layers were a distinctly different color than those stacked above it. I sniffed the air at different levels close to the smoker to test my increased senses. To my absolute delight, I could tell another definite difference in the smell of the layers of meat—those closer to the heat were ready to eat.

When I walked around the back, I found a flap of wet cloth covering the access. I flipped it up so I could poke around inside, took out the bottom three rows of meat, and rearranged the top three layers onto the bottom so they would cook faster. I flipped the cloth down to recover the hole and walked back to my family with my arms full of skewered meat.

Sandra rushed over and delicately plucked a giant skewer from me with one hand and slid the meat off onto my slate with the other hand. I watched in awe as she did this with each one. It was like some beautiful, bizarre dance as she held a perfect rhythm, one after another.

When she took the last one from me, I fought the desire to clap and jump up and down like a little child who's been pleased.

But while I managed to stop myself from acting on this impulse, I couldn't stop the image of myself doing it from flashing through my head. Aleks started laughing at my mental applause and his sister gave a little bow.

"I'm getting a little sick of this," Deema grumbled. "You all can read each other's minds, but I cannot read anything from any of you!"

"Well, sorry. But if it makes you feel any better, I can only hear what they push, so I'm mostly in the dark like you are," I offered.

He mumbled something too fast and quiet for me to understand, so I just ignored him. He had every right to be a little pissy with me. After all, I'd been pretty rough on him ever since last night. So I turned back to my fresh pile of food and proceeded to eat my fill.

After several hours and a small nap, the meat was ready to pack and the sun was starting to set. I took one last walk down to the creek for some water and pondered along the way. How many times, in my previous life here, had I made this walk? Would this be the last time in this life? If I ever returned here again, would it be as an immortal? An immortal angel with a half-breed child—*what are the odds?* I thought with a "humph." Aleks joined me once I reached the creek and he filled some skins with water for me before tying them all to his waist.

"Are you ready?" Deema grumbled as we emerged from the tree line.

I turned my gaze the sky and sighed. "As ready as I'll ever be. Is she carrying the meat since he is carrying the water?"

"Yes," Deema replied flatly. "You can take off whenever you're ready. I'm not carrying you the same way as I did on the way here." He looked me up and down. "I don't want your stomach compressed for so long," he said with a sigh. Without another glance at me, Deema took off straight up into the sky. Once he got far enough away that I could barely see him, he stopped and just floated. I was afraid to make him impatient and I was all too anxious to get home—so I crouched, flapped, and pushed off to join them in the sky.

CHAPTER 51

We turned west to chase the setting sun and after several minutes, I started to worry about Deema. How angry was he with me? Just how long was he planning on making me fly and waste energy?

Before I had too long to distress over his new attitude toward me, I heard my son ramble off a string of Russian words far too fast for me to understand. Deema seemed upset by his comment or question and rattled off his own set of lightning fast words. Aleks stared at him strangely before he turned his baffled expression on me.

Before I could even open my mouth to ask someone to explain all of this to me, Deema was in his favorite flight position—underneath me and inches from my face. He clasped my cheeks in his frigid hands and gently kissed my lips. Over and over he kissed me.

Every time he pulled back to gaze into my eyes, I would open my mouth to speak. And every time, he would seal my lips with his before I could start my inquiries.

After at least ten minutes of this nonsense, he finally spoke. "I promise to love you and protect you for all of time. I promise to watch over you and care for you when no one else can. I promise to never let you die. I promise that I will follow you anywhere you ask me to and give you peace when you ask for it. I promise to be everything you need me to be and everything you never thought you would have in a partner. I promise you all of this, because I ask you to be my wife again. Ana." A tiny kiss. "My only Hope." Another light kiss. "White Eagle, will you be my wife for the rest of eternity?"

His gaze never broke from mine as he spoke. His words were slathered with sincerity, but I barely heard the sentences they formed. I was far too lost in the depth and beauty of his eyes. He had beheld me with love in his eyes before, but this was far beyond that. The emotions in his eyes were so complex that I forgot to answer him while I was figuring it out. There was hope and truth beneath the love, along with a huge splash of absolutely pure happiness. But there was also something else layered deep beneath all the rest that I couldn't place at first. *Could it be doubt?* I wondered as it continued to grow. I suddenly realized he was waiting for an answer, and every second that I delayed was making him more anxious that I would decline his request for marriage.

"How could you ever doubt my answer?" I cried out as I wrapped my arms around his neck.

"Well, you certainly took your time answering me," he muttered while I finished giving in to him. "Now you agree, and I agree. So we are married again. Our children and God have witnessed it."

I dropped my wings and let him support me as he flew with his back to the ground. He wrapped his arms securely around me and I nuzzled closer to his granite body.

Breath after breath, I sucked in his scent and tried to pick out the undertones of it. Certainly, it was woodsy—a little musky with some various tree smells. Pine was the most prominent of the trees, but some of my favorites were in there, too. Cedar, oak, and the faintest hint of maple, I decided. But his scent was even more complex than this bouquet of trees. There were the various smells of water—morning dew, ocean air, and, without a doubt, my sweet spring water from his castle. And lying side-by-side, with his perfumes of woods and waters, were the aromas of wildlife. But before I had a chance to start deciphering those subtle notes of flavor and fragrance, he interrupted my thoughts.

"Just what are you doing, anyway? Are you…smelling me?" he asked incredulously.

Aleks stifled a laugh while I permitted myself a small giggle.

I blushed. "Yes. But there are so many layers to your scent, so many subtle flavors to figure out. Just like your eyes. There are so many layers of emotion in those sparkling stones you call eyes. I got a little lost in them earlier and I didn't really notice you had stopped talking," I confessed.

We all had a good laugh at my childlike fascination with my newly heightened senses.

We flew for about five hours with little conversation until we reached the western edge of Europe. I was feeling the void in my belly again. We landed for a little while so I could eat and drink. I managed to consume almost half of the meat as well as all of the water. It took another twelve hours to cross the ocean and I was beyond thrilled when we landed on the roof of the New York apartment.

I staggered down the stairs with the help of my children while Deema bolted down to unlock the door. I collapsed on the daybed while Deema filled a large glass of water for me and my daughter started to unwrap the remaining smoked venison. I drained the glass in a few large gulps and then I scarfed down the meat so fast I almost choked. I slowed down enough to drain another glass of water, and then I resumed my consumption at a more reasonable pace. Once I'd polished off the last of the deer meat and a third glass of water, I fell back on the bed and slept like the dead.

CHAPTER 52

When I awoke hours later, I was sore all over from sleeping on top of my wings. I noticed the faint light of dawn creeping through the window before I glanced around the apartment. I was alone. I tried to sit up too quickly and got overcome by a wave of vertigo. Once I regained my sense of balance, I stood and stretched. I picked up my glass and shuffled into the kitchen for some more water. As I was filling it for the second time, my vampire family emerged from one of the bedrooms.

"Are you ready to go home, my love?" Deema asked sweetly as he strolled to my side.

"Yes. The sooner we get there the better since I'm out of food now." I frowned as I looked up into his sparkling black eyes. "This is Saturday, yes?"

"Yes. We should be home in twelve hours."

I sighed deeply and turned to the door. "Well, let's hit the road. Or the sky, I guess," I corrected with a small smile.

We dove off the roof and flew for only a few seconds this time before Deema took his place in front of me—or rather, underneath me—and took the burden of flying away from me. I was still quite tired, so I wrapped my wings around my immortal lover and dozed off and on for several hours until we reached southwestern Colorado. I was fairly surprised at how fast we seemed to get there, and I realized that I must have slept longer than I'd thought. I reminded Deema to land in my practice valley since it was mid-day. I was thrilled to find my brother, Will, sitting by a fire with a large ham cooking on a spit.

"Taniya called me this morning and asked me to wait for you here," he said casually as Deema and I approached the small campfire. He must have registered the sound of extra feet because he jerked his head up and stared in shock at the immortal teenage twins. "Who the fuck are you?" he demanded suddenly.

"These are my children from a past life," I said wearily as I plopped down in my tall chair. "Aleksandra, Aleksander, this is my brother, Will. You will meet the rest of our family later." I turned to my lover and silently asked him for something to drink. I was so tired, hungry, and thirsty I just couldn't bring myself to move again. Even though I hadn't been expending vast amounts of energy by flying, I still felt as drained as if I had been training non-stop.

"What happened to you? Why are you back so soon? Why do you seem so…" He waved his hand at my unusually distorted body.

"Pregnant? Because I am. I have a little over a week before I give birth to some kind of mutant child. Some half-breed that has never been seen before. Half angel, half vampire. We had no idea he could father children as an immortal, so we took no precautions," I babbled quickly while I stared at the ground and toed a small rock. "I will live," I assured him as I glanced up to see his wide, frightened eyes. "But we do not know if I will survive as a human. I may already be slowly changing into a vampire because I ingested Deema's blood when I broke my spine in a flying accident."

Without looking at her, I silently told Sandra that my people need not know it was at her hands that I was injured. I didn't want to give them any reason to not like her. I noticed a quick nod out of the corner of my eye and knew she understood.

Will stared at me in shock. He was utterly speechless. While he tried to recover and readjust his view of the world yet again, I drained the two skins of water that Deema had handed me during my little exchange with my brother. Deema then proceeded to slice off the outer layer of the ham and serve it to me on one of the metal plates. I was so hungry that I didn't even care that the meat burned my mouth and throat as I gobbled it down. In record time, my plate was empty and I turned to Deema with questioning eyes.

"The rest is not ready yet, love," he told me quietly. He spared a quick peek at my brother before he returned his full focus back to me. "Perhaps you'd like to 'call' Taniya? Or would you like to return home? If you fly home first, the twins can hear you if it is safe or not for us to follow you. If it is not safe yet, then we can wait until dark?"

I didn't think I'd ever seen him so unsure of himself. "Yes," I said hesitantly. "I think I'll go home and make some phone calls. They need to know I'm back. I'd also like to sleep some more before I visit with the elders tonight."

My brother snapped out of his deep thoughts and jumped up from his seat, casting his gaze aimlessly around the camp. "This changes everything. None of this is possible!"

"I'm sorry, Will, but 'impossible' doesn't seem to exist anymore." I placed my hands on his shoulders to stop his pacing and stared into his eyes. "Please, calm down. All will be well. This does change things, but it will not stop me from saving or protecting out tribe."

He watched me blankly for a few moments before he gave me one slow nod. "Okay," he said slowly and doubtfully.

"I'm going home now," I said to my immortal family. "Listen for my voice and, if it is safe, Deema will bring you home." I didn't bother waiting for a reply before I pumped my wings and took off into the sky. It took a quick minute to reach my house and I was only slightly surprised to find Brian and Taniya waiting for me.

"I see she spoke the truth," my brother said by way of greeting. "You certainly appear pregnant. But how are you *so* pregnant?"

I shuffled over to my pallet, flopped down on my pile of pillows, and settled into a comfortable position.. "It is developing twenty times faster than a normal child," I mumbled.

"I got you that stuff you asked for," Taniya said quietly before she sat on the floor next to me. "You look like hell," she observed after a few moments of examination.

"Would you mind?" I mumbled to her as I started to lose consciousness.

I pushed her the image of her slathering my growing abdomen with cocoa butter and vitamin E oil. I heard the crinkle of plastic as she opened the seals, but I was passed out cold by the time she started to rub down my belly.

CHAPTER 53

I awoke around dusk to a growling stomach and the realization that I'd never "called" my children. My hands instinctively went to my belly which was noticeably larger as well as extremely slick with oil.

I glanced around my trailer and saw that my vampire family had already joined me. I smiled weakly at them and silently asked for water and food. My throat was so dry I wasn't sure if I could speak. In a flash of movement, the twins had me propped up. She put a skin of water in my left hand and he placed a large platter of meat, fruit, and vegetables next to my right hand. I drained the skin and then proceeded to stuff my face.

Between mouthfuls of food, I asked Deema to call Brian. "Tell him to bring the truck and call the elders. We will meet them at the Hall in an hour." He gave me a nod and picked up my phone on his way out the back door.

Within half an hour, the sun had finished setting, I had finished my giant plate of food, and my brother arrived with the mattress in place in the back of his truck. The twins lay next to me in the back of the truck while Deema joined my brother in the cab. A few more minutes passed and we had arrived at the Hall of the Elders. I tried to ignore the panic that was rising inside of me as I climbed from the back of the truck and shuffled into the Hall.

"Why have you called us here?" the chief asked calmly as I entered the room behind my brother. I peeked over my shoulder and realized that the vampires were waiting outside until I could explain the story of the twins. I scanned the room and saw that the younger elders were there as well. They all stood behind their grandfathers. My heart stuttered for a moment while I gathered my thoughts.

"I have some shocking news," I said as I turned to my grandfather. He gestured for me to continue after a few moments and I sucked in another deep breath. "I am pregnant and it is developing twenty times faster than a normal child. I will give birth in less than ten days, and I may not survive as a human. But I will survive!" I assured them as they gasped and murmured. "I also have returned with two more protectors. They are my children from a past life, and they, too, have vowed to protect this tribe as if it were their own. Sandra, Aleks, could you come in here please?" I turned to the door and watched my immortal children glide into the room behind their father. More gasps and murmurs ran through the room as the elders took in the sight of my vampire family.

"How? H—how did this happen, child?" my grandfather stuttered.

"When we returned to our human home in Russia, they found me in the woods. I'm sure you can see the resemblance between us," I said as I put my arm around my daughter's shoulders.

"Indeed we can," said the chief. "But how is this—this isn't possible. Genetic traits do not pass through the soul, and you cannot be related by blood if you all died 500 years ago," he argued.

"Well, I cannot explain it other than by saying that impossible doesn't exist anymore. I look like his wife and their mother. I have memories of this past life. I can speak the old Russian dialect without even thinking about it. We share many other unusual traits other than our appearances. "Grandfather." I turned back to the old man. "Everyone has always been baffled by my skin. I am lighter than the rest of the tribe, and I have never gotten any darker. I cannot tan or burn and, in life, the same was said of my children."

"Yes. The same was said of us when we were human, only

we were darker than our people. But we had the same skin our mother has now," my eternally teenage daughter said in her musical voice.

"I don't understand," the youngest elder whispered.

"Well, this may never be explained, but I suppose we must just accept the way things are," the chief said after a long, silent moment. "There is nothing we can do to change the past, and we must accept what is coming. How will this child grow? How will it develop once it has been born? Will it be immortal like the rest of you and remain an infant? Or will it continue to age rapidly?"

"We don't know yet," Deema answered for me. "We will just have to see. There has never been anything like this before. Vampires do not produce—we cannot make bodily fluids. We don't have tears or sweat, and I've never met a vampire who could experience a release during intercourse. In my 500 years, I never have. But when I lay with my wife—" He smiled sweetly at me. "—I did. Her dreams showed us pieces of what would happen, but we don't know the whole story."

"Then wait we shall. Can you promise not to harm any of our tribe?" my grandfather asked as he turned to the twins.

"We promise," Aleksander replied. "We can read minds like our father, so we will hunt as he hunts. We also learned to hunt animals, so we can help feed your tribe. We would never do anything to cause harm to our mother or those she is sworn to protect." He smiled broadly and bowed regally to the room full of elders.

"Well then, I suppose we just wait and see," the chief concluded before he waved us from the room.

CHAPTER 54

I decided to fly home since the vampires were going to head off to Las Vegas to hunt.

"We will be back by dawn. Do you need anything while we are out?" Deema asked as we exited the Hall of the Elders.

"Yes, love. I'm out of food at home. I still want fresh pineapple and strawberries and…well, I'm getting a little bit sick of venison. Can you bring me some beef? Or bison if they have it."

"Sure. We'll go to the store before we leave Vegas." He gave me a tender kiss and the three of them took off into the sky.

I flew home alone and called Taniya once I landed in my back yard. She agreed to come over after she dropped her son off with Will so we could talk. While I sat upwind from her on my patio, I rolled up a joint for her. I told her everything that happened while I was in Russia. I explained my dreams and my fears of the future. I told her all of my recovered memories of my past life and the deep love I felt for my immortal children.

By the time I finished my ramblings, Taniya was quite stoned.

"Well, to be honest, honey, I just don't know what to say," she said after a couple minutes. "This is all so…" She seemed at a total loss for words.

"I know," I sighed. "I'm so scared, but there's nothing to do now but wait. Wait for this child to be born, wait to see how it develops, and wait to see when the world will fall. I've never felt so lost and scared and confused," I confessed.

"But you're not alone, you know. We're all here for you. And Deema will not let you die. He loves you more than his own life."

"I know," I choked out as I burst into tears.

Taniya wrapped her arms around me and held me as I sobbed.

Once I ran out of tears, I realized how tired I was. As I lay down on my pallet, I asked her to stay with me until morning.

"I want you to meet them when they get back. And I don't want to be alone," I confessed.

She agreed and I fell asleep to my best friend softly singing the birth song in our ancient language.

I awoke several hours later to the sound of hushed voices. The faint light of dawn was creeping through my windows.

"Deema?" I murmured as I stretched.

The voices stopped.

"Are you really awake this time?" he whispered from across the room.

"Yes. Have I been talking a lot?" I struggled to push myself up to stand, but my arms felt like Jell-O.

"All night, my love." He appeared at my side and helped me stand. "Are you hungry?"

"Of course. Is that a roast in the oven I smell?" I asked, inhaling deeply. "With carrots, potatoes, onions, and red wine?"

"You have a good nose," he said with a loving smile.

I snorted a laugh. "Yeah, thanks to your blood donation. But I'm not sure if I want dinner for breakfast. I think what I really want is pancakes, bacon, and eggs."

Aleks pursed his lips and his eyebrows drew together. "What are pan…cakes?"

Taniya laughed. "I've got stuff at home for pancakes if you don't have it here," she offered.

"Do I?" I asked Deema.

"No, sweetheart. I didn't think to buy stuff like that. But I did buy several pounds of bacon since you said you were out before we left." He turned to his son who was still waiting for an answer. "Pancakes are a sweet batter that is cooked into round flat cakes in a skillet rather than in an oven like other cakes. Most people put butter on them and then pour maple syrup onto them," he explained.

"Maple syrup?" his daughter asked with a similar confused expression.

"Yes. It is the sap of a maple tree that is drawn out in the spring and then boiled down so it is thick and sweet. It tastes like a maple tree smells, only much sweeter. At least, that's how it has been explained to me. Of course, I've never tasted it myself."

"Of course," Aleks drawled.

"So...pancakes?" I asked Taniya hesitantly when no one moved for a few moments.

"Oh! Yes. Sorry," she said with a slightly embarrassed smile. "I'll be right back." She disappeared out the door and I heard my old car start.

"I should sign my car over to her since I can't drive it anymore and she doesn't have one," I commented as I heard her drive away.

"I'm sure she'd appreciate that," he said absently as he caressed my face.

I stared into his eyes and got lost in them again as I tried to decipher the layers of emotion that lay behind them.

"I'm not sure I deserve you," I said quite suddenly.

He opened his mouth to protest, but I clamped my lips to his and he soon forgot what he was about to say.

After several seconds of being attached to his face, I heard the back door open. I jerked back and saw the twins walking out to the back porch.

"I think we are making them uncomfortable," Deema said with a guilty grin. "They are not used to displays of affection."

"So, how is this going to work now?" I whispered. "If they never sleep, and they only go hunting with you...I mean, how will we ever have time alone?" I pressed against him to illustrate my meaning.

A small moan escaped his lips before they found mine again.

"I don't know, lover. But maybe we shouldn't until you heal from giving birth," he replied after several minutes of passionate kissing.

I pouted in response to his words, but I knew I couldn't argue with him. I would never do anything to endanger my child or to push away my immortal children. I sighed heavily and backed away from him as I heard my car pull back into the driveway.

"Well, I guess I should put some more stuff on my belly while Taniya cooks breakfast."

"I don't mind cooking for you." He pulled two skillets out of the cabinet. "I don't mind rubbing oil on you either," he said with a wink.

Taniya walked in the front door with several bags of groceries and a big grin while Deema was laying me down on my pallet. She mixed up the pancake batter and started cooking them while he saturated my skin in cocoa butter. By the time the pancakes and bacon were done cooking, I realized I still needed to gather eggs. I rushed out to the henhouse, found they were out of food, and all of the chickens sat on multiple eggs. I put them all in my flat basket and hurried back inside.

"You can come back in now if you don't mind the smell of food cooking," I said to the twins as I rushed past them.

They followed me inside without a word and watched with interest as I scrambled and cooked half of the eggs I'd gathered.

CHAPTER 55

We developed a rough routine over the next several days. It mostly consisted of my vampires taking care of me by cooking all my food while I watched TV and slept. I wasn't allowed to fly, so I didn't even bother going outside. They took turns going to Vegas to hunt. The twins always went together, and Deema tried to only go while I slept. Taniya was also around most of the time so that she could sing songs to my belly that we'd learned from our mothers.

On the thirteenth day of my pregnancy, the child shifted into position to be born. A few hours later, I started having labor pains. They continued all through the night. After fifteen hours of labor, I managed to push out the child. It was extremely unusual. The placenta stretched to fit around my baby, but it didn't break until Deema ripped it open with his teeth. The amniotic fluid splashed all over both of us as well as the linoleum floor, but I couldn't have cared less. I was anxious to see the child that Deema announced was my daughter.

She was incredibly, shockingly beautiful. I'd heard skin described as milky before, but her skin truly looked like milk—an almost translucent white. It was perfectly smooth and as soft as silk. Her black hair was several inches long and matted against her head. Her eyes were the same lavender that mine had changed into. She stared at me with them, wide-eyed, as Deema held her out to me. She took slow, startled, broken breaths that caused me worry at first until I felt her confusion.

"It's okay, baby," I said with a smile. "It's just air. You don't have to breathe liquid anymore."

She grinned back at me and I was shocked to see her full set of teeth. I moved to wipe some goop off of her face, but she bit my hand. I cried out in shock and Deema snatched her away from me.

"I guess she's hungry," I mumbled as I lay back. I fell into unconsciousness within seconds.

I awoke several hours later, feeling more physically refreshed than I thought I should. I wasn't in pain, my insides didn't feel out of order, and I instantly felt wide awake. I licked my lips and felt an odd effervescent feeling. *Where have I felt that before?* I wondered.

I shot up from the floor in half a second when I realized that it was the same taste and feeling as when I had drank Deema's blood. My eyes quickly scanned the room and found only the twins.

"We are sorry," Sandra said quickly. "He took the child to hunt in the city. You didn't stop bleeding and we were scared. You wouldn't wake up. I knew we couldn't seal your wounds without changing you, so we fed you a few swallows. Not a lot," she said when she saw I was about to protest. "Not even as much as last time. We just wanted you to not hurt anymore. We are sorry." She moved toward the back door as if to leave.

"Please, don't go," I said as her brother started to follow her. "I am not angry. Just surprised is all."

They stopped and turned back to face me.

"How long ago did he leave? When do you think he'll get back?"

"We're back now," Deema said as he slid the glass door open. "She's fed, full, and sleepy. I don't think she'll bite you now." He smiled lovingly as he passed me the yawning child. She nestled into my arms and petted my neck before drifting off to sleep.

"What should we name her?" I wondered aloud.

"Have you called the elders?" he asked as I walked over to my chair.

I sat down. "No, I've only been up for a couple minutes."

"No!" he cried out as he rushed toward me. I felt my eyebrows draw together in confusion as the baby stirred in my arms. "Isn't that painful? You just gave birth. You should not sit down."

"I didn't stop bleeding after you left. The twins could not wake me and feared I would bleed-out and die. They fed me just enough blood to heal me. I don't feel any different than I did before. I still have the same acuity to my vision and hearing, so…" I trailed off and shrugged one shoulder.

He sighed deeply and, after a long moment, he shrugged as well. "Okay, well, we need to call your family. She's not even twelve hours old yet and has already changed so much."

"Yes, I can see that. Will you call them? And some baked chicken would be wonderful. I'll call Taniya and Brian if you'll call the Hall. Someone should still be there. It's not quite seven o'clock yet."

I leaned back against the wall and focused my thoughts toward my best friend. I found her at the store. *'Perfect luck.'*

'What's perfect luck?' I heard her say in my head and saw her smile at the loaves of bread.

'I want some baked chicken with rice. Can you also get some sour cream, butter, and some cream of mushroom soup? I guess we can kill one of my chickens, but if they've got organic meat there, that'd be awesome. Save me some trouble, you know? I guess you can't see me because you shouldn't draw attention to yourself by going in to a trance in the store, but I gave birth several hours ago. You might want to come over here as soon as you get done shopping.'

'Okay. I'll be done here soon and I'll be at your house in thirty minutes.'

'Great. I'll see you then. I've got to call my brothers now. Actually, if you've got a cell, it'd be great if you called Will. I don't know if he can get these *kind of calls.'*

'No problem.'

She smiled at the irony of the two of them getting along before I broke the connection to search for my big brother. I found him sitting at the table in the Hall of Elders with a few old men and a few young men as well.

'*Brother.*'

He held up his hand to the men around him, closed his eyes, and spoke aloud for their benefit. "Sister," he acknowledged. "I see you have given birth."

The room around him fell silent.

'*I have. I passed out right after and just awoke a few minutes ago. It is time for a gathering. We need to name the child and I don't want her to have a Christian name. Taniya should be here in thirty minutes and she's calling Will, so he should be here soon. If you could gather the rest of the elders, that would be great.*'

"We'll be there before an hour has passed," he replied.

I nodded before I broke the connection.

"No need to call, Deema," I said as he picked up the phone he'd finally found. "Brian was at the Hall, and they'll be here within an hour. Taniya will be here in thirty minutes to start cooking dinner. Will should be here soon as well."

"Yes, I think I hear his truck. He'll be bursting in shortly," he said teasingly.

I laughed as I heard the Jeep's engine cut off in the driveway. "He does have a tendency to over-react sometimes, doesn't he?"

A few seconds later, my younger brother burst through the door. He stopped halfway across the room when I held up my finger to my lips.

"Shhh. She's sleeping," I whispered.

CHAPTER 56

"S he? I have a niece? I'm an uncle?" Will walked over to where I sat with my new daughter in my arms. "Can I?" He held his arms out toward the sleeping marvel I held.

"Okay, but you should know that she drinks blood and has a full set of teeth. She's already bitten me once, and if she wakes, she may bite you. So, you've been warned," I said as he pulled her against his chest.

He stared down at her. "She's the prettiest baby I've ever seen."

"Isn't she, though?" I stared into her perfect little face and grinned from ear to ear. "She's growing very fast. It hasn't even been twelve hours yet and I can see a difference in her."

"What's her name?" he whispered without turning his eyes away from her.

"I don't know. The elders will be here in less than an hour. We will name her then."

He nodded in understanding.

"Taniya will be here soon, too. This has all happened so fast, I can't quite wrap my head around the fact that I'm a mother now."

"Yeah. It's weird, isn't it? Having parenthood thrust on you so suddenly?" He huffed a short laugh through his nose. "Yeah. She called me and I was out the door before I even hung up. The cordless phone is in my passenger seat."

The baby stirred and peered up at her uncle with curious eyes.

"Baby, this is my brother. His name is Will. He is your uncle."

She stared at me and, after a moment, held her tiny arms out to me, grabbing the air between us with her little fingers. I laughed as I took my daughter from my brother's arms.

"Don't bite me, okay, baby? You only bite people Daddy says you can." I felt like she understood, so I lifted her up to my face and covered her satin skin in kisses. "My baby, my baby," I murmured between kisses.

She seemed to drink up my love and affection, enjoying every bit of my doting. After several minutes, she put her little hand on my neck and rubbed it with longing.

"How much did she drink? Do you think she can eat people food?" I asked my lover.

"She drank until she was full. But with that tiny stomach, it wasn't much. I would imagine that with her rapid growth, she may need to feed more often than a normal baby," he informed me.

"Good point," I muttered. "What should we do? You can't be flying to Nevada over and over again every day so she can feed."

"Can she kill a chicken?" he suggested.

I thought about it for a moment. "Yes," I said hesitantly. "I suppose she can *this* time. We'll likely need more meat than Taniya will buy. And then she can try people food. Does she produce waste? She doesn't feel like she's wearing a diaper." I patted her bottom to be sure.

He suppressed a smirk. "No. She's not wearing one. She hasn't yet and I figured she might not since neither of her parents do."

I rolled my eyes at him before I turned my attention back to my new daughter. She grinned at me and patted my neck again.

"Okay, baby girl. Let's go get you something to eat."

Her smile widened as we walked out the back door.

"Sandra, could you give me a hand?" I said over my shoulder.

"Sure, Ma," she said as she followed me.

We walked out to the henhouse and I pointed out the oldest chicken. "That one. Break its neck so it doesn't scratch or bite her, and then hand it here," I instructed her.

She did as I asked and the child watched with great interest as her big sister killed the bird. Sandra handed me the twitching chicken and we held it in front of the baby. Without hesitation, she wrapped her little fingers around its feathers and pulled its neck to her hungry mouth. The child sank her razor sharp teeth into the bird's flesh and drank in deep, greedy gulps. I could actually feel the chicken getting lighter as she drained it completely of blood. When she finished and let go of the chicken, her tiny face scrunched up and she shook her head quickly.

"I know, little sister. It is bitter, is it not?" Sandra laughed. "Bad people taste best, you will learn, and animals that eat meat taste good. Deer are okay, but birds taste bad, don't they?" she cooed at the baby in my arms.

"Would you like to hold her?" I asked as I held the child out to her.

She gingerly took the baby from me before we walked back into the house.

CHAPTER 51

I walked into the kitchen and plucked the chicken while everyone oohed and aahed over the little miracle I'd birthed. I had just pulled out my cleaver to start chopping up the bird when Taniya arrived. She had her arms full of grocery bags.

"Will, can you grab our son and the last bag of groceries out of the car? I'm going to help your sister." She set the bags down on the counter, flashed me a smile, and turned her attention to my daughters. "Oh!" Taniya exclaimed as she met the infant's sparkling lavender eyes. "She's so beautiful! She's perfect! Can I hold her?" she asked Sandra.

"Of course," I answered when the vampire looked at me for an answer. She passed the child to my sister and Taniya proceeded to coo at the baby.

I returned to the kitchen and, in record time, I had the chicken boned, chopped, and ready to bake. I pulled out some rice, dumped it into the biggest mixing bowl, and searched the grocery bags for the rest of my ingredients. I poured in the large tub of sour cream, three cans of cream of mushroom condensed soup, two cans of water, and a few tablespoons of butter. I mixed it all before I added the chicken. I remembered that the elders would be arriving soon, so I chopped up the boneless/skinless chicken breasts that Taniya brought and added it to the mix. It took two large pans to hold all the food and they barely fit into the oven.

Once I finished preparing the food, I went back to the living room to reclaim my daughter. But Taniya had passed her to Aleks so she could put away the rest of the groceries and he was in the middle of speaking Russian to her. *No reason for her to not be bilingual*, I thought. I checked the clock—7:32— and watched my family for a few minutes. Despite all of our differences—age, culture, race—it looked like any happy family after the healthy birth of a child.

"Do you want her now?" Aleks asked me when he noticed me watching them.

I glanced at the clock. It read 7:50. "Not just yet." I rushed into the kitchen and stirred the pans of chicken as quickly as I could. When I walked back into the living room, I had my arms spread to embrace my newest child. As soon as I had her clutched to my chest, the door rattled with knocking.

"We're here," came Brian's muffled voice.

"Come in," I called back.

Brian opened the door and held it for the chief while he entered, followed by my grandfather and the rest of the elders. Some of the younger men carried lawn chairs and they quickly set them up so the older men could sit down.

Once everyone was settled, my grandfather rose. "We should have been called while you were in labor. It is tradition that the elders sing the birth song outside while an important tribal woman is giving birth," he said in a stern tone.

"I *am* sorry," I said with a touch of shame. "I didn't think I had time. I kept thinking that the pain couldn't get any worse and that at any moment she would be born. I figured that since her gestation was accelerated, her birth would be as well. But—" I hesitated as I glanced at Taniya. She nodded that, yes, I should say it. "Almost every night of my pregnancy, Taniya sang it to me as I fell asleep so that the baby would be healthy as it grew so quickly."

My grandfather sat back down and turned to the chief, who thought for a few minutes. "I suppose that is fine. At least the child was still in the womb when the song was sung. It will have to do. Now, when did you have the child?" the chief asked me. "When exactly?"

I glanced at Deema, hoping that he knew the exact time.

"She was born at 8:46 this morning," Deema answered without hesitation. "She has a diet similar to mine, but as soon as the food it done cooking, we will see if she can eat human food like her mother." He abruptly turned to the youngest elder. "Yes, I am reading all of your minds and answering your most common questions.

"She has grown about three inches in length since she was born eleven hours and fifteen minutes ago," he continued. "She has a very developed mind and I expect she will be able to speak within a week or so. See how she already holds up her head? She also has advanced motor skills for a child of her size. The food should be ready in about 30 minutes, so if there is another song to sing, would you like to do it now? Or after?"

"The first song takes fifteen minutes," the chief said. "The naming ceremony could take much longer, though, so we will do that tomorrow. Hope, your brother said you don't want her to have an English name?"

"Right. I don't want her to have a name like us. Hope, Brian, William, Taniya. I don't want my child to have a name like that. I want her to only have a tribal name, like her cousin, Dancing Bronco."

"I understand," the chief agreed. "Well, elders, shall we sing?" The timeworn man grumbled as he rose from his chair and headed for the back door. The other old men followed while the young men carried their chairs. I trailed after them with my daughter in my arms and my vampires right behind me. Taniya, her son, and Will were the last to leave the house.

CHAPTER 58

We gathered around the massive drum that they must have carried out back before they'd come in the front. There was a very tall, empty chair on the closest side of the drum that the chief gestured was for me. I sat down and propped my new daughter on my knee. She reached down to the drum without hesitation and gave it three pats—bink, bink, bink—right at the edge.

"This newborn child is a member of this tribe," the chief began. "She is under tribal protection and any tribe member who causes this infant harm will be punished. To let our ancestors know, we now sing the healthy child song to celebrate her birth."

He began to beat the drum slowly and rhythmically. Three of the other old men joined him and we all—except the vampires—began to sing the healthy child song in our ancient tongue. The baby smiled, closed her eyes, and turned her head toward the drum she was still touching with her fingertips. About four or five minutes into the song, she started tapping my hand in time with the simplest drum beat. By the end of the song, she was also swaying with the music our voices created.

Some of the old men, who weren't drumming, closed their eyes as they sang, but most of the younger men kept their eyes open.

"She is, indeed, very advanced. I saw her keeping the beat with her hand, and swaying to the singing," came a voice behind me.

A small chorus of agreement followed the young elder's observation.

I nodded and handed the baby off to Deema. "Yes, she's definitely something else. Please, excuse me. I must check on dinner." I opened the oven and pulled out both pans of chicken. The chicken all seemed to be cooked, but the rice wasn't quite done yet. I stirred a can of corn into each pan and popped them back into the oven. "Fifteen minutes," I announced as I took my daughter back from Deema.

She patted my neck again to let me know she was hungry.

"Not just yet, baby. It'll be ready soon, and then we can eat. And if you can't eat food like me, then your daddy will get you a nice deer to drink from. Okay?"

"Does she really understand you?" Brian asked as he made his way to the front of the group.

"Yes, I think she does. Don't you? You understand me, baby?"

She gave me a big smile that I took for a yes. It seemed to be enough for Brian as well. His eyes lit up as he asked to hold this amazing child.

I passed her to him, then excused myself again to retrieve more chairs from the bedroom I never used anymore. I placed them around outside for the others to sit on while they ate. By the time I had finished, almost twenty minutes had passed. I pulled the pans out of the oven and it was perfectly cooked. I set out all of my plates and bowls, laid all of the spoons and forks on the counter, and pulled out the loaf of bread Taniya had brought me.

"Food's ready," I told everyone as I dished out a heaping serving for myself. I grabbed a couple slices of bread, nodded to Deema to follow me, and strode out the back door. I sat down in the hammock and he sat down next to me. One by one, people flowed out of the house with plates or bowls of food and sat around my backyard while I tried to feed my baby.

"It's good, baby. See?" I took a bite of chicken and rice and made an "mmm" sound.

She seemed a bit more interested, so I got some rice and

sauce on the spoon. She allowed me to feed it to her, but made a shocked face.

"Is it too hot? I didn't burn her, did I?" I asked Deema in a panic. He shook his head and I relaxed enough that I was able to pick up on what she was feeling—confusion. She mushed it around in her mouth and eventually swallowed it.

"More?" I asked her as I held out the spoon.

She opened her mouth and swallowed her second bite more quickly. For her third bite, I gave her a small chunk of chicken that I'd shredded with the spoon. She made her own little "mmm" sound and I laughed.

"That's the chicken you drank earlier," I told her and she gave me a big grin after she swallowed. I shredded some more chicken for her and she made grabby hands toward the plate.

"I'll tell you what. I'm going to make you a little pile of food here," I said as I pushed it toward her. "If you can feed yourself, I'll let you." I picked up a chunk of chicken with my fingers, placed it in my mouth, and chewed it to show her how. She showed me her dazzling smile and imitated me perfectly.

Brian laughed from the other side of the patio. "Hey, Mikey, I think she likes it."

"Yep. She can eat normal food," I called over my shoulder to the elders.

"Good," boomed the chief's voice. "One less little monster killing things," he mumbled under his breath.

"I heard that, Chief. And so did all of them. They are here to protect us, you know. I truly wish that you could let go of the misinterpretations of the old stories. If you do not get over the bad ways of thinking of my family, you may end up driving all your protectors away and being defenseless."

"How dare you threaten to leave your tribe?" my grandfather bellowed as he stomped over to me.

"I threaten nothing. I was—that is the only way I could see them as being bad for our tribe—if they left. And why *should* they stick around if they constantly have to hear negative, mean thoughts and words about themselves pouring from the brains and mouths of those they are here to protect? What if one day their annoyance with all this negativity outgrows their

love for me? What if you are left with only me? If I'm inca-
pacitated by caring for a small child, I can protect you from no
one."

"We will never leave you, Mama. No matter how mean
they are to us," Sandra said in a tender tone from behind me.

"We would only leave if they tried to kill us," her brother
corrected.

"But they will not, because they need us," she snapped
back.

"No. We will not do you harm, and we ask that you forgive
us for being stubborn old men. These are stories we have been
told our whole lives and it will take a while for us to change
the way we were raised to think." He set his empty plate on top
of the grill. "I suppose it's lucky for you that only the men
here—" He gestured to the gathered elders. "—know these
stories." He picked up his plate and walked inside, returned
with a glass of water, and sat in his seat without further comment.

I shook off the tension that had developed and returned to
feeding myself and my daughter. She ate heartily and even ate
almost half a slice of bread on top of all the chicken and rice.

By the time everyone had finished eating, it was just past
ten at night. I stood and turned to the elders. "Should we name
her tomorrow? It's getting quite late."

"That's fine. Come to the Hall at noon. We will eat lunch
and then name her," the chief said. "She is so lovely. She looks
a lot like you, but I see she has her father's hair and skin. I
wonder if she will grow wings like her mother."

He kissed my forehead and then kissed my baby's forehead.
"Goodnight, Hope." He gave Deema a nod and walked
through the house to leave. The rest of the elders followed
him, chairs in tow. My brothers carried the drum around to the
front and hoisted it onto the mattress in the bed of Brian's
truck. I waved goodbye to the cars full of tribal elders and
wished my family sweet dreams as they left as well.

CHAPTER 59

W hen I went back into the house, the twins had already finished almost half of the dirty dishes. "Thank you," I told them as I got a glass of water. The baby yawned widely, laid her head on my shoulder, and fell fast asleep. I carefully passed her to Deema and told him I'd be back in a while.

I pushed off into the warm summer sky and flew lazily to my valley. I dipped and dove my way around it for a while until I was satisfied. I wasn't quite tired, but I wanted to get some exercise since I hadn't flown for over a week. After a couple hours out, I went back to my trailer.

The baby woke up after another hour and wanted some blood. The twins offered to take her out to feed and I thanked them with a smile. As soon as the back door was closed, Deema's mouth was on me like white on rice.

"I've missed you," he mumbled as his lips moved down my jaw and to my neck. A small moan escaped me in reply. In a snap, we were both naked, our clothes in piles of shredded fabric. The hours passed much too quickly with our passion. Right around the time I was too exhausted to continue, Sandra's voice came into my head saying they would arrive in twenty minutes. Deema found some clothes for us both and we got dressed before I lay back down on my pallet to go to sleep.

When the twins returned around four in the morning, the baby was getting tired again and my son had a large hog in his arms. He tied it to the porch post while his sister handed me my baby. I fell asleep, more comfortable than I'd ever been. I held my child—my own flesh and blood child—in my arms while her father held me. I was flanked by my immortal children keeping watch over us and I felt incredibly safe and happy.

I awoke at eleven a.m. and started to get ready for the ceremony. The twins took the baby outside to feed from the hog while Deema helped me bathe and wash my hair in the sink. He parted my hair expertly and braided it as a new mother's hair should be braided. He then helped me wrap my braids in the same leather strips my mother wrapped around her own hair after she'd given birth to me and my brothers.

At a quarter 'til noon, the twins came back in to get some knives and ask their father if he'd like to finish off the pig's blood. He thanked them and quickly drained the hog before he took the baby from our son.

"Ready, lover?" he asked as he went out the back door again.

I strapped on my bokken and followed him. "Ready as I'll ever be."

We took off into the hot, clear day and arrived at the Hall of the elders a couple of minutes later. They welcomed us warmly and we started lunch immediately. It was such a large spread that it made me feel a little ashamed that I hadn't fed them all better the night before. Roast beef, a spiral-cut ham, three kinds of potatoes, two kinds of bread, apples, peaches, and several platters of vegetables were spread out on a folding table along the back wall. They had also brought in extra chairs along with two more folding tables so we all had a seat while we ate.

"Where are the twins?" Brian asked as we settled down to eat lunch.

"They are butchering a feral pig they...I don't know...found, I guess." I laughed at the face my brother made. "It'll taste just as good as store bought pork, maybe even better since it lived a happy and free life."

"Yes," said the chief. "Happy animals do, indeed, taste better."

"Would you like a ham, Chief?" I asked him out of courtesy.

He laughed. "No, my dear. You keep it all. I'm sure you and your family will have it finished within a week."

I pouted for just a second at his little joke before I brushed off the feeling of being mocked. *They aren't being mean*, I told myself, *only practical*.

I returned to cutting up bits of pork and beef to feed my daughter. She didn't think much of the beef and honestly, neither did I. But, she loved the pork and made some more "mmm" sounds while she gobbled down the little pile I gave her.

"That's good, yeah?" I asked her. "When we go home later, we'll cook some more like this. It's from a pig, the animal you and Daddy drank from before we came here." She beamed up at me and I could feel the love and satisfaction emanating from her. I gave her some potatoes and she treated them with a general indifference, so I let her just eat the meat.

"I think she only wants the protein right now for her growing muscles," Deema commented. "I bet she gets most of her vitamins and minerals from the blood she drinks."

"I bet you're right," I replied with a mouthful of roasted vegetables.

CHAPTER 60

By the time we all finished eating, nearly an hour had passed. We went out the back door and gathered around the sweat lodge. The chief, my grandfather, and three of the other oldest men sat around the drum while the middle-aged men prepared the lodge.

The youngest men, still "elders in training" so to speak, stood behind the old men at the drum to study the beat and help sing the naming song.

Once the sweat lodge started to fill with steam, the elders emerged to touch the child. "We cannot find the name for a child we've never held," one of them explained as he reached for her.

They passed her around between them before handing her off to the men around the drum. Once all of them had held my baby, she was passed back to me and we were led to stand between the drum and the lodge. Deema stayed in the shadow of the Hall. The elders re-entered the sweat lodge and the drumming began.

After only ten minutes of drumming and singing, sweating and meditating, the elders had a name for my newborn daughter. The different drum beats merged into one rhythm, escalating in speed and pitch as they lifted the sticks lower and lower, beat them closer and closer to the edge. At the exact moment the drum beat ended, the elders exited from the lodge.

"Do you agree?" asked the first man to leave the hut.

"We agree," answered the chief. "The name of your daughter's soul in this body is White Buffalo. We knew quickly. Within the first minute, I'd say. But, we—we had to be sure of—do you know the story of the white buffalo, Hope? It is a common story amongst many of the native peoples. Her birth heralds the start of a new war, followed by a new era of peace that will last 1000 years. The birth of the strong, healthy, and long-lived white buffalo is another sign of the times, but we always expected an actual buffalo." He smiled wryly. "I suppose we were wrong again."

"Did you hear that, baby? You've got a name and you are known as White Buffalo. Do you like that? White Buffalo?" I asked her. She looked me in the eye and quite distinctly gave me a nod. "Oh my god! Deema! Did you see her nod? She's progressing so fast!" I was stunned and even a tiny bit terrified.

"I did see that, Mama," he said with a wink.

He opened his mouth to speak again, but he was interrupted by a tiny, tinkling voice like delicate silver bells on a bracelet.

"Ma-ma. Da-dee. Eat. Seep." To emphasize her meaning, White Buffalo pointed at us, then her stomach, followed by a yawn.

"Um," Deema mumbled after a few moments of silence. "Do you think she meant 'sleep'?" he whispered.

"Of course, she did. Cut her some slack. She's only a day old," I said in a whisper. It was all I could force my voice to do.

I was thoroughly shocked and trying to do the math in my head. If she developed twenty times faster in the womb, I had figured it would be the same after she was born. So, if she was about thirty hours old, she should be less than a month old. But babies that were three weeks old didn't talk, didn't eat solid foods, or point and understand things like she did.

What if she's developing 100 times faster? I wondered. That would put her closer to six months old than a month. Six-month-olds could talk sometimes, I reasoned to myself. But what if she kept growing at this rate? I worried. What if she wasn't immortal and died in a matter of months of old age?

Deema must have noticed the panic starting to grow on my

face, because he placed his hands on my shoulders and stopped me mid-thought.

"We should go home, shouldn't we?" he said gently.

"Yes, yes. Of course," I replied, shaking the negative thoughts from my head. "Thank you, Chief, Grandfather, elders," I said as I bowed my head to them. "Thank you for gathering today to name my child. We thank you with all our hearts."

Deema bowed lightly to show his gratitude as we backed away to take our leave. We pushed off into the sky at the same time and went straight home.

CHAPTER 61

The twins were waiting for us, frying up slices of ham. We described the ceremony to them and then told them what happened afterward. They didn't seem too surprised that the baby had spoken.

"Wasn't she making sounds while she was eating? Saying 'mama' isn't that much harder than saying 'mmm' right?" Aleks said matter-of-factly.

"I suppose," I said slowly.

"And I can't imagine that she would die if she is half immortal. At the very worst, I bet she'll live for hundreds of years, not only a few," Sandra chimed in as she read the worries in my mind. "I think she is growing quickly to get through the vulnerable stage of childhood. Once she is an adult, I bet her growth slows or stops."

"I hope so," I muttered.

"Eat," came the tiny silver voice again.

Sandra rushed into the kitchen and grabbed some of the ham that was ready. She tore off a small bite and gave it to White Buffalo, beaming at her the whole time. The baby ate it greedily and grabbed for more, making her yummy noises all the while.

I stood quite still while she ate then decided to call Taniya. I found her at home, playing with her son. She felt my presence and put her play-time on hold. '*Will you come over and stay for dinner tonight?*' I asked her.

'*Of course. We'll be there in ten minutes,*' she replied.

I snapped back to my physical surroundings and found my baby munching on her third chunk of ham. Deema was feeding her and the twins had returned to taking care of the meat. Aleks was on the back porch loading a smoker that looked like my little brother's. Sandra was sealing ham steaks and bacon in freezer bags and stacking them in the refrigerator to await smoking.

"There's a big ham in the oven baking for dinner, too," she said once she felt me return to myself.

"Awesome. Taniya's on her way," I said to no one in particular.

White Buffalo smiled at my words before she grabbed another piece of ham from her father.

I handed her over to him and grabbed the hollow book off the shelf. Once I had a couple of joints rolled up, I flew up to the roof to smoke while I waited for Taniya. I was halfway done with the first one when she pulled into the driveway.

"I wish I lived closer so I could just walk over here," she called up to me as she pulled her son from his car seat.

"That would be cool," I said as I jumped down to greet her. "We named her today," I nearly whispered as I hugged her.

Taniya pulled back and waited with expectant eyes.

"She is White Buffalo," I said quite seriously.

"Oh," she breathed. "Oh. Oh! Do you know what that means? Did they tell you the story? The White Buffalo," she mused, her voice filled with awe. "Oh, wow! She's not a buffalo at all! This is incredible. The elders named her?"

"Yep. Sweat house, drum, everything. The full shebang. Come on, let's get out of the sun."

We walked into the house to find Deema rocking the baby to sleep. "She should sleep as often as she eats, I think," he whispered as we approached.

"She's so much bigger than yesterday and practically bursting out of her clothes!" Taniya gasped. "She's like, as big as my boy was when he was three months," she whispered in disbelief.

Sandra came out of the kitchen and quietly explained her theory.

"I guess that makes sense," Taniya said after a moment of thought. "I hope you're right."

"I hope so, too," I murmured as I stared into the baby's perfect little slumbering face.

"I'm sure she's right," Deema assured me. "It *does* make sense. Why would she die quickly if she is half immortal?"

I sighed dejectedly. "I guess we just wait to find out."

"If she continues aging, we can always turn her," Aleks suggested as he entered the house.

"Yeah!" Taniya exclaimed just a bit too loudly.

The baby stirred in Deema's arms, but she did not wake. Once she was deeply asleep again, I carefully took her from her father and went out the back door. I sat in the hammock facing my backyard and arranged my wings so I could lean back a little bit. I rocked and rocked until I started feeling sleepy, too.

A little while later, I woke up from my dreamless nap to the sound of my daughter's tiny silver voice. "Mama," she said more clearly than before. "Dink, Mama."

"Okay," I said sleepily. "You thirsty, baby? You want some water?" I asked her.

"No." She pursed her lips and thought for a second. "Bad man," her voice tinkled.

"Could you settle for some meat for now? We can't go hunting for bad men until after dark. Your dad and the twins can't go out into sunlight around humans like you and I can," I told her before I called for Deema to come outside. He was by my side in a flash. "Can you stick your arm into the sun to show her?" He did as I asked without hesitation.

White Buffalo said "Ooh" when she saw his skin become clear in the bright afternoon desert sun. "Me! Me!" she cried as she reached her arm toward his in the sunlight. I leaned forward and held her out to the sunlight. Her skin appeared slightly glittery, but didn't become any more translucent. It reminded me of those lotions that made your skin shimmery.

"See, baby? You can still pass for human. He can't. At least, not in the sunlight. So, is meat okay for now?" I asked her again.

She pouted, but gave me a firm nod in response.

I jumped up and we all went back into the house. The twins were just finishing telling Taniya and her son the story of their lives. I stood in the kitchen and handed my baby bits of fried ham until she was satisfied. She fell asleep again and woke up about an hour before dark. "Dink, Mama," she said after she yawned and stretched.

"Okay, White Buffalo. It takes two hours to get there. That's a long time. Do you want to eat a little meat to hold you over until you can have blood?" I asked.

She thought about it for a minute before she bobbed her little head up and down. She ate three more slices of ham before we changed her into the largest set of clothes they'd brought back for her on their last visit to the city.

I also changed my clothes to a long white skirt and a billowy white blouse I hadn't worn in years. We had to cut big slits in the back to fit my wings through, but it looked so cool once it was on that I just didn't care.

Deema asked me why I was doing all this and I just blinked at him for a moment. When he didn't seem to understand on his own, I heaved a sigh.

"I'm coming, too. If I'm going to be around so much death, then I need to get used to it. I need to fulfill my role as a protector."

He stared at me strangely, but before he could ask me what I was talking about, the twins started explaining. "I will hunt alone so I can go shopping and buy White Buffalo some larger clothes and a good digital camera with a good printer for it," Sandra started.

"The rest of us will hunt together. She will—" Aleks paused to cast me a sideways glance. "She will 'judge' them before we 'execute' them."

Sandra put her hand on my shoulder. "I think it's nice of her to help us. We *should* hunt as a family. Soon, we'll be hunting together for the rest of time."

"Okay."

"All right then. Shall we go?" Deema asked us.

"Sure. Let's go." Aleks enthused.

CHAPTER 62

We took off straight up into the sky and turned west to chase the setting sun. The vampires pushed themselves to the limit, flying as fast as they could so they could feed. "And so she can feed," Sandra called back to me. I smiled and felt all fuzzy inside that the twins were so wonderful, so accepting, so anxious to be a part of her life.

Since I could fly three times as fast as they could, I didn't have to push myself very hard to keep up with them.

"You wanna have some fun while we fly?" I asked the child in my arms.

She gave me a big grin as an answer, so I started doing dips and loops and spirals in the sky. At first, she was a tiny bit frightened, but that quickly passed. Soon she was having just as much fun as I was, which was quite a lot. I flew high over the vampires and got far ahead of them before I dove toward the ground. I spiraled over until I was facing the ground, and began my ascent back to the vampires. One more tight barrel-roll and we were back behind them as if we had never left.

"Wasn't that fun?" I asked the giggling baby in my arms.

"Fun! Fun!" her tiny silver voice shrieked over the wind. "More!" she demanded.

"Okay, baby," I laughed. I did the giant loop over and under the vampires again and again until we reached Las Vegas.

Deema, Aleks, and I landed on the roof of some fancy hotel while Sandra kept on flying toward a sleazier part of town. It only took Deema a couple of minutes to find someone who deserved to die. He jumped over the edge of the roof and landed halfway down an alley that our victim would soon pass by. Aleks was quickly at his father's heals and the trap began.

Deema pretended to vomit in the alley while Aleks "drunkenly" hollered about what "big winners" they were. I ran to the edge of the roof and dove off, gliding down slowly and silently. The thief walked past the mouth of the alley and took the bait. He walked quietly up to the "drunk and rich" men he thought he would rob and most likely kill. I pulled his name from his head along with a few other rotten thoughts that glinted through. I landed silently behind him, but he felt the wind my wings created. He spun around a split second before I started to speak.

"What are you doing, Harold?" I asked him in the gentlest voice I could muster. I kept my wings spread and fluttered them slightly so that they were quite obviously real when he looked at me.

"I was—I was gonna help them?" he stuttered doubtfully.

"No, Harold. You were going to rob them and kill them just like you have done to so many others," I told him in a soft, sad voice.

His eyes flickered down to the baby in my arms who was watching him with contempt. His eyes filled with longing, while mine filled with disgust at the perverted thoughts that flashed through his head.

"As punishment for your life of sin and defiling the innocent, you will now die at the hands of this child," I told him in a tone slathered with the disgust I could no longer contain.

He fell to his knees as he begged and pleaded for me to spare him while I shook my head back and forth.

"Stand up," I demanded.

He obeyed, but shook in his boots the whole time. I took a few steps closer until he was within arm's reach and I held the hungry baby up to his shoulder. She sniffed him.

"You're a bad man," White Buffalo said quite clearly.

"I know," he replied quietly.

"Are you sorry?" asked Deema from half a step behind the murderer.

"No, I'm not. I did what I had to do so I could survive," he retorted as he stuck out his chin.

"No, you could have made different choices. You could have lived an honest life, but you chose not to. And where have your choices gotten you, now?" I asked him. "About to die in an alley at the hands of an angel and her spawn."

As if we had planned that as the cue, White Buffalo jumped forward in my arms and ripped out the side of Harold's neck with her tiny hands. The blood sprayed across the wall to my right in one arching spurt before she had her tiny mouth clamped over his jugular. She made a "num-num-num" noise while she fed. Once she was full, he was still mostly full of blood, so her father latched on to the wound the baby had made. He finished off the thief in a matter of seconds, emptied Harold's pockets, and tossed him into a nearby dumpster before straightening his clothes and turning his attention to his daughter. "Was that good?" he asked the bloody-faced baby in my arms. She beamed as she made grabby hands at him. I handed her over and then checked my own clothes to see if I had become bloody. *Luck must be on my side*, I thought with a smile. Not a single drop of blood had marred my flowing white clothes.

"Shall we find another so you two can feed?" I asked Deema once my inspection was complete.

"That's okay. We can hunt alone now. She's sleepy after all that blood. I think maybe you should take her home. I'll come back with a crib," he said while he wiped the blood off her face with his sleeve.

"She doesn't need a crib. She's growing too fast to need it longer than a week, and with three of you that never sleep, I would think that you all wouldn't mind holding her sometimes. What would be great is if you went to a blood bank and brought home a backpack full of blood for her." I nodded to the yawning child he passed to me. "She wants blood every day, and she should have it several times a day. You know, whenever she craves it."

"Okay. We'll do that. I'll see you at home in a few hours, okay, lover?" he asked me after a tender kiss.

"I'll be waiting," I said in a slightly shaky voice.

He chuckled quietly at my tone before he flew up into the warm night sky to search for another person who deserved to die.

"I'll see you later, Ma," Aleks said.

After a quick kiss on our cheeks, he left his baby sister and me standing in the alley to join his father or, perhaps, to find his twin sister.

CHAPTER 63

I shifted White Buffalo in my arms, shook a few loose feathers out of my wings, and pushed off into the night sky. I found east easily and sped back toward my house. In about forty-five minutes, I was landing in my backyard with a slumbering baby in my arms.

Much to my surprise, I found Dancing Bronco sleeping in my hammock on the back porch. His mother and father were sitting downwind from him in a couple of lawn chairs, smoking the joint I'd left behind earlier. I gently laid my sleeping child next to her cousin in the hammock and pulled my stool over the short wall so I could sit with my family.

They passed the joint to me without a word and I smoked it until it burnt my fingers while I told them of my little excursion.

"That's kinda fucked up," my brother informed me once my story was complete.

"Why? She's gonna be one of them someday," Taniya said matter-of-factly. "Shouldn't she get used to the idea of hunting with them? And her baby isn't going to be a baby for very long. She's, what? A day and a half old? And she's already speaking, eating solid foods, and physically she's the size of a four or five month old. Mentally, she's probably already closer to an adult than a two day old baby. If she keeps growing at this rate, she'll be past being a toddler within a week. She'll be a teenager or maybe even a fully grown adult by the end of the year. Shouldn't Hope do everything she can to be around her own daughter as much as she can?" Taniya spouted off, edging closer and closer to anger as she went.

"Okay, okay. Settle down there, Sparrow. I can see your point, I just—look, this whole vampire thing is still kinda weird for me. You've had over a year to get used to this freaky shit, but it's gonna take *me* some getting used to..." Will trailed off and shuddered.

"Well, you'll get used to it," I sighed, stoned and content. I leaned back and stared at the stars for a while, marveling at their beauty. I was glad that they let me have silence so that I could consider how I would prepare myself for the coming war as best as I could. I was so overwhelmed with where to start. Really, I didn't know what to do to get ready other than flying, learning to use a sword, and storing food for my tribe. I sighed before I stood up and faced them. "They'll be back in an hour or so. I'm going to go inside and give her a bath so she's nice and clean for her new clothes," I said after ten minutes of quiet contemplation.

"Yeah, I'm gonna go home. I've got to go to work in the morning," my brother grunted as he got up and returned his chair to the patio.

He waved goodbye as I picked up my sleeping child and tried not to disturb my nephew. I gave her a quick bath in the sink while Taniya basted the ham one last time.

"This is going to be *so* good," she said after she closed the oven. "We can eat it anytime you want. Unless...do you want to make some vegetables or potatoes? There's a package of frozen dinner rolls if you want."

"If there's any sliced bread left, that'll be fine. I think potatoes would take too long, unless we fry them. And I don't know if I have any canned veggies, but there might be some in the garden if you wanna turn on the flood lights and check."

"Do you have any potatoes? Or are they in the garden, too?"

"There are some in the garden, but they're probably still new. You'll have to check the cabinets to see if I have any in here. I don't really know," I said with an embarrassed chuckle.

"Nope. There are no vegetables of any kind in your cabinets," she informed me after opening every little door in my kitchen. "I'll go see what you've got." She flipped the switch next to my back door and the garden lit up like midday. She returned a few moments later with a small red onion, several red new potatoes, some carrots, celery, and six ears of corn. "I figured we could fry all this stuff together while the corn boils."

"Sure, that sounds good." I let her do the chopping and cleaning and cooking while I swaddled my daughter in a towel. We returned to the hammock to await the return of the vampires. White Buffalo fell asleep while I rocked and her cousin only stirred once when I sat down.

By the time we had finished eating our midnight dinner and started the dishes, the vampires landed in the back yard. Deema walked inside carrying Dancing Bronco, Sandra carried White Buffalo, and Aleks carried two huge backpacks and a large cooler.

"What's with the heavy load?" Taniya asked cheerfully as she watched Deema take her son down the hall to put in my room where we wouldn't wake him.

"One pack is clothes for the baby. The other is blood for the baby. Cooler is blood, too," Aleks explained as he unburdened himself. He opened the pack with the clothes and pulled out a variety of baby clothes. "She grows so fast, we got sizes up to ten years old. They get bigger as the pack gets deeper," he informed me.

"Camera things are in front," Sandra chimed in with a proud grin spread on her face. "I got the most expensive they had. The man said it is the best photo, best printer and paper, too."

"You're looking extra rosy tonight, Sandra," Taniya commented.

"Yes," she said. "I had to kill three men tonight. The first man had enough money for clothes and camera paper, but no camera. The second man was plotting evil, but he had no money. Still, I had to stop him from hurting that girl. The third man who needed punishment was a—what is man who sells women and takes their money?"

"A pimp?" Deema asked and raised one eyebrow.

Sandra nodded. "Yes, a pimp! But he was yelling about 'gonna beat you bitches' if they didn't give him more money, and he hit at least two of them." She paused, as if remembering her most recent kill. "To the humans, I seemed like I appeared from nowhere. I was not there, and then I was standing between him and a woman. I told him he was not allowed to hit women anymore, and I ripped off his arm.

"The *minyetka* ran away as fast as their silly little shoes would carry them, so I took him up to a roof to drink his blood and find his money. He had many thousands hidden all over his body. His last thought was that he hoped I wouldn't find his money hidden inside his belt." She sighed and shook her head in an almost disappointed manner.

"He must have been very greedy to be thinking of nothing but his money as he lay there dying," Taniya remarked.

"Oh, yes. He was very, very greedy. And very cruel to his bitches," she said with a grave expression.

My eyebrows lifted and I bit back a laugh. Nothing was funny about her story, but the seriousness with which she'd said bitches was almost too much for me. "The proper term is prostitute," I said. "A bitch is a female dog, but it's used as an insult to women and frail or weak men."

White Buffalo yawned and stretched, still wrapped in a towel, in her sister's arms. "Blood," she requested slowly, trying the word for the first time.

"Would you like to get dressed first?" I asked as I took the bundle of my baby from Sandra.

"What if she gets blood on the clothes?" Aleks asked as he pulled a frozen pint of blood from the other backpack. He tossed it into the water in which we had cooked the corn and turned the stove on to thaw the blood. "Of course, how silly of me," he said before I could even open my mouth. "She'll never wear these clothes again after a few hours, but you will want to use your towel again." He smiled and shook his head at his oversight. Lucky for him, he could read everyone's thoughts. "Not everyone all the time, but you do project a lot," he said as he opened the freezer to put away the blood he'd brought.

I dressed my daughter in a loose shirt and pants that were too long while he stacked the bags of blood in my freezer. While I rolled up the legs so that they'd fit her, I glanced at the clock. "It's almost one in the morning. In eight hours, she will be two days old." I sighed. "Let's see how long it takes her to outgrow these clothes," I said with a forced smile. "And while your blood is thawing out, we can take some pictures." *So we don't forget what a cute baby you were*, I finished in my head.

White Buffalo gave me a stunning little smile and posed for pictures with everyone in the house.

After thirty minutes, her blood was ready and Aleks pulled it from the boiling water. He mopped the water off of it and sloshed it around in the bag to even out the temperature. The baby did her usual grabby hands at her food until she had a hold of it. She continued her little routine by making yummy noises while she slurped down the blood. She drank the entire pint without spilling a single drop and tossed the empty bag into the trash with an eerie accuracy. She pulled back her perfect little lips, stained ruby from the blood, and yawned widely before slumping in my arms.

"I think that's a good idea. I'm pretty tired, too. Can I—" Taniya started to ask.

"Of course. I was going to insist. He's already asleep in there, so you might as well. It's not like I can sleep in there," I said with a flutter of my massive wings.

Once Taniya was settled in my room, the twins returned to their still unfinished task of smoking and preserving all of the meat from the feral pig. I handed White Buffalo to Deema and lay down to arrange myself on my pallet. Deema lay down beside me and I quickly fell asleep, holding my baby and her father.

CHAPTER 64

I awoke around nine in the morning to the sounds of bacon frying, Dancing Bronco laughing, and White Buffalo telling me to wake up. In the eight hours we had slept, my daughter had grown another month's worth.

"Mama," her little voice rang while she patted my cheek. "Mama, eat! Da-rink!" she demanded.

"Well, hungry *and* thirsty. That's a first," I yawned as I untangled my legs from Deema's and stood up.

"She did wake up in the middle of the night and eat a few pieces of ham," Aleks informed me through the screen door. He was busy placing more slices of pork and a large ham inside the smoker on the back porch.

"Well," I said with a jaw cracking yawn and a lengthy stretch. "Let's get to it. I'm hungry, too."

We ate a nice breakfast of smoked bacon, eggs, toast, juice, and fruit. White Buffalo loved the fresh strawberries and oranges. She wound up eating so much fruit that she even decided to not drink any blood. Luckily, we had waited to heat up her blood, so there wasn't any wasted by her not drinking.

I rolled down her pant legs and changed her shirt so that we could take some photos before she grew any more. While we were in the middle of taking pictures with my daughter, I was startled by a knock on my front door. I peeked out the window and saw a car in my driveway I didn't recognize.

"Taniya, can you answer the door?" I asked over my shoulder. '*I don't know whose car that is,*' I told her with my mind.

She walked over to the door and opened it a crack while I stood in the hallway behind the door. Dancing Bronco ran up behind her and peeked around her legs to see who had interrupted our photo session. His face lit up at the same moment Taniya breathed a sigh of relief and swung the door open.

Nallia and Bob walked in, surveying the room to take in their surroundings. When Nallia's eyes found me, her legs couldn't carry her to me fast enough. She gave me a big hug and asked why I hadn't called her.

"Oh, girl, so much has happened since we left the valley. I'm not even sure where to begin."

"Who are the teenagers?" Bob asked when it became apparent I wasn't going to continue.

"They are my children, and so is the little one. We named her yesterday with the elders."

"You didn't say you had kids. And how can they be yours? They've got to be at least sixteen," Nallia observed.

"We *were* sixteen when we died, but that was 500 years ago. We are Deema's children from when he was alive, and the soul inside of White Eagle is the soul that was in our mother. They came to our castle in Russia, found us, and brought us back here to help protect the tribe," Sandra told her.

"Yes, these are my Sashas. This is Aleksander, or Aleks. And this is Aleksandra, or Sandra. The baby is White Buffalo. She is two days old and growing about 100 times faster than a normal child. She is also Deema's child. I was pregnant with her for only two weeks," I explained.

"Oh my god! That's—that's just not—I mean, how?" Nallia stuttered.

"Impossible doesn't seem to exist anymore," Deema said with a laugh. "We understand very little about how or why much of this is happening, but we just have to accept it. Times are changing rapidly. The world around us is changing almost overnight, it seems. Just like you change overnight," he said as he smiled at our baby.

White Buffalo beamed up at her father from the arms of her sister. "Daddy," she chimed as she reached for him. "Drink, Daddy, drink," she told him as he took her from Sandra.

"You thirsty, baby? You want some fruit juice?" he asked her as he rocked her lightly from side to side.

"No," she said with a pout. She reached up, rubbed the side of his neck, and I sensed her thoughts about the taste of blood in her mouth.

"Son, will you start some water boiling to heat her up something to drink?" Deema said over his shoulder.

Aleks did as he was asked while I resumed taking pictures of my daughter. After I got shots of her with everyone there, I showed Bob and Nallia the pictures I'd taken the night before.

"I can't believe she's only two days old," Nallia marveled as she glanced back and forth between the photos and the child in my lover's arms.

"I know. She's growing so fast. I mean, this is all happening so fast. Who'd've thought, ya know?" I paused and shook my head in disbelief. "If someone had told me a month ago that I would have a husband, a baby of my own, and two full grown kids, I would've told them they were crazy. But, here I am. And here they are." I laughed. "It's even crazier to think that every fifteen minutes she ages a whole day."

We continued to chat while the bag of blood warmed on the stove and I explained in further detail what had happened in the last two weeks. When Aleks handed the warmed pint of blood to his baby sister, Nallia choked on the water she was drinking.

"That's not milk," Bob said in a disgusted voice while he patted his fiancée on the back.

"No, it's blood," Aleks said as if he couldn't believe that someone would assume his little sister would drink milk.

"I'm not producing milk, and she has shown no desire for it," I explained with a touch more tact. "The first thing she did after she was born, though, was bite me. She can eat food, but she needs to drink blood as well. She *is* half vampire, after all. And half angel, too. She may even grow wings someday for all we know."

CHAPTER 65

S peaking of wings…um, Hope? Can you tell me what it felt like when your wings were growing?" Taniya asked.

"Yeah, it hurt like hell. My skin broke open and it bled for almost a day," I replied while I stared at my daughter suckling from a bag of donated blood. "Why?" I asked as I looked up and saw the expression on Taniya's face.

She seemed worried, scared, nervous and even guilty.

"I…well, see…I…um…" she stuttered.

Bob smirked. "Spit it out, girl."

Taniya ducked her head with a touch of shame. "I just—I don't want to steal your thunder, or anything, but—" She turned around and lifted the back of her shirt to her shoulders while she kept the front down with her elbows. In the exact spots where my wings had emerged, my friend had two little nubs that pushed her skin out and stretched it thin.

"Holy shit! What is that?" Bob exclaimed.

"How long? When did the tingling start? When did the bumps appear?" I demanded as I lightly traced around and over the protrusions on her back.

"The tingling started when you came to my apartment. The bumps just pushed my skin out late last night. It was when I lay down that I felt them," she replied.

"They will push through the skin very soon. We must consult the elders. They might have been expecting this. Or maybe something has changed." I paced back and forth a few times while I thought hard. "Oh!" I stopped in front of Deema.

"Have I been dreaming? What's coming? I remember nothing."

"I'm sorry, love. You have not been dreaming of the future. You have only been dreaming of the past," he replied with a dismal countenance.

I took my baby from him and resumed my pacing. After a minute or so, she finished her pint of blood and showed off her skills by throwing the bag across the room. She turned and smiled at the "new" people after she watched it fall into the trashcan.

"Amazing," Nallia whispered.

Bob just stood there with his mouth open.

I sat in my tall chair, fixed my wings so I was comfortable, and leaned back against them. I searched for my brother and found him in the Hall once again.

'*Brother, we may have a problem,*' I began without preamble. '*Taniya appears to be growing wings, as well. Does the story tell of two angels? Is that why you wondered if my daughter would grow wings? Are there supposed to be two angels?*' I demanded.

'*Greetings to you as well, little sister. You should come to the Hall. We will discuss this with all who are a part of this. No need to repeat ourselves over and over again,*' he replied.

'*We'll be there in fifteen minutes,*' I told him before I jumped up from my seat and broke the connection. "We're going to the Hall. Taniya, you can drive. We will fly. But we need to go now," I announced as I shot down the hallway to my bedroom. I laid White Buffalo on the bed while I quickly changed into a halter top and shorts. I scooped her up again, and I was out the back door in a flash. As soon as I was clear to open my wings, I flapped furiously and pushed off into the sky.

'*What about Bob and Nallia?*' Taniya's voice asked in my head.

"They can hang out with the twins if they want. We'll have lunch when we get back," I said aloud. I lacked the focus to project my thoughts and I didn't want to do anything risky while flying with my little baby.

I arrived at the Hall first and stood outside the back door for a moment to gather my composure. It helped that Deema landed about thirty seconds after I did. He stroked my face and muttered soothing words in Russian while we waited for Taniya to arrive.

"Should we wait for her out front?" he asked after a few minutes.

"No. You can hear my car from back here and this road is too central for us to be at the front door for long." I slumped in his arms. I was suddenly exhausted for no good reason. I decided that maybe I'd just gotten sluggish from my stretch of not flying and all that sleeping when I was pregnant.

"I think I should go flying after lunch and maybe after dinner, too. I shouldn't be getting so lazy and sleeping so much just 'cause there's a baby to take care of and watch grow," I said as I heard a car stop out front.

I closed my eyes and searched for Taniya. I saw her getting her son out of the car so I walked in through the back door of the Hall. Deema walked around front and escorted Taniya and Dancing Bronco into the room where the elders sat.

"Welcome, Little Sparrow," the chief said as she entered the room. "We understand that you are now growing wings as well?"

"Yes, Chief. Hope said they should emerge very soon." She turned around and showed them her back. She had changed into a spaghetti strap top that showed the bumps on her back. "But what do the stories say of this? Are there supposed to be two? Or am I growing wings because she will become a vampire someday?"

"The stories say that there *may* be more than one, but it isn't specific about how many winged women there will be. We wonder if the child will grow them as well, but that will only be answered by waiting."

"Is there any mention of men with wings? Do I need to worry about this happening to my son or his father or uncle?" she asked, on the verge of tears.

"No. There is no mention of men with wings like yours. We have no worry that your son or either of Hope's brothers will grow wings," he said. "We think that the aggression of men would prevent them from being both peaceful negotiators *and* ruthless defenders. But a woman's heart is capable of both, and our protector must be both."

"But you are peaceful men. You are wise men with calm temperaments. How could you say such a thing when you yourselves are so peaceful?" Deema asked politely.

"We are old men," the chief replied with a wry smile. "But men in their prime…well, it is hard to calm the rage when it must be quieted immediately. And the men of this tribe have other…" He trailed off and looked away from Deema's inquisitive gaze.

"*Really*?" Deema exclaimed after a moment of digging in the old man's brain. "Really?" he repeated quietly after a few more moments.

"Yes, really. Please respect our ways and our wishes. You are an outsider here and keep in mind what we have allowed," my grandfather said sternly.

The vampire bowed deeply to the gathered elders. "Yes, sir. Of course. You have my word."

"What is this all about?" I demanded. "What are you keeping from me now?" I seethed at my brother. I was infuriated at him for not telling me that others might grow wings, too. If I'd known that I might get help someday, maybe I wouldn't have been so scared over being so clueless about my mission to protect my tribe.

"It is not for you to know. It is the business of the men of this tribe and the women need not be concerned," Brian answered calmly and smoothly.

'*Why won't you tell me*?' I asked without speaking.

"It is not for you to know," he repeated aloud.

Suddenly, I picked up a stray thought from one of the men in the room. I couldn't track it to the source, but at that moment I didn't care where it came from. It was the revealed secret that mattered the most.

"You're shapeshifters?" I asked the chief. I was outraged, awed, shocked, and speechless.

CHAPTER 66

The chief shot a glare at my brother but he denied telling me. One of the other men must have confessed mentally because the chief seemed satisfied after a moment.

"Well, there's nothing we can do to take it back now. I suppose she should know since she is hosting creatures that drink blood. We can't have them killing tribal members just because they think it's an animal," he told the other elders.

"I suppose you're right," my grandfather said after a moment.

"We turn into different animals. It is our own personal spirit animal and it varies even among families," the chief stated.

"I am a wolf," my brother informed me.

"And I was a bear when I was your father," Dancing Bronco chimed in. "Now, when I grow up, I will be a horse."

"I was a falcon," my grandfather said quietly.

"Was?" I asked him gently.

"Yes, dear. I am too old to change. Shifting is a young man's game. I am too old to fight, too weak, so I am too weak to become an animal," he explained.

"So, Great Falcon was a falcon, Dancing Bear was a bear, Silent Wolf is a wolf," I said slowly.

"Yes," the chief replied.

"So would I be correct in assuming that Red Elk is an elk?" I said meekly.

"Yes, I was," Red Elk said regally.

"What of the men who do not have animal names? What

about you, Red Shadow? And you, Tangled Tree? What about you, Tall Grass?" I asked three of the men sitting before me.

"We do not become animals," Tangled Tree answered me. "It does not happen for every generation. Sometimes it skips all of the children for one or two generations, and sometimes it only skips one child. We don't know why or what triggers the change, as it happens at different stages of development. My brother could not change either, but his sons can. My oldest son started to changed when he was eighteen, my youngest changed when he was only ten, but my middle son never has."

"Wow," was all I could manage. "I promise it will not leave this room. I will tell no one."

"The twins will need to know. There are over 1000 known shifters in this tribe of 10,000. We cannot be having them killed to satisfy the vampires' thirst. So when they hunt, they must still try to read the minds of the animals. When we are in animal form, we still have human thoughts—a human mind. And if we are killed in animal form, we will turn back into a human," the chief told me.

"Oh good," I blurted out. "I was starting to worry about all the deer and the feral pig we have butchered. I certainly don't want to be eating my tribe members."

For some reason I couldn't quite grasp, everyone seemed to find my comment quite hilarious and the room erupted with laughter. After everyone gained control of themselves, the chief spoke again.

"It is quite unusual that women are given animal names. Before your parents died, they asked us to name you shortly after we named Little Sparrow. We tried, but we did not agree with the name of your soul. Perhaps once every 100 years or so a woman will be born with an animal's name, and to have two girls so close in age, so close in spirit and in life to be named after birds—well, it's just unheard of. Now we understand. Now it makes sense. You are both birds because you both can fly with birds' wings."

"This is just too much," Taniya muttered as she slumped in a chair, already crying silently. Her son climbed up into her lap and rubbed her cheek in a comforting manner.

"Taniya, do not fear," her great uncle said from across the room. "All will be well, and you will be safe. The more protectors we have, the safer we will be. And most of the shifters are animals that can defend us. There are many wolves and birds of prey. There are mountain lions and a few black panthers. And, keep in mind that we have not named everyone in the tribe yet, so the one in five men that we know are shifters— well, it could be even more. At the next tribal meeting, we will start making appointments with the unnamed men. Then we will name the rest of the women. If any of them have bird names, we will keep an eye on them to grow wings as well."

His words seemed to comfort her. Her breathing became less ragged and her heartbeat calmed.

"Thank you, Tall Grass," she said as she wiped the last of her tears from her eyes. She smiled at her son and he slid to the ground.

I got the feeling she was ready to leave, so I asked her if she'd like to return home with me and eat lunch. She nodded quietly and rose to her feet.

I thanked the elders again, and the five of us left. I carried my daughter through the sky with Deema on my trail and we arrived at home in a couple of minutes.

CHAPTER 67

When I walked in the back door, Bob sprang to his feet. "What's the story?" he inquired anxiously.

"She is growing wings," I replied. "The prophesies say there *may* be more than one, but it does not say how many more. Do you two have tribal names?"

"Um, no?" Nallia replied cautiously.

"Bob, you need to make an appointment to be named soon. So do you, Nallia. First of all, you two should not be getting married if you are not named. The ancestors must be acknowledged and asked for protection," I told them with complete sincerity. "And any children you two have should be named quickly after their birth as well," I said as an afterthought.

"Okay. Can I ask why?" Bob asked cautiously.

"At the next tribal meeting the elders will announce the need for everyone to have a tribal name. It is imperative that everyone be named so that the ancestors will help protect us all. We cannot have masses of unnamed people who are not under their protection," I said matter-of-factly.

"Oh," was all they could say.

Not ten seconds later, Taniya walked through the door carrying her toddler and they turned their attention to her. Before she could even close the front door they were bombarding her with questions.

"Does it hurt?"

"How long 'til you can fly like Hope?"

"What about your son?"

"Yeah, will you need a sitter for while you practice?" Nallia asked sweetly.

"I meant, will he start flying someday, too?" Bob smirked at his fiancée.

Taniya sighed deeply before she started to answer them. "Yes, it hurts. I have bones about to puncture through my skin from the inside as well as growing pains. I should be able to fly in, what? A year or so?" she asked as she turned to me. I nodded and she continued. "No, my son will not grow wings because only women become angels in the flesh. And his father or his cousin can watch him while I am out flying. If White Buffalo grows 100 times faster than a normal child, she would age 100 years within one year," she explained. They gasped. "But since she is half immortal, we all expect her to stop growing when she hits her prime. If she doesn't, then they will turn her into a full-blown vampire. And she should grow twenty-five years in three months."

They looked at my daughter again and pointed out that she had grown noticeably in the last hour.

"Yes. She grows a touch over a day every fifteen minutes," I whispered.

I was trapped in my worry again. I hadn't let myself do the exact math before as to when she would be fully grown. My little baby would be my size, my age, before I had known her father for even four months. It was a terrible thing in my mind. Children should have long, normal childhoods. I felt like I had so little time with her. I was so lost in thought that I didn't notice Taniya messing around in the kitchen until I heard her say that lunch was ready.

We had leftover ham, a salad, and leftover fried potatoes. Bob and Nallia commented often about the baby gobbling down the meat. I tried to be a polite hostess, responding when warranted. But, it was hard. I was still lost in thought. The gears were turning throughout the whole meal and, toward the end, it hit me. I could just keep having kids. The vampires could feed me blood, I would heal, and all would be well. After all, the elders *did* say that the more protectors we had, the better.

So if I popped out a kid once a month, well, I'd have my own little tribe of half-breeds within a year.

"I can almost see the light bulb. If only I could see the idea," Deema mused as he stared at me.

"I'll tell you later," I said with a sly grin.

He smiled back at me predatorily, and I assumed he was thinking about sex. *Well, he's got part of it right*, I thought to myself.

After the twins started washing the dishes, the rest of us went out to sit on the patio. Dancing Bronco wanted to play with his cousin, so I set her down in the yard. The five of us settled into our seats and enjoyed the breeze while we watched the kids interact.

Taniya's son took my daughter by her hands and lifted her to her feet. For having never stood before, she was exceptionally steady. He kept a firm grip on her hands and walked slowly backward. She watched her tiny bare feet and tentatively followed him. When she didn't stumble or swagger at all, she glanced back at me for approval. I beamed at her and she returned my grin. He took a few more steps backward while she followed him without hesitation. After walking the small circle around a cluster of parsley in the yard, she gently pulled her hands away from him and stood on her own.

"Can you?" he asked her doubtfully.

"Yes," she said to him before turning to me. "Mama," she sang in her silver voice.

I leaned forward in the hammock and opened my arms to invite her to walk to me. She took a cautious step and then another. Her third step was more confident and, by the time she reached me, she had no more hesitation or doubt. I lifted her up and covered her satin face in kisses.

"You did so well!" I exclaimed.

Her father agreed and ran his hand over her thick head of hair. She reached out for him and I reluctantly handed her over. I just couldn't bear it when I was separated from her. Every moment I wasn't holding my rapidly aging child was a moment of her brief childhood I was missing.

"Well," I said after White Buffalo decided to go back out to the garden and practice walking. I stood up and stretched before I went back into the house to retrieve my bokken. "I'm going to go flying for a while," I said upon my exit. "I'll come back when I get hungry or tired," I told Deema.

"You don't want me to come?" he asked, confused.

"No, you should spend time with White Buffalo. She's growing so fast." I stared at her walking back and forth in my yard. "I won't be gone for too long," I said with a smile as I turned back to him. '*Maybe the twins can take the baby hunting when I return.*'

"Sure, Mama," Sandra called from inside the house where she was slicing smoked bacon to freeze.

I smiled at her, even though she couldn't see me, and gave Deema a kiss. I thanked Bob and Nallia for stopping by and told them they were welcome anytime.

CHAPTER 68

I turned toward my yard and ran for my take-off. I went to my valley, but decided to fly past it toward the Navajo reservation. There was a forest there near the Grand Canyon and I wanted something physical to slash at with my practice sword.

I reached the forest without being seen and proceeded to dip and dive over the trees. I practiced tight turns and evasive maneuvers for several hours until my stomach started rumbling.

I arrived home just in time for dinner. My brothers had both shown up while I was gone and picked everything ripe from my garden. Brian was outside grilling corn and Will was inside frying more potatoes with veggies. We finished off the ham from the day before and it reminded me to thank my brother.

"Will," I said as we dropped our plates in the sink. "Thanks for loaning me your smoker. They're still trying to smoke all that pork." I laughed. "Would you guys mind taking some home and freezing it? You can eat what you want of it, but I'm likely to ask for some back. Taniya, of course you're welcome to take some home, too."

"Yeah, I've got a feeling I'll be needing it," she said glumly. "Did you start eating a lot right at the beginning?"

"Not really. Well, sort of," I answered slowly.

"Beginning of what?" Will asked with a touch of confusion.

"She's growing wings, Brother," I told him gently.

Little Sparrow turned around and showed him the little

nubs on her back. I watched the panic spread over his face and laid my hands on his shoulders.

"There's nothing to worry about. The more protectors we have, the safer we all will be," I tried to soothe him.

"Oh, yeah!" he scoffed. "I'm sure the five of you will make a world of difference in protecting all 10,000 of us." His voice shook with a panic I'd never seen in my brother before.

"Calm yourself," I said more sternly. '*Does he not know? Will he not change?*' I asked Brian silently. He shook his head slightly. "There may be more of us. And at the rate White Buffalo is growing, she will likely be able to fight as well."

"How will there be more of you?" he asked, suspiciously eyeing the vampires.

"Not more of *them*. More of *us*," I said as I pointed to myself and Taniya.

"Oh. How? I mean, how do you know? And how many more?"

"We don't know how many more. But we went to the elders today to ask them why she was growing wings. They told us that the prophesies say there *might* be more than one woman to grow wings, but it doesn't say how many more," I explained.

"Oh," was all he could manage.

There seems to be a lot of "being stumped" going around today, I thought with a small chuckle.

We all turned our attention back to the kids, who were now chasing each other around the backyard in the fading light. Once the sun sank behind the western horizon, Brian said he needed to get home and get some sleep. Will also decided to leave and asked Taniya if she wanted a ride home.

"No, thanks. Your sister gave me her car since she can't drive it. I guess I won't be able to drive it for much longer, either."

The twins came out the back door as the others left and asked White Buffalo if she wanted to go hunting.

"Bad men?" she asked as she ran to her big sister.

"Yes," Sandra said with a smile. "We can get you some new clothes, too. You want to pick out a new outfit?"

The baby nodded enthusiastically and followed Sandra into

the house. They picked out an outfit that would fit her until she fed and another to change into afterward in case she got bloody. Aleks checked the smoker and rotated the shelves one last time before they left. Sandra winked at me as she turned and ascended into the night sky with her siblings.

'*Go make me another little sister,*' she cheerily said inside my head as they flew out of sight.

I turned to Deema and tried to tell him my idea while he smothered me in kisses and carried me into the house. "If I keep having babies, I won't have to miss having a baby. I mean, if she's gonna be an adult in less than three months," I said while his lips grazed my skin and his fingers removed my clothes. "I want to have a baby longer than a week. I want more kids," I said with a serious expression and stern tone.

His lips stopped in their tracks and he stared at me, slightly stunned. "Well, what's stopping us?" he asked after a moment. He gave me a playful smile before he placed his lips back on my neck and his hands on my chest.

We made love for almost five hours straight. By the time I got the "call" from Sandra that they'd be home soon, I was already on the verge of sleep. I awoke shortly after nine in the morning and found my baby crawling out of my arms.

"Where are you going?" I yawned.

"I am hungry, Mama. Sister will make me eggs. You can sleep, Mama," she said clearly in her silvery, wind chime voice.

"Well, what if I'm hungry, too?" I asked her in a teasing voice.

"Then come eat breakfast with me, silly," she said while she rolled her eyes. She skipped into the kitchen while I stared after her.

"Deema," I whispered with a touch of terror.

"It's okay, lover. All will be well," he said with a smile and a light pat to my abdomen while he helped me stand up. "We shall do as you wish."

I returned his smile and followed my toddler into the kitchen.

CHAPTER 69

The next few days that passed were fairly uneventful. Taniya's wings broke through her skin. White Buffalo aged another year. When she was a week old, she was bigger than her almost-two-year-old cousin. She could walk, run, sing, dance, and even move with inhuman speed. Her sleeping evened out, as did mine, and we only slept at night like normal people. By the time she was two weeks old, she was the size of a kindergartener and had the mind of a grad student.

It was on that night, two weeks after she was born, that White Buffalo saw the entire tribe for the first time. We flew to the meeting at the casino and arrived several hours early for a meeting with the elders. We had sandwiches for lunch and we ate while we all caught each other up to speed.

"My wings are coming along nicely. I've even started to grow some feathers on them," Taniya said between bites of roast beef on rye.

Her great uncle smiled. "You don't seem upset anymore."

"No, I'm not. I think it's pretty cool that I'll get to fly around with Hope someday."

"And how are you coping with the growth of your child?" my grandfather asked me.

"I'm coping."

Deema gently nudged me with his elbow.

"I'm also four or five days pregnant, so I'll be having another one soon," I grudgingly admitted.

My grandfather sighed. The chief shook his head in disbelief.

"Will you ever practice flying? Or will you just keep pushing out these half-breed children?" one of the old men mumbled at his plate.

"I am still flying every day and at least every other night. I am still practicing, and I will continue to practice even if I am pregnant half the time," I replied as calmly as I could manage.

"Or you could use protection like normal people," the teenage elder, Quick Coyote, said with a classic teenage snottiness.

"We tried. His—it's too—" I looked at Deema, asking him with my eyes to explain.

"Not that this is anyone's business but *ours*," he said as he put his arm over my shoulders. "But, we did try using condoms once. I shot *through* them. I even tried layers with no luck. And I will *not* deny my wife physical love if she wants it. I will also not deny my wife children if she wants them," he told the gathering of tribal leaders.

"So it shall be however it shall be," the chief said to the murmurs of disapproval that arose in the room. "As I've found myself saying a lot lately—the more protectors we have, the better off we will be. And as some new food for thought, what if these half-breeds can also breed? What if her sons mate with our women? And what if her daughters can carry a child as any woman can? Only her children will live the length of many lives because their father is immortal. What if this infusion of fresh blood and fresh magic is just what this tribe needs? Our old stories say that every man used to shift, and now that magic is waning. We have had infusions of other native blood into this tribe in the past, but none were magical as we are. None could become animals as we could. And now only twenty percent of our men can shift. We are a magical people. Why should we not welcome more magical blood into our tribe? Should we not be thinking of the welfare of the generations ahead?"

Everyone seemed touched by the chief's little speech and no one argued with him or me ever again about my desire to keep popping out babies.

After our little lunch meeting, we went out to the stage area to await the arrival of our tribe. The elders went out front to sign everyone in while Will, Taniya, and their son went down to sit in the front row. The vampires stayed backstage with me and watched me play games with my child to pass the time.

"Do you wanna race?" I asked her with a playful smile.

She didn't even pause to agree before she cried out, "Go!" and took off running across the stage. I ran after her, but I couldn't catch up. Deema stopped me in the middle of the stage with a firm grip on my shoulders.

"No," he said gently. "Flying is one thing, but I will not have you racing on foot. Your body is changing rapidly, and I can't have you falling and risking injury to our child." He stroked my hair while he spoke and I read the concern quite clearly in his eyes.

"Okay, lover. I guess you've got a good point. Do you wanna fly with Mama?" I asked the small child who had started to run circles around me and her father. She skidded to a stop and sprang at me. I caught her in my arms, laughing at her enthusiasm. She wrapped her arms around my neck, her legs around my growing belly, and gave me a kiss on the cheek. I returned her affection and gave her a little squeeze as I pushed off into the large and empty theater. I did some dips and dives, some spirals and barrel rolls, but I could feel the boredom coming off my child in waves of discontent.

"I don't like this," she admitted after a few minutes. "I want to fly outside," she said with an unshakable attitude. "I like the wind and the smells of outside. Flying in a room is just not right."

"Okay, I'll see what I can do," I said and landed at the back of the theater.

We walked out the double doors and strolled through the halls of the casino, passing a few early birds who wanted good seats for the meeting. We reached the outer doors and I asked the elders if I could fly outside until the meeting started.

"I don't see why not. We'll let you know if any outsiders enter our land while you are in the air," my grandfather replied with a smile.

I returned his smile, as did my daughter. She jumped into my arms again and I pushed off into the sky. As we gained altitude, I heard scattered cheers below us coming from those who were filing into the theater.

CHAPTER 10

I did a few circles around the casino and waved to the string of cars pouring into the parking lot. I did a few barrel rolls to the great amusement of White Buffalo and she squealed with delight.

"Higher!" she demanded, so I climbed higher and higher into the atmosphere. "Faster!" came her wind-chime voice.

I folded my wings and dove for the ground, gaining speed as we neared to parking lot. I opened my wings and swooped down over the parking lot that was rapidly filling with cars and tribal members. They cheered again as I soared over their heads and my child laughed loudly with glee.

It felt like we'd only been flying for a few minutes, but after two hours of amusing my child, my brother's voice boomed in my head. '*Almost everyone is here and signed in. You might want to come back inside,*' he informed me.

I peered down at the parking lots and saw that they were indeed nearly full. I turned toward the ground as I told my little girl that we had to go inside now.

"I'm thirsty, Mama," she told me as soon as my feet touched the ground.

"What are you thirsty for?" I asked her as I set her on her feet.

She gave an exasperated sigh before she rolled her eyes and said, "Blood, of course."

We walked through the doors and started down the hall to the theater where we held our meetings.

"Well, we're going to be here until past dinner time, and there is no one here that you can feed from. Everyone here is a member of our tribe, and we are forbidden to drink from fellow tribe members. Also, since the meeting is about to start, we don't have time to go home and heat you up some blood." I frowned. "I'm sorry, baby, but you're just gonna have to tough it out." She returned my frown, creasing her satin face in an unpleasant way. "We can maybe see if there's any meat here for you to eat, but that's as good as I can do."

"I'd even settle for a bird," she said with a grimace as we walked past some confused people. "Can we go get me a chicken, Mama?" she pleaded.

"I'll see if your sister will take you, okay?" I said as we entered the theater. We walked down the center aisle, getting more than our fair share of odd looks, and up the stairs that led backstage to where the vampires were waiting for us. "She's thirsty," I told them once I reached them. "Can you rush home, let her kill a chicken, and gut it real quick so it doesn't rot? The meeting will start soon, and it will last for hours," I asked my oldest daughter.

"Of course," she replied and scooped up White Buffalo.

They rushed out the back door in a blur of movement. About ten minutes later, they returned just in time for the meeting to start.

The chief stood up, walked to the microphone, and asked for quiet. The tribe fell silent, anxiously awaiting another influx of information as to what the hell was going on.

"I'm sure many of you saw White Eagle flying around this afternoon. And I'm sure you all are wondering about the pale child in her arms. The child is White Buffalo and she is very, very special." He motioned for us to join him on stage, so I strolled over to where the old man stood.

My child opted for a more flamboyant entrance. She waited until I was halfway to center stage and then she ran past me at an inhuman speed. Some murmurs of confusion started drifting through the massive theater.

"This child is only two weeks old. She grows about 100 times faster than a normal child. Her gestation inside of her mother was only two weeks, instead of the normal forty weeks."

With every sentence, the murmurs of confusion grew louder and louder. The chief held up his hand, asking for silence again.

Once the quiet had spread to his satisfaction, he asked Deema to join us on stage. "This man is many centuries old, and he is the child's father. He is an immortal who has vowed to protect our tribe as if it were his own."

Someone called out "Pahana" from one of the balconies and cheers erupted throughout the theater.

Once he was able to quiet the tribe again by shouting, "No, he is not Pahana. That is another." He waved the twins to come out onto the stage as well.

"These are also the children of the immortal and they will add to our protection. All three are able to fly without wings, and they are mind readers as well as blood drinkers. They have sworn to never feed from any natives and they only drink from animals. So any farmers who need to slaughter livestock, please contact us and we will send one of them to drain the animal. Waste not, right?"

CHAPTER 71

There were only a few outraged cries from the crowd, but most seemed to accept this unusual revelation without batting an eye. I saw Taniya trying to calm someone who was freaking out right next to her, and I focused on hearing her words. She asked him what harm he saw if they would never drink from anyone in our tribe. He thought about it for a second and quickly saw the wisdom in her words. Similar scenes were happening all over the theater but once everyone was calm again, the chief continued to speak to the tribe.

"We have nothing to fear from these immortals. They would gladly die before they ever harmed a single one of us."

The vampires adamantly nodded their heads to agree with his assertion.

"We ask that all here accept them as if they have lived here our whole lives. The man is Deema, the boy is Aleks, and his twin is Sandra. In less than three months, we believe that White Buffalo will be fully grown and she will aide us in defending the tribe. Then, of course, we have our own warriors already. About twenty percent of the men in our tribe have been named by our ancestors as warriors and they all know who they are. Those who have not been given tribal names will need to be named as soon as possible. Only two women have ever been named as warriors in the history of our tribe, and both of them are here tonight—White Eagle and Little Sparrow. As that is the case, we would like the unnamed men and boys named first. When that is complete, we will name the women and girls just to be sure that all are protected by our ancestors and every available warrior is aware of their special abilities."

"Abilities like what?" someone called from a few rows away.

"Well, some of us can read minds, or see something in our minds that is far away and happening at that moment. Some of us can dream the future or communicate with animals. There are many talents in this tribe as we are a magical people. And if we are all to last through these trying times, we must be sure everyone who is capable of helping knows how to help.

"After the meeting is over, we ask that all unnamed men remain behind to make an appointment to be given a tribal name. If you are unable to stay behind tonight, then we ask that you call us on Tuesday or Wednesday to set up an appointment. There are over 2000 people in this tribe who do not have tribal names, so we will have to do as many as we can every day."

The next few hours were filled with the experienced elders taking turns and telling tribal legends. My grandfather told the story of the winged woman and the story of the white buffalo. Taniya's great uncle told our creation story, which was quite long. Red Elk told the story of Pahana, followed by the story of the bear who became our first tribal chief. Then the chief stood again and told the story of why we live where we live and why our land is sacred. An hour after dark, the meeting finally finished and we left through the back doors to fly home.

"I'm not tired yet," my child said after we landed. "I want to go hunt. I'm big enough that I can lure them by myself," she asserted. "Who's coming with me?"

I looked at the vampires and they all seemed willing to go. "I guess we all are. Let me go get changed first. Do you need to put on some bigger clothes yet?"

She reluctantly joined me in the house and dressed herself in a looser outfit while I put on the white flowing clothes that I wore to "hunt." I strapped on my bokken, scooped up my daughter, and took to the sky. Since I could fly so much faster than the vampires, they hadn't bothered waiting for us to change to leave for Sin City. I caught up with them quickly and entertained my daughter during our two-hour trip with my crazy flying patterns. We landed on the roof of a brothel and the vampires started searching for victims.

"Why can't I fly?" White Buffalo asked me with the innocence one would expect from a child her size.

"Well, baby, it took your dad and the twins 500 years before they could fly, and I can only fly because I grew wings," I said quietly.

"Can I grow wings and fly like you do?" she asked hopefully.

"I don't know. I hope so because I won't be able to carry you for much longer. In a few days you'll be too heavy for me to carry on long trips since I don't have the strength the rest of you have. Plus, in a little over a week, I'll have a new baby to carry, so your dad or your brother or sister will have to carry you," I explained.

She grinned at me. "I hope I grow wings, too. I like how you fly better, Mama."

"Shh!" Deema hissed. "We've got one." He pointed out a man who stood on the corner at the end of the block, waiting to cross the street. Then he pointed at me and the child and made a motion for us to fly.

I scooped up my daughter and threw myself off the roof to follow him. I saw an alley ahead and turned to land in it. Setting my daughter down, I stepped back to hide in the shadows. White Buffalo sat down at the entrance to the alley and started to cry when her victim was close enough to hear her. He took the bait and stopped to gawk at my daughter. "What's wrong, little girl?" he asked her sweetly while nasty, despicable thoughts ran through his head.

"I lost my mommy," she sobbed into her hands. "Are you my daddy?" she asked as she peered up at him.

His eyes lit up. He picked her up and started to walk down the dark alley. "Yeah. I'm your daddy. Come down here, child. It's a shortcut home."

As soon as I saw the vampires blocking his escape from the mouth of the alley, I stepped out of the shadows.

CHAPTER 72

"What are you doing with my child?" I demanded as I stepped forward and spread my wings to touch the walls on both sides of the alley. "Do not lie to me, Timothy. I can see the evil sins in your mind and your heart," I said when his thoughts started churning for an excuse. "Set her down. Now!"

He complied and tried to back away from her.

"No. You will come here," I told him sternly.

"Are you here to judge me? Am I going to die?" he asked, panic creeping into his voice.

"What? Do you really think I should let you live?" I scoffed. "You have defiled countless children and scarred them for life. You were about to rape my little daughter. There is no stopping you without killing you," I said in a disgusted tone.

"No, please. I will stop. I promise," he begged as his eyes caught sight of the sword handle sticking up from my waist.

"There is no stopping you," I said again. I drew my bokken—just to draw his attention—and White Buffalo used the opportunity to spring on him. She sank her teeth into his neck and he fell to his knees. She drank deeply and nearly killed him all by herself. But she was still too small to kill alone, so her brother stepped up and finished him.

"Well done," Deema congratulated us as he threw the drained body into a nearby dumpster. "Do you want to go home now? Or do you want to go shopping with your sister?" he asked our now rosy daughter.

"I'm sleepy, Papa." White Buffalo yawned. "I can buy more clothes tomorrow before we hunt. But can we go farther away next time? I want to see the ocean," she said sheepishly.

"Sure. We can go to Los Angeles tomorrow night."

White Buffalo beamed at her father before she sprang into my arms. She laid her head on my shoulder and said, "Let's go home, Mama."

I told my vampires that I loved them before I pushed off into the sky.

Since she was in no mood for fun, I flew as fast as I could toward the reservation. It took a little over thirty minutes and, when I landed in my backyard, my child was already asleep. I lay down in the hammock with my daughter and fell fast asleep.

I awoke at dawn and found my house a bustling center of activity. The twins were setting up a massive smokehouse between the chicken coop and the back edge of my property. Deema was talking to some tribal members—a contractor and his crew—about what he wanted done to my house.

"What's going on?" I asked sleepily as I rolled out of the hammock.

"We hit the jackpot last night in Vegas," he said with a wink. "We're going to build a house and get rid of your trailer. With our help, it will get built very quickly. We will have enough room for Taniya to stay here. And of course, we'll need extra room for all the kids we'll be having." He walked over to me and rubbed my growing abdomen while he gave me a soft kiss.

I beamed up at him, at a loss for words.

"We can stay with Taniya tonight, or we could rent a room somewhere. We will pack up everything in your house today and they will remove your trailer first thing in the morning tomorrow. Then they will start building your house immediately. You'll lose some of your garden space, but the neighbors will surely agree to let us transplant the plants into their yards."

"Can we stay by the ocean?" White Buffalo asked hopefully from where she still sat in the hammock.

"Sure, baby. We can stay by the ocean tonight and tomorrow you can go play on the beach. Of course, if it's sunny outside, we can't go with you. And your mama can't go with you regardless," he replied.

She pouted up at us, clearly unhappy that she'd have to go alone.

"Can Aunt Taniya go to the beach with me? So I can play with my cousin?" she asked after a moment of thought.

"Well, we'll have to ask her, I suppose," I replied. "But you know she's growing wings, too. If they can't be hidden, she can't come," I told her reluctantly. She pouted at me again, but knew there was nothing else to say.

While I cooked our breakfast, the building crew marked the outline of my new house and finished talking to Deema about how many rooms there would be, their dimensions, etc. After White Buffalo and I ate, the crew left and I called my best friend. She agreed to come over, help us pack my house, and even said we could store my boxes at her house until construction was complete.

CHAPTER 73

"White Buffalo, was there something you wanted to ask Taniya?" I prompted the child while we were packing up my bookshelf.

"Will you come to Los Angeles with us tonight and take me to the beach tomorrow? I've never seen the ocean and I don't want to go alone." She gazed up at Taniya with puppy-dog eyes, and started saying "Please, please, please," when she saw her hesitation.

"Well, I'll have to find something that covers my back," Taniya said hesitantly. "I certainly can't wear only a swimsuit on the beach." She thought for a few more moments before her eyes lit up and she smiled down at my little girl. "You know, I think I've got just the thing. There's this knit jacket type thing I've got that I could cut the sleeves off of and, well…yes. Definitely. I'd love to take you to the beach."

"Yay!" White Buffalo cried as she jumped up and down, squealing like any excited child would. "I can buy a swimsuit tonight after we get there. When can we leave?" she asked me anxiously.

"As soon as we get the house packed and emptied, we can leave," I said with a wide grin. "If you want to speed it up, you can help us pack," I jokingly suggested.

"Okay. What can I do to help?" she asked. She stared up at me with such seriousness, I couldn't even laugh at her. It would've seemed like an insult to her helpful intentions.

"Um, well, here," I said as I walked down the hall. "Take

all the clothes out of my drawers, and stack them in these suit-cases." I pulled a few suitcases out from under the bed I never slept in anymore and opened them on the floor. "Once the drawers are empty, take all the clothes out of the closet and put them in suitcases, too. Then if there's any room left, take all the towels out of the hall closet and the bathroom and stack them in there, too. Do you think you can handle that?"

"Yep. I bet I can finish that before you finish the living room," she said teasingly.

"You know what? I bet your right," I said with a loving smile. I leaned over and gave her a kiss before I turned and left the room. I went back into the living room and helped Taniya finish packing the bookshelf. "Don't worry about taping them yet," I said after we'd finished another box. "White Buffalo can do it when she's done packing my clothes."

We'd finished packing the living room before I realized that we'd need Brian's truck to move all my furniture. I sat down for a minute and searched for my brother with my mind. Once again, I found him sitting at the Hall with the other elders.

'*So, do you not work anymore?*' I teased.

'*No, actually, I don't. My share of casino profits pays my bills and between my garden and yours, I do all right with food. What's up? Another emergency?*'

In my mind's eye, I could see his eyebrow raise while he suppressed the teasing smirk that wanted to shape his lips.

'*No,*' I thought with a laugh. '*I just need your truck after a while so I can move all my stuff over to Taniya's house. They're hauling my trailer away tomorrow and Deema's pay-ing Black Panther and his crew to build me a house. I'll need the room if I'm going to keep popping out kids, and I'd like to have Taniya closer, so she'll probably live here, too.*'

'*Okay. I'll come over around lunch time and we can start hauling stuff over there. Where are you going to stay while the house is being built?*'

'*We're going to LA tonight and we'll probably stay there a couple nights while they dig and pour the foundation. Then I'll stay with Taniya and the vampires will help build the house to get it done quicker.*'

'*All right. I'll see you around noon then,*' he said before he broke the connection.

I stood up and found my daughter taping up the boxes in the living room. Taniya had moved on to the kitchen and she was busy wrapping plates in newspaper. I glanced at the clock and saw it was already ten in the morning. "What does everyone want for lunch?" I asked as I started wrapping glasses in paper.

"How about we order a pizza?" Taniya suggested. "I bet she's never had pizza before," she said with a nod to the little one in the other room.

"No, she hasn't. But I don't think I really want a delivery person coming here. Would you mind going to pick it up?" I replied.

"Well, what if we order from that place Tall Grass's kid owns? We can ask that a tribal member delivers so we won't have to worry about anyone out of the loop coming to your house," she said after a pause.

"That's cool. Are you hungry yet? Brian will be here at noon, so if you can wait, we'll call in about an hour."

"I'm thirsty, Mama," White Buffalo said as she tugged on my shorts.

"Okay, baby." I grabbed a pint of blood out of the fridge and tossed it into the water on the stove.

"Can I have two?" she asked hopefully.

I smiled and pulled out another bag of blood. "Of course you can."

By 11:30, we had everything packed, except for a few changes of clothes and my water-skins. I called to order the pizza and a guy I went to high school with delivered it a few minutes after Brian got there. The twins loaded the truck in a matter of minutes and rode with him over to Taniya's to unload it. At three o'clock, my trailer was completely empty and the last load was on its way to Taniya's house. Once the twins got back, we finished the last details of getting ready to leave. I filled the auto-feeder for my chickens, Aleks strapped on the backpack we had our clothes in, and Deema helped me into the snuggly to carry Dancing Bronco.

"What are you doing, Mama?" White Buffalo asked me as I picked up her cousin and strapped him in.

"Well, baby, this is the longest flight we've done since you were born. I'm afraid my arms will get too tired from holding you. I don't want to risk dropping you, and since you're too big for this, I can't carry you. But Daddy can carry you and Sandra can carry Taniya. Is that okay?"

She shrugged and nodded before she walked over to Deema and jumped into his arms.

CHAPTER 14

We took off into the sky and headed west toward California. It took us four hours to get there, but the smog was too thick and nasty to breath for us to fly around over the city until the darkness hid us. We decided to drop Taniya in the city to get a hotel suite and then we went back to the country to wait until dark. Once the sun had set, she sent out a mental beacon for me to follow to her location.

We landed on the balcony and went into the hotel room to get ready for the hunt. I changed into my usual white garb and White Buffalo picked out an all-white outfit, too. The vampires were anxious to find some killers, so we went to the worst part of town and waited in an alley. It took only a couple of minutes for the vampires to find someone worthy of death.

I stepped out of the alley and blocked the path of their intended victim. "Hello, Jack," I said in a kind voice. "Could you come with me, please?" I took him by his bleeding, needle-poked hand and led the baffled, intoxicated man into the dark alley.

"What you want with me, lady? How you know my name?" he slurred as he struggled to focus through his heroin haze. His scrawny arm jerkily moved to brush his greasy brown hair from his eyes.

"I am no lady," I said after I stopped and turned around. I opened my wings and stretched them toward the sky.

"Bullshit! That ain't real! Ain't no angels real!" he insisted as his muddy brown eyes grew wide.

"This *is* the City of Angels. Did you really think you could keep getting away with your crimes unjudged? Many have died at your hands to feed your many addictions. Tonight, you will die by *my* hands," I informed him.

"Whatever," he mumbled as he turned around and started stumbling back toward the street.

Deema jumped in a huge arch over both of us and landed between Jack and the mouth of the alley. "Oh, no you don't," he said as his feet touched the ground. He latched onto the killer's throat a fraction of a second later and quickly drained him.

"You'd better ask your god for forgiveness. This is your last chance to do so," I told him a few seconds before he died.

Deema emptied the corpse's pockets and threw his driver's license back onto his chest. When he turned to walk out of the alley, I stopped him. "Why did you do that? You always hide the bodies," I said, confused.

"He is wanted by the police for many crimes. They will be happy to find him. Usually, we kill people who are not likely to get caught for their evil deeds. But not tonight. We will feed well in this city and when we leave, the police will be secretly happy to be rid of some of their most dangerous criminals," he explained.

"I love you," I said out of the blue. "I'd kiss you if I didn't think you'd taste like his blood."

"I'll settle for a hug," he said as he embraced me.

"Later, can we?" I asked as I barely pressed my hips into his.

"Oh," he groaned. "You know we can't until you give birth," he whispered reluctantly.

I pouted at my immortal lover, but I knew I couldn't argue with him. I turned to my little girl and asked her if she was ready to feed.

"Yes. I'm thirsty, Mama. When can *I* kill a bad man?" she asked impatiently.

"In just a minute. Here comes another one. How about you stop him this time?" Deema said to our small child.

She beamed up at him before stepping out onto the sidewalk. She focused on the man who stopped in front of her and just stared at him.

"What are you doing out here all alone, little girl?" he asked as he crouched down in front of her.

"I'm thirsty," she told him simply.

"I can help you with that. Are you all alone?" he asked her again.

"No. I have an angel watching over me," she said proudly as she turned and walked into the dark alley.

CHAPTER 15

He followed her into the darkness without hesitation. His mind was bent on the sick, disgusting things he planned to do to my baby girl. He stopped dead in his tracks when he saw the body of Deema's victim. "Who is that?" he asked in a frozen voice.

"My daddy, he—" she started to say, but her victim cut her off.

"Well, I guess your angel wasn't looking after him," he said with a nod at the dead man.

"Nope. She led him here to die, just like *I* led *you* here to die," she said matter-of-factly. He turned to face her, just in time to see her spring on him. She latched onto his neck and no matter how hard he fought, he could not shake her off. After she took several deep draws from his neck, he fell to his knees.

Once she was done, he was still alive, but too weak and stunned to move. I stepped out from the shadows and stood over the man as he bled on the dirty pavement. "You die here tonight for your sins. If you have a god, ask for forgiveness now. Her father is not lying over there dead. Her father killed him for being just as evil as you are. And now, he will kill you, too," I told him.

Deema immediately moved in and finished draining him in a matter of seconds.

"Are you ready for bed, White Buffalo?" I asked my two-week-old toddler.

"Yes," she yawned. "I'm sleepy. But I can drink again in the morning, can't I?"

"Of course, baby. You can drink from anyone here who is evil and, in a city this size, there are a lot of them."

"And I get to see the ocean tomorrow?" she asked as I hoisted her onto my hip.

"Yep. Taniya will take you after breakfast," I told her with a smile. "I'll see you all later at the hotel," I said to my vampires.

I pushed off into the sky and flew back to our room. Taniya was waiting for us on the balcony and welcomed us with a smile. Once we entered the room, I could smell burgers and fries.

"Did you go get some food?" I asked as my eyes roved the room, searching for the source of the smell.

"Nope. We got room service. They'll make anything you want at any hour of the day or night," she said with a huge grin. "Hungry?"

She handed me a menu and I perused it for a few minutes. I picked out enough food to feed a whole family and then I took a shower while I waited for it to arrive.

The hot water felt so good on my skin and my hair that I just stood under the huge shower head for several minutes and let it relax my muscles. After I finished washing my incredibly long hair and stepped out of the shower, I found a fluffy robe hanging from the back of the door. I wrapped up my hair in a towel before I put the robe on backward.

It was awkward to tie it closed, but it was so soft, I just couldn't bear to *not* wear it. I poked my head out of the bathroom and saw that my food had just been delivered. I rushed over to the balcony and stepped outside for a moment to shake the water from my wings. I went back into the room and sat down at the bar to dig into my food.

"Is she asleep?" I asked with a nod at my daughter.

"Yep. She tried to stay awake, but I told her that we needed to get up early so we could spend the day at the beach. She jumped up onto the couch and was out in a couple of minutes," Taniya said with a chuckle.

"She still needs a swimsuit," I reminded her after I swallowed a few fries.

"Yeah, so do I."

"I wish I could go, too," I said reluctantly.

"Well, you could fly out there and just stay far out in the water. If you let your wings just float on the water behind you, and you were the farthest out, no one would see them," she suggested.

"I can't though. I'm just too afraid I'll make the news again. But if you buy me a swimsuit, too, I'd be willing to go for a swim after dark tomorrow."

"Sure," she said with a grin. "One piece or two?"

"Better make it a two piece. Something with ties will be easier to put on around my wings," I said after a moment of thought. I was finishing my huge meal when the vampires landed on the balcony. "You all look like you had your fill."

"Oh, yes!" Sandra exclaimed. "It's too bad you didn't stay. We never even had to leave the alley and we each got two of them."

"So, will you not have to feed tomorrow night?" I asked hopefully.

"Well, we won't *have* to, but we'd *like* to," Aleks answered. "Why?"

"I want to go swimming after dark. I've never been in the ocean before and I figured you never had, either. The water will be wonderfully warm just after the sun sets," I explained.

"Sure, we can go swimming. Then we can hunt after," Sandra said.

"Sounds good to me," I said with a yawn. "But I'm gonna go to bed now. Where should I sleep?" I asked Taniya.

She led me to a bedroom and said it was all mine. I left my child on the couch because I didn't want to disturb her, but I asked Deema to join me in the king-sized bed.

"There aren't enough pillows and I need to be propped up," I explained and rubbed my distended belly full of growing baby.

"Of course, my love," he said as he appeared at my side. He scooped me up and carried me into the room. He hopped into bed and gently but quickly flipped me around so I could lie down comfortably.

"I hope I dream tonight," I yawned. "I need to know what's coming next for me as well as what's next for the tribe."

CHAPTER 16

I awoke the next morning to White Buffalo jumping on the bed, saying, "Mama, wake up!" over and over again.

I smiled. "Hey, baby."

Deema grinned. "Sorry. I told her to let you sleep, but she wants you to eat breakfast with her."

"That's fine. I can always take a nap later," I said before I crawled out of bed and stretched. We walked into the main room of the suite and found Taniya and her son already eating.

"Sorry," she said with a mouthful of food. She finished chewing and swallowed before she explained, "We were too hungry to wait. But you can still order whatever you want." She handed me the menu as I set my daughter on the counter of the bar. I sat down on a stool next to her so that we could inspect the menu together.

"I don't know what most of this stuff is," White Buffalo said with an exasperated expression. "What is French toast? And hash browns? What is an English muffin?"

"I could spend all morning explaining this stuff to you, or we can order a lot of food and I'll explain everything to you when it gets here," I said to my child.

She rolled her eyes at my convoluted statement, but said, "Okay, Mama. But tell them to hurry. I'm hungry."

I picked up the phone and ordered a massive amount of food. Twenty minutes later, they delivered several carts of food while I hid in the bathroom and the vampires stayed in the shadows. The young man who delivered our meal wanted so badly to ask Taniya how they would ever eat all this, but he was too well trained to let his judgmental thoughts leave his head. Once the door shut and the hotel employee was gone, I burst from the bathroom and pounced on the food.

"Wait! Wait!" White Buffalo cried. "What are you eating?" she demanded.

I explained to her what every dish was as we ate, and she tried a plethora of foods she'd never eaten before. We had French toast, eggs Benedict, hash browns, cantaloupe, honeydew, sausage, grits, oatmeal, as well as other things she had eaten before like scrambled eggs, bacon, and toast. She enjoyed all of the foods she ate and soon we had everything polished off.

"Are you ready to go now?" Taniya asked White Buffalo.

The child jumped down from the stool she was on and ran to the door in her excitement. Deema handed my friend a wad of cash and suggested that she buy the little girl some new clothes as well.

"Sure," she agreed. "She's growing so fast, it's hard to keep her in stuff that fits, isn't it?" she asked as they walked out the door.

"Do you think you need some cocoa butter?" Deema asked me as I walked back to the bedroom.

"Sure. I think I'm gonna take a nap, though. I want to be plenty awake later for my midnight swim," I replied. I lay down on the bed and Deema lifted my shirt. He slathered my growing abdomen with cocoa butter and softly sang until I fell asleep.

I awoke in the middle of the afternoon because my stomach was growling. We got out of bed and I shuffled into the main room to look over the room service menu. I picked out another large selection of food and placed my order. I closed all the shades in the room so the vampires would not be exposed to the sunlight before I sat down at the bar to wait for my food.

"There's a lot of stuff in the minibar if you must eat immediately," Deema said as he rubbed my shoulders lovingly.

"Yeah, but who wants to pay $5 for a candy bar," I said gloomily.

All the vampires burst into laughter before they reminded me that money was never an object. They each emptied their pockets and threw wads of cash onto the bar in front of me.

"There's at least $2000 right there, plus all the money I left with your brother to pay for the construction of the house. We also get more money every night when we hunt," Deema said with a touch of laughter left in his voice.

"Well, okay. I could go for a Coke and a Snickers, I guess." I felt a little foolish that I'd forgotten that my family had acquired so much money—money that they would never need for food or shelter.

"How much is this room, anyway?" I asked Deema as he handed me a soda and candy bar from the tiny refrigerator.

He looked at me skeptically for a moment before he replied, "It's $1000 a night."

My jaw dropped in shock and he reached out playfully to close it for me.

"A thousand dollars?" I squeaked.

"Doesn't matter, remember?" Deema said as he grazed my cheek with his lips. "Eat, love." He opened my soda for me. I tore open my candy bar and ate it in three big bites before I drained my pop. I set down my can just as a knock came at the door.

"That was fast," I commented as I headed for the bathroom. "I figured it'd be at least another ten or fifteen minutes." I left the door open a crack and listened as Deema answered the front door.

CHAPTER 11

You're not here with our room service?" Deema asked the man at the door flatly. He already knew what this man—the hotel manager—wanted since he could read his mind.

"No. It will be up shortly, but we wanted to make sure that there's nothing funny going on up here. One woman checked in all by herself and paid for the room in cash. Then room service has been ordered several times in less than a day, but it is far more than one woman could eat. I see there are many more people here that just her. We wanted to make sure all is well," the strange man said to my vampire. He sounded less and less sure of himself with every sentence he uttered.

There was a silence that stretched on far too long in my opinion before Deema finally replied. "The woman who checked in yesterday is my sister-in-law. Her flight got in before ours did, so she came to rent the room. She also got four keycards when she checked in. Funny, you ignored that fact. We arrived hours later with my wife, our children, my nephew, and our cousins. Some of them are at the beach right now, but Taniya called and asked that we have a late lunch or an early dinner waiting for when they got back. We pay for everything in cash because we hit a jackpot in Vegas. Does this hotel require that we pay for our food in advance? Or as it comes? Isn't it customary that we pay the bill when we leave?" he asked in a chillingly calm voice.

When the man spoke again, his voice shook. "We usually

have a credit card on file that we charge at the end of your stay. But—she—I—I'm sorry," he stammered.

"Here is $200. Surely that will cover what we've ordered today. We'll come down later to pay for another night's stay and the rest of the food we have ordered. But for now…" Deema trailed off.

I peered through the crack of the door and saw that the twins were now flanking their father, hovering over the man much too close for comfort.

"T—thank you," the hotel manager stammered. "I'm sorry about the inconvenience and the misunderstanding. I will let the front desk know to have the bill ready for you…um…after dinner? Is that all right?"

"Yes, after dinner will be fine," Deema replied as he opened the door to usher the man out. The extremely nervous man exited into the hallway, never taking his eyes off of the ominous vampires. Before Deema closed the door, he stuck his head into the hallway. He must have seen the carts of my food, because he stepped back and swung the door open wide. A minute later, the young man delivering my food pushed one cart into the room and pulled another cart in behind him. Deema handed him a $20 tip after he signed the ticket.

As soon as the front door was closed, I threw back the bathroom door and made a bee-line for the carts of food. I picked up a sandwich and began to eat it as I asked the twins questions with my mind. '*How could you intimidate him like that? We're trying to keep a low profile, aren't we? He's going to tell everyone here how wrong you felt, how inhuman you felt!*'

"No, he won't," Sandra said smugly. "We could all read his mind, and he thinks we must be a mafia family or something. He was certainly scared of us, but not because he thought we were unnatural. His mind didn't even consider that we were not human. You know? People see what they want to see. They only think things are real if they believe such things are possible. We pass so easily for human because most people don't believe in vampires. And, if they do, they certainly don't believe we can be awake during the day." She laughed. "Being seen during the day, even if out of sunlight, is enough for most people to 'know' that we are just plain-old, pale humans." By the time she finished speaking, I had finished the sandwich and started on a pile of French fries.

"Okay," I mumbled skeptically around my food.

"She's right, you know?" Deema assured me as he picked up my plate and led me over to the bar to sit down. "He won't say anything to anyone. He wouldn't want to draw attention to himself any more than he already has."

I relaxed a bit more at his reassurance. I finished my food in silence while the vampires discussed their plans for the next few weeks.

"When the house is done being built, we can put all our money toward stocking up food for the tribe," Sandra declared.

"Yes, and until then, we can dry the meat that she cannot eat," her brother said with a nod at me.

"And what of grains? The three of us could plow fields as quickly as any machinery," Deema asserted. "We can get permission from the elders to plow fields around the house and other parts of the reservation."

"What would we plant? What will grow in the winter?" Sandra inquired.

"Winter wheat, of course. On the plains, where grain is usually grown, it would be planted in the fall, but not sprout until spring. But in the dessert, it should grow over the fall and winter and be ready for harvest before the spring rains as long as we water it," Deema explained.

Sandra and Aleks gave him a nod of understanding before they slipped back into silent thought.

By four in the afternoon, I'd finished my food and Deema rolled the carts back into the hall to be taken away. Shortly afterward, Taniya returned with her son and my daughter.

"Mama!" White Buffalo exclaimed as she jumped into my arms. "It was so much fun! I wish you could've come! Are you still going later? Can I come with you?" she said in a rush while I hugged her and gave her a few kisses.

"Sure, baby. Do you wanna take a nap first?" I asked the enthusiastic child in my arms. "Have you all eaten?" I asked Taniya over my daughter's head.

"Yeah. We had hot dogs and burgers. She'd never had soda before and she tried some of mine," she informed me.

I raised my eyebrows in questioning and Taniya started laughing.

"It's too sweet," my daughter said while she made a disgusted face. "I don't like it at all."

"Well, that's good! Most kids want nothing but soda once they taste it," I told her with a smile.

She made another funny face to show her disapproval and we all laughed.

"Are you tired? Do you want to sleep for a while before we go hunting and then go swimming?" I asked her as I set her down.

"Okay. Are you sleeping, too?" she replied after a moment of thought.

"Sure. I could probably use another nap. Where's the cocoa butter?" I asked as I turned to Deema.

He walked to the bedroom and held the door open for me and our daughter to enter. He smiled at me lovingly and told me to show him my belly. I complied and he slathered my growing abdomen in cocoa butter before he carried me to bed. Once we were settled, White Buffalo jumped up onto the bed and snuggled up underneath my wings.

"Are you sleeping back there?" I asked her over my shoulder.

"Yep. I'm too big to sleep on top of you now," she asserted. "Besides," she said after a big yawn. "It's soft and comfortable."

CHAPTER 18

I awoke just after dark when Sandra entered the room to hang my clothes on the door. "Sorry," she whispered when I opened my eyes and looked at her.

"No, it's fine. We should probably get going, huh?" I said as I crawled over Deema and set my feet on the floor.

White Buffalo yawned and stretched behind me before she jumped off the bed. She ran into the other room and dug through some bags that Taniya had brought back with them earlier while I got dressed.

My friend had picked out a cute swimsuit for me as well as another white outfit for hunting. The swimsuit was blue camouflage with ties on the sides of the bottom so it would fit as my belly grew. The dress was white, gauzy, and backless with a flowing skirt that brushed the floor.

By the time I finished dressing and went back into the main room, everyone else was ready and raring to go. Taniya decided to remain behind since it was almost bedtime for her son, so I dove off the balcony with the vampires right behind me. Sandra carried White Buffalo and Deema quickly moved into his favorite flying position underneath me. Within a few minutes, we landed on the beach in an isolated spot.

"Aren't you thirsty?" I asked them as they walked to the water's edge.

"Yes, but there's a shark about 200 yards out. I think I'd like to try that," Deema said with a wink. He dove into the water and swam so fast he was a blur. After a moment, there was a lot of thrashing followed by calm waters. After another minute passed, Deema emerged from the water a few yards from the beach. He was grinning from ear to ear. "That was interesting," he told the twins.

"What did it taste like?" Sandra inquired.

"Have you ever had a large jungle cat? Or maybe a lion?"

"I've had a few tigers over the years," she replied.

"It kind of reminded me of a jungle cat, but it also had a similar flavor to a dolphin," he remarked.

"Well, that's interesting," I said to no one in particular. "So is it safe for us to swim now?" I asked Deema as I wrapped my arms around his waist.

"No, Mama. I want some blood, too. Won't you hunt with me?" White Buffalo asked with a sweet innocence.

I smiled down at her and asked her where we should hunt. She thought for a few minutes before she ran across the beach and then cleared the road in two bounds. I took to the sky and followed her while Deema and the twins chased after her on foot.

After she reached a rundown part of town, she came to a skidding halt and scanned the sky to find me. The vampires stopped behind her and ducked into a nearby alley. It was their sign to her that a criminal was near. I remained aloft and watched my child's victim approach. As the pedophiles she hunted always did, he stopped and spoke to this lovely child who seemed to be alone and lost. She led him into the alley where her father and siblings waited and I landed behind him.

"What are you doing, Aaron?" I asked as he leaned over to pick up my child.

He quickly spun around and gawked at me in shock. "Who are you?" he asked with a shaking voice.

"I am her mother," I told him as I spread my wings to block his view of the street. "And I know what you are thinking. I can even hear the panic inside your thoughts. You will never touch another child again. You will never harm another soul," I told him as I walked toward him.

"Are you really real?" he whispered as he reached for me. I folded my wings forward and brushed some feathers against his outstretched hand. He stumbled backward as his mind spun and he tripped over White Buffalo.

"On your knees," she commanded in her silver voice.

He did as she instructed and gazed up at me. "Please," he begged me. "I can change."

"I don't think so," I said as I stared him down. "Your thoughts betray your words. You only say that out of fear, not out of sincerity. You will die here tonight." I gave my daughter a nod and she pounced on him from behind. "Let him suffer," I told her as she fed. "He feels no sorrow for the terrible things he has done to children."

In his panic to escape, he groped around for a make-shift weapon. Aaron's fingers closed around an empty beer bottle, which he promptly threw at my face. It broke on impact, but I was only cut across my cheekbone. I reached up and wiped away the fresh stream of blood before I met his eyes again. "Like that would really convince me to let you go," I scoffed. "Kill him, baby."

White Buffalo looked up at me then and a firm sense of justice spread to her eyes. She reached her slender little fingers around to the front of his neck and slowly wrapped them around his windpipe. Her fingers dug in deeper and deeper until they were completely around his trachea. As his eyes got wider and he struggled to breathe, she ripped out the front of his throat.

Deema was in front of me in a flash and blocked the spray of blood that would have surely ruined my brand new dress. By the time she was done feeding, Aaron was drained and dead. She dropped him in the pool of his blood and grinned up at me.

"I could almost hear his thoughts." She was almost giddy at the prospect of getting to be a telepath, too. "I couldn't hear the words, but I could feel his emotions. When he got scared, I could feel it." She wiped the blood off her face and sprang into my arms. "Ready to go swimming?"

"I'm ready if you are."

I glanced at Deema and he touched my cheek.

"Does it hurt?"

"Not at all."

He wiped away the blood and gaped at me. "It's already healed! There's not even a scar."

"Must be the vampire blood," I said with a small shrug. "Maybe that's also why my stomach isn't ripping open from this rapid growth. I bet your blood keeps healing me."

"That's cool, but let's go," White Buffalo said as she impatiently bounced in my arms.

"We'll catch up with you soon. There's a group of thieves headed this way." Deema walked out of the alley toward his intended victims and the twins followed.

White Buffalo wrapped her arms and legs around me, so I pushed off into the sky. I flew back to the beach and landed in the water. It was so warm and felt so good I almost couldn't believe it. I let her go and she swam away from me, laughing.

"It was nice during the day, but this is better," she sang as she swam. "See the stars, Mama? Aren't they pretty?"

"They sure are," I said with a smile as I gazed out away from the city to the sparkling sky over the ocean. I let my wings relax and float on top of the water while I slowly swam over to her. We splashed and played for a few minutes before the vampires arrived.

"You got your dress all wet," Deema chided me. "And her clothes are all wet, too." He frowned as he looked over at our daughter.

"What about your clothes?" I teased as I spun around.

"Mine are on the beach," he said. He jumped up out of the water for a moment to show me he was wearing only boxer shorts.

"Okay, but what does that matter now, anyway? You soaked them earlier when you ate that shark. And they're all bloody from her kill." I was starting to get mildly irritated.

"So what?" White Buffalo chimed in. "Clothes can be washed and dried." She splashed me with the warm sea water and we all had a good laugh.

We played in the water for several hours before my child yawned and declared that she wanted to go to bed.

Deema gathered his clothes and carried our sleepy daughter

back to the hotel. The twins remained behind with me while I struggled to fly with my sopping wet wings. I pumped my wings as hard as I could, but they felt like they each weighed a ton. Sandra noticed my struggle and cocked her head to one side. "Would it be easier if we carried you? Those seem like they will take a long time to dry," she said after a few moments of observation.

"Well, okay. But, remember," I said as I stroked my distended belly, "you've got to treat me like I'm made of glass."

Aleks smiled. "Of course. We'll be extremely careful," he assured me.

We flew back to the hotel, and I immediately took a shower to wash the smell of ocean off of me. Once I had dried my body, Deema helped me dry my wings with the blow drier.

I went to bed and soon fell into a blissful sleep with my lover holding me and my child snuggled beneath my wings.

EPILOGUE

The coming war and battles had been the last thing on my mind lately. All I'd cared about was my growing family. Visions of a big house and lots of kids filled my dreams that evening. Only the end of my sleep that night was disturbed by visions of darkness. But it made no sense to me. All I saw were a pair of dark green eyes, flecked with blue, and filled with menace.

It'd been a long time since I'd woken up terrified. I did the next day, though. I was shaking with fear and unable to explain myself to Deema.

"Why could I not see into your mind just now? How was your nightmare shielded from me?" he wondered as he stroked my hair to calm me.

"I don't know," I muttered. I pulled away from him and stood up to stretch. It was awkward. My movements felt jerky and I realized I was still trembling from the vision of those eyes.

"Do you think someone—somehow—could someone else control your thoughts and your dreams? Could another have kept me from seeing what you saw?" He paused and gave me a speculative look. "What did you see?"

"I saw an enemy. I think. I guess I don't really know what I saw. Maybe it wasn't what is to come. Maybe it was from the past. I just don't know. Only the future will tell," I murmured before I walked away from him. "Only time will tell just how much I'll have to give up for my tribe."

"What do you mean by that?" he asked with a touch of worry in his voice.

I turned around and just blinked a few times while I tried to understand what he'd asked me. "I—I guess I don't really know. It just kind of came out," I finally replied with an uneven voice.

"Well, whatever happens, I promise I'll be at your side when they come to attack your people," he swore as he enfolded me in his arms and made me feel safe again.

"I'm so lucky to have you." I sighed against his chest. "To think that we were together 500 years ago, and that we've found each other again now. You must be my soul mate or something."

He gave me a squeeze as he agreed, but part of me was distracted. It almost felt like there was someone else behind Deema that I couldn't see. For just a second after I'd spoken, I felt like there was a terrible sadness in the room with us. But then it was gone and I decided I'd imagined it. After all, how could I possibly be sad when Deema loved me more than anyone else who'd ever existed? Well, I couldn't.

I let him lead me back to bed and he massaged my wings until I thought I'd melt.

Yeah, I told myself. The war could wait. I had other things to tend to.

About the Author

Janelle Samara lives in Kansas City, Missouri, with her husband. When she is not busy writing, her favorite pastimes include devouring classic books on her tablet, growing organic vegetables, and creating new recipes for her family. When she needs to get out of the house, she has many interests, ranging from watching ballet to fishing with her brothers.